Clasping her hands, he held them to his chest. "Renee, look at me." When she did he saw how heavy and dark her eyes had become. He'd never seen a more beautiful woman in his life and struggled to find his voice.

"Baby, I don't want to take advantage of you or of our situation. But I need to know that you're sure this is what you want . . ."

Renee cut him off extracting her hands from his and reaching up to his face. Wordless, she pulled his head down to her lips. She kissed him thoroughly and passionately answering him in a way she knew he understood. She felt his heart beating wildly under her hand and knew her own heartbeat marched his. Everything in Renee was alive and she had never been more sure of anything in her life, despite her history of making bad decisions. No second-guessing, no self-doubts, just feeling and living in the moment.

A moment that was becoming unbearable . . .

PROMISES MADE

BERNICE LAYTON

Genesis Press, Inc.

INDIGO

An imprint of Genesis Press, Inc.
Publishing Company

Genesis Press, Inc.
P.O. Box 101
Columbus, MS 39703

Copyright © 2008 by Bernice Layton

ISBN: 13 DIGIT : 978-158571-334-9
ISBN: 10 DIGIT : 1-58571-334-1
Manufactured in the United States of America

First Edition

Visit us at www.genesis-press.com
or call at 1-888-Indigo-1

DEDICATION

To my husband, Derrick, and my daughter, NaTiki, thank you for your ever-present love and encouragement; without your constant support and guidance, this book would not have come to fruition.

All things are possible with love and friendship, and the endless possibilities of past, present, and future encounters.

ACKNOWLEDGMENTS

To my family and friends: thank you for your love and support, and thanks for understanding when I couldn't make it to dinner or a cook-out.

To my friend, Danise (Lu) who has blessed me with a lifelong friendship, love and support for the past twenty plus years . . . thank you, you're sister is my heart. And to my mom, Susie, who always has plenty to read, thank you . . . okay, so that's where I get it from.

Thank you, Angie, for your support, now you finally get to read the whole book. I have to thank my editor, Deborah Schumaker, at Genesis Press, Inc. for giving me a chance. Thank you to Doris Innis for your edits, some of which had me laughing. But you gave me a lot to think about, and work with—hope you like the finished product.

If I have forgotten anyone, please know that your assistance has been heartfelt, thank you.

CHAPTER 1

Renee Richards practically jumped out of her skin when the shrill cry of a police siren pierced the noonday quiet. Standing on the steps of the local courthouse for the past twenty minutes and rethinking the foolish decision she'd made a week ago to meet Craig Lemar Thompson, she had reason to be jumpy.

Although she hadn't seen Craig in almost seventeen years, last week he had called her out of the blue with a proposition. Actually, it was to keep a silly teenage promise they'd made years ago.

Craig was her brother Bryant's best friend when the two were teenagers. They remained friends until Bryant died of leukemia when they were sixteen. His death had been hard on her family. Renee was twelve then and she remembered watching him get sicker and sicker. Each time he came home from the hospital, he was less and less able to bounce back to his once lively self. Bryant was always excited to see his friends from school. They would drop by the house, bringing everything from comic books to junk food to . . . oh, yeah, she smiled, remembering the time she walked into Bryant's room and caught four or five of his friends crowded around the TV set watching a dirty video.

She also remembered what a tattletale she was back then. It was not an usual sight for her family to see Craig chasing her or teasing her about her ponytail or those funny sneakers she used to wear. Craig knew the drill when he caught up with her. He had to bribe Renee to keep her quiet, usually with bag of gumballs in hand. Renee would just melt from head to toe during those encounters. She drew in a breath and held back a tear.

Of all her brother's friends, Renee thought Craig was the sweetest and the cutest. Her family was so thankful that he kept coming to see Bryant long after the other boys had stopped. Because he was four years older than Renee, Craig never saw that she had a major crush on him . . . but everyone else in her family knew. She laughed now, thinking back on the days she would see him coming on his bicycle four blocks away and would run to her room to brush her hair and put on her sister's lipgloss, but Craig never noticed her efforts. He would just come in the house, call out to her, "Hiya, Squirt," and then would fly up the stairs to Bryant's room.

When Bryant died, Craig and his family were supportive and helpful to her family. The day of the funeral, when everybody returned to her house and she saw Craig sitting on their porch swing all alone, her grief-stricken heart broke a little more. Renee didn't know what to do, so she sat down beside him and slowly began to rock the swing until he looked at her. His voice barely a whisper, he sniffed back tears and said, "How ya doing, Renee?"

She was stunned. Craig had never uttered her name before. "Oh, I'm okay, I guess. What about you? I guess you're real sad about Bryant, too, huh?"

"Yeah, I am, and I'm gonna miss him, a lot. I'm gonna miss you, too," he said, looking past her at a sleek sports car turning the corner.

"Miss me? Why? I'm not dying or going anywhere. What do you mean by that?"

Craig was absently admiring the sky blue sports car as it slowed down and pulled into a driveway across the street. "I bet you anything that car is really fast."

Renee tapped his shoulder. "Craig, what did you mean that you would miss me, too?"

"Huh? Oh, sorry . . . my folks found the house they've been looking for. It's nice and way too big, but they like it. Anyway, we'll be moving next weekend."

Moving? No, please no. I'll miss him. Renee's heart was breaking, and all she could do was look down at his hands. Craig had nice, clean hands she thought. "Well, I guess I'll miss you, too. You'll still be in the neighborhood, right?" she asked, hoping he would say yes.

"Naw, we're moving out of Houston, going up to Dallas cause my dad got that job he's been wanting. It's only a couple of hours away. I'm glad we're moving."

Swallowing the huge lump in her throat, Renee pulled in her bottom lip. "Why?"

"Well, I kinda broke up with my girlfriend. Anyway, you wouldn't understand what I'm talking about; you're just a kid. See, this girl I liked a lot . . . well, I broke-up with her." Craig returned to admiring the sky blue sports car, and didn't see the shimmer of tears in Renee's eyes.

"Why did you break up with her?" she asked quietly.

"Look, I don't expect you to understand any of this, Squirt, but I found out she's really a sleaze, that's all. I'm just better off by myself—forever. Who needs girls, anyway?"

"Oh, don't say that. You're a really nice boy, and Bryant really liked you." Renee wanted to keep talking; she liked his voice, and this was the first time they'd ever really talked. "Besides, you don't really want to be by yourself all your life, do you?"

Drawing in a deep breath and turning in the swing, Craig saw the sadness on her face. "I don't know, I think being by myself will be good, and I'll never get that hooked on a girl again." He reached up and teasingly pulled her ponytail, causing the swing to move slightly.

"Well, what about when you get older and you meet someone really nice and pretty, wouldn't you want to marry her?" Her breaking voice touched him.

Craig smiled and smoothed back her ponytail. "Tell you what Squirt, since I like you and you're really nice and pretty, when I decide I want to get married, I'll look you up, okay? Is that a deal?" He held his hand out for her to shake, giving her his widest grin . . . soothing her broken heart.

"Craig, you're being so silly," she said, smiling down at his hand. He had said he liked her and that she was nice and pretty. But he was still moving away.

"No, I'm not. It's my promise. Is it a deal or not, Squirt?" His smile was contagious, and it touched his red eyes and her tender soul.

Smiling back, Renee grabbed his hand and shook it hard. "Okay, it's a deal." Craig placed his arm around her shoulders and rocked the swing and she knew with the certainty of a twelve-year-old that she would miss him a lot and would probably never see him again. She could only mumble, "I'll miss you Craig, with all my heart."

"Yeah, I'll miss you too, Squirt, but I have something for you." Then he reached inside the pocket of his bomber jacket and pulled out a big bag of bubblegum balls, all for her. Renee's delighted squeal could be heard a block away. She just loved bubblegum, and she loved him for remembering that on such a sad day for them.

Renee swallowed the lump in her throat and willed her tears back. She felt that painful ache of losing her only brother all over again.

Now, seventeen years later, Craig Thompson had called her out of the blue. He expected her to make good on that promise she had made all those years ago when she had that stupid crush on him. They had agreed to meet on the courthouse steps but the darkening sky and the wind signaled an incoming storm, forcing Renee to wait inside the courthouse. She figured he must have been just joking with her when he called and invited her to lunch. He was always such a jokester and tease. She couldn't imagine why he wanted to meet there at the old courthouse, but it was convenient for her since she worked downtown, anyway.

Finding an empty wooden bench below a high window, Renee sat down and remembered how Craig looked the last time she had seen him on that porch swing. Would she even recognize him after all these years, she wondered, looking up as someone passed by. Surely he wouldn't recognize her. She looked nothing like she did as a skinny twelve-year-old. Her father described her then as all legs, arms and a ponytail.

But that was then. Renee had blossomed into a beautiful woman. Still single and unattached, she never failed to draw admiring looks from males everywhere. Her golden complexion was set off by expressive, exotic brown eyes, attributes she shared with her father, Harold Richards. Although she was slim, she had a curvaceous body, and she could literally eat anything without gaining a pound. Her two older sisters, Meg and Cecelia, hated her for that.

Gazing out the window, Renee saw several men walking toward the courthouse entrance. She wondered if one of them could be Craig. After all, she was relying on how he looked at sixteen. She realized she was nervous.

Okay, so where is he? she wondered, looking at her watch again. They had agreed to meet at noon, and it was now twelve-thirty. Suddenly apprehensive, she looked out the window again. Not seeing Craig among those rushing up the courthouse steps, Renee decided to use the ladies' restroom at the end of the marble hallway.

CHAPTER 2

Craig Thompson hated to be late for anything, especially for something important, and this meeting was important. It was a stroke of luck that he had remembered that promise he'd made all those years ago to his best friend Bryant Richard's skinny little sister, Renee. *Lord,* he thought, *how old were we then anyway?* He realized how often he had thought of her over the years. From time to time, his mother would tell him that she had received a birthday or holiday card from the Richards' family and that everybody was doing fine.

But whenever he thought about Bryant, he would remember Renee's sadness at seeing her only brother so sick. She used to say that she was going to be a nurse and take care of sick people like Bryant. As he drove into downtown Houston, two things struck him: It was hot as hell for early June, and he was somewhat nervous. Craig wondered if Renee had become a nurse. He laughed, picturing her in a nurse's uniform with a long ponytail and with that shiny pink lipgloss on her lips. Hadn't he seen her like that many times before?

He had seen Renee's sister, Cecelia, at a charity function a few months ago. Cecelia was much, much heavier than he remembered her. He could only imagine how

Renee would look. He also remembered that Renee's mother was on the heavy side, too.

Oh well, he figured he only needed to be married for three months, tops. Destined to remain a bachelor until he really had to get married, Craig was thankful he had dodged that bullet. Unfortunately, the ladies he'd been involved with all seemed to be marriage-minded from the start, and that was always his red flag not to get involved beyond the physical level; otherwise, they end up mad at him.

Now he had to get married; that is, if he wanted to get the inheritance left him by his grandfather, Reginald Thompson. He looked heavenward and spoke aloud, "Good old Granddad, I just know you're up there just laughing, watching me jump through hoops to get my hands on that money . . . money I need to buy that advertising agency."

Craig had an opportunity to buy Davis Franklin Advertising, the advertising agency he'd been working at for the past seven years as an account executive. He had been good at securing new business, but for the past few years business had been only trickling in. Not good. Not good at all. The agency's staff of twelve worked as a team, and he didn't want to see anyone in jeopardy of being laid off. Craig had seen it before, and it wasn't pretty. Definitely not pretty for the employee who got the pink slip. And those who were fortunate enough to keep their jobs, well, they just felt like heels . . . lucky heels, to be sure, but heels.

Davis Franklin, the agency's owner, was retiring. He'd started the agency back in the eighties and had made huge profits with strong advertising campaigns, but Davis admitted he was burnt out and had finally told the staff that he was planning to retire.

Everyone immediately looked at Craig to take over the reins. Then Davis met with Craig privately and offered him the opportunity to do just that. How could he have said no? Craig reflected. He was doing a job he loved, and he had a great creative team behind him. But what he didn't have was the capital to buy the agency.

Now that word had gotten out that Franklin Advertising was up for grabs, every other agency in town was looking to take it over. The agency's history was that of creating marketable campaigns that got products into the minds and homes of consumers. It was a very attractive acquisition.

Craig had Davis Franklin in his corner and he was keeping the wolves at bay, so to speak, thus giving Craig time to raise the funds needed to buy the agency. Time was running out, and so far, banks were reluctant to advance him that kind of money. They weren't willing to risk it . . . risk it on him, that is.

Craig remembered a conversation he'd had with his grandfather when they were trout fishing one summer afternoon at their favorite stream. He'd told Craig that he was leaving him an inheritance, his entire fortune that he'd built from good investments. He had said, "Now, boy, don't you dare touch it until you really, really need it . . . and if you squander it away on foolishness, I'll come back down here and whup your butt back up there with me."

He'd told Craig that only his mother knew about it, and that he'd sworn her not to tell anyone; especially, Craig's father, who had lost more money on gambling and on get-rich schemes than he could remember. "Craig, I made sure you, your mama, and sisters wouldn't lose that big house you all are living in. Trust me son, I know your daddy and how he is with money in his hands. You know, I tried to warn your mama, but like you, she's stubborn, and I guess she was in love. Anyway, son, you remember what I just told you and when you need it, that money, I mean, well, you just go to your mama, and Lord forbid if something happens to her, then you just go to my old bank down on Seventh Avenue. You go there and see Miss Lilly and just have her pull my account card. Everything you need will be there when you need it. Who knows, you might find the love of your life and decide to get married and have a bunch of babies running all over the place. I sure would like to see that," he said, grinning at Craig's embarrassment.

Disturbed by the prospect of his grandfather ever leaving, Craig didn't want to hear talk like that. He had said, "Okay, Granddad, but I really don't want to talk about this. You're going to live forever, I just know it. Now can we move farther downstream, where I can see the fish looking at us and laughing? And besides, I'm not going to marry nobody. Girls are stupid and funny acting." He knew the response he would get from his grandfather, and he sure got it.

"Boy, you're a mess. You just wait, but I love you through and through." Then he turned serious and looked at Craig eye-to-eye. "Now promise me you'll do as I said."

"Well, okay then. I promise, Granddad, and I love you through and through, too."

A wide grin spread across Reginald's face. His mind was twirling. Yes, he couldn't wait to go see Miss Lilly down at the bank later. Oh yeah, and he will also add a little line or two to that account for his grandson. *Um, hum . . . a stipulation, that's what I'll add.* Reginald smiled when his grandson threw his fishing line in, just as he'd shown him when he was only five years old.

Craig didn't remember pulling into the parking garage across from the courthouse, but he was glad for the dim lighting inside that hid the tears in his eyes as he remembered that wonderful day. Just a couple years later, his beloved grandfather had died.

Craig had called his mother just two weeks ago, just as his grandfather had instructed him to. He could not understand at first why she had insisted on coming to town to speak with him first. After all, he just needed the account number. But when they had met over lunch, Craig still had no idea how much money awaited him, only that it was in the Wayland Bank. But his mother did give him the account number. Then she had cleared up a couple of questions for him. Mainly, how was it that he and his sisters were able to attend the colleges of their choice. His parents were not rich by any means, but they never went without.

His mother explained that his grandfather didn't trust his own son with money, and that years before he had put several thousand dollars into a bank account under her name. He then taught her how to save and make that money grow to the point they were finally able to buy a house. All the while, she never told Craig's father about it.

Craig sat back, smiling at his mother. "Mom, you were a sly one, weren't you?"

"No, Craig, not sly, just smart. You see, when you all were just babies, your father would blow his whole paycheck before he came home from work. There were so many times I had to go to his father for money to pay the rent and to buy food."

Craig was stunned to hear the story. "But you stayed with Dad. Why, Mom?"

"Because, in spite of his faults, I loved him and he was a good father. In the early days he just kept trying to get more money for us, but he only ended up losing it, time after time."

Craig parked his car and sat for a minute, looking at his reflection in the rearview mirror and thinking out loud. "Okay, I've come this far and there is so much at stake. I just hope Renee is still the sweet girl I remember, and if she's a little heavier like her sister, Cecelia, well, that's okay, too. Besides, it's only for three months. But first, I've got to talk her into keeping that promise she made to me, and I've got just the bargaining chip I need," he said, grinning, as he patted his pocket and got out of his car. With that, he laughed and headed out of the garage.

CHAPTER 3

Renee was combing her hair out. "I must be out of my mind for even agreeing to meet Craig. But he was such a cute boy back then, and he always seemed to be thinking about something."

All he ever did was chase her. Her mother would just laugh at them. Sometimes he'd chase her up the block and leave her, only to return to the house without her. Only she wouldn't know until thirty minutes later when she came out from her hiding place. He would sometimes give her a ride on his bicycle when he was on his way to their house and saw her walking from the school bus. Renee could still remember the feeling of flying when she was perched upon the handlebar, and his sixteen-year-old legs were pumping the pedals really fast. That was when she had become aware of Craig's body. She was scared at first, but when Craig talked her into letting go of the handlebars, saying, "Let go. I've got you and I won't let you fall . . . just let go, Squirt." And when she did, Renee had never been happier in her life.

Renee didn't even try to suppress the smile creeping across her face. She could still feel his arm draped across her shoulders that day on the swing. Thinking about the swing brought her back to why she was standing there.

She didn't even recognize his voice. The deep voice that came across the line the night he called had washed over her in warm waves. "I mean, come on, only a crazy person calls somebody after almost eighteen years and expects to hold that person to a stupid preteen promise. And that is exactly what I'm going to tell him, too. I know he was being his usual teasing self, that's all this is." Embarrassed for talking to herself, Renee ran from the ladies' room.

Craig didn't see Renee on the courthouse steps. She must have gone inside, he thought, as a light rain began to fall, promising to cool the city down some. He stood in the brightly lit, marble hallway, looking up and down, but didn't see her. He saw several people mingling about, but no Renee, or anyone resembling what he thought she might look like. "Hum, the Squirt chickened out on me," he said aloud. Smiling, he opened his suit jacket and thrust his hands onto his hips. Just as he turned around, a young woman came rushing out of the ladies' restroom and ran smack dab into his chest. And she literally took his breath away.

Renee saw gray pearl buttons inches from her eyes, and just as she was about to mumble an apology, she found herself staring up at the sexiest mouth and the most beautiful eyes . . . eyes she had looked into only a thousand times. She couldn't speak at first. She could only bat her eyes several times, before finally croaking, "Craig . . . Craig Thompson?"

Looking down into her familiar brown eyes, Craig went from smiling to a full laugh. "Squirt?" He was dumbfounded and felt foolish for calling her that familiar pet name he'd given her. Narrowing his eyes and rubbing his very close-cropped hair, he couldn't take his eyes off her. "Oh, ah . . . wow," he stammered, staring down into her face and beyond.

Frowning at being called the nickname after so many years, she reached out and pinched his arm. "How about Renee, knucklehead?" She knew she must look pretty silly standing there grinning up at him, showing all her teeth. He'd grown up to be one handsome piece of eye candy, and it didn't escape her notice that a defined six-pack lay under those pearl gray buttons.

"You're right, Squirt no longer fits you. Renee, wow, look at you." Craig took her small hands and stood back, admiring and drinking in every detail of her. "Oh, my God, Renee you, you've grown up to be so beautiful . . . I'm stunned." He honestly was. She had none of the physical attributes of her mother nor sister. But her eyes were the same as he remembered them, brown, seeking and full of hope; and, oftentimes, sad.

"Thanks, I think. You didn't turn out so bad yourself. How big are you? I mean, how tall are you, anyway?" she asked, looking from his wide shoulders down to his powerful thighs. She blinked self-consciously for her all-out staring, but she was tempted to reach out and touch his biceps, which were quite visible under the tailored suit he wore so perfectly.

"Oh, around six-one, but I haven't measured myself lately." Then Craig cringed at the play on words and coughed to cover his embarrassment. Then he grinned and reached out for her, bringing her into the embrace of his muscular arms.

Before Renee knew what was happening, she was being lifted off her feet and spun around as he circled the marble floor with her in his arms. Thank goodness she decided to wear pumps; otherwise, her shoes would have been left on the floor somewhere below her. Laughing, she put her arms easily around his neck. Inhaling his masculine scent, she immediately experienced shivers of pleasure running up and down her chest. She also noticed that her heart was thumping loudly. When he finally set her down, Renee was dizzy, heated and still laughing.

"You're stunning, Renee. You filled out well, nice . . . oh, baby, just sweet. Not heavier at all." Frowning slightly, he guided her to one of the wooden benches lining the walls of the hallway.

"What?" she asked, smiling as he sat down beside her.

"Oh, sorry, it's just that I saw your sister Cecelia a while back and, well . . ." He trailed off, covering his gaffe with another convenient cough.

"Oh, really? She didn't mention it when I talked to her a couple weeks ago."

"Hum, well, I saw her. She may not have recognized me, though. It was at a charity function and it was pretty tight in there. My mom told me that Cecelia's married with a couple of kids." Craig was fighting to keep his eyes off her exposed thighs and her breasts under the cream colored blouse that matched the short skirt. He coughed again and forced his eyes up to hers, but then her mouth captured his attention. Gone was that shiny pink lipgloss.

"Cecelia and her husband have three children, and they're all spitting images of both of them and way too cute. Oh, and she's real self-conscious about her weight, so if you see her again, act like you don't notice it." She waved her hand as a distraction because she couldn't stop looking at his handsome face.

"Don't worry, I won't. So, Squirt, I talked to my mom recently and she said you're still single. I can't understand that, but I'll bet you've got guys lining up outside your door, huh?" Craig recognized he was fishing and hoped she hadn't noticed. Single meant marriageable in his mind.

"Hum, not really. As I told you on the phone, I'm still single, and Craig . . ." She looked up, forcing him to take his eyes off her chest. "I plan on staying single, so enough with the joke that got me here today, okay?"

"Oh, no you don't, Squirt. You made a promise. What kind of person makes a promise and then breaks it, huh?"

The look on his face told her that he was serious. But that wasn't the problem. Renee thought he was positively the finest brother she'd ever laid eyes on, and that was her problem. She couldn't keep her eyes off him as she tried to keep the conversation on track.

"Craig, look, I was twelve. How could I be expected to make good on a promise that you now expect to collect on?" she asked frowning.

"Renee, you promised me, we shook hands on it and you accepted the gift I offered, which technically sealed the deal. You know, many contracts are binding based on a handshake." He spread his hands in a gesture of finality.

"Besides, I have two things in my pocket to make sure it happens." He touched a curl resting on her forehead, his hand straying down to caress her cheek. "You are so beautiful." And he thought she was really sexy, too.

The warmth of his hand on her cheek radiated throughout her body. Her eyes widening, she studied his serious face, then down at the hand now covering his pocket. Renee's curiosity was piqued. "What is it? What's in your pocket?"

Smiling, he said, "Always were a curious little bee, weren't you?" He reached into his left pocket and pulled out a folded sheet of paper and handed it to her.

Renee read her name, date of birth and address on a document, a marriage license application, in fact. She looked up at him dumbfounded. "Craig, th-this is a real legal document. Are you nuts? Have you grown into a deranged lunatic or something?"

"Yes, that's a real legal document, and no, I am not deranged or a lunatic. And I want to get married immediately. Today, if possible, but if not, I can wait until early next week. You know, in case there are things that you need to do, or whatever it is that brides need to do before getting married." His smile and soothing voice weren't melting her one bit. This was not going as he had originally planned.

"Well then, you're just right out crazy. Craig, I am not going to marry you, understand? Now stop joking and read my lips . . ." She never finished her sentence because Craig's lips suddenly covered hers, pulling Renee into an abyss that she didn't know how to escape from, and in that moment, didn't want to. Suddenly, her body burned from head to toe as if someone had turned the thermostat way up in the old courthouse. She felt his large, warm hands move up her arms and slide around her back as he pulled her closer to his body. Renee didn't resist him; she couldn't. This was Craig, the cutest boy ever, and he was kissing *her*. She saw flashes of lights behind her closed eyes and sent up a silent prayer. *Lord, have mercy, what is happening?*

This was not turning out as Craig had expected. He knew she was single, and like her sister and her mother, he expected her to be a plus size young lady of thirty. He expected her to still have that little crush she'd had on him when she was twelve. But he never, never expected the woman he was holding in his arms to be his Squirt. This sexy, attractive creation was all woman. She was no longer the little skinny girl who used to love wearing colorful sneakers and matching tee shirts. She thought he was crazy, and he would have thought the same thing if she had been the one to approach him about the promise made. She's smart, too. Craig's mind raced as he continued kissing her. Damn, how was he going to convince her, this other Renee to marry him? He deepened the kiss and captured her bottom lip. She melted instantly into him and was kissing him back.

Think, man, think. Ending the kiss, he was stunned that he couldn't pull away from her and, when he did, the look on her face made him want to kiss her again, so he did, and again she didn't resist.

Girl, you have lost your mind? Renee thought as her hand curved inside Craig's jacket to ease around his waist. Why did this simple kiss between two old friends create such a drugging effect on her? she wondered. When she inched one eye open to look up at him, she saw that his eyes were closed, but she also noticed people grinning at them as they passed and tried to pull her mouth from his, but Craig seemed to be lost. "Craig, stop," she mumbled, finally able to pull back from him. "People are staring."

Craig was warm, feverish in fact, right down to his, well . . . he knew if Renee got up to run away from him at that very moment, there was no way he could go chasing after her. So he held on to her hand, just in case she did plan to run. He desperately wanted to kiss her again. To Craig, that kiss was sweeter than he'd imagined kissing her would be. He had to press on.

"You know, Renee, it's no shock that we'll be married, even Bryant joked with me about it." He didn't want to go there, back to his best friend; when he saw the shadow pass over her face, he wished he hadn't.

"What? No, he didn't. When we made that promise or whatever it was, Bryant had already died." She tried to pull her hand from his, but Craig held firm, his thumb caressing her fingers.

"Not then. It was on his birthday, and Bryant was too sick to be moved to the first floor, so the party was moved up to his room. Remember, when he wanted to give you a hug?"

"Yes." She remembered the day clearly.

"And I helped lift him up and put his arms around you?"

Sadness threatened to return. "Yes, I remember that. Oh, Craig, you were such a good friend to him." She patted his hand, which still covered hers.

"Well, Bryant saw how upset you were when you ran into the hall crying and I ran after you. Remember? I told you how happy Bryant was that you decorated his room with balloons and all those cards and stuff while he was at the hospital getting his treatment?"

Renee couldn't speak, so she just nodded.

"Well, after you calmed down and went to get his presents, I went back in and he said, 'Man, I sure hope when you finally catch up with her that you'll marry her and take care of our Squirt.' I swear he said that, Renee, just ask everyone that was in there . . . your family and mine. They all saw how embarrassed I was when they all said, 'ooh and aaw.' I was a mess. Everybody teased me." Craig smiled, remembering his friend.

Renee looked at him for several minutes then spoke in a quiet voice. "He was such a brave guy, wasn't he? Bryant could make me laugh no matter how bad he was feeling, especially after one of his treatments." She bit back a sob as she looked down at her hands, still held within his. "But, Craig, you don't owe anything to me or Bryant because of what he said when he was so sick or because of that silly promise we made on the swing that day."

Craig was biting his bottom lip, remembering the feel of her lips on his and how she pulled his body toward hers. "Oh, yes, I do. I owe you both and, sweetheart, you did accept the gift. That in itself sealed our promise, and we shook hands, too." He held his fingers to her lips when she was about to speak again. "And you said it yourself . . . if and when I was ready to get marry, then you would be that so nice and oh, so pretty girl who would marry me, didn't you? Now, guess what, baby, I'm oh, so ready." Having said that, he leaned forward and captured her in a kiss again.

After initially enjoying the kiss, Renee pulled back abruptly and held her hand up to his chest to stop him from moving toward her again. "Wait a minute. There was no gift, Craig. I accepted no gift from you, so ha, ha . . . no promise, no obligation. I'm free." Renee crossed her legs, then crossed her arms under her heaving breasts and turned up her nose at him, grinning.

Sexy and adorable popped into Craig's head. "Oh, my dear, I beg to differ. I even brought you another one. Go ahead, check out what's in my right jacket pocket." Craig couldn't contain the laughter that erupted from her expression. His Squirt didn't want to go anywhere near his pocket. None of them.

"Come on, Squirt, you're stalling. I've seen this tactic of yours before, like just before you took off running. It's not a mouse trap or anything like that." He turned a little to allow her to reach her hand into his pocket and, when she finally did, he laughed at the wide-eyed, open-mouthed expression that lit up her face.

Renee removed the bag from his pocket cautiously and then stared down at a clear cellophane bag of colorful bubblegum balls. And just as he expected, she squealed and giggled. "Craig, you're so stupid," she managed to say between fits of giggles.

He laughed with her. "Oh, Renee, I've missed you. I'm so glad to see that you're well and have grown into this wonderful, beautiful woman." He touched her chin affectionately, and then glided his hand down to where he watched her pulse race at the base of her throat.

Sobering up, she met his eyes. "Craig, all kidding aside . . . I still can't marry you."

"Why not? You're not married."

"Craig, you're practically a stranger to me. As far as I know, you could be gay and just looking for a wife as a cover or something. Maybe you need a wife as your alibi for a crime."

Craig frowned, processing what she'd said. He thought for a second before answering. "Let me make this perfectly clear: I am definitely not gay. I've never, ever had any interest in my own sex, and I've never committed any crime. I am not crazy, because if I were, my mother would have told your mother. Baby, you are so sexy, and I should tell you that your skirt is rising up when you swing your foot like that. And, lastly, I just want the girl who promised to be my wife one quiet, sad day when she sat down beside me on her front porch swing." Craig then leaned forward and placed a very large diamond solitaire on her ring finger. He kissed her palm briefly and then kissed her lips tenderly.

Renee was stunned into silence. She didn't know if she had lost her ability to speak because of the kiss he'd pressed onto her lips or because of the gleaming diamond that was casting prisms all over the front of her cream-colored blouse. Pressing her other hand to her chest, she found her voice. "Craig, th-this is insane. You must know that, don't you?"

"No, I don't. Do you like the ring?" He honestly wanted her to like it.

"What?" She glanced down. "Yes, it's very beautiful, really it is, but I . . ."

He just watched her and knew everything she was feeling, and suddenly, out of the blue, he couldn't catch his breath and started feeling overly warm. His chest tightened. *What the hell?* "Look, I need to use the men's room." He inched his face close to hers again and stared deeply into her golden brown eyes. "Renee, please don't run off on me. Promise me that you'll be right here when I come back." He was serious. She knew that because there was that look he used to have when he was deep in thought.

"Oh, okay. That I can promise you, because I don't think my legs can move right now. I'm in shock." She looked at the ring again, then up at him.

"Okay." Craig walked to the restroom. Once inside, he was thankful for the coolness of the vacant room. He wet a couple of paper towels and held them to his flushed face. Then he looked at his reflection in the mirror and talked aloud to himself. "What the hell is going on?" he said, pulling in several deep breaths. "I-I just don't believe this. Renee was supposed to be fat and homely and just say yes. Damn. We would get married, I'd buy the agency and then, in three months, the marriage would be annulled. Done deal. But I'm out there, unable to control myself and keep my hands off her." He paced the tile floor. Then stopped and looked again to make sure no one was in any of the four stalls then yelled out, "Thanks a lot, Granddad. Real freaking funny, man! When I get up there I'm going to kick your ass for that damn stipulation; I can't believe you did that." Craig frowned up at the large ceiling light fixture. He was almost afraid it would fall on him any minute and stepped from under it.

His grandfather had indeed added a stipulation clause to the inheritance he'd left for Craig. That's what Craig found out when he went to see Miss Lilly at the bank as he'd been instructed to do. The clause stipulated that for Craig to have access to his full inheritance, he must be married. The money, totaling almost three million dollars, had been gaining interest all these years, and it would be all his. That is what he needed to buy the Davis Franklin Advertising Agency. Actually, his inheritance was way more than enough. He only needed half, and the other half and interest, well, that was just sweet butter cream icing on the cake.

Calming down, he looked into the mirror, Renee on his mind. "I never expected this . . . she's sweet and hot. Oh, God. I'm so screwed. Well, she just has to say yes." Just then two courthouse bailiffs entered the restroom and Craig quickly washed his hands and walked out. Thankfully, Renee was still there, standing now and looking out the window, as the sun had come out. He was struck by how sexy she was from behind. He looked upward and muttered through tight lips, "Oh, Granddad, just you wait 'til I get up there. And, you, too, Bryant, old buddy."

Craig looked at Renee's slim profile as the sun touched her hair and face. His heart seemed to pump more blood through his body, making him lightheaded just looking at her. Looking upward again, he just knew they were up there together, laughing down at him.

Craig came up behind her and wrapped his arms around her shoulders, and she automatically brought her hands up to his forearms. Her faint perfume drifted upward, causing desire to surge through him again. He quickly stepped back from her. "Hey, you said you were off for the rest of the day; have lunch with me. And don't tell me you still eat like a bird, or was that just around me that you acted shy?" She glanced up at him sideways, emboldening Craig to kiss her cheek, now warmed by the ray of sun. An unsettling feeling jolted him.

"Well, okay, if you're sure." She felt him moving away.

"I'm sure, but excuse me while I call work and let them know I won't be returning." Renee watched him move away. She thought Craig had grown up to be a fine man, and he was so attractive, too. She also liked him kissing her and realized that she'd always wondered what it would be like if he kissed her. She suddenly remembered that one Christmas when her sister Meg had hung up mistletoe above the entrance to their living room in the hope of sneaking a kiss from Marcus, her geography class study partner. Only it wasn't Marcus who came through the door. To their surprise, it was Craig who walked in with a tin of baked cookies from his mother. Meg was on him in a flash, and he kissed her back. Truth be told, Renee stayed mad at Meg well into the next year for kissing Craig.

Later, Meg told her sisters that she really liked kissing Craig. She said he had nice lips, and she could feel all of him when he kissed her. Renee still fumed about that. She smiled when he reached for her hand, and side by side they walked along the marbled hallway, her heels echoing off the walls. Renee watched Craig's profile and thought Meg was right on both accounts.

Craig chose a restaurant frequented by courthouse regulars. He fit right in, Renee thought. But she felt out of place in her simple cream skirt set, which she had set off with her purple passion stiletto pumps and matching purse.

As they were being escorted to their table overlooking a wonderful garden, Craig saw her faltering steps and her tentative glances around. He leaned forward and whispered, "Baby, you outshine all these overdressed and overpaid women in here. Now, move on, woman, 'cause I'm hungry," His warm breath sent shivers up and down her spine.

After they were seated and ordered pasta and salads, Craig surprised her by ordering a bottle of champagne, telling their waiter that he'd just asked her to marry him. After shaking Craig's hand the man scrambled away with a wide grin on his face.

"Craig, I can't believe you told him that." Her scowl was lost on him.

"I told him the truth, and I did just propose, so this is our celebration lunch. It's supposed to be special and include champagne." He watched her intently, planting his elbow on the table and resting his cheek against his palm. "I've missed you, Squirt. Have you missed me?"

His serious tone drew her eyes to his. "Yeah, I guess so."

"I mean, did you miss me at all?"

"I missed all of you. But I didn't miss your father teasing me whenever I came over to study with your sister Annette." She smiled at him, but he didn't smile back.

"Dance with me." He stood and held out his hand.

She looked up at him. "Dance? Are you nuts? Craig, this is the lunch crowd and nobody dances at lunchtime." When he began tugging at her hand, she had no choice but to get up, as she didn't want to risk having all eyes on them.

He smiled when she stood and eased her in front of him. He then escorted her to an alcove area. Not really a dance floor, but he didn't care. He desperately wanted to feel her body against him again. When the dance ended, he helped into her chair and noticed that their drinks had been served. Craig promptly made a toast. "To us, Renee, and to promises made."

She hesitated and then took a small sip. She was spared from responding to his toast by the arrival of their lunch, quietly and elegantly served by their waiter.

"Renee, did you miss me?" He was still waiting for her response.

She looked out into the restaurant, then back at him. "Craig, why do you keep asking me that? Besides, I told you that I missed everybody, and I guess that includes you, so yes." She surprised herself by getting angry. "But did you miss me? No. You didn't even bother to come back to our house and say good bye, did you?"

"I wanted to."

Her cheeks were turning red. She was getting upset.

"No, you didn't." She waved her hand in angry agitation. "You guys just packed up and left without saying good bye to me . . . I mean to us. And don't you dare say I'm wrong. It's true. I took the bus over to your house that Saturday, and just as I got there, the moving van was driving down the street. I only went there to bring some traveling treats that my mother and I made for your family. And you guys had just left." Renee prayed that the subtle lighting in the restaurant would mask her now pain-filled eyes, which meant tears were pooling in them. "I even saw the mailman, and he gave me the forwarding address. So I sat there on your old steps and wrote a note to your family . . . and to you, to say good bye." She pursed her lips and swiped at the tear that fell to her cheek.

"I wanted to say good bye, to you especially, but I did see you that day, Squirt. We were in the minivan several cars behind the moving van. I saw you walk up to the front door. Let's see, you had on blue jeans, a bright yellow tee shirt with a hideous big flower across the back, and those awful matching yellow converse tennis shoes." He made a face and watched realization spread across her face. "And I wanted to get out of the minivan, but my mother said how hard it was for you to see us go. She said it was hard for you to see *me* go, and wouldn't let me get out of the minivan. I saw you walk up to Mr. Jackson, our old mailman." Craig reached across the table and covered her hand.

Renee stared back at him at first, then brushed off what he'd said. "Oh, well, that was eons ago. Anyway, we were kids." She moved her hand away from his and placed her cloth napkin on her lap. Then saw a white envelope with her familiar scribble on it, right down to the red quarter-size heart in the corner with Craig's name written in. Tears welled as she continued to stare down at the envelope, almost afraid to touch it. It was exactly as she had given it to his mailman that day. Only it had been postmarked, opened and read. She sat back in her chair and looked across at Craig, embarrassed and sad.

"Renee, I never knew what a crush really was until my mother explained it to me a few months after we moved. She then gave that letter to me. I don't know why I've kept it all these years, but I have and since I was coming to meet you today, I wanted you to know that I did get it and I've read it many times. I guess you missed me, Renee, just as much as I missed you." He tried to take her hand again, but she pulled it back.

Renee ran her fingers over her scrawny writing and she traced the red heart. "Craig." She could barely speak. Tears fell and she didn't bother to stop them.

He was instantly at her side, taking an empty chair at their table. He pulled her into a warm embrace and felt no embarrassment at all for doing so in such a public place. He lifted her face and wiped her tears away with his finger, and then kissed her tenderly. They remained that way for several minutes, forgetting all about their lunch—until, that is, the waiter brought to their table a beautiful one-layer cake with *Congratulations* scripted on it in bright yellow icing and yellow rose petals, complete with green leaves. Craig and Renee laughed tentatively and were somewhat each taken aback by the applause from the lunchtime diners.

But they were soon caught up in the impromptu mini-celebration, and Renee saw no point telling these people, strangers to her, that she was not marrying Craig. She smiled and accepted the piece of cake he fed her.

The headwaiter insisted the happy couple take a picture for their wedding album. Soon one picture became six or seven or maybe ten. It was hard not to believe the happy couple was anything but that. As they were leaving the restaurant, the waiter handed them a container with the rest of their cake and the pictures.

Outside, she looked at Craig. "I feel awful. How could we do that to those nice people in there?" she asked him, looking back at the restaurant.

"What are you talking about? We didn't do anything but let them celebrate with us." Craig slid his arm around her waist, pulling her closer to him.

"Look, we didn't get a chance to talk about well, you know, about that promise, and I think we need to talk, like right now," she said, trying to sound dead serious.

"All right then, how about following me out to my house and you can see where you'll be living. I'll even let you redecorate if you want to." Grinning, he kissed her before she could say anything else, then grabbed her hand and walked quickly across the street to the garage.

"Are you parked in the courthouse garage?"

"What? Oh, yes, I am, but I don't want to leave my car there." She was distracted by the idea of spending more time alone with him.

But once inside the garage, she stopped him. "Tell you what, I have a better idea; you follow me back to my apartment. One, it is closer, and two, I can always chase you out with my stun gun. Deal?"

"Deal. Lead the way," Craig smiled, watching her shapely legs and nicely rounded derrière when she moved ahead of him to walk to her car.

As he followed Renee in his car, Craig received a call from Justin, one of the creative writers back at the ad agency, who related that some bigwigs had come in to see Davis. He also reported that the men carried briefcases, like the ones containing money, or more likely acquisition papers. Craig had Justin transfer him to Davis' office. He knew that pressure was on for Davis to sell the agency, and fast.

"Hi, Davis. Look, I'm so close to having all the funds to buy the agency. I'm hoping that everything will be settled by next week at the latest. You remember what I told you in confidence about my inheritance?"

"Yes, of course I remember. Craig, you do what you have to do; do what's right for you, understand?" Davis said to the young man he liked and had mentored for seven years.

"Yes sir, I do, and thanks, Davis. Have a good weekend." Craig closed his cellphone and looked into the back window of Renee's car as he drove behind her. "Renee, you have to say yes and marry me." She was no pushover, and he knew his work was cut out for him. But if she was still determined and refused to budge, then he was going to have to backtrack and call on an ex-girlfriend to be his temporary wife in this marriage of convenience.

Exiting the expressway and slowing down behind Renee, he immediately recognized her neighborhood. Most of the large, three-story buildings had been converted into apartment units with very large rooms. Most had ornate moldings and other original details specific to the period in which they had been built, the 1930s and 1940s.

He was so deep in thought he hadn't noticed Renee had gotten out of her car and was now tapping on his window. "What are you doing? Come on in and I'll show you why I rented this place." He looked up at her just as a light breeze lifted her hair, and he was again struck by how beautiful she was. She literally took his breath away.

Craig got out of his car and followed her inside the building. He was immediately drawn to the large iron radiator in the foyer and the detail of the wide banister. He ran his hand along an original interior column and then followed her up the steps. Again his eyes were drawn to the sway of her hips. That is, until she stopped abruptly and turned around, staring down at him from two steps above.

He grinned sheepishly, then nudged her back around. "Hey, I'm an appreciative man, so fire me."

Once inside her bright and airy apartment, he could see all of her feminine touches. *Okay,* he thought, *she likes blue and white.* Renee pointed to the three huge windows. The one bay window was an array of color. The entire window contained original stained glass. In intricate designs was a mix of odd patterns and shapes. Craig was drawn to it immediately. "Oh, wow," he said, as he moved closer to inspect the window's details. "This is beautiful, and especially with the late afternoon sun coming through. Oh, yeah, baby, I can definitely see why you rented this apartment. Nice."

"Why don't you make yourself at home and I'll get out of these shoes and get us some iced tea."

He turned from the window and took off his suit jacket. "Sounds great, thanks. By the way, Squirt, what's up with those purple heels?" he asked her quizzically, but really liking the shape of her legs.

When he sat down on the couch, Renee stomped over to him. "Now, what's that supposed to mean? They're beautiful shoes."

Craig couldn't help laughing. She was almost pouting. At any minute he expected her to punch him in the arm. Not giving her a chance, he reached up and pulled her onto his lap. For several minutes, he did nothing else except look into the depths of her eyes.

Renee's eyes went right to his mouth. He had beautiful full lips, and his teeth were white and very even. She could remember every single time in the past when she had sat somewhere staring at him when he wasn't looking. With her heart beating wildly, Renee lifted her hands and cradled his face, letting her fingers trace his thick but neat eyebrows. She liked that the hair on his head was in the just-barely-there style; it made him look even sexier. At sixteen, he had a mop of curly hair that she had dreamed of touching.

Saying nothing, Craig sat quietly and let her tour his face, but he was aching to kiss her again. He thought about the crush she had on him. He remembered what his mother had said about Renee that day in the minivan. "Craig, she's so young and impressionable. You're a few years older and you have the potential to hurt her tender little heart because you're growing into a young man in high school. She's not even out of middle school yet, and if ever the time comes for you two to be more, then let time find you when you're both older." His sisters had agreed. They, too, saw how hurt he was watching Renee sitting on their old front steps, her face sad and her arms folded. All he wanted to do then was to hold her in his arms, like now. Craig didn't know why he hadn't told Renee that back at the restaurant.

Slowly, he eased his hands around her, bringing her into his embrace. He kissed her forehead and guided her head onto his shoulder. Then he said, "I'm sorry for not stopping by your house to say good bye to you, Squirt."

Renee lifted her head and looked at him and the emotion in his eyes floored her. She remembered him fighting to hold back his tears when Bryant died, and now he was sorry for something he knew was important to her. "Oh,

Craig, I'm just . . ." She couldn't finish what she started to say. The pull was so great that she leaned forward and kissed him, tentatively at first, then with a passion she didn't know she possessed, as her arms circled his neck.

Craig was having difficulty believing this was the skinny little ponytailed sister of his late best friend. She had grown up and filled out in all the right places. He reached around her back, pulling her against his chest. His roving hand found the sides of her breasts. Her beautiful eyes expressed her emotions . . . and she was one sexy babe. In that moment, he was fighting the urge to flip her under him and make passionate love to her. *What?! Make love to the Squirt? Whoa . . . hold up!* Craig's mind screeched to a halt. That startling realization shook him to the core, and he set her back from him, effectively ending their passionate kiss.

Extremely embarrassed, Renee scrambled up off his lap and retreated to her bedroom and closed the door. "Oh, my God." Her body was aflame with desire. She kicked off her shoes and paced the floor, then stopped when she caught her reflection in the full-length mirror hanging behind her closed bedroom door. Immediately, her eyes flew to her breasts, and the one Craig had held within his hand was aching, seeking more of his touch. But realization forced her to look into her own eyes. *I have lost my damn mind.* She recalled feeling him come to life under her hips and knew that he wanted her, too. "Oh, Lord," she whimpered, still studying her reflection in the mirror.

Back in the living room, Craig went over to the fireplace. His desire was not subsiding, but how could it when she kissed him like that, and moved against him like that? Damn. This is not what he expected. He wasn't complaining, he just couldn't believe how things were going, definitely not how he had planned. He walked to her bedroom door and knocked. "Renee."

He knew she was probably embarrassed, so he tried another approach. "Renee, I know your mother taught you how to treat a guest in your home. Come on out, please." He waited and still she didn't come out, so he turned the knob and opened the door. Looking around the large, neat room, he stood dumbfounded. The room was empty. "Hey, Squirt, where are you?"

Renee had gone in her private bathroom. And into the walk-in closet. She never heard Craig call out her name. She quickly changed into a pair of jeans and a tee shirt. She was walking barefoot back into her bedroom and gasped when she looked up and saw Craig standing at a bureau. He seemed to completely fill the space in her large bedroom.

He was standing by the bureau and looking at pictures of Renee's family. But he was drawn to a picture of him and Bryant, taken before Bryant became too ill to go outside. The picture showed them in the Richards back-yard during a Fourth of July barbeque.

Craig remembered that one hot day well. He and Bryant ate so many monster-sized burgers they ended up sick and had to drink glasses of Alka-Seltzer, courtesy of Mrs. Richards. Other pictures showed Renee and her sisters at various stages of growing up. He was amazed. It was as if the snapshots were somehow a chronicle of how

Renee had grown into the beauty she was now. He turned when he heard her gasp, drawn to her again.

"I'm sorry I came into your bedroom, but I called out a couple of times and got worried when you didn't respond."

"I have a private bathroom in here. Got check it out. It's like three times the size of the one in the hallway off the living room." She didn't move when Craig walked over to her and ran his hand along her heated cheek.

"I don't know about this, Squirt. You and your sisters would have screamed bloody murder if I had dared to even tap on the bathroom door while you guys were in there."

"You're safe today. Go on in." She needed to get him out of her bedroom fast.

Craig returned and whistled. "Beautiful. That tub—man, you could fit four people into that thing. Or," he said, moving closer to her again, "cozy enough for just two people."

Renee didn't know if it was his sexy eyes or what he'd said, but she felt an irresistible pull towards him. "Well, I wouldn't know. I only take baths by myself, and that's quite nice, too. How about that iced tea?" She darted around him and left her bedroom. Craig followed.

Watching the movement of her backside in the jeans, Craig said, "Iced tea sounds good, and maybe we can eat more of our prenuptial cake." *Yes, stay on track.* Craig reminded himself. His career—and that of eleven other people—was depending on him staying on track. But he couldn't explain why his libido was going haywire around her.

Renee headed to the kitchen to prepare the tea. Her breath caught in her throat when he followed and had rolled up his shirt sleeves to help her. He had strong muscular forearms. She couldn't remember having seen anything so sexy before. She watched as he sliced the cake.

"We can take everything out into the living room."

"Sure. So, Renee, tell me why haven't you settled down and had a couple of kids yet? Oh, by the way, did you ever become a nurse?"

⌒

Renee was glad to announce that the iced tea was ready. It saved her from having to answer him. But once they had settled in the living room, he asked her again. "So, are you going to answer me or not, Squirt?"

"Okay, in short I'm not married because I haven't found anyone I'm willing to entrust my heart to, and that's why I don't have any children. And no, I never became a nurse. I just didn't want to see all that sadness and pain in other people that I experienced watching my only brother die. So I became an accounting major in college. I work for an investment and accounting firm downtown. I'm one of three senior accounting specialists there."

Eating his cake, Craig sat back and listened to her give an abbreviated account of her career. "Ah, sexy and smart, I like the combination."

"Okay, my turn. What do you do?" she asked.

"I work as an account executive at Davis Franklin Advertising Agency. I've been there seven years, going on eight."

"Oh, the Davis Agency? I've heard of it, not too much lately, but I've heard of it."

"Well, we've had some major advertising campaigns in the past, and a few years ago we won several advertising awards. It's been a little of a struggle, you know, competing with bigger, newer firms, but the Davis Agency is well known in the field. Actually, I . . . nothing." He couldn't explain why, but he wanted to tell her what he planned to do.

"What?" She was intrigued and she liked them talking.

"I was just thinking that one day I might buy that agency and take it over." Craig bit his lip and wondered why he had told her that. Damn.

"Well, I think that would be great. Are you successful at what you do?" She could tell by his custom-tailored suit, his watch and, of course, his car, a jet black top-of-the-line Mercedes Benz, that he was financially well off. Besides, he looked loaded.

He laughed briefly as she just stared at him, thinking he'd lost his mind. "You know what, I think that was just your way of asking me if I'll be able to take care of you financially after we're married. Well, the answer is yes."

She set her glass down on the coffee table. "Okay, enough of this already, Craig. We're strangers who haven't seen each other in seventeen years, and here you call me out of the blue and expect me to marry you? We're back to where we were at the courthouse . . . You've lost your mind. That's it, isn't it?"

"Baby, you did not kiss me a while ago like we were strangers. We're old friends, just getting reacquainted, that's all." He set his plate on the table and watched her.

"Old friends? Craig, you never gave me the time of day way back then. Well, except to chase me through the house and up and down the street. So you really don't know me, nor I you, and that makes us strangers."

"Hum . . . what about the kiss, then? Do you kiss all strangers you meet like that?"

"Oh, shut up." She, too, was wondering about that kiss, especially her response to it.

He smiled. "So how would you feel about moving in with me after we're married? I mean this apartment is very nice, but I already have a house out in Highview Canyon. It's large and has nice rooms." He glanced around the room, and then looked up at her. "I have a housekeeper and a gardener who comes out once or twice a week," he added, taking a sip of his iced tea. "And you wouldn't be that far from work. I think just two or three exits away and you're downtown."

"Craig . . ." She could see he was dead serious. She listened as he explained that, while he wanted to get married right away, he wanted to wait to tell their families. She held up her hand to stop him. "Craig, we are not getting married. Understand?"

"Oh, yes, we are, Renee," he said calmly. "You promised me."

"Okay, you're now freaking me out. Craig, I'm not marrying someone I do not love or someone I shook hands with when I was twelve years old."

"We made a promise to each other, Renee. And the moment you shook my hand, it was sealed. I'll bet you chewed all that gum, right down to the ones you saved until last. The ones you really didn't like, those nasty pink ones." he grinned up at her.

Renee swallowed, thinking, *Lord, this nutcase is serious.* This was no longer funny.

"You're thinking I'm crazy again. Well, I'm not, and I know you must also be thinking 'he's serious as a heart attack,' and you'd be right, I am." He stood up, taking her by the arm and brought her body closer to his. "And you do love me, and I love you. We always have, haven't we, Squirt? You even wrote that in your letter to me," he said.

She couldn't speak. She forgot what he'd said the moment his lips came down on hers in a light kiss. She didn't stop him, and felt powerless to do anything except give into the intense passion he had once again ignited. Craig effectively inched his tongue into her mouth, and resting his hands on her hips, he pulled her up against. Her entire body reacted immediately to feeling his body pressing against hers. The kiss was a full body experience, and to top it off, he tasted like cake. Renee's hands went around his waist, holding onto him for support. Her legs were weak with the knowledge that he actually wanted her. When Craig backed her to the couch without breaking contact with her mouth, she unsuccessfully fought for control over her body.

This was not part of Craig's plan. No way did he want any entanglements, so what was he doing, he wondered? Here she was, a total honey. He angled their bodies so that he was on top of her on the couch. He ran his hands up her short tee shirt, reveling in the feel of her skin. His fingers flitted across her breasts. Her reaction was immediate. Craig dragged his lips from hers and moved to her ear, then to her neck, where he kissed every inch of exposed skin. Her sighs were propelling him to sample all that she offered, so he lifted her tee shirt and slowly feasted on her breasts, first one rosy tip, then the other. "Renee, you're so beautiful," Craig murmured. Her arms held onto him tighter as she gasped, seconds before his mouth found hers again. Craig desperately wanted to feel more of her. His fingers sought the exposed skin below her tee shirt, then he found and unfasten the snap closure on her jeans.

Blood pulsated in Renee's ears. She didn't hear her own cautionary inner voice. Instead, she only heard his voice and felt his heavy breathing, hot on her face and neck and moving lower. Where was her inner voice, she wondered? The one that always told her to stop and think before doing something she'd regret later. But it all felt too good; he made her feel too good. Craig was the cutest boy she'd ever known, and he wanted her. She reveled in his caresses, then his lips sought hers again feverishly. Renee clutched at his shoulders, just as his wandering hands were seeking more of her. That's when her inner voice called out to her. "Oh, my God, Craig . . . I . . . stop. We can't . . ." Renee never finished her sentence. The telephone, on the end table, just inches above their heads, rang twice. She and Craig just stared at each other, unable to speak. Then they heard the voice of her mother, leaving Renee a message on her answering machine. The result was so effective that they might as well had been caught doing something terribly wrong. Within seconds, Craig had pushed himself up off her. Renee jumped up as well and began trying to adjust her bra and snap her jeans closed, a simple act made harder by perspiring, trembling hands. Her mother's message was forgotten.

Seeing her struggling, Craig moved her trembling hands aside and expertly adjusted her bra and snapped her jeans. Embarrassed, she couldn't meet his eyes, so she turned her back to him.

Craig adjusted his own clothes and was grateful that Renee's back was to him. He was embarrassed, too. Taking a calming breath, he reached out to touch her shoulder but she pulled further away from him. "Renee, we didn't do anything wrong here. I mean, it's not like we're teenagers and your mother walked in a caught me with my hand down . . ."

She turned and glared at him. "Why don't you just shut up, Craig. This isn't me," she said, pointing at the couch. "What are you, anyway, some kind of master player? You get the ladies on the couch and put your hands all over them and then what, huh?"

"Huh? Excuse me, but I didn't feel you trying to stop me. In fact, I think you were enjoying it just as much as I was." She moved near the window and he followed, softening his tone. "I think we probably would have, well, had a very good time this afternoon had that call not come."

Renee couldn't believe him. Actually, she couldn't believe how far she had let things go with him. "Craig, I'm not some innocent, ditzy bobble-head who doesn't recognize when a man is putting the moves on me. Trust me, nothing was going to happen here this afternoon. Besides, I think it's time you left." And she really did want him to leave then. She wanted to be alone to process what could have happened and why she had felt powerless to stop him. More importantly, she wondered if she was so starved for love that he was probably right in saying they would have had sex on her couch.

Craig's cellphone rang, robbing him of an immediate rebuttal. Anyway, he knew the exact moment when she was about to surrender to him, regardless of what she just said. "Hello." He turned aside when he heard Miss Lilly's voice on the other end of the phone. She was calling to see if he was still coming to the bank to complete the processing of his inheritance. "No, that's not going to happen this afternoon, unfortunately." He turned and watched Renee pick up their plates and glasses and go into the kitchen. Craig listened as Miss Lilly reminded him that since she was retiring, Tuesday would be the last possible day for her to assist him.

Craig swallowed hard and closed his eyes. His main thought was the eleven people counting on their jobs; in effect, counting on him. Davis' words replayed in his head: Do what you have to do for you. He looked toward the kitchen, where Renee was. "I'm sorry to have kept you waiting for me all afternoon, but I'll call you on Monday."

"Oh, Craig, you're so sweet, just like your grand-daddy knew you'd turn out to be, and tall and handsome, too, just like he was." Her giggle made him smile broadly, remembering that his grandfather did enjoy keeping company with Miss Lilly.

Renee returned and caught him smiling at whatever his caller was saying. It was obvious to her that he was talking to a woman. She pointed to the door, indicating for him to leave.

"Well, thank you. Bye." Snapping the phone closed, Craig turned and saw where she was pointing. "Renee, sweetheart, you made a promise with me and I expect you to keep your end of that promise, just as I plan to do. Now, I'll give you the weekend to think over things like living with me. I mean, I like your apartment, but I have a house and a pool." He smiled as her cheeks reddened. "Used to like swimming, didn't you?"

Renee's eyes were slits as she stared at him. "Out. You're crazy, and I think you need some type of mental health counseling."

Unrolling his shirt sleeves, Craig continued on as if he had not heard her speak. He picked up his jacket from the chair and shrugged it on. "Renee, I'll be waiting for you at the courthouse on the very bench where we first kissed, ten o'clock sharp on Tuesday morning."

Renee tried to breeze past him to open the front door, but he was much too quick for her. Grasping her arm, he firmly repeated his charge. "Renee, Tuesday, ten A.M. sharp, and if you don't show up, my next stop will be to my attorney, one block up from that courthouse. I'll be in the company of a shitload of people who witnessed and participated in our prenuptial celebratory luncheon. Let me see, there were attorneys, judges, business people . . . all there with us. I'll file a breach of contract lawsuit against you so fast it'll leave you spinning in your purple heels."

Renee pulled her arm from his grasp and glared up at him. "Try it and I'll sue you for harassment so fast it'll be *your* big head spinning in the face of a lawsuit."

Craig edged on as if he had not heard her. "I guess I should have evidence to show my attorney, right?" He leaned forward and kissed her lips quickly, then placed two of the six or seven Polaroid pictures on top of the marriage license, leaving them on the coffee table. Then he walked to the front door. "You don't look so harassed to me in those pictures. I'll see you Tuesday." With that, he left.

For a full minute, Renee stood rooted to the spot in her living room. She finally edged her way to the couch. Her breathing was labored. "Attorney? Lawsuit? Oh, no." She was genuinely flustered. *I absolutely cannot get involved in another pending court case.*

She flopped down on the couch and pulled a chenille-covered pillow to her chest. The scent of Craig's cologne immediately jerked her back to his demand and threats. If she didn't follow through, could he—would he—actually sue her? He must be crazy, she reasoned. But she didn't think so at all. Renee sat up abruptly and picked up the marriage license from the table; the pictures from the restaurant fell onto the floor. She picked them up and looked at the first picture. She was sitting on Craig's lap, each of them holding a champagne glass. They looked very happy. His arms were around her waist and the ring on her finger shone brightly. In the second picture they were blowing out the candles on the cake. *Congratulations!* glowed boldly in yellow icing. The servers had encouraged them to make a wish before blowing out the candles. In a court of law, she guessed, the pictures would be powerful evidence. "Oh, Lord," she said, staring up at the ceiling in an effort to block the tears threatening to fall. She walked into her bedroom and retrieved a thick file from her nightstand drawer. Sitting down on her bed, she began pulling out various documents, reports and receipts.

To Renee, the folder represented her personal humiliation and embarrassment. It was the product of letting her guard down and trusting a man she thought loved her. It had cost her dearly. It cost her her heart, her self-esteem, and her life savings. Thirty thousand dollars—money given to her by her parents—gone in a flash, stolen by an unscrupulous man who pretended he loved her. Charles Hunter had said he loved her, and had convinced her that he did, for all of two months. It happened one night when he stayed over at her apartment, which was not unusual for him to do. After sharing the night together, she awakened very late the next afternoon and Charles was gone . . . and so were her bankbook and bank cards.

It had been a Friday, and the staff at her bank seemed unconcerned at first. Renee had sat in the office waiting for the bank rep to check recent transactions against her savings account. Her heart sank lower as she watched each printed page land in the paper tray. It confirmed what she'd only assumed. She sat in the manager's office, staring at a large colorful poster advising customers to protect their identity and guard their bank cards and pin numbers. She also remembered dissolving into tears when the bank rep returned to the office with the senior bank manager. The little slip of paper she held in her hand matched the sad look on her face. "Dear, I'm so, so sorry to have to tell you this, but your account balance went from thirty-three thousand to twenty-five hundred dollars in a span of twenty minutes around nine fifteen this morning."

Renee's sobs drew the attention of a police officer, who happened to be in the bank. "But how could that have happened? I trusted him. That was all the money I had," she wailed. The bank manager contacted the other branch where the transaction had been processed, some twenty miles away, out on the interstate. Charles Hunter had her account number, her checkbook and her pin number. They surmised he must have had an accomplice at that bank branch, because armed with just that information, he was issued a cashier's check for an account that he was not even on. A Houston police officer, Detective Skinner, who happened to be in the bank, offered his assistance. He made a few calls in an attempt to locate Charles. He also found out that the bank teller who had processed the cashier's check could not be located. Renee realized that Charles had done his homework. She was later taken to the police station by the detective to file a theft-by-deception police report. She did file criminal charges against Charles Hunter and hired a private investigator to find him. She filed the charges without hesitation, and she also signed documents for the police to issue an arrest warrant and promised to assist the state's attorney in prosecuting Charles when he was apprehended. When she met with the PI, Simon Donovan, he immediately told her she had been the victim of a con artist, not a lover or boyfriend.

That was some eight months ago, and Charles continued to elude the police. He kept moving from state to state, and the police were still looking for him to serve the warrant and arrest him. At that point, she had been told, he would be extradited back to Houston for trial. Whenever that was, Renee intended to be right there. He had to pay for what he'd done to her.

Looking down at the documents again, she felt like a fool all over. She spread out on the bed eight months worth of bank correspondence, police reports, and letters she had to write to the courts, as well as letters she had to write to all of her creditors. Feeling like a fool, and embarrassed for being deceived in such a way, Renee had told no one except for the PI what Charles had done to her. And although she longed to tell her parents, who gave her that money, she had not. Renee thought about other times she had made bad choices in her life and her parents and her sisters, although loving and supportive, had reminded her that she had been reckless and thoughtless when making decisions.

"All of this would become known to Mom and Dad and my friends if Craig files any kind of lawsuit against me. He can't do that, can he?" She blew out an angry breath.

Renee was too embarrassed to tell anyone, particularly her parents, about what had happened with Charles Hunter. Harold and Lena Richards were working middle-class folks who loved their children. They vigilantly and tirelessly fought the insurance company to pay off on Bryant's death, which was only settled three years ago. Her parents' generous nature dictated that they divide the money, including the large penalty the insurance company had to pay, equally among themselves and their three daughters.

Renee paced her bedroom and thought about calling her parents and telling them everything. She even played out scenarios in her mind about how the conversation could go. *Mom and Dad, listen, I fell into the clutches of a con man and . . . I didn't know he was a con man at the time, but I fell in love with him. Anyway, one night he drugged me and I don't have the money you guys gave me.* Renee cringed; it even sounded stupid to her own ears. And she was sure her parents would once again tell her that she had been reckless and used bad judgment. She didn't think before she leaped. Yeah, another decision she didn't think through. Her family always told her she jumped into action before she thought things through. They were usually costly mistakes for her. No, she couldn't tell her parents.

Saturday afternoon the ringing telephone pulled Renee from the work she had brought home. Thinking it was her sister, Meg, Renee quickly picked up the handset in the living room. Only it wasn't her sister. It was someone Renee had become increasingly frightened of . . . especially in the past month.

It was Charles. He said nothing at first. Then Renee said she knew it was him because she recognized his breathing. "You sound so scared, Charles and you should be." He had called her before to threaten her into calling off the private investigator. Then Renee had pushed him to another anger level.

It was then Charles's frustration came to a boil and he had shouted, "Renee, shut the hell up and listen to me! This is not a game. If you don't call whoever you have on my ass off, then I'm coming back there and I'll personally take care of you myself; that is, after I take care of him. You understand what I'm saying to you, or do you need me to spell it out? Now, let it go, because if you don't . . . I'm warning you. Don't push me, Renee, or you will regret it. I promise you that. You know what a promise is, don't you? Now, you call your dog off my ass."

With a mouth gone dry, Renee said, "I'll see you in jail for a long time, you coward. You pathetic coward."

"How you gonna see me in jail if you're dead, Renee? Call him off!"

"What? You have a lot of nerve threatening me. I'm calling the police," she screamed through her fear. She couldn't believe Charles had threatened her life.

"Renee, sweetheart, listen. It's over and done with. Let it go. You were my mark. I studied you . . . your routines, your habits, everything. I'll bet you're pacing the living room floor, right now, and biting your bottom lip." Charles blew out a breath and said, "Last warning, Renee. Call him off my back, or else."

When Charles slammed the phone in her ear, Renee double-checked every window and door and closed every curtain. Then she collapsed into a trembling heap onto her couch, and her eyes connected with the pictures and the marriage license Craig had left on the table. After slamming them into a drawer, she called Simon, her private investigator.

When Simon arrived at her apartment an hour later, Renee had calmed down somewhat. She was relieved to see his smiling, reassuring face.

In the course of his investigation, Simon had followed Charles from South Carolina, then up to Canada, and that is where the trail had gone cold. Simon told her he expected as much. "Renee, this guy is a predator. He knows how to survive and he knows how and when to lie low. I'm sure he's still in Canada. Don't worry, he'll come back to the States."

"Simon, he threatened me and you, and now I'm scared, I really am," Renee said.

"I know, but don't be. Right now, he's edgy. He has latched onto his next victim and doesn't want to screw that up. We'll get him," Simon told her confidently.

"So what do I do now? Just wait for him to make good on his threats and come for me?"

"No, Renee, you get on with your life," he said, watching her pace her the floor. "Here it is, a beautiful Saturday in June, and you're in your apartment working. You're a beautiful, smart young woman who should be out there dating and having fun. Instead, you're frittering away your life in this apartment. Don't let that dirt-bag con artist Charles Hunter do that to you. You're letting him take control over you again."

He indeed had told her that before. "You know, Simon, it's funny you mention me getting out. An old friend from way, way back when, well, he called me and we had lunch, yesterday. I think he wants us to have a few dates." Renee didn't dare tell Simon about Craig's demand that she marry him.

Simon clapped his hands. "Great, do it! Go out, and if he starts to act up, just call me," he said, grinning at her. "Don't forget my wife, Rhonda, is a cop, so when I do come to punch him out, she'll be with me as my backup."

The weekend was long and drawn out because both her cellphone and her apartment phone rang constantly. The few times she answered, it had been Charles calling with more threats.

When Renee finally drifted off to sleep in the wee hours of the morning, she held in her hands the pictures of her and Craig at the restaurant.

On Saturday, Craig remembered the look in Renee's eyes before he left on Friday. He remembered her teenage temper, and he'd bet anything that she'd gotten worse as she got older and he had seen some of it yesterday. But then Craig had seen something else in her. He'd seen, felt and sampled her passion . . . and he was craving more of it, of her. That realization shook him. He didn't want a serious relationship or involvement with anyone. Period. His focus was on building his career and purchasing the advertising agency. Period. He couldn't wait. Craig had already begun working on ideas that he knew would bring in big business and get the agency back on track. To do that, he needed access to the money that was almost within his grasp.

That's why he had sought out Renee Richards. Craig knew he could have called on any one of his ex-girlfriends, but he didn't want to marry any of them. He also knew that's exactly what they wanted of him, and if that happened, then he would be permanently trapped and deep into a marriage he didn't want in the first place. Then he was sure his wife would end up pregnant. No, no, he didn't want that at all. He figured three months, tops, would be enough time to stay married, and there would be absolutely, positively no sex. Okay, he realized that was going to be extremely difficult, especially if the ex-girlfriend he chose to be his temporary wife was one he'd particularly enjoyed previously. He figured it wasn't a sacrifice for nothing.

He still couldn't believe his reaction to Renee. Bryant's scrawny little sister wasn't so scrawny anymore, he thought, a smile tugging at the corners of his mouth. And she had passion burning inside her. But he was genuinely happy to see her. He did miss her.

Craig always knew when Renee was at their house, because she always came looking for him, and she always had a little smile for him. He laughed now remembering the time when he chased her and his sister, Annette, into the backyard with a frog. Only he ended up tripping over a rock, falling and breaking his arm. Then he felt ten times worse, trying not to cry like a baby, when the two of them did everything they could to bandage his broken arm until his father came out of the house and rushed him to the hospital.

Craig hoped she'd be at that courthouse on Tuesday, but just in case she wasn't, he needed to move to Plan B. That meant making some calls and doing some fast talking.

He took out his palm pilot.

CHAPTER 4

Tuesday morning was a beautiful, sunny June day. Perfect for a wedding, Renee thought, frowning. She'd had one of the longest weekends ever. She barely ate or slept. She tried to reach Simon, but he was called out of town on a family emergency. All she did was try and think . . . think of a way out of the mess Craig was forcing her into. She found none. What was clear to her was that Craig had told her that he was now ready to get married, but he didn't say why *now*. That was a significant question Renee needed him to answer. She didn't really think he was crazy, or a lunatic. He appeared to be of very sound mind; a likable, well-off, sexy guy. So what was up with him, she wondered. That question continued to plague her as she pulled into the parking garage across from the courthouse, her pulse quickening and her heart fluttering as she once again relived their near tryst on her couch. It was 9:45 in the morning and she was fifteen minutes away from meeting her groom.

As Renee climbed the steep steps of the courthouse, she hoped all the while that this would prove to be a Craig joke. Craig was always joking and teasing her, wasn't he? *Yes, of course, that had to be it.* Then she remembered that he had stopped all that just before

Bryant died. Besides, she had a feeling he was serious. This all-grown-up Craig was not joking.

Renee reached the top landing and rested her head against the cool marble of the column flanking the heavy brass doors to the courthouse. She stood there for several minutes, wondering why she kept thinking about how Craig kissed her and how wonderful she felt in his arms. Then her trembling started again.

Pulling herself up to her full five feet, six inches, Renee walked through the brass doors and went up the few steps to the main hallway. At first she was too afraid to look in the direction of the bench, but slowly she finally peeped around an interior column and realized for sure that Craig wasn't joking. There he stood with his back to her talking to another man. Fifteen or twenty steps . . . that was about the number of footsteps it would take for her to reach him; or she could turn around and take ten steps and be back outside . . . where she would start running and just take her chances that Charles would be captured before he had the opportunity to kill her.

The guard on duty at the security desk was watching her with a quizzical expression on his face. Perhaps he sensed her dilemma. When he smiled and waved her in, she walked in and even managed a tentative smile at him. Then she slowly took twenty-two steps exactly, and was now standing directly behind Craig.

He knew the moment she had stepped into the court-house. Of course he did because he had seen her walking up the courthouse steps. Craig smiled with relief. But his relief came mainly from not having to make another call to an ex-girlfriend. Now he knew that Renee was standing behind him. He could feel her body heat and could smell her perfume. He also felt a tight pulling sensation in his stomach; he was excited to see her again. Craig shook the hand of an attorney he knew and said goodbye. Then he turned to face Renee and was floored.

Renee was stunning, a vision in a brushed silver skirt and jacket set with matching shoes and purse. Her engagement ring sparked against the fabric as she clutched her purse. Her hair was piled high, and several brown ringlets bounced around her face. She took his breath away. Craig was speechless, totally at a loss for words, a first for a fast-talking, wheeling-and- dealing ad man.

Renee had taken extra care dressing that morning. After changing her mind four or five times, she'd finally settled on the silver outfit she had purchased several months ago but had not yet worn. Looking down at the outfit now, she wondered about her choice because he hadn't said anything. "Am I overdressed?" she asked quietly.

"Huh?" Craig still hadn't been able to find his voice, but he was vaguely aware that she'd asked him something. Finally, Craig took her hand and leaned down to kiss her cheek. "Renee, you're beautiful." He spun her around. To touch her again was warming and soothing to him.

She was aware that he'd started walking slowly while holding her hand, and she was now walking with him. *Say something.* "So, how is your family?"

"Fine, yours?" His eyes drank in the sight of her. "Okay, here we are . . ."

Renee looked up at the gold letters on the door: Room 112 Marriage Ceremony. She looked up at Craig. "So you were serious about this?"

"Were you serious when you dressed in this outfit this morning?" He opened the door and held it for her to proceed him. Once in the room, Craig led her to a private waiting area and sat down beside her. After a few minutes of silence, he said, "Where's the license, Squirt? Please tell me you brought it with you." He watched her pull her bottom lip in.

This is your opportunity, she told herself. All she had to do was say she left it at home, or better yet, that she misplaced it while cleaning up. She looked up into his face, and after several tense seconds ticked by, she snapped open her clutch purse and passed the document to him. "Craig, why are we doing this again?"

"Because you promised me." Craig opened the document and looked at it, and then handed it back to her, along with his pen. Renee took the pen, noticing his name was scripted on it and swiftly signed her name. She passed the document back to Craig without a word or look of protest.

Craig signed his name and then got up and took the license up to the counter, where a clerk waited to assist him. When he returned to his seat they sat quietly, saying nothing for a few minutes. Just as each was about to say something, the quiet outer office became noisy when a just-married couple emerged from the marriage chapel with their wedding party. Flower petals were tossed above the couple as they kissed to the shouts and hoots of those with them. Renee watched the scene unfold as if in slow motion. Some of the red and white flower petals had landed on her short skirt. She just stared at them, not bothering to brush them off. *This can't be happening. What am I doing? I don't believe that Simon had to leave town like that.*

Craig reached over and plucked the petals from her skirt, holding them in his hands for a few seconds before tossing them into the wastebasket beside him. He wondered what she was thinking about. She was biting her bottom lip. What was it he had heard said about women's dreams of their wedding day? He couldn't remember, but guessed it was a bigger deal than he was aware of. He was pulled from his thoughts when the court clerk announced they were next and that their witnesses were already inside the chapel.

Craig stood and held his hand out for Renee. "It's going to be okay, Renee."

Renee drew in a breath and accepted his hand and stood.

Once inside the chapel, an older woman came up to them. She had a flawless cocoa complexion and had her hair done up in a beautiful salt and pepper French twist. She looked happy to see them. She also looked familiar to Renee, but she couldn't place her. The older man was white, and she didn't know him at all.

Craig introduced Renee to his boss, Davis Franklin, just as Miss Lilly reached for her hand. Renee put on the barest of smiles and shook their hands. The kind woman pinned a yellow rose boutonniere onto Craig's lapel and kissed his cheek. Then Miss Lilly shyly handed Renee a beautiful bridal bouquet. Renee stared down at the floral arrangement of yellow roses, green ivy, baby's breath and streamers of lace and pearl clusters. The woman held onto Renee's trembling, cold hands. "Honey, do you need a few minutes, maybe to freshen your lipstick? And I can put some extra pearl clusters in your hair. Oh my, you are such a beautiful little thing, Renee."

"Oh, okay, thank you." Renee followed the kind woman into the ladies' room within the chapel. She would have collapsed against the wall were it not for the woman holding onto her. "I'm sorry. I haven't eaten much in the last few days." That was not a lie. Her weekend had been filled with stress and little food, if any at all.

Lillian laughed lightly and patted her own hair. "Oh, honey, I understand. I was first married when I was nine-teen, and I was so nervous. I hadn't eaten anything at all. I almost passed out right there in front of my groom and the preacher. Boy, oh boy, that was funny. But that night, I was not laughing. It was just perfect." She smiled at her own memories and helped Renee over to the vanity stool and went about taking some of the pearl clusters from the bouquet and placing them fashionably in Renee's hair.

Renee looked up at her reflection in the mirror as the woman stood behind her fussing with her hair. "What happened that night?" Renee asked, absently, dazed almost.

The woman let out a laugh. "Whoa . . . girl, I had the time of my life. We didn't have much money, so my

Bobby and I just went to a justice of the peace when he lived up in Baltimore. Oh, this was back in the fifties." Miss Lilly, as she was affectionately known, enjoyed retelling the story of her wedding to her first love. "Then our friends threw us a big old party in the back yard. We had so much food and wine that night . . . well, let's just say, our daughter, Laurel, was born exactly nine months to the day Bobby and me got married." She finished and smiled at Renee in the mirror. "There, you're all set . . . just lovely, honey." She rested comforting hands on Renee's shoulders.

That's when Renee met the woman's smiling eyes in the mirror and it came to her. "Wait a minute. I know you." Renee swung around on the vanity stool, her eyes lighting up with recognition. "You're . . . Miss Lilly? Miss Lilly from The Wayland Bank?"

Miss Lilly laughed and hugged her. "Well, who did you think I was, baby?"

Renee hugged the woman to her and broadly smiled for the first time since entering the courthouse. "Oh, I don't know. I haven't seen you in years. You look wonderful, Miss Lilly. Oh, my goodness . . . your Bobby was Mr. Bob. Oh, he passed away years ago." Renee touched Miss Lilly's arm with compassion.

"Yes, that's right. Now, look, we can talk later. You've got that man waiting out there to marry you. Now freshen your lipstick and come on. I've been waiting to see him get married for a lifetime, then to find out he's marrying little Renee, well . . ." Emotion made her eyes water. "Well, let's just say, I'm truly happy for both of you."

Before Renee knew what was happening, she was ushered out of the ladies' room and was standing beside Craig and he was holding onto her hand. She looked back at the door, twice, wondering if someone was going to burst in and tell her she was on Candid Camera or one of those "gotcha videos." Only nobody came running in during the simple ceremony, during which Renee vaguely remembered mumbling, "I do," promising to be Craig's wife. *This is such a farce,* she thought, never meeting his eyes. But she knew he was staring down at her; she felt his eyes touching her, everywhere. She kept her eyes focused on the bouquet in her hands. Suddenly, she felt Craig's warm hand lightly tugging at her hand and realized that he was sliding a matching wedding band onto her finger. The band was a full circle of sparking diamonds and now she had something else to stare at. This was good, she thought. Look at anything but him or the judge or their witnesses. Renee wanted to cry, but she didn't.

Craig tried not to focus on Renee's expression. If she understood why he had to do this, he was certain she would have said, "Oh, Craig, I understand." Then he thought he wasn't so sure now. This was not the little teenage Squirt whose eyes were always on him. This Renee was a woman, and now was about to be his wife. He smiled over at Miss Lilly, knowing she had the bank checks made out as he had requested them . . . one for one million dollars even, the other for the balance, well over two and a half million dollars, including interest. He'd told Miss Lilly that he and Renee had been quietly dating and decided to get married. The fact that his inheritance included a stipulation that he must be married in order to get his hands on it, well, he just hoped neither she nor the bank folks would put two and two together.

Craig heard his name and looked immediately at the judge. "Excuse me, sir?" he said, embarrassed for letting his mind wander. He looked at Renee, who was now looking at him.

The judge, his clerk, Miss Lilly and Davis all laughed as the judge reached out to take Craig's shoulders and turned him to face Renee. "I said, you may now kiss your lovely bride."

"Excuse me? Oh, okay." Craig swallowed nervously and wondered why he was suddenly perspiring. Even his hands were damp. He thought, *This is crazy, I am definitely not the nervous type.* Still holding onto Renee's hand, he gently pulled her into his embrace and kissed her, and it was not the brief kiss he'd intended, either.

Renee was determined to just accept the ceremonial kiss and, hopefully, get out of there. All she wanted to do was go home and have a good cry, or have yet another cry. Then Craig's lips touched hers and memories of Friday flooded her like snapshots. Memories of his hands caressing her face when he kissed her, like now, created waves of longing she thought was long gone . . . as in gone like her life's savings and gone like Charles Hunter. That sobering thought snapped her back to the present and she broke off the kiss with Craig. Her husband. She was so shaken she would have run back into the ladies' room if he had not pulled her to his side, his arm going around her waist as if he had read her mind and knew she was about to flee. But he held onto her while accepting congratulations from the well-wishers in the room.

The clerk had sectioned off an area to take pictures of the bride and groom, and she was trying to talk Renee into taking at least a few pictures. But when Renee told the clerk that wasn't necessary, Craig and Miss Lilly spoke simultaneously. "Oh, yes, it is." Then Craig led Renee over to the area to take their pictures, where he announced he wanted the full package.

To Renee, it looked like a lunch menu written on a poster board in a deli. *Chips, soda and pickle included.* Renee almost laughed at her wandering thoughts. *I'm becoming delusional.*

The clerk, whose name tag read Verna, was excited and fussed all over them to get the best pictures and poses. "You know, Mr. Thompson, you weren't supposed to see your bride before the wedding," Verna said, continuing to snap pictures of Craig embracing Renee.

Craig and Renee looked at each other, then Craig told the woman they had not seen each other since Friday. Renee agreed by shaking her head no, her curls bouncing.

Now Verna was embarrassed, then she laughed. "Oh, it's just . . . well, Mr. Thompson, your wife's outfit is a perfect match to your light gray dress shirt. And these will be very nice pictures, that's all I meant." The clerk laughed when Renee reached up, touching his shirt, and Craig looked down at it, then up at Renee. Maybe it was the tension of the moment, but they both laughed together for the first time, and Verna couldn't have been happier as she continued taking many more pictures, more than what was normally included in the full package. And she wasn't alone; Miss Lilly pulled out her new digital camera to capture the special moment as well.

After the pictures were taken, their marriage license was signed and handed to Craig. He briefly separated himself from Renee to speak with Miss Lilly. "Thank you so much for being here, Miss Lilly. You've made this day extra special for us, and I will always be grateful for that."

Miss Lilly smiled. "Thank you for inviting me to take part in this, but Craig your family and Renee's family will be heartbroken that you didn't allow them to see the two of you get married. I just know your mama and hers are going to skin you both," she said, reaching into her purse and handing him the two envelopes containing the checks.

He smiled down at the envelopes. "Thank you, and now I have a gift for you." Craig put the envelopes in his inside jacket pocket and took out another one, which he handed to Miss Lilly. He looked up to see that Renee was still talking to the clerk, who was writing up the picture order.

"What's this, Craig?" Miss Lilly looked up at Craig in surprise. She grinned when he told her it was a little something to kick-start her retirement, then she stared wide-eyed at a check made out to her for fifteen thousand dollars. Her jaw dropped. "Oh, my, Craig, you didn't have to do this. I mean, this is a lot of money and you're just getting married and all." Her eyes misted.

"It's just a little cushion if you need it. Besides, I wanted to do it." He looked up and saw Renee now standing just behind Miss Lilly.

"What's wrong?" she asked quietly, looking from Craig to Miss Lilly.

Miss Lilly noted the sudden tension on his face and said, "Girl, these are happy tears for two wonderful, beautiful people. I wish you both all the happiness in the world. But I just wished your families could have seen you two get married, finally." She touched Renee's hand when she saw the look of apprehension on the young woman's face. "Well, look, I've got my retirement party to get to. I do wish you two had planned a celebration party or a dinner, but . . . anyway . . ." She kissed and hugged them, and then whispered to Renee, "now, remember what I told you in the ladies' room and have a ball, honey."

Craig smiled watching her go out the door. "Can you believe that she won't be in that bank anymore? Second desk on the left."

Flustered by what Miss Lilly said, Renee mumbled, "She was always so nice." Renee didn't get a chance to say anything else, because at that moment Craig's boss came up to congratulate her again.

"Young lady, you've got yourself one fine man here. Hardworking, determined and caring, and I have the utmost respect for Craig as a businessman and friend. I hope you two will be very happy. And, Craig, I expect you to take a few days off and take your bride on a well deserved honeymoon." He smiled and kissed Renee lightly on the cheek before asking to speak to Craig in private.

Renee was glad to be alone for a few minutes. She was tired and hungry. She looked up at Craig. He looked happy, and he was indeed a fine man. Today, especially, he looked handsome in his black Armani suit. Even his boutonniere still looked fresh. She, on the other hand, felt hot and frustrated. She was sure she probably looked like the saddest, sorriest-looking bride ever.

Renee closed her eyes and was immediately transported back in time. Back to that day she and Craig had sat on the swing talking. She was sad then, too. How could she have gotten to this place? But then she remembered why . . . it was nothing like a little death threat to force one to seek protection. Inhaling deeply, she opened her eyes and glanced down at her bouquet. It was still fresh and fragrant. Lifting her eyes, see saw Craig hand an envelope to his boss, who in turn handed Craig a thick packet of papers. To Renee, it appeared to be some type of legal document with blue backing. The two men shook hands, and then Craig looked over at her, just as the clerk, Verna, was handing Renee the sample packet containing six pictures.

Craig rushed over to pay for the pictures. He smiled nervously, or so Renee thought. It was almost noon when Craig and Renee left the courthouse. She walked away from him and stood on the sidewalk and waited to cross the street to the parking garage. But he said, "Excuse me, but where are you going, honey?" He stretched out the word honey and added a wide grin.

Hand on hip, Renee turned sharply and looked up at him, exasperation clearly visible on her face. "Look, you, you bully . . . you got what you wanted, and this was a colossal mistake. I must have been out of my mind to make yet another bad decision." She stared up at Craig and shook her head. "This is just crazy. I'm crazy, and I'm out of here." She finished with an angry huff and thrust the bouquet at him. Then she turned back to face the street, again waiting for the light to change so she could cross.

He thought she looked adorable and wanted to kiss her again. "Wait, who's a bully? Not me." He reached for her hand to prevent her from crossing the street. "And what do you mean you're out of here?" Craig lowered his voice and, lifted her hand and gave her back the bouquet when he noticed several passersby looking at them.

"And what part of any of that didn't you understand?" she asked, waving her hand in front of his face. She blinked when she realized just how handsome he was. The early afternoon sun was showing off his brown complexion. He was positively one sexy piece of eye candy. *Girl, stop this,* She chided herself.

Craig laughed and lifted her free hand to his lips. "Well, dear, I didn't understand any of that. I expect us to live together, as in, now what did that judge say?" Craig pursed his lips and then put his finger up to his temple as if truly trying to remember something. "Oh, yeah, as in 'holy matrimony, my little sweetheart, sealed with our circle of rings.'" For emphasis, he held up his hand and wiggled his ring finger at her, before placing his hand over his heart in some kind of grand gesture, all the while grinning down at her.

Renee blinked at his fingers in front of her face. She didn't remember him putting a ring on. She wondered if she had put it on him. Then looked up, realizing he was still talking to her.

"What about the celebration luncheon I've planned at our favorite lunch spot, at our favorite table?" He waved his hand and pointed at the restaurant across from the courthouse where they had lunch on Friday afternoon.

Renee looked over at the restaurant then up at him, her eyes narrowed into slits, her lips tight and her face red. "Craig, go celebrate with yourself." With that, she snatched her hand from his and walked quickly across the street to the garage. Once inside, she stopped and peeped around a cement column to see if he'd followed her. Thankfully, he hadn't, but he was still standing on the sidewalk watching her, when she glanced back at him.

Craig watched her retreat to the parking garage. "Oh, my beautiful wife, we need to stay married for at least three months. If not, than I lose everything I did all this for." With that, he patted his inside breast pocket, which now held just one envelope with a check. He checked his watch and spoke aloud. "Okay, I'll give her time to cool off; in the meantime, I've got a stop to make." Craig headed down the street to his attorney's office, where he would try to catch Davis. The transfer of the agency would be completed today, before Davis left for his vacation, and since all the paperwork was in order, the agency was his . . . all with a court stamp of official transfer. With air in his steps and a smile on his face, he walked with confidence that things could only get better from this point on.

∽◦

While Renee headed to her apartment, and Craig and Davis sat in his attorney's office signing several documents before they headed back to the courthouse to complete the agency transfer, Miss Lilly had just arrived at the catering hall that was several blocks up from the Wayland Bank. Her retirement party would soon be underway.

Arriving a little early, she saw all the decorations and preparations set up for a grand affair. "My goodness, I didn't know I even knew two hundred people."

Miss Lilly sure hoped her outfit was appropriate. Looking down at her pale green lace and satin dress, she waved her hand in the air. "Shoot, I look darn good, good enough to be included in a wedding party, as a matter of fact." She looked up towards the ceiling for a moment. Her eyes danced as a thought hit her. Miss Lilly cleared her throat and reached for her cellphone to call on some folks she hadn't seen or talked to in quite a while.

∽◦

Renee couldn't get home fast enough. Once inside the safe haven of her apartment, she let out the breath she felt she'd been holding since she left her apartment earlier that morning. She kicked off her gray satin shoes and walked into her bedroom and sat on her chaise lounge. She fought the urge to throw something. "Damn, why did Simon have to leave town?" Just thinking about Simon, Renee was forced to close her eyes and force away what he would say if he found out what she had just done. But then she looked at her flashing answering machine, it also brought home how scared she really was . . . sixteen messages since she had left home earlier that morning. She only listened to one. *Charles.*

"What the hell have I just done? How could I have done this to myself? First, Charles walks out of my life with all my money, and now Craig walks into my life, and, and . . . what? He wants a wife 'as in holy matrimony.' What a crock." As her ranting went on and on, Renee realized just how tired and hungry she was and went to the kitchen and remembered Craig in her kitchen with his shirt sleeves rolled up, slicing cake. *Cake.*

Walking back to the living room she sat on her living room couch, wishing she hadn't taken the day off from work. At least there, she would be so busy she wouldn't have time to think about what happened today. With exhaustion claiming her, she rested her head on the back of the couch and, within a minute or so, she was fast asleep. She never heard her phones ringing.

Several hours later Renee awakened, but didn't get up from the couch. It was now dark outside. The only light inside her apartment came from the guest bathroom near the front entrance. Something felt odd. She didn't move. *Oh, God . . . Charles.* Then she realized that a blanket covered her and didn't think Charles would cover her with a blanket if he was going to kill her, like he had threatened. "What the . . ." She reached behind her and turned on the table lamp. That's when her breath caught in her throat. Her eyes widened. And if she hadn't recognized him, she would have screamed and thrown the lamp at him.

Craig sat in a comfy chair across from the couch, watching her. His long legs stretched out in front of him. Like her, he, too was still dressed in his wedding attire.

He'd arrived at her apartment almost two hours ago. He had knocked several times and when she didn't answer after a few minutes, he tried the knob and found the door unlocked. Once inside, he found Renee sound asleep on the couch. He went to get a small, colorful blanket he'd seen in her bedroom the last time he was there. He watched her until the sun disappeared in the sky, then got up to turn the bathroom light on. He smiled at her. "Hi, baby."

Relief swept over her like a cool breeze. It wasn't Charles. She watched Craig. Something in the simple endearment caused a longing in her heart, but she shook her head in an attempt to ignore the feeling. In a weary voice, she asked, "What are you doing here, and how did you get in here?" She sat up keeping the small blanket over her thighs because her short skirt was not only twisted, but it had ridden up and was practically meeting her panty line. "Well?"

"Well, I came here to pick up my wife, and I did knock, but you didn't answer," he explained in a calm voice as if explaining something not at all unusual.

"So you just decided to come into my apartment?" she stared across at him, angry that she must have forgotten to lock the door. And in the face of Charles's most recent call, she should have known better, she chided.

He only smiled. "Renee, how many times did I just walk into your home in the old neighborhood? And you did the same thing in our house."

"That's different, and that was a long time ago. We were kids."

"Guess you're right, sorry. Are you ready to leave?" Craig hadn't moved. He still reclined in the chair, looking very relaxed, resting his chin on his palm.

"Leave? I'm not leaving. I live here. You don't, so guess again who's leaving." She pointed to the door.

"Renee, we were married today, and I told you I expect us to live together, in that union. I'm only continuing the promise that you made to me. Now, what's the problem with that?" he asked, stretching his arms above his head and rolled his shoulders back to ease the tension in them.

She stared at the full length of his body and swallowed hard. Angry at her distraction, she looked at him as if he'd suddenly grown two heads. "What's the problem with that?" she mimicked his deep voice, cringing when he grinned at her. "I'll tell you what the problem is, you clown. I don't want to live with you, and I don't want to be married to you, either. Craig, please tell me, did you have to get married?" she asked point-blank.

"No, I was ready, that's all," he lied, point-blank.

"I don't believe you, and if I find out that you've pulled me into some crazy drama you've got going in your life, well, all I'll say is that you'd better watch your back. I promise you I'll make you pay. Oh, but then won't I get to sue you for alimony, too? Yeah, so trust me, it will be on." *But what about my own drama?* she thought.

Craig pinched the bridge of his nose. "Money is not an issue for me, Renee, and it won't be for you. So put that out of your mind, because I plan on taking care of you, my darling wife," he said, his lips tightening as he erased what she had said about his drama. He'd just cross that bridge if he had to, he thought.

"I'm not your darling anything. Now get out of here." With that she angrily threw the cover from her and stood up; unfortunately, her skirt stayed up, giving Craig a full view of her thighs. Looking down at her skirt, then over at him, Renee only smirked and yanked her skirt down before turning and walking barefoot into her bedroom. But she did see his eyes darken as they trailed from her thighs and up to her face.

Craig wasn't even affected by her attitude at that point. He felt he'd done what he had to do. In the long run she was going to benefit from being married to him, but she didn't know that yet.

After the ceremony, he'd decided to give her the time to cool down, before coming to her apartment. He expected her to be angry and probably throw something at his head. He didn't expect to walk into her apartment and find her sleeping, hugging her pillow. Standing over her, he didn't expect to feel his chest tighten at the very sight of her. Already, he felt so protective of her, and when his eyes moved over her as she slept on her side, he thought, this Renee was all woman . . . his Squirt was long gone.

Craig stood and stretched his frame and then walked right into her bedroom without bothering to knock. Again, she wasn't there, so he walked into her master bathroom. He found her sitting on a footstool, clutching a towel to her face, crying. Oh, damn.

He braced himself before speaking. "Renee," he said hesitantly. He did not expect to see her crying, and that broke his heart. "Squirt."

She couldn't believe that he'd invaded her privacy again and looked up at him with red and swollen eyes. "Craig, get out of here, and keep on walking until you're out of my apartment and my life, because in the course of two days, I've had enough of you." She threw the towel on the sink and stormed past him in her stocking feet.

He followed her back into the bedroom and, when she was about to go out into the living room, Craig reached for her hand and stopped her. "Come here, Squirt, sit down, I want to talk to you." He sat on the side of her bed and encouraged her to sit with him, and after a few minutes of his tugging and her hesitation, Renee sat down beside him.

"Listen, baby, I'm really sorry about the way things have turned out."

Sniffing, she asked, "What does that mean, Craig? Are you telling me that you're now sorry for forcing me into marrying you?"

"Renee, I'm not going to keep saying this, but I didn't force you. You could have said no, but you didn't. What I'm sorry about is that you're angry because you obviously didn't want to."

She saw that he was searching for the right words; for what, she didn't know. "Then why did you demand that I make good on that promise?"

"Because of that, because you promised that you would marry me when I was ready."

"Well, what about me, you goof? I don't love you, Craig, so tell me what kind of marriage this is?" She yanked her hand from his and stood up, waiting for him to answer.

"What? You don't love me? Wow, I'm crushed and heartsick," Craig said placing his hand over his heart and assuming a fake hurt look.

"I don't want this," she said loudly, and began pulling at her wedding rings.

Craig reached up and put his hands around her waist. In one quick move, he pulled her down onto the bed and eased his large body over hers, effectively pinning her under him. "I want this marriage, and I want you living with me in my house, and as long as we're husband and wife, you, Mrs. Thompson, will keep those rings on your finger, okay?" He looked down into her beautiful face and she closed her eyes. Tears slipped from her closed eyes and ran sideways to her ears, and again he felt that odd tightening in his chest. "Baby, look at me, please." He pulled a handkerchief from his breast pocket and dabbed at her tears. His voice softening, he pleaded. "Come on, Squirt."

How could she not look at him? His deep, smooth voice in her ears and warm breath feathering her face was as powerful as any caress. Besides, the length of his body was flat against hers. Such intimate contact alone was causing her imagination to run amok. Her eyes fluttered open and she looked into his chestnut brown eyes. Her heart began beating faster. Or was it his?

When she opened her eyes, Craig realized he had never really looked at them as a teenager. "You're so beautiful, but listen, Squirt, I'll take care of you. You'll want for nothing, trust me."

"This is all about you, Craig, and about what you want. I can take care of myself, and I don't need you to make me happy. I was crazy showing up today and falling into this senseless arrangement." But Renee knew it wasn't all about him. She, too, had a reason of her own for showing up. She just had not thought her plan through past the 'I do' part.

Releasing the breath he'd been holding, Craig thought that he might just be what she'd called him, a bully. But he had a responsibility. He had to keep the agency from a takeover. And admittedly, he knew it was an opportunity he might have never gotten again. All because Davis had given him a chance many years ago. He knew that Davis didn't want the agency to be turned over and lost with the larger firms. But, with a stamp of transfer, Craig had turned the larger firms away and he had secured employment for a lot of people. He forged ahead. "Our arrangement, our marriage, is not just about me. A marriage is between two people." Yeah, that sounded like something he'd heard before.

Renee was having difficulty keeping her thoughts straight, because his body was heating hers from the inside out. "Get up off me." She began futile attempts to get out from under him.

"Renee, when I leave this apartment, either tonight or tomorrow or the next day, whenever, you're going with me. And we will live in my house, but I will make you a deal." He gazed down at her, liking the feel of her body squirming under his.

She met his eyes. "I don't want to leave here and give up my apartment. And, Craig, I don't want to be your wife."

"Do you want to hear the deal I have for you or not?"

"Get up off me first," she said heatedly.

"Oh, no, I think you'll probably grab that heavy lamp on your nightstand and hit me over the head. So no, we stay right here and talk. Besides, I kinda like this." Craig dipped his head and kissed where her pulse was beating at her throat, beckoning him. He inched toward her lips, but Renee turned her head and his lips connected with her ear, so he kissed her there. "You're lovely and you smell wonderful. You were the most beautiful bride I have ever seen." Craig was trying desperately to still blood surging from his brain to his groin. "Okay, here's the deal. Stay married to me for, ah, let's say three months, and if you can't get past the ogre you think I am, then I'll release you from your part of the promise and we'll get divorced and move on. Deal?" Then he lifted his head.

Renee didn't believe him, and her expression showed it. Her mouth dropped and her eyes narrowed. "Three months! No! No way am I staying in this joke of a marriage with you that long. No deal, now get off me." She began to struggle again.

Craig closed his eyes and lowered his head again, nuzzling her neck, feeling her move under him. He grinned, realizing she had no idea how much he was enjoying her movements. But after a few minutes, he knew he had to say something. Letting out a sigh, he said, "Ah, baby, if you don't quit moving under me like that, then, dear wife, we'll end up consummating our marriage right here, and right now." Craig moved his hips against her so that she could feel just what he meant.

Renee stilled instantly and didn't know if it was because of the heaviness and warmth of his body against hers or the fact that he'd mentioned consummating their fake marriage. Her mind raced. Surely, he didn't think for one minute that they would . . . oh, no, he won't. Suddenly, a deal of her own formed in her head. It started as a sizzle and exploded in her brain. If Simon was stepping up the investigation like he said he was, then there was a strong possibility that Charles would be captured within the next three months. He just had to be, she thought. Okay, accept Craig's deal because it would ensure her protection for the next three months under his roof, then give him one of her own. "About your deal . . ." When he began kissing her ear, she reached up and pulled his ears back, forcing him to lift his head.

Craig rolled off her and onto his side, grinning boldly. "Okay, lay it on me, baby. Whatever it is, I say yes, but that's only if you come live with me," he said, pointing to himself.

Renee smiled for the first time then turned on her side. And like him, resting the side of her face on the heel of her palm and tugging at her skirt. "You meant what you just said, honestly?"

He couldn't remember what he'd just said, because he was still thinking about kissing her. But if she agreed to live with him as his wife, then the three months would fully satisfy the stipulation attached to his inheritance . . . and he would be home-free. "Real smart of you, Granddad," he inwardly fumed, causing his nostrils to flare briefly. Although Miss Lilly had retired, the bank manager had told him yesterday that they planned to make sure he satisfied the stipulation and that he wasn't trying to pull the wool over their eyes. Yeah, right, he thought at the time, but then his attorney had rattled on about bank fraud and what could happen if Craig had committed any type of fraud. He, too, was surprised by Craig's announcement of marriage. Craig had all but dismissed such concerns.

"H-e-l-l-o?" Renee called out through his musings.

He remembered her question. He really needed to stop dwelling on things that didn't matter at the moment. "Yes, I honestly meant what I said." Craig really had no idea where she was going; his eyes were busy taking in the swell of her breasts above her now-wrinkled jacket and matching shell top.

"Okay then, I'll accept your deal and live with you, Craig, but nothing will be consummated. That way, when I file for an annulment at the end of the three months, there won't be any hard feelings, and I'll even go so far as to not sue you for alimony. Deal?" She held out her hand for him to shake. Three months under Craig's protection, while Charles Hunter was apprehended and arrested appealed first and foremost to Renee's sense of safety.

Craig became fully alert and wondered what the heck had just happened and what it was she wanted him to agree to. "What? Wait a minute." He sat up on the bed and looked down at the hand she still held up, but his eyes strayed once again, this time to her exposed thighs.

Renee didn't move, noticing the direction of his eyes. "What's wrong? Aren't you going to shake on that deal?" The doubt in his eyes told her she'd hit a nerve.

Craig cleared his throat. "So, then nothing will be consummated, huh? So then I shouldn't be expecting you to jump my bones in the middle of the night, huh?"

"Only in your dreams. Do we have a deal?" She still waited for him to shake her hand.

Craig chewed on his lower lip, thinking, but he finally shook her hand. "All right then, Mrs. Thompson." Still holding onto her hand, he leaned in closer and ran a finger along the side of her face and down to her neck. He kissed her slowly and tenderly. When she didn't push him away, he increased the intensity of the kiss and eased her onto her back and under him. This time he wanted her to feel all of him, his intent clear. A twinge of conscience made him hate what he was about to do, but it didn't stop him. Just when he felt her hands sliding up his arms and she relaxed her body, Craig bounded up off her and walked out into the living room.

It took Renee several minutes to pull herself together before she could drag herself up from the bed. Despite the fact that her body hummed everywhere his body had touched hers, her mind was still working. "Ha! Three months is a walk in the park, and I can outlast you far longer than that, old friend," she muttered. But there was still something else she needed to sell him on.

Craig paced the living room floor, his eyes from time to time straying to his ring. He couldn't believe he was wearing a wedding band, no more then he could believe he was actually married. Not that he had anything against people getting married. Some of his best friends were married. It was just that that type of confining relationship wasn't for him. He preferred the freedom of having no formal attachment. When Renee emerged from her bedroom, he remembered his newly minted marital status and altered his thinking. *My former freedom.* "Ready?"

"Well, um, no. Craig, I need time to pack, so how about I move into your place, say in a couple of days. What do you think?"

"Well, um, no, Renee," Craig replied, mocking her. "I just don't think that's going to be acceptable."

"What do you mean, no? You really can't expect me to pack up my stuff and move in with you tonight, do you?" she asked, her face turning red.

"Yeah, sure I do. In fact, I'll help you pack. The sooner you move in, then the sooner the three months will start counting down." He thought that sounded plausible, reasonable.

Her eyes blazing, she snapped, "No, I can't move in tonight." She then crossed her arms over her stomach and stared at him until his own stare wavered.

Craig found a spot somewhere above her head and took in a deep breath before looking back at her. "Renee, I'm hungry and I've arranged for dinner at my house," he said. "In fact, I believe it has been delivered and is just waiting for us. So look, just pack a few things, then we'll come back in a day or so and pack up the rest of your stuff." He admitted to himself that he must sound like a brute, but he needed her to live in his house to establish at least the appearance of a real marriage. One thing he knew for sure, Renee was going to be hell to live with for the next three months. He wasn't worried about the deal they'd made to not consummate the marriage, but he did wonder how much of a toll that was going to take on both of them. In any case, he didn't intend to risk having to return almost three million dollars, and lose the agency, by getting caught in a compromising situation . . . like in the arms of a woman not his wife. He gathered her to him and hugged her tightly. "Renee, it's going to be okay. I promise."

Renee wiggled out of his embrace and took a step back from him. "Craig, don't ever promise me anything again." In an icy voice she added, "Our marriage today just proves that a promise made can come back to bite you in the ass." She turned and stormed into her bedroom.

"Ouch," Craig said, following her, but Renee slammed the door in his face, telling him she didn't need or want his help.

c2~

Renee had insisted on driving her car and following Craig home. When she pulled up to his house and into the driveway, she was surprised. He lived in a new development in a traditional home with large windows on both floors. With lights spilling out from some of the rooms inside, she would have thought a family lived there. A normal family, she thought.

When she exited her car, Craig was there to assist her by reaching for her hand and walking her up the walkway. When they arrived at the front door, Renee was so taken by the landscape of beautiful hedges, she couldn't understand why he hadn't opened the open door yet. He just watched her, waiting for her to get it. When she didn't, he simply lifted her up in his arms and carried her over the threshold into the house. When she fumed and squirmed and threatened to punch his lights out, Craig finally set her down in the large, open foyer. He then gave her a tour of the house, which had three large bedrooms, three bathrooms, and an upstairs loft-style library. A combination den and sunroom, which he used as his office, had a large window that looked out on a waterfall. The large formal dining room was sectioned off by a curved glass block wall, and a state-of-the-art kitchen opened out onto a full patio. The huge backyard captured Renee's attention immediately. It was complete with a full outdoor cook station, spa and pool.

Back inside, he led her to the top level, where he showed her the bedrooms, stopping first at the master bedroom, his bedroom, with her one suitcase. "What?" she blurted, taken aback by the way he was staring at her, like a moron.

"This is the master bedroom, Renee," he said, smiling at her tight lips.

Glancing at the closed door and then up at him, she said, "Forget it, Craig. If I stay here, then I'll take one of those guestrooms." She pointed in the direction of the other two bedrooms. "Preferably the one on the end."

He looked down the length of the wide hallway, knowing full well that she was referring to the bedroom nearest the library, and farthest from his bedroom. "Afraid you're going to get tempted during the night and need a little distance from me, Squirt?" he couldn't help teasing her. Her face was so serious, and adorable.

"Again, only in your dreams. Now, it's either that room or your office downstairs. It has a futon, and I happen to like that aquarium."

"Okay, the lady chooses room number three. Come on, I'll show you the room."

Talk about odd. The room she chose had been decorated in the same colors as her apartment, in various shades of blues and white, with touches of yellow here and there.

The room was quite feminine, and had vases of fresh yellow and white roses. The blue and white bed linens were thick and beautifully quilted, with plush-looking pillows piled high at the headboard. She was drawn to the matching cream-colored armoire that also matched the chest of drawers and two nightstands. She ran her hands across the slightly raised hand-painted yellow and blue flowers that were on the drawers. "So beautiful," she said quietly. Craig was standing behind her and heard her comment.

"You like this room, or do you want to see the other one?" He smiled at her back, his eyes straying to her backside, which was accentuated by her snug-fitting jeans. Beads of perspiration popped out on his forehead.

"No, I don't need to see it. This one is fine. And, yes, I do like it."

He set her suitcase down and turned to walk out. "Good, I'm glad. I had to rely on my memory of the color scheme of your apartment to get this room decorated the way I thought you might like it. Why don't you take a few minutes, get settled in and then come on down to the dining room for dinner." He left leaving her staring at his back.

Renee's eyes swept the room again and then his words sank in: *I had to rely on my memory of the color scheme of your apartment.* "But how did he know I would choose this one?" She was suddenly too weary and too hungry to think about it any longer. She checked her voice-mail and listened to a message from Simon, telling her he was going to be away longer than he thought, maybe a week and a half, at the most. He also hoped she was 'getting out.'

Downstairs, Craig sat at the dining room table waiting for Renee to come down. His mind wandered back to the vision of her in those sexy jeans and a cotton shirt. Draining his glass, he chuckled when he recalled how she had stood on the sidewalk outside her apartment waiting for him put her bag into the trunk of her car. Then she announced she was driving her own car and would follow him. He didn't trust that, so he gave her directions to his home, then he followed her. Craig had a feeling that the next three months were going to be interesting.

He looked up to find her watching him, and shook the eerie feeling of déjà vu before he stood up and led her to the chair next to his. "You weren't trying to find an escape route from the second floor, were you?" He chuckled when she rolled her eyes at him and plopped a kiss on her forehead.

"No, I was checking out the library." She glanced around the traditional dining room and at all the food he had delivered. "This is a lot of food, Craig," she said, sitting down.

"Like I told you, I'm hungry. I'll fix our plates if you like." She nodded and Craig complied. "I'm glad you like the library. I want you to feel comfortable here, so please feel free to make any decorating changes you want. I'm agreeable to anything and any color, except that whole black and white checkerboard thing, or anything pink or orange. As for everything else, I'm good," he said, returning to his seat.

"Three months, Craig. Trust me, I won't be making any decorating changes during that time. Besides, it is perfect just the way it is." She picked up her fork, ready to dig in, but he took her hand and stopped her. "What? You said you were hungry."

Still holding her hand, he said, "I am, but it's still our wedding day, and I think a toast is appropriate, don't you?" Her expression told him what he could do with his toast. "Indulge me, please." He lifted his champagne flute and waited for her to do the same.

For some twenty seconds, Renee hesitated, then, seeing his serious look, she lifted her glass to his and managed a phony smile.

"That's my girl. Now what shall we toast to?"

"To promises and deals. Cheers," Renee said quickly, not giving him a chance to respond. She tapped her glass to his and gulped down half the contents. Then she picked up her fork and began eating, feeling his eyes on her. Ignoring him, she concentrated on the full-course meal of roasted chicken, seasoned shrimp, and many vegetable dishes and assorted dinner rolls.

Craig stared at her bowed head then said, "Cheers."

They ate in silence for several minutes, each hungry and each deep in thought. He then told her that he had arranged for them to be off from work the next day so they could go get the rest of her stuff, or he could take her shopping, or they could just hang out at the pool.

Renee looked at him as she reached for a dinner roll. "Sorry, but I'm not off tomorrow."

"Oh, I think you are. In fact, I know you're off because I called your assistant, Tracy, and told her you were taking another day off," he said, reloading his plate. "I hope you like these dishes, Squirt. I kind of just ordered a variety of things from the restaurant's menu." He looked up from his plate and caught her staring at him with narrowed eyes. Craig set his fork down and prepared himself for whatever was coming. "Okay, what now? Come on, bring it on," he said, gesturing with his hand.

"You called my assistant and said what exactly?"

"Well, I told her the truth, Renee. I told her that we were married today and that you wouldn't be in tomorrow, either. Once she stopped giggling and shrieking, she said congratulations. Oh, yeah, and she said she would tell Leslie somebody and that they'll plan a party or something for you at work." He resumed eating, but looked up when her chair scraped the floor. She had stood up and was now glaring down at him. Furious, she was practically breathing fire. She had his full attention. "Oh, shit . . . what? Did I say something wrong again?"

"Yes, you did. You took it upon yourself to call my job and talk to my assistant and change my work schedule. I don't appreciate that, and I'm telling you now, don't you dare play that boss man crap with me. I don't like it, so don't you ever do that again, are we clear?" Renee fumed, shaking a finger at him.

While she ranted and raved, Craig refilled their glasses and promptly drained his. His mind rambled. *Three long months of this . . . all for that freaking three million dollars.* But he knew it was worth it. When her rant ended, he realized she had asked a question; he had no idea what. So he simply answered, "Yes." Then he stood and waited for her to take her seat.

The meal was finished in strained silence. Craig cleared the table and put away the food. "Why don't you make yourself comfortable in the living room, and we'll sit and talk."

And so she did, but her attention was drawn to his family photos on the built-in glass enclosed bookshelves flanking the fireplace. Moving closer, Renee noticed that he had several pictures of her family and of her on the mantle. One photo showed her sitting on the swing in her backyard alone. Renee remembered that day, but she didn't know that someone had taken a picture. She was about nineteen. There were other pictures of their families at outings together. Her eyes moved to one particular picture and her throat swelled with emotion. It was of the last birthday she'd shared with Bryant. Craig referred to the picture on Friday. Everyone, including her parents, sisters, and Craig as well, had all climbed onto and around Bryant's bed. She was unaware that one of Craig's arms was draped across her shoulder. They were all smiling with colorful party hats on.

Craig now stood beside her. "I like that picture. Everybody looks happy, and Bryant was happy that day. We spent a lot of time laughing," he said, remembering his friend.

"I remember. What did you laugh about?" she asked.

"Everything . . . guy stuff. You were a girl; we couldn't tell you everything we talked about." He reached out and tucked a stray curl behind her ear, letting his fingers linger on her warm cheek. Smiling, he picked up the picture of Renee on the swing. "Mostly, we talked about girls and sex. But definitely sex if I'd managed to sneak over a couple of dirty magazines or videotapes stuffed in my backpack."

Renee laughed. "Oh, that's right. I do remember that time I walked into Bryant's room and caught the two of you watching a dirty video."

He laughed out loud, startling her. He sure did remember what happened when she had walked into her brother's room—she shrieked and ran out, threatening to tell her mother. "I chased your butt for almost two solid blocks," he said, still laughing. "I just remember seeing those colorful sneakers of yours dipping and darting around trees and hopping over hedges."

"Yes, that's right; that is, until you got all winded and ran back to the house like a scared little chicken." Renee couldn't help but smirk at him.

"Scared my ass; I had to run back and stop that damn videotape before your mother or one of your nosy sisters walked into Bryant's room. I realized I'd run out of the house chasing after you with the damn VCR remote control in my hand," he said. He picked up the picture of Renee on the swing again. "Don't you want to know how I got this picture of you? We had long ago moved."

Renee glanced at the picture again. He was right. His family had moved away. "You're right, so how . . ."

"My mom went to visit your mother and she saw you in the backyard and snapped the picture. She sent it to me while I was away at college." His voice softened and he desperately wanted to kiss her. "It's my favorite picture of you." He leaned closer; she moved away.

"Do you have any pictures of your family?" Renee felt the need to move away from the magnetic pull she was feeling toward him.

He said, "I sure do. Hang tight." He went into his den, returning with two large photo albums. He sat beside her on the couch.

For the next hour or so, Craig and Renee looked through the photo albums and talked about the old days. After Bryant had become too weak to do more than lie in bed, Craig remained his constant friend and companion. She now wondered how he'd really handled his grief, and the picture of him sitting all by himself on the porch swing appeared in her head.

Craig closed the photo album and looked at her. He saw a softening, a sadness, really, in her eyes and he ached to touch her. He wanted to hold her, but wouldn't let his mind go there. "I ordered us a cake. Nothing fancy, just a small single-layered cake. Say yes, cause I know you like cake." He got up, suddenly needing some distance from the heat of her body.

"Oh, okay, but I'll help. I'm not used to anybody waiting on me hand and foot."

"I'm not just anybody, Squirt. I'm your husband, and I'm supposed to wait on you hand and foot." Their eyes connected for a few tense seconds.

Before following Craig, Renee picked up the remote to turn the stereo off but ended up muting it, and then the television came on. When they returned to the living room, Craig's eyes flew to the TV; the business channel was on and there was his picture flashing on the screen. He knew the story had to be about his acquiring the agency. Renee looked from him to his face on the screen, then back at him, her eyes wide. Neither seemed aware of the ringing telephone sitting on the coffee table. Craig looked at Renee for a split second then their eyes flew to the answering machine. He hoped she hadn't picked up anything more than his face on the business channel. He didn't think the story would break so fast. He turned the TV set off. Suddenly, his mother's excited voice filled the living room. Craig and Renee eyed the answering machine and listened to his mother's happy, tearful voice.

"Craig, oh, honey, we just don't believe it. Well . . . we're just overfilled with happiness. I'm so happy for you and Renee, our little Renee. Oh, Craig, that little sweetheart has had a crush on you for as long as we can remember, and now the two of you have fallen in love and have gone and gotten married. I told you it would happen one day. I'm just so happy . . ."

Craig and Renee looked at each other, baffled, then back at the answering machine. They heard muffled voices and movement taking place on the other end. When Renee heard her own mother's voice saying pretty much the same thing, she flopped down on the couch, still holding their dessert plates.

How long, Craig wondered, was his answering machine going to keep recording? He frowned at it, hating the thing. Then he heard his father's voice.

"Way to go, my boy. I don't know how you finally caught up with that little skinny gal you were always chasing around, but I'm glad you did." He laughed heartily.

Craig flopped down on the couch, too, when the call finally ended. His first thought was to replace his answering machine with one that had an internal voice mail ASAP.

"Oh, my God," was all Renee could say at first. Then she looked up at him accusingly. "You told them, didn't you?"

"No, I didn't."

"Well, who would have told our families? Who would . . ." Then realization dawned. They'd forgotten somebody.

"Miss Lilly," they said in unison.

"But, Craig, why would she do that?" Renee asked, closing her eyes and already hearing her family saying how impulsive she was.

"Probably because Miss Lilly has a kind heart, and remember when she said how disappointed our families were going to be for not being there?"

"Well, what do we do now? I didn't want anybody to know." Renee's headache was in full throttle now, and she rubbed at her forehead and cut her eyes at him.

Craig poured their coffee and then walked over to the glass and marble bar in an alcove off the dining room. He grabbed a bottle of scotch and poured a good amount into their cups. Then he placed her cup in her cold hands and laughed when she took a hefty gulp and cringed.

Craig drained his cup and, ignoring her protests, refilled both of their cups with his mixed brew of scotch and coffee. "We have to plan some evasive strategy for when these folks get all up in our business."

Renee leaned forward and pressed the red flashing message button to replay the message. When it ended, she finally drained her cup, hiccupped and looked at him.

Craig was beginning to feel the effects of the scotch, for which he was thankful. He grinned at Renee. "So you did have a crush on me, huh?"

"Oh, shut up," Renee said, reaching for her dessert plate and attacking her wedding cake.

Craig decided to eat his cake then said, "Hey, Renee . . ."

She'd seen a look in his eyes. "Forget it, Craig . . . I am not sleeping with you."

He was still laughing when Renee announced she was turning in.

"Okay, I have some work to do, so I'll be down here in the den for a while if you need anything." He wanted to say *if* she needed him. But she was already climbing the steps.

Five minutes later, Renee came back downstairs and picked up the photo albums and carried them upstairs with her. She wanted to look at the pictures again, alone . . . mainly his pictures. She did glance in the direction of his den, briefly wondering if Craig was as shaken by the phone call as she was.

Renee did wonder what that business story was all about she had seen on TV involving Craig. But with her parents now knowing about the marriage, she had more pressing things to worry about.

The following day, as Craig and Renee slept the morning away, their respective families were gathered at the Richards' house to plan a proper wedding reception, to be held the coming Saturday. They had three days. When Miss Lilly rang the doorbell, they were delighted to have an extra pair of hands. But more than that, Miss Lilly came with the extra set of wedding pictures of Craig and Renee's marriage. She'd had them enlarged to eight by tens.

The two families gathered around the table and beamed down at the smiling faces of Craig and Renee on their wedding day. The pictures had captured the couple in intimate moments, looking happy . . . looking completely in love. Anyone looking at the pictures would not have believed otherwise. Miss Lilly pointed at a picture she said was her favorite. Renee's hand was touching Craig's shirt and his hand had covered hers; they were laughing. The dads just looked at the pictures, each swelling with fatherly pride.

The pictures gave Cecelia an idea. "Hey, you guys, I just got our color scheme for the reception." She held up one of the pictures. "Yellow and white, those are our colors."

命

When Craig finally got up the day after the wedding, it was one in the afternoon. He had been up until almost three in the morning working on several plans to put the Davis Agency back on the fast track.

His first order of business was a meeting that had been originally planned to officially inform the staff that his ownership of the agency was now final. Now that the news had already hit the media, he needed to speed that plan up. At about one in the morning, Craig drafted a memo to his staff telling them that he'd purchased the agency and stressing that he was still their team leader and needed the expertise and skills of everyone there. He expected the e-mail to finally put to rest everyone's fears of a takeover.

He made breakfast while waiting for Renee to come down, then worked at his laptop computer on the countertop of the center island in the kitchen. He'd been reading some ninety-two congratulatory e-mails, with more coming in. His staff responded first; they all told him that they were with him all the way. He found this especially reassuring, as he hadn't known how they were going to take the news. Most were aware of his attempts to secure funding to prevent a takeover. He recalled overhearing a conversation in the lunch room between two staff members who were talking about getting home equity loans to assist him if they had to. He couldn't let that happen. They had children and other obligations.

Craig was well aware other people in the business world still had issues with an African American taking over a traditionally white business or becoming a head of department. They would not be pleased to hear he had purchased a well-known, well-established agency. But Craig was also ambitious and recognized his own motives. He wanted the agency to be a success under his direction. He wanted to push the agency further into the future, someplace Davis had seemed hesitant to go. Craig knew he had the energy and drive to do it, but he needed his current staff's skills to accomplish all that he was prepared to do to make the agency flourish once again. He felt pretty good reading another e-mail, and could not contain a smile.

"Feeling pretty good this morning?" Renee asked from the doorway.

Craig closed his laptop and slid off the stool. "Yes, as a matter of fact, I do, and guess what, dear wife . . ." He walked her over to the sliding glass doors. "It's afternoon already." He watched her twitch her lips, frowning.

Adorable, he thought, dipping his head and kissing her lightly on her pouting lips, liking the taste of her toothpaste. "I fixed breakfast on our first day of marriage." He opened the patio door, letting the warm afternoon air caress her face. "I thought we could eat out here today."

Renee took in the full table setting out on the patio. "Thank you."

Craig noticed two things about Renee immediately. One, she didn't have any shoes on, and two, her hair was damp, which meant she'd just gotten out of the shower. As he fixed their plates, an image of her in the shower invaded his thoughts to the point that he sat down quickly so that she wouldn't see the obvious sign of where his mind had drifted. "So, how'd you sleep?" he asked, mentally shaking off the memory of the two of them on her couch.

When he handed her a plate of bacon, scrambled eggs, and sliced fruit, she saw his hand shake. "I guess I slept well, considering how it's afternoon already, and I was sleeping in a strange bed," she said. She had slept well, something she had not done in months. She looked over at Craig. He was truly a handsome man, and had been impeccably dressed in suits the two times she'd seen him. But today he had on beautifully fitting jeans and a gray polo shirt that clearly outlined the taut and flat muscles of his stomach. The smooth, black hairs on his medium brown arms lay flat and circled his forearms. Renee's hand was itching to touch him. Suddenly feeling slightly voyeuristic, she quickly picked up a piece of bacon and took a bite.

Renee looked out at the not-so-ordinary backyard and patio. "You really do have a beautiful home, Craig, and then you added this outside haven. Nice," she said. "This patio has a cook station, a bar, and you still have plenty of lawn." She could also see a water fountain that was overlooked by his sunroom.

"Thank you, and I hope you are comfortable here." He saw the now-familiar narrowing of her eyes and quickly changed the subject. "So, I see you still like to go running around barefoot," he said, his amused eyes on the foot she had tucked up under her bottom.

She immediately dropped her foot to the patio floor, mumbling, "Yes, well . . . the need to wear shoes all the time is highly overrated, anyway."

"Hmm . . ." was all he could manage, because suddenly the image of her legs wrapped around him and her warm feet touching his back popped into his head. Shaken by the thought he got up so quickly his knee bumped the table, causing Renee's coffee to spill over the rim of her cup. "Sorry, I forgot the, um, orange juice. It's in the fridge."

He hurried into the kitchen, and closed the patio door behind him. He had never been so thankful for air conditioning. "Come on, man, get it together," he said aloud as he poured orange juice. Before heading back outside, he rolled his glass across his forehead in an attempt to cool down his internal flame.

Renee was now sitting on the edge of the pool, her bare feet dangling into the cool water. She felt overly hot, and it wasn't the afternoon sunlight, either. If it were just the outside heat, her heart wouldn't be pounding so furiously, and her breasts would definitely not be reacting as they were. She looked up as his shadow fell across her.

"Juice . . ." he said, but when she reached up to accept the glass, Craig immediately saw that her little cotton shirt couldn't hide the fact that she wasn't wearing a bra or the fact that her nipples were erect. His mouth watering, he relived the feel and taste of them on her couch Friday afternoon. *Honey . . . yes, that is what they tasted like.* His mouth went dry and he gulped his juice down before Renee had a chance to take her glass. Then he drank hers, too. When he looked down at her, she was staring up at him quizzically. "I'm still growing and need extra juice. I'll, ah . . . go get you another." When she smiled up at him, it touched him all over and settled somewhere in the center of his chest.

Renee laughed and didn't know what was going on with him, but whatever it was, it was making him look silly. He had that mischievous look on his face that he used to get as a boy.

Craig made a hasty retreat back inside to refill her glass, just in time to hear his answering machine pick up a missed call. It was his most recent ex-girlfriend, Cynthia Gaines. Damn, he thought, she must have gotten his Friday message to call him as soon as she got his message. He'd said that he had an interesting proposition for her, and she was leaving him a message in her sultry Southern voice.

"Hi, Craig baby, it's Cynthia. I was so glad to hear from you. Hum. So you have an interesting proposition. Anyway, I had to fly up to New York on business, and I just checked my messages. But look, I'll be back in town this weekend. I'll call you and we can get together to discuss your interesting proposition. Bye for now, kiss, kiss." Her giggles could be heard as she hung up the phone. Craig turned from the counter and realized that Renee had come back into the kitchen and had heard the message.

"Guess you have a busy weekend planned, huh?" Renee walked past him to put her empty plate into the sink.

He watched her back as she went about washing the dishes. "No, I don't—that is, unless you and I make plans for a busy weekend." When she didn't stop washing the dishes, he walked over and took her hands, "Renee, listen . . . that call was from an ex-girlfriend. She, ah . . ."

Renee looked up at him as if staring at a blank wall. The smile she had given him outside was gone. "I know, I heard. 'Craig, baby, it's Cynthia.' " Perfectly mimicking Cynthia's Southern drawl, she extracted her hand from his and picked up a tray to collect the rest of the items from the patio table.

After she slid the patio door closed, Craig glanced at the answering machine. "Fucking answering machine! Note to self . . . replace today." Then he went to help Renee clear the table. Gone was their earlier warm conversation and hot glances, replaced by a cold front moving in very fast. "Hey, do you want to go shopping? There's a really large mall near here or we can go to a movie." She called a curt "No" over her shoulder as she went back into the kitchen.

The cold front moved onward into the kitchen, but he wasn't giving up. "All right, how about a drive in the country, and maybe have seafood at a waterfront restaurant?" He stood behind her, rubbing her shoulders. "Come on, Squirt, it's a weekday. How often do you get to play hooky from work and just enjoy the day?" He wasn't giving up.

"Gee, I don't really know. Maybe that's what usually happens when people get married at ten in the morning. Look, go do whatever you want to do. I brought my laptop and I have some work to do." With that, Renee headed up the stairs.

Shaking his head, Craig watched her go into her room and close the door. He picked up the cordless phone in the kitchen and dialed the phone company. "This should take care of that."

Renee stayed in her room for the remainder of the afternoon, working on a client's ledgers that she'd packed in her suitcase. It was a tedious, time-consuming task. But she was actually glad to focus her attention on something else besides her new husband and his ex-girlfriend, Cynthia, who, to her ears, didn't sound much like an ex. She let her mind go down a path that she knew she should have stopped, but she didn't. Cynthia was probably like the girls he liked at sixteen—those hot-and-fast wenches who were pretty and had large breasts.

Renee had fallen asleep in the middle of the bed, surrounded by papers, pens, rulers and erasers. She awakened, turned on her back and saw it was getting dark outside. She was surprised that she had fallen asleep again; that rarely happened at her apartment. Then she heard a knock on the door. "Come in," she said groggily. She didn't bother sitting up or fixing her hair when Craig walked in bearing a glass of juice and a plate of cookies.

"Hi, I was worried. Here's that glass of juice I owe you." He walked in and turned on the night-table lamp and thought she looked beautiful with sleepy eyes.

"You don't owe me anything, but thanks," she said, sitting up and reaching for the glass. "I guess I fell asleep. I haven't slept much since Friday." She met his eyes briefly. That was the truth. Between calls from Charles and her constantly checking the doors and listening for every sound, Renee had gotten little sleep at all over the past few weeks.

"Yes, I can imagine. I haven't slept much myself since then. Actually, I don't think I've slept well in a couple of months, perhaps longer," he said absently.

She drank half of the juice and handed the glass back to him. "Why haven't you slept?" she asked, eating a sugar cookie.

He met her eyes. "Work mostly. We lost a couple of bids that could have been very profitable, and that was very disappointing." He pulled his attention from her pink lips to answer her question about what the disappointments were. Craig sat down on the edge of the bed, and realized that she seemed genuinely concerned. "Well, the advertising business has gotten more cutthroat and competitive, and the larger companies go around trying to gobble up the smaller firms, like the Davis Franklin Agency."

"But that place has been around forever. I even remember an ad and the commercial." She pursed her lips, thinking. "Let me think, oh, yeah . . . it was about those talking pillows. That was so funny. It was about those fabric-softener sheets. Remember that one? It was really cute." She said, recalling the cartoonish talking pillows.

"Remember it? I created it. That was one of my first campaigns," he grinned.

"You're kidding. Well, I did buy those fabric-softener sheets just because of that commercial," she smiled.

"Then I accomplished what I created that ad to do— send consumers out to buy and use the product. The manufacturer was so happy about the profits they not only paid the agency, but they sent us a shitload of those damn dryer sheets. I'm sick of them now."

"I can't believe you did that," she said, amazed. "Tell me another one you did that I might know." She sat up further, waiting, and ate another cookie.

He was caught up in her excitement and leaned further back on the bed, stretching his legs out and eating a cookie himself. "Oh, okay, ah . . ." He began humming a catchy tune, waiting for her to guess the product. "Hurry up; my lips are itching with all this humming. Oh, okay, I'll whistle it." Then he saw recognition on her face.

"The soap! It's the one for softer, well . . . everything, right?" He nodded and asked if she bought it. "No, but my mother sure did; in fact, I'm pretty sure she still uses it sometimes."

He touched her face and ran his hand down her bare arm. "Do you use it?"

"Actually, I do. But not as much; it has changed." Renee swallowed, looking down the length of him, suddenly aware that they were lounging on the bed together. The moment seemed very sexy to her, and when his hand touched her bare arm, a sizzling sensation hit her stomach.

"What do you mean? How has it changed?" he wondered, his thumb caressing her neck.

"Huh?" She swallowed, distracted. "Oh, well, it just used to be a good moisturizing soap and then they went and added extra fragrance and now the original, plain old moisturizing soap, that I used to like is gone. So I don't use it that often anymore."

"That's an excellent observation, Squirt. You want to work for me?" He laughed when she shook her head no. "Then how about you help me rework a campaign to re-promote it?"

"You're not hearing me, Craig. It doesn't need an advertising campaign. It's the soap itself; it has changed. The original scent had just the barest hint of roses. Now it has this overpowering, almost sickening smell. That's what the problem is. So, I think whatever is making the scent too strong is probably making the soap extra sticky and it gets all slimy in the soap dish. Now, if you can do anything about changing that, then I'll bet you anything that soap will be hard to keep on the shelves again."

He was processing everything she'd said. "You know what, I'm going to do just that. I need to be writing this stuff down." He reached across her and picked up one of her notepads, but Renee snatched it away from him before he had a chance to look at it.

"Sorry, but I have important numbers scribbled on this. Here," She tore off a couple blank sheets and passed them to him. He began writing quickly, almost filling up the two sheets of paper. While he jotted down what she'd said, Renee glanced down at her writing pad and saw that she'd written *Craig Lemar Thompson* and *Renee Thompson* several times on the notepad. She immediately grabbed a heavy black marker and blacked out the names.

He looked up and said, "Done. Renee, this is good. You're a very observant consumer. You would do well as a survey participant." He looked down at her mouth and reached for her glass. "You want this?"

"No, go ahead. Help yourself."

And so he did, only it wasn't the juice he wanted; he wanted to kiss her. And although he knew he shouldn't, he couldn't help himself.

Renee saw his face becoming a blur. His lips connected with hers, and she didn't stop him when she knew that she should. But she remembered she no longer needed intimacy in her life. There was no place for it. In her experience, intimacy came with a price. For her that price tag was thirty thousand dollars, her heart, and her self-esteem. The ever-painful thought caused her to turn her head away from Craig, ending the kiss.

He didn't apologize. He just sat and watched her fumbling with her papers. "Hey, are you hungry yet?" He was missing her company while he worked alone in his den, knowing that she was upstairs, mad at him.

"I am. Maybe I can fix us something. I saw that well stocked fridge." She looked up at him. "I mean, really Craig, how much food do you need for one person?"

He started laughing and didn't stop as he flopped back on the bed, grabbing his stomach.

Renee shook her head. "Did I say something funny, or is this your lunacy showing?"

Between bouts of laughter, Craig managed to say, "Oh, Renee . . . I-I sent my housekeeper to the market to load up the refrigerator, the deep freezer and the pantry just for you." More hearty laughter erupted from him.

She recalled trying to push the juice back into the fridge earlier. "For me. Why?"

Oh, shit, he thought. He knew he had to tell her, but his laughter continued in ripples as he watched her staring at him. "Well, remember I told you that I'd seen your sister, Cecelia, at a charity? Well, she was, ah, larger than I expected. She was much more, well . . ." He spread his arms out about his body.

Renee's eye narrowed. "Fatter, and maybe more homey-looking?"

Oh, no. "Well, yeah, kind of. I mean she was still as pretty as ever, but come on, Squirt, I can remember that every time I saw Cecelia she was primping and acting cute and messing with her hair, and only picked at her food . . ." He couldn't go on when the laughter took over again. He held his stomach, but one look at Renee and he started laughing again.

Renee threw a bed pillow at him. "She'd just had a baby, you clown, and she had a difficult delivery, and besides she's working on losing that baby fat. Now I haven't seen her in a few months, well, not since they moved to San Antonio, but anyway, she and her husband didn't expect to get pregnant so fast after having the second child. Look, I'm not making any excuses for Cecelia. She's still a beautiful person. But what does your seeing her at that event have to do with all that food in your refrigerator and . . ." Renee's eyes narrowed, then widened when realization dawned on her. "Oh, I get it now. You thought that I was heavier and that I . . ." That's when it really hit her. She bounded up off the bed, shoving her papers aside and flying from the room, with Craig hot on her heels and still having fits of laughter.

Renee raced down the carpeted steps barefoot, her mass of hair swaying as she flew to the kitchen. She threw open cabinet doors and the refrigerator doors and then looked up at him. She pointed to a door in a corner of the kitchen. "Is that the pantry?" She didn't wait for an answer; instead, she just pushed past him and opened the door to the large walk-in room and flipped on the light switch. White, open shelves that reached the ceiling lined three walls of the room. Her eyes swept over the items stocked in there. She turned and glared up at him as he stood in the doorway, his laughter finally subsiding. "Well, I'm impressed, Craig. Everything I see is on every list of what not to eat because it's loaded with trans-fats, salt and sugar. But, if you've just got to have junk food, oh, let's just see what we've got here." She turned and reached for a pack of double-stuffed crème filled cookies and threw them at him, one by one.

Craig ducked his head as the packs of cookies flew by him, landing out onto the kitchen floor. "Come on, Squirt. Look, I-I just wanted you to be comfortable, and, you know . . ." He was at a loss for words to explain himself.

"Fat, and fat, you goof." She walked to the freezer chest inside of the pantry.

Craig came into the pantry then, stepping over the stuff on the floor, but she'd yanked open the freezer door before he had a chance to stop her. "Renee, stop this." Then he cringed when she looked back at him. He backed up to dodge whatever she was about to throw next.

"Wow, deep-dish pies, pizza and fruit." She threw them at him, and the last one connected with his stomach. Then she turned to start again.

Craig had had enough. Besides, that last box had hurt, but he also knew she was hurt. He walked over and picked her up and slung her over his shoulder, stepping carefully to avoid tripping over all the stuff on the floor. He sat her down on one of the stools and dipped his head to look her in the eyes. "Okay, you've made your point, and I'm truly sorry for . . . what the hell am I sorry for, Renee?" He spread his hands.

"I don't believe you, Craig. You thought I was overweight; in fact, you thought I was obese and you stocked your house with all that stuff," she yelled as she pointed toward the pantry and the floor. "Why? To kill me, if I did have a weight problem, which I don't!"

"No, no, that's not it at all. Look, I only wanted you to be comfortable here, and if you needed something, well, I didn't want you to have to go all the way to the store to get it, that's all. Honest." He remained hunched over her, looking into her troubled face.

"No, you wanted it right under my nose so that I could kill myself! I mean, why burn calories going to the store for that stuff? So you thought I was a mirror image of my older sister and my mother, didn't you?" Renee was breathing fire. She watched him nod. She was on the verge of tears but refused to give into them. "You insensitive goof. You know what, Craig, your father used to trick us kids out of our spending money. I can't think of anyone who lived in our neighborhood who he didn't trick out of their lunch, spending, or church money to play that stupid shell game or card trick. But I never thought you were a mirror image of him. Did any of us think that? No." She turned her head and stared out at the patio.

She had struck a nerve and it hit home for him, far deeper and more painful than the frozen pizza to his chest. Craig was aware that everyone knew that his father dabbled in gambling when he was laid off from work. He was just so embarrassed by his father's money tricks that he thought it was forgotten. But he was wrong. "My father tricked you out of your lunch money, Renee?" he asked quietly.

"No, but he sure got my Saturday spending allowance, more than once." Then she saw the pain in his face and wished she hadn't said anything. Her words had hurt.

"I'm sorry that my dad did that, and I'm sorry that I did this." He waved at the floor and began picking the stuff up.

Renee felt terrible. "Look, my mother would be horrified to know that I was throwing food onto the floor." She slid from the stool and reached down to pick up a pizza box and then glanced at his back. "I really do like pizza, though."

Craig continued picking up the items, which he piled onto the island and counters, then looked at her feet. "Renee, this floor is cold. Why don't you go put some shoes on?" Then he disappeared into the panty.

Renee walked out of the kitchen and up to her bedroom. A few minutes later she went to window and saw his car backing out of the driveway. As it disappeared around the bend at the end of the street, she sank down to the window seat. "I always go too far," Renee chided herself.

Renee stayed in her room until she heard his car pulling back into the driveway about an hour later. At first her excitement surged, then she remembered why she was in his house in the first place. Still, she couldn't forget the look on his face before she left the kitchen. A few minutes later, he knocked lightly on her door. "Come in," she said, looking up hesitantly at him standing in the doorway.

For a full ten, seconds they only stared at each other. He spoke first. "I'm sorry, Squirt, for everything, including my father's stupidity at that time. He has changed, and I didn't mean to insult you or Cecelia or your mom by stocking the house with all that stuff. I won't do it again. I picked up dinner, so whenever you're ready, I'll be downstairs." With that, he turned and left her doorway.

She didn't say anything; she couldn't. Remorse was plain on his face and in his posture.

It only took her a couple of minutes to shut off her computer and join him in the kitchen. He was at the island, watching a baseball game on the TV in the kitchen. "Hi," she murmured and got up on the stool beside him.

"Hi." The smile that appeared briefly on his face didn't reach his eyes, which went to her feet. "Where are your shoes, Squirt?"

"I'm fine, really." He went into the laundry room, located next to the panty and returned, lifting her foot and placing it against his stomach. Renee watched him unroll a clean pair of his thick cotton socks and slipped them onto her feet. That simple act of him putting her bare foot against his stomach was one of the most sensual things she'd ever experienced. Her hands itched to reach out and touch his bowed head.

He glanced up and met her eyes. "There, that's better." After a few seconds, Craig realized he was still holding her foot in his hand and reluctantly released it.

Shaken by the moment, she murmured, "Thanks."

He pointed at a large, covered silver dish. "Dinner." He lifted the lid to reveal a large cheese pizza. "You said you liked pizza, so I went with the plain cheese. Well, okay, I got extra cheese," Craig explained, grinning sheepishly at her.

"That's fine," she said, glancing up at him as he placed a slice onto her plate before his attention returned to the ballgame and his own slice. Renee remembered that he and Bryant used to play baseball. That thought brought home the fact that they really didn't know each other. Sure, everybody said he was a fine man. But so was Charles, or so she thought. Shaking her head, she took a bite of her pizza.

Craig saw her shake her head and offered to go grab one from another pizza place. But he relaxed when she told him it was good. Then she asked about all the junk food.

"I took it to a soup kitchen downtown, not that they needed all that stuff either. Then I wrote out a donation check so they can buy some healthy foods. I had a thought while I was out," he stated, pouring her a glass of wine. "If you've finished your pizza, grab your glass and I'll bring the bottle and we'll go sit out on the patio and talk."

They left the kitchen and walked into the balmy early evening. She could hear the water trickling in the fountain just outside the den. The effect was very calming. When Craig sat across from her, they spent the next hour talking about their lives.

Craig thought again how beautiful she was, especially with the light from the candle flickering across her face.

"Craig, did you have to get married for some reason?" She sipped her wine and stared at him above the rim of her glass.

Craig knew this was an opportunity to tell her about his inheritance. "Renee, I told you that I was ready, and I remembered our promise so I said, why not look up the Squirt."

"And you didn't have a special lady in your life?" She doubted it, but he'd said he had been so focused on work he hadn't had time for a social life. "What about Cynthia?" Renee had been curious about the woman whose voice she'd heard leaving him the message earlier.

Cynthia. "Cynthia and I have a past involvement, but I ended the relationship awhile ago, and I guess she was just calling to say hello."

"I heard her message, Craig. She said she missed your call." Renee sat forward. "Look, that is your business and it really has nothing to do with me."

"You and I are married, Renee. We took vows in the eyes of God, well, via the courthouse judge, but nevertheless, we're married and I plan to be faithful to those vows." To himself, he said, *I also plan on taking a lot of cold showers during the next three months.*

"And me?" she asked, watching him.

Craig smiled. "Well, naturally I would expect the same of you. But if your needs are that great, then honey we can easily . . ." He'd inched closer to her just as his neighbor, Steve, came through the privacy fence door and called out to Craig.

"Yo, yo, Craig . . . I got barbeque baby-back ribs, hot off the grill, buddy." Steve stopped in his tracks when he saw Craig sitting with a beautiful woman. "Oh, I'm sorry."

Craig got up and took the tray from Steve. "No problem. Steve, come on in. I'd like to introduce you to someone." Steve took Craig's seat, and pulled it even closer to Renee.

"Well, you are some kind of beauty. Would you like some hot ribs, Miss . . ." Steve asked, grinning from ear to ear.

"Renee." She couldn't help smiling at the friendly man who turned and took the tray back from Craig and pulled up a succulent rib for her without taking his eyes off her face.

"Oh, Renee, I like that name. I'm Steve, and I'm . . ."

"Married, you idiot," Craig said, watching his friend trying to put the moves on Renee.

"Steve! Hey, Craig, is that fool over there with the food?" a woman's voice called out from the next yard.

"Fran, please come over here and collect your husband," Craig answered as a pretty woman came through the gate. It suddenly occurred to Craig that people needed to know that he was married, just in case anyone from the bank suspected his marriage was only temporary. He couldn't risk that, because the first people questioned would be his neighbors. Craig made introductions.

After the shocked neighbors stammered out congratulations, they all but ran back home.

The minute they were out of sight, Renee and Craig fell back in their seats and dissolved into fits of laughter. "Craig, they seem adorable," Renee said.

"They are. They're also very much in love and they have twin daughters and a new puppy. Renee, that is why I have the pool gated off—in case the twins come wandering over here. I also keep the privacy gate locked, but you saw how Steve can reach over and unlatch it."

"I'll have to remember that over the next three months." Her eyes connected with his before saying, "Well, tomorrow's return-to-work day. I have a feeling I'm not going to get much work done at the office."

"I know what you mean. I'll clean up everything." He stood and watched her go inside.

It was almost midnight when Craig showered and fell into bed. But just as he was drifting off to sleep, he heard banging and then something fall. *Renee.* He hurried down the hall to her room. He paused for a second before knocking on the door. "Renee, are you okay?" When she didn't answer, he went in and found her standing on a chair reaching for the air conditioning vent on the upper wall. "Hey, what's wrong? What are you doing up there, Squirt?" He reached up and helped her down. His eyes traveled up the length of her sexy legs sticking out from under her short nightshirt. *Nice thighs.*

"Oh, I didn't mean to wake you," she said.

"You didn't, but what's wrong?" Then he saw that she was shivering and was holding her blanket tightly around her shoulders. He checked the vent and felt the very cold air blowing into her room. "Oh, damn, Renee, I'm sorry. I should have adjusted the thermostat in here," he said and vigorously rubbed her arms under the blanket, and then went into the hall to turn the thermostat down. Returning, he reached for her and began alternating rubbing her arms and holding her against his body. "That thermostat was set low for the library. I am so sorry, baby." As she turned and walked toward the bed, he noticed she was limping. "Did you fall?" He knelt down, checking her foot for bruises or a cut or something.

"I stumped my toe when I jumped up and tried to hit the vent lever with my shoe. When that didn't work, I pulled the chair over and that's when you came in."

"Well, let me take a look at it," he said, reaching down for her foot.

"No, it's fine." She wanted distance from him. Just looking at his naked chest and dark red nipples was causing her to get heated despite the still-cold room. The same hair that circled his forearms also covered his chest lightly and was slightly heavier and thicker as it swirled together in some kind of pattern downward, disappearing into his pajama bottoms. Frowning, she pointed to his chest and asked, "What's that?"

"What's what?" Craig looked up from examining her foot to where she pointed. There, in the center of his chest, was a four-inch oblong purplish bruise just above his stomach. He just smiled and rubbed the area. "I think that's from the frozen pizza." His dancing eyes met hers.

Renee didn't know what to say, but she felt terribly sorry for her behavior and reached out to touch the bruised area, which looked painful. "Craig, I really didn't mean to hit you."

His hand covered hers and he held her hand to his chest. "It's fine. I get banged up all the time." He felt the warmth of her hand against his bare chest, and it created a slow flame down to the pit of his stomach. It didn't help knowing that she only had a sleep tee shirt and yellow panties on under the blanket. In the cold room, a fine bead of perspiration spread out across Craig's forehead. He swallowed thickly and, before he knew what was happening, he was kissing her on the mouth. He was unable to stop; it felt so right.

As for Renee, she wanted Craig to kiss her, but she didn't let it happen. She turned and walked away from him, clutching her blanket around her shoulders. They were still strangers, and that meant they would not cross the line that she'd drawn for the three months she was there.

Craig cursed his weakness and stared at her back. He had frightened her, and now he felt worse. "Renee, I'm sorry. Good night." Back in the safety of his room, Craig felt the need for another shower, only a cold one now. Instead, he stretched out on his bed, trying to control his breathing and praying for control over his heated body. When that didn't help, he just closed his eyes, only to see Renee's face as he drifted off to an uncomfortable, restless sleep.

Renee fared no better when visions of Craig filled her dreams. Only it wasn't the grown- up Craig she dreamt of kissing her; rather it was the sixteen-year-old Craig sitting beside her on the swing who kissed her so tenderly.

CHAPTER 5

Over the course of the next two days, Craig was buried knee-deep in work. He had nonstop meetings and conference calls and ad campaigns to approve or send back to production for revisions. Both he and Renee often worked late and he surmised that, like him, she was avoiding any close contact so as to avoid a repeat of what had happened in her bedroom. He honestly didn't know how he was going to survive. For someone who was basically a stranger to him, he yearned for her. A simple kiss thrilled him beyond words, and now he couldn't even do that without wanting to make love to her.

Their living situation was making them both miserable, with each trying to avoid the other. With the day being Friday and with the weekend looming, he expected this time at home to be a test of wills that would either make them stronger or as vulnerable as ever. In any case, he was prepared to put up additional walls to keep a manageable distance between them. He decided to call her at work and test the waters early in the day.

Renee was just about to dig into something sinful when her office line rang. Her 'sin' of choice was an ice cream fudge sundae purchased from the cafe in her building. "Oh, crap," she said, frowning at the ringing phone. She grabbed it up quickly. "Renee Richards."

"Shouldn't that be Thompson?" Craig asked, picturing her pursing her lips. "Renee?"

"Yes, I'm here." She looked longingly at her sundae. "What's up?" she asked, watching the melting ice cream.

"Nothing, I just thought that is what spouses do. You know, they call each other at work to say, 'How's it going, what's for dinner, or can I bring you a sandwich for lunch.'"

"Craig, why did you call me?" She didn't like his sarcasm. He apologized for getting in late last night and missing dinner with her. "You have not had dinner with me for seventeen years, so I was fine." She was sure he had probably been out relieving some of his sexual tension with an ex-girlfriend. "I'm going out with some coworkers after work, thanks to you," she angrily whispered into the phone.

"Me? What did I do?" Craig asked.

Lowering her voice, Renee spoke through clenched teeth. "You told Tracy about our marriage, and guess what? They've planned a little bridal shower for me. Doesn't that sound like fun?" Although Renee had a private office, she still looked up through her half-glass wall to see if anyone in the area could overhear.

"Yes, it does." He heard her snort. She was angry. "Renee, I . . ." She cut him off.

"Don't you say dare say you're sorry again," Renee ground out. Something snapped and now she was angry at him. She didn't want to lie to her coworkers, and now she had to sit through a party because they were genuinely happy for her. Her office was proof of that. She had returned to work to find it filled with congratulatory cards, balloons, streamers, and cute wedding trinkets. "I've had it up to my ears with those two words, 'I'm sorry,' and I'm sick of hearing it." Hearing the harshness of her words replay in her head, she regrouped. "Look, what I meant to say was . . ." Her tone softened when she pictured his face.

"I understand. Enjoy the rest of your day, Squirt," he said, ending the call.

Renee hung up the phone and flopped back in her chair. She stared at the melted sundae for several minutes. She thought the sundae was much like her life at that exact moment—a sticky mess. Yep, she'd jumped from one mess into another, she thought.

One hour later, Renee got off the elevator and approached the reception desk at the Davis Franklin Advertising Agency. It was an impressive suite of offices. The entire wall behind the reception area was covered with colorful posters of various advertising campaigns, all featuring cartoon characters. She was so busy trying to recall the products they were created for that she absently mumbled to the receptionist that she was there to see Craig.

Before the receptionist replied, Craig could be heard coming down the hall.

Craig was coming back from the production department with his assistant, Alex. As they neared the reception area and were about to go down another hallway, the receptionist called out to Craig. Looking up, he saw Renee and a wide smile immediately spread across his face. "Hi," he said hesitantly, searching her face.

Not knowing what else to do, Renee held up a brown paper bag up to his face and whispered, "Lunch." Then she added, "And a peace offering."

Lovely, he thought, reaching out and drawing her into a warm embrace. "Thank you. You brought me you. Best lunch I could've hoped for."

"Your old favorite," she said, pointing to the bag. "Fried bologna and grape jelly. Yuk."

He had to kiss her. Hell, it had been years since he'd had one of his favorite sandwiches. That she remembered it was his favorite made it all the more special.

When she'd gotten off the phone with him earlier, Renee felt awful that she had snapped at him. She vaguely remembered he had said something about lunch. Squirming out of his embrace, she saw curious faces openly eyeing them. "Craig, your coworkers are watching us."

He looked up to see everyone beaming at them and quickly introduced Renee to his staff, and then he practically had to pry her away from the well-wishers to escort her to his office. Once inside, he put his reserved face back on, not wanting to upset the seemingly calm front.

"You really didn't have to come all the way up here to bring me lunch, although I appreciate it." He opened the bag, saw the two sandwiches and grinned. He watched her walking around, but when she commented about how nice his office was and that she could only imagine how his boss's office looked, tension flitted across Craig's face and he felt himself begin to perspire under his dress shirt.

Craig's eyes darted to the door; thankfully, his name as president and CEO hadn't been added yet. He looked back to Renee. He had to get her out of there before somebody said something or she picked up a sheet of the stationary which did have his name and new title on it. "Baby, I wish I had more time, but I have a meeting that I have to been in, so I'll walk you out."

If Renee thought he was trying to rush her out of his office, she didn't let on as he escorted her down to her car. "Thanks again for my lunch," he said as she slid into the seat. "Have fun tonight at your bridal thingy." He ached to kiss her lips, but ended up kissing her cheek. He stepped back when she nodded up at him and then backed her car out of the parking spot.

Craig relaxed as soon as she drove off and hurried back up to the agency. Although the official announcement of his new position had come out, he was keeping everything hush-hush. As he told his staff, he didn't want any competitors to know what he was up to. "Let's keep them guessing for a while." But he also went on to say that he didn't want to send his bride running because of his workload. They understood; that is, after they got over their initial shock over his marriage announcement.

Several hours later Renee pulled into the driveway and hauled all her gifts inside. Since Craig wasn't home, she ended up bringing everything inside and then carrying it all up to her room. By the time she'd finished, it was almost one in the morning and he still hadn't come home, so she took a leisurely bath and promptly went to sleep.

CHAPTER 6

Craig woke up barely able to open his eyes. Lifting his head from his pillow was too much to think about, much less do. Nonetheless, he tested how bad his hangover really was by attempting to sit up. It was pretty bad; he couldn't. Then he drifted off again. Minutes later, Craig was forced awake when an insistent buzzing filtered through his fuzzy head. He realized it was his front-door buzzer and fumbled on the bed for the remote control.

Craig's home security system was state of the art and complete. Images from any of the cameras mounted around his property could be seen by turning the TV on and switching to the access channel. Once he located the remote at the bottom of his bed, he used his foot to kick it up to his hand. With some effort, he raised the remote and turned the TV on and clicked on the channel to see who was at the front door. His blurry eyes popped open, and his mouth dropped.

Craig sat up on the bed, his head now pounding full throttle as he stared into the grinning, happy faces of his and Renee's parents on the 42-inch flat screen. "Aw, damn," Craig mumbled, his teeth chattering. He jumped up from the bed and flew to Renee's door, knocking impatiently and with great effort to hold his arm up. When she didn't answer, he let himself in and saw that she was still sleeping, sprawled out and hugging the pillows. "Renee, wake up. Renee." His voice was croaked and dry, and he couldn't speak any louder without the sound vibrating in his sore head, so he just shook her until she stared up at him.

Renee didn't want to get up; she was exhausted. She was still enjoying getting a full night of restful sleep. "Stop it. Go away. It's too early to get up, and it's Saturday, dummy," she mumbled into the pillow.

"Renee, you've got to get up now!" he bellowed, his teeth chattering again.

She flipped over, this time glaring up at him. "Why?" Then she took in his rumpled appearance. "And what happened to you?"

"Impromptu bachelor party," he said, ruffling her hair with one hand and with the other searching on the bed for the remote to the TV in her room. "Where the hell is the remote for this set?" he asked. He finally found it under her bottom and yanked it out. "This is why . . ." he said, turning the TV on. Renee glanced at the screen, then back at him.

"Yeah and . . ." she said.

"Renee, they're at the front door. Right now."

"What? That's a TV show. You're still full of booze."

Craig would have laughed—if he could. "Renee, that's the security camera on the front porch." He pointed back to the TV screen. "They're all outside."

Realization hit Renee like a pail of cold water. "Huh? Wh-what are they doing here?" She scrambled up, unconcerned that she only had on a tee shirt and a pair of panties. "What do we do? We can't let them stay out there . . ." She looked up at him, looking hopeful. "Can we?"

"No, we can't. Besides, our cars are in the driveway. But Renee, we've got to move your stuff into my room, like now." Then the door buzzer sounded again, and they tried to ignore the speculations coming over both TV sets as to why they hadn't answered the door yet, all to the great amusement of Craig's father. "Oh, that's my boy! We Thompson men take our time!"

Glaring at Craig, Renee ran from her room to his with an armload of her clothes. This went on for two or more trips, then throwing the comforter over her bed when they heard his sister Sarah say, "Oh, I'll bet they're in the hot tub making out . . . that is supposed to be very sexy, I hear. So who wants to be brave enough to go check?" More laughter erupted.

Craig and Renee only exchanged embarrassed stares before running to the bathrooms to quickly gargle with mouthwash and throw clothes on. They ran down the stairs two at a time and slid to the front door, just as his father's face appeared in the side window. That's when Craig felt like throwing up. But he managed to keep everything together, literally, as he opened the door and their families spilled into the house, beaming and kissing all around.

Lena Richards reached her daughter first. "Renee, girl, you've always so quick to do things, girl, anyway, we're just happy it is Craig you married." Lena gave her a stern look, just seconds before her father and sisters embraced her tightly. Renee was able to stretch her neck and see that Craig was having the same experience a few feet away. Then, as everyone switched places, Renee and Craig looked over at each other and smiled.

Renee's mother walked about the living room. "My, my, what a nice house. Oh, Renee, all you probably need to do is change the curtains. The ones in here are way too heavy for the summer, but otherwise it's just a lovely home, just lovely." She turned to the couple. "You two, what are your plans today, this afternoon, actually?"

Craig looked at Renee, and shrugged. She did the same.

"Well, good, because we've planned a little something for the both of you back at our house and we're here to escort you." Lena Richards gushed all over her daughter and touched Craig's face. "Oh, Craig, you were always such a good boy. I just know you'll make our Renee happy. I just know it." She pulled tissues from her purse and dabbed at her eyes. "Well, look, you two go on upstairs and change into something to wear for a garden affair," she said, waving away their objections.

"Yeah, sure hope we didn't interrupt anything that could have caused our grandchild to pop back in, if you know what I mean, son?" Craig's father said as he carried a large fruit basket to the kitchen, grabbing an apple and biting into it before setting it on the island counter. "By the way, this basket was delivered by your neighbors as we were driving up."

Craig couldn't believe his father. But then, yes he could.

Craig's mother, Jean, popped her husband on the back of his head. "Shut up, you old fool, or you'll be going to the hospital to have that apple surgically removed from inside your body."

Renee grinned at Craig's embarrassment as they climbed the stairs together.

When he closed his bedroom door, Craig rested his pounding head against it while Renee nervously paced and looked around his bedroom.

This was her first time really seeing his bedroom. It was enormous. It included a sitting area with a loveseat and side chair arrangement as well as a built-in fireplace. Turning to him, she said, "I guess I should go shower and get dressed, huh?"

"Yeah, me too. Hey, what is all these bags and packages and stuff? I don't even remember bringing them in here." He was pointing to twenty or more gift bags and boxes on the floor in front of the dresser.

"Those are the presents from my bridal shower. The theme of the party was 'After the Wedding', and I have pictures." She made a sour face at him and opened the door.

Two hours later, their parents ushered them into Renee's family's house.

Neither was aware that the entire backyard had been transformed into a sea of balloons and other decorations in yellow and white. The rented tables had been covered with white tablecloths, and each had centerpieces of fresh yellow roses in little glass vases. Tiny white lights had been strung up everywhere, promising a twinkling and dazzling effect when the warm summer sun turned into night. No fewer than four food tables had been set up buffet-style with sternos ensuring that the food would stay warm. The dessert table was just past the food tables. In its center was a three-tiered wedding cake adorned with confectionary yellow roses complete with green leaves. Last was a large table already overflowing with wedding presents.

Craig and Renee were escorted into the large dining room. Her father and mother then welcomed Craig into the family by way of an old tradition that Renee's great-grandmother started, long ago. They had to record the marriage into the family Bible. Renee looked up at Craig and held her breath after her mother handed him the plume-handled ink pen.

Craig vaguely remembered Bryant explaining the significance of keeping family records in the Bible. He'd stood with the family when they recorded Bryant's death, but then he retreated to the front porch. He caught Renee watching him. "Well, this is a special acknowledgment, isn't it?" Everyone nodded agreement. He saw that the Bible was opened to a page scripted *Marriages*, but his eyes strayed to a tab that read *Deaths*. His finger lightly lifted the pages to see his friend's name—Bryant Harold Richards. Craig traced Bryant's name with his index finger and immediately closed his eyes when Bryant's laughing face floated in front of him. When he opened them, Renee reached for his other hand, enclosing it in both of hers. Something in that moment made him want her to stand beside him forever. With emotion in his voice, he finally spoke to the assembled group. "Well . . . the last time I was here, in this house, it was a very sad day—for you, surely, and for me, as well. We had buried my best friend that day, and it was the last time I saw Renee as the little Squirt that I always saw her to be." He pulled her closer to his side. As his emotions and the remnants of the hangover almost overwhelmed him, she gave him strength. "Anyway, I want to say thank you for accepting me into your hearts once more. Please know you've always been in mine. Always." Craig looked down into Renee's eyes, now brimming with tears.

But for the family standing around, the tears flowed freely as they watched Craig sign his name in the Bible and pass the feathered pen to Renee to sign her name, which she signed as *Renee Richards Thompson*. When she looked up at him quizzically, Craig picked her up and, holding her in his arms, kissed her as everyone applauded.

"Wow, I still can't believe that you two are married, I'm just so happy for you," Cecelia said. Then she shooed everyone from the room, leaving Craig and Renee alone.

Craig was still blown away to see the slim and stunning Cecelia. "You know, I thought I saw you at a charity event downtown a few months ago." He closed his mouth when Renee tugged on the back of his shirt.

Cecelia thought for a minute. "Oh, right, my husband Gil and I did attend a charity event a while back. Oh, Craig, I'm glad you didn't see me. I was huge then." She fanned out her arms around her. "I tell you, after I had the last baby, my weight just went haywire, but as you guys can see, I've lost it all, and I eat well now. But you watch Renee, she has a sweet tooth, too."

Renee cringed when Craig pinched her bottom and smiled down at her.

"Oh, you don't have to worry about her, Cecelia. Renee has forbid me to buy anymore junk food. She's already punished me severely." Craig rubbed at his chest, which still sported a purplish-red bruise. He knew Renee was getting steamed; he felt it rising up from her body.

Cecelia laughed at her baby sister's embarrassment. "Well, you two, this is the wedding reception you properly deserve."

Craig and Renee looked at each other for a second and followed Cecelia out onto the back porch, where white tulle and yellow and white roses lined the trellis, forming an arch between two large white columns. A large yellow paper bell hung above them. They stepped out onto the porch to thunderous applause, and walked on yellow rose petals lining the porch, steps and walkway. The couple was equally stunned to see the smiling faces of so many peoples including all of their families, friends and their coworkers.

Some two hours later, the wedding reception was in full swing. The stone patio had been turned into a dance floor, with speakers placed throughout the yard. Many danced the late afternoon away. Craig looked up at the back of the house and saw Renee looking out the window of Bryant's old room. Filling up two glasses of punch at the rented fountain, he carried them into the house as Renee's grinning parents looked on.

"Hey, you . . ." Craig walked in the room and reached around her, handing Renee one of the glasses. "To us." He turned to look about the room, nodding his head at the colorful room. "I like the room like this. You?" He watched her nod her head.

"What's wrong? Come on, talk to me." He took her hand and listened as she told him it was wrong of them to celebrate a marriage that was not real.

He stood behind her and rested his chin on the top of her head. "We are accepting this with open hearts, because that's how they planned it for us. Should we leave and say, thanks, guys, but we really don't want to be here?" he asked quietly. "Besides, the food is kickin.'"

"But we know that we're lying to them. We even signed the family Bible. Oh, Craig, how could we do this to them? Then, in three months, one of us has to come back and sign under the divorces." She dropped her head to his chest.

He lifted her face to him. "Let's not talk about what's going to happen in three months. Let's go back out there and have a good time for us and for them. They even got paper napkins with our names printed on them." He grinned, desperate to see her smile, and bent his head to kiss her, and just hold her in his arms. Then he turned her back around to look out the window. "Besides, look at that gift table," he whispered, pointing past her with one hand, the other around her waist, holding her close to him. "I'll bet you anything there are at least four toasters and five irons among them." His rumbling laughter tickled her back, making her laugh with him.

"Look, Meg is signaling for us to come down and cut the cake." He turned her to him again. "I heard one tier of the cake is red velvet; you used to love that."

Renee raised her eyebrows. "I still do," she said and walked out of the room. Craig didn't follow her immediately. Instead, his eyes were drawn back to the room—the room he had spent many hours in, comforting and watching his friend die. He closed his eyes and, for a brief moment, he heard Bryant laughing.

When the sun finally settled, the reception became the dazzling affair they had all hoped for. Craig and Renee danced together many times to the whistles and shouts of their guests.

That Saturday afternoon found Lawrence Jennings down at the Wayland Bank. As the vice president of the bank everything crossed his desk, and he had the final say on which loans were or were not approved. To Lawrence, his position was power. Lawrence preferred using other people's money for his pleasures. He sported a tan from his ten-day cruise to the Bahamas, having returned just the day before. His goal was to purchase that nice piece of property he'd been using as his vacation home. Like the astute businessman he professed to be, Lawrence decided to stop by the bank and ran the usual reports that showed the day-to-day activity reports, including large deposits, withdrawals and special customer requests. He sipped coffee and flipped through the reports, absently scrolling through his e-mails. He also ran, rather secretively, the report showing account balances and transactions of his bank employees. He believed that one could never be too careful when employees were surrounded by money. All that temptation was something he was well aware of.

He was still sipping his coffee and humming a catchy little tune he'd picked up in the Bahamas when something made Lawrence stop. "Whoa . . . now where did she get that kind of money?" Lawrence looked up at the recently vacated desk of Miss Lilly James. He thought the woman had been a fixture at that desk for far too long and couldn't wait to hire another account associate. Someone younger and pretty, he thought, a lecherous glint to his eyes. He shook that distracting thought from his head and returned his attention to the employee transactions sheet, specifically, the now much larger savings account balance of Miss Lilly. Upon closer inspection, he saw that she'd made a deposit of fifteen thousand in the form of a cashier's check from the bank. He wondered where she had gotten it, then just shrugged. "Oh, well, probably from some old fart she knows." He put the sheets in a compartment in his desk and locked it.

Lawrence was a master at locking things up and hiding them, especially hiding what he did. And what he did, and had been doing for some twenty years, was to skim money from some of the heavily padded accounts . . . mainly those dormant accounts that just sat and collected interest and dividend payments for years. That money had paid for his four-star vacations and other expendi-

tures. Of course he always replaced the money he withdrew. These accounts he called his babies. There were
only two, but these were the one that he had used as if
they were his own personal accounts. The holders of
those accounts pretty much didn't exist. They were his
best kind of customer. They never came into the bank,
and their statements were mailed quarterly to a post
office box that he'd set up. Over the years, that money
afforded Lawrence all the benefits of having lots of
money at his disposal. Only it still wasn't his money, but
he treated it as though it were. Four years ago, that
money had enabled Lawrence to wine, dine and finally
marry the beautiful and sexy Vivian.

Almost twenty years his junior, she could easily pass
for thirty, and he liked that. And he liked the fact that
she'd loved him and never rejected him, despite him
pushing almost fifty-nine. But, he thought to himself, he
wasn't so bad in the looks department. Truth was, he
wasn't. Lawrence had curly salt-and-pepper hair, a
smooth cocoa complexion and a neatly trimmed goatee.
He stood five feet, ten inches tall and was somewhat
stocky. He remembered meeting Vivian when she came
to the bank to inquire about cashing in a pitiful one hundred dollar savings bond. She'd practically offered herself
to him on a platter. Lawrence, a recent widower then, was
receptive to her every tactic. Within four months they
were married, to the chagrin of almost everyone he knew.
He didn't care. He loved her and she loved him.
Lawrence had spoiled Vivian with expensive things. She
was from the so-called wrong side of the tracks, and he

gladly showered her with nice things so she could forget from where she had come. He would have given her the moon if he could. She could have had any man she wanted, but she'd said yes to him . . . the moment he'd put a four-caret diamond ring on her finger. Lately, though, he'd noticed that she seemed distant, but she seemed to have had a good time on the cruise.

As Lawrence continued to click various keys on his keyboard, his train of thought came to a screeching halt and he stared at his computer monitor with large, rounded eyes. His coffee mug slipped from his fingers to the floor. "Oh, Lord, this cannot be right." Someone had been touching his babies. "No, no, this cannot be right." Beads of sweat popped out on his forehead and his hands trembled, causing him to punch the wrong keys, thus locking up his computer. "That was probably a wrong account. Calm down, breathe . . ." He talked to himself as he rebooted his computer and waited for the thing to hum back to life. *It was the wrong account, that's all,* he told himself. *Everything was still A-okay with his babies . . . it had to be.*

While Lawrence waited for his computer to come back up to the bank's logo, he pulled a file card from another compartment in his desk. It contained numbers only he knew the meaning of—a post office box number, where he had bank statements for those dormant accounts sent and the last account balance of his main baby account, the one with the invisible inheritance benefactor. The balance was just as he expected it to be— a little under three million dollars in cold hard cash was in his bank, at his fingertips, drawing interest. This account funded his lifestyle, and he wasn't about to let anything change that. The beeping of his computer forced him to put the card back into the compartment, locking it securely. Then he turned to log onto his computer. "Okay, let's do this again . . ."

He started again, sure the account balance would be what he had just seen. He started humming that catchy little tune again as he plucked up a handful of tissues and blotted the drops of coffee on his shoes. He logged back onto his computer and brought up the activity of his main baby account. Lawrence rubbed his hands together and adjusted his bifocals. He scrolled down the electronic ledger, line by line, reviewing the activity for the last six months. He saw all the withdrawals he'd made, usually in increments of two to three thousand dollars, to coincide with the interests and dividend payments. The last withdrawal was just like the others he'd made before taking a trip or making a major purchase—twelve thousand dollars. Lawrence simply transferred money from his other baby, the account of a dead woman down in Florida.

He remembered when she called and went on and on about asking her dim wit of a grandson to take over management of the scholarship fund. She mentioned that ridiculous plan of wanting to withdraw all the money from the Wayland Bank and transferring it down to some bank in Florida to hold in a trust for yet another charity scholarship fund. That woman was out of her feeble, aging mind, he had thought as he forced himself to listen to her prattle back then.

Lawrence wiped the sweat from his forehead with the back of his hand and retuned his full attention back to his computer. "Now where was I . . . oh, yes, last Friday, no problem; Saturday, no problem. I know I was just imagining things when I thought . . ." Lawrence bolted upright in his worn leather chair, almost sliding from it to the floor, his eyes bulging from their sockets. "No. Good, Lord, no . . . th-this can't be true." He stared at the final transaction from Monday. It was a stop of all interest and dividend payments on the account as of twelve o'clock midnight. He read further, rapidly clicking the computer keys, and scrolled down to the attached electronic bank note. He became sicker as he read the note.

Customer Craig L. Thompson presented in person to inquire about the inheritance in File #112294 and was assisted by Mrs. Lillian James, who processed the customer's request, to withdraw the full balance of $2,755,430.25. Balance confirmed by president, James Tinsly, and head bank teller, Ms. Marian Henley. Both signed off on the customer's request to withdraw, providing customer Craig L. Thompson provides documentation that substantiates stipulation of the inheritance. Same was reviewed with Mr. Thompson.

Lawrence didn't know how he had managed to read the note without punching his computer screen. He kept rereading the same line: *withdraw the full balance of . . .* His blood boiled with such anger that he banged his fist onto his desk. His trembling finger hit the scroll down key again so that he could continue reading the notes.

Tuesday, transaction of withdrawal complete as customer requested. Two cashier's checks processed and made payable to Craig L. Thompson. Stipulation of inheritance provided and accepted: one marriage certificate and proper ID copied for the transaction. At customer's request, the checks were hand delivered to him by Mrs. Lillian James. This electronic note will mark this as the final bank transaction processed by Mrs. James, who has officially retired as of Tuesday's date from the Wayland Bank.

Lawrence sat as if made of stone; only his shifty eyes moved. They slid over to Miss Lilly's former desk. He was physically sick and would have gotten up to go to the bathroom had he not looked at the large wall calendar near her desk and seen Tuesday's date circled with a blue and red marker. He squinted further and saw that someone, most likely the woman herself, had written, "Last day, bye all," on the calendar. He dropped his sweating head down into his hands and let out a sound that would have drawn looks of fear . . . had anyone been in the bank.

By the time Craig and Renee arrived home it was after midnight. When they'd finally finished unpacking the car with the help of two sets of the neighbors who had been invited to the reception, all of their presents were piled into the living room. Exhausted beyond words, they collapsed on the couch. But sleep would be a long time coming.

"I'm glad Meg had an extra pair of sneakers I could wear," Renee said, grinning and pointing her toes in the blue and white sneakers.

Craig laughed. He thought she looked adorable. "I'm glad. Hey, I have something to show you." He went into his den and returned with the packet of wedding pictures. To Renee the pictures, although beautiful, were deceiving . . . she and Craig looked like a couple deeply in love, with all the promises and hopes for the future. "They really look nice, don't they?" he finally said quietly.

She changed the subject. "So now we know for sure who told our families—Miss Lilly. I was glad to see her there today. Did you see her dancing all evening with Mr. Stewart?"

"Yeah, I did. Who was that old dude, anyway?" Craig asked, leaning over and picking up one of the many presents scattered around the living room and shaking it. "Toaster," he said.

Grinning, Renee said, "That old dude was Mr. Stewart. He owns that garage down on Glen Road." She watched as he picked up another box.

"Annette and Meg are coming out here tomorrow to help us open these gifts and write thank-you cards." She knew they would have a ton of cards to address and send out, and reflected they would have to be returned in three months.

Deciding to turn in, they climbed the steps, said goodnight and turned towards their respective bedrooms.Not bothering to turn on the light on his room, Craig went in and flipped on his stereo to a quiet jazz station. When he turned to walk into his bathroom, he tripped over something . . . many things, and ended up falling against the dresser and down onto the floor. "What the hell . . . ?"

Renee heard a loud thud, followed by a string of profanity, and ran down the hall to his room. She slid to a halt in the doorway and turned on the bedroom light. Then she saw him sitting on the floor among all the gifts from her bridal shower. "Oh, no . . . Craig, we forgot," she said in a pitiful voice, walking in and reaching down to help him up.

Craig looked around him at the bags and boxes and then up at her. He braced one hand on the carpeted floor to get up, but a flaming red, see-through nightie caught in his watchband. Renee, meanwhile, was trying hard to hold back her giggles.

He looked at the dangling item and then up at her. "Renee, what is all this stuff and why is it in here? And stop laughing," he said, his teeth clenched.

She pulled his arm up and, with nimble fingers, began to untangle the tiny ribbons of the garment from his watchband. Her fingers making contact with the smooth black hair on his forearms was distracting.

"What's on your mind, sweetheart?" Craig asked with a lecherous glint in his eyes.

Renee looked up from examining the item. "What? Oh, please, all of this stuff is from that shower thingy. I wouldn't buy anything so . . ." She stopped when she saw his look.

"What, sexy? Let me see it; I'll be the judge." He took it from her fingers and held it up to the light. "Well, it leaves nothing to the imagination. But it's beautiful. What else you get?" Craig was only mildly curious about her gifts; what he liked was her being in his bedroom.

"I thought you were tired. Anyway, I can't imagine you would want to look through this stuff," Renee said, glancing around his room and seeing her things among his things.

"I guess falling down on my ass has awakened me, so come on, let me see your gifts." Craig sat down on the loveseat and watched her debate what to do.

Renee was excited about her gifts, and she had really opened just a few of them before the male strippers took over the club. She smiled, her cheeks reddening.

Neither was lost on Craig. He sat back and stretched his legs out. "So tell me all about the bridal shower. Was it one where oily male dancers popped out of cakes?"

Renee rolled her eyes at him with attitude. "No, that's what happens at male bachelor parties." When he only grinned, she crossed her arms over her chest and walked over to him. "Oh, that's right. You know, Craig, you were looking all kinds of hung over this morning . . . and I swear I could smell some cheap perfume on you when you woke me up. So, tell me . . . did an oily fake-hair hoochie pop out of a cake at your shindig?" Renee knew she shouldn't have asked, but her curiosity jumped into high gear around him.

"Actually, it was several of them, and they were not hoochies, and I didn't think their hair was fake, but I know for sure some of their boobs were. Oh, and they didn't pop out of a cake either, but they all danced around a poll. Next question?" He grinned.

"And how would you know their boobs were fake? You sampled them?"

"Curious or jealous?" he asked, watching her closely.

"Neither," she answered, curling her lips.

"Liar."

"Did you sample them or not?" Renee was insistent but really didn't want to know. But she did like the easy banter with him—anything as long as they were not fighting.

"Did not. Besides, I've had better. Now, are you going to show me your hoochie wear or not?" He did have better, he thought, last Friday on her couch. It was still fresh in his mind.

"Well, okay, if you're sure." Her excitement growing, Renee sat on the floor among the gifts and began pulling out a variety of sexy nightgowns, flimsy robes, toiletries, books, sex games, CDs and two videotapes.

"Whoa, what's with the videotapes?" he asked, reaching down to pick one up. But she grabbed it and wouldn't let it go. "Hey, come on. What's it about?" When she wouldn't let go, he tickled her and her hold on the tape loosened, enabling him to grab it. He read the title aloud: Pleasing Your Mate with 101 Positions. Craig laughed. "I didn't know there were that many, did you?" It was a loaded question, and he reached down for the second tape, but she'd rolled over onto her stomach with the videotape under her. He laughed heartily at her antics. "That one must be better than this one. Show me, Squirt."

Renee only shook her head stubbornly and mumbled, "No way."

Craig inched closer to her until he was lying beside her on the plush carpet. "Let me see the tape, or are you embarrassed about it? Hell, I can't wait to see this one with the 101 positions and trust me, I'll play is slowly and count them." When she refused, Craig slid his hand under her stomach until he felt the tape. He moved closer and kissed her just below her ear. Within minutes he had slipped the tape from under her. Then he turned her over onto her back, continuing to kiss neck. The tape was forgotten as his lips moved further along her neck.

Renee was burning at the point where his moist lips kissed her neck. All day long at their reception, he had touched her constantly. But as his body moved over hers, and he kissed her ear, then his lips sought hers, Renee could want for nothing more. Well, almost nothing more, she inched her arms around him to caress his strong, muscular back.

Craig was dizzy with desire. Kissing her, he thought she tasted as sweet as their wedding-reception cake. The minute she held the sheer garment up, he imagined her wearing the little red number. He thought the minute he moved on top of her she would probably bolt and run, but she didn't. And when her hands moved up and down his back, his desire for her mounted so quickly that his breathing became labored. He kissed the pulse area in her throat and brought his hands up to her breasts, caressing them. Craig moved his body against hers and was thrilled when her breath caught audibly in her throat.

Her tongue explored the contours of his mouth and kissed him back with all the frenzy and passion that he kissed her.

Craig ran his hand down her body to her thighs. He loved the feel of her and just then the image flashed of her that morning when he went into her room to awaken her. His Renee had grown up and filled out. His mouth found its way to the tops of her breasts, which rose above the sundress with the low V-neck bodice, while his hands continued to slide downward to the hem of her dress, then slowly moved upward caressing her bare thigh.

Renee knew she should stop him. After all, she'd made a deal with him and now, in her weakened state, she was about to give into the delicious waves of pleasure he was giving her a sample of. Then his fingers trailed a heated path along her thighs at the same time his mouth claimed hers again. His touch elicited a moan that tore from her throat. Renee was literally clinging to him for the sweet relief that she knew he could give her. She could feel his body pulsating against her.

In one swift move, Craig rolled over so that she was on top of him, her hair tumbling around them. Their lips remained locked in the midst of a passionate kiss. One hand now rested on her hip, while the other began to unbutton the bodice of her sundress. When his eyes looked up into her face, he'd never seen her look so beautiful; arousal made her look even more beautiful.

"Renee?" Craig could only whisper her name past the pounding of his heart.

When she opened her eyes, Renee sat up so that she was straddling him. Her breathing was as labored as his when she reached down to touch his heated face. "Craig," she whispered to him. "I-I can't believe that you want me like this, but this isn't going to happen." She moved her hips against him and was delighted when he sucked in his breath and grabbed onto them.

When he was finally able to speak, Craig drew her closer to him. "Why wouldn't I? You're so beautiful and sexy." Renee's eyes connected with his, each realized they'd crossed into another realm of their relationship. A place they'd never been before. Renee moved forward to kiss him back. He rolled over with her so that once again he was on top of her, and it was exactly where he wanted to be. Holding her, kissing her as her hands caressed him everywhere, beckoning him, encouraging him. He felt her tugging his polo shirt from inside of his jeans, then her hands ran a heated trail up his back. He was so lost in his ever-mounting desire, Craig was unaware that the buzzing he heard in his head was actually from his front door and not from his rapidly beating heart. When the insistent buzzing continued, he realized what it was and forced himself to break off the kiss with Renee. Weakened, he could only sag against her. "Who in the world . . ." Craig said breathlessly, reluctant to get up and leave her.

Renee brought her hand from under his shirt. "Guess we have company again."

Craig looked up at the ceiling. "Probably Steve with a tray of hot ribs for you." He grinned down at her. "I should go get it." He kissed her again and then hoisted himself up and stood watching her, not wanting to move or to leave her.

Renee's breath caught in her throat as she ran her eyes down his body. Her hands flew to her stomach to quell the tightening she suddenly experienced.

Craig saw the direction of her eyes and quickly turned and left his bedroom. Muttering incoherently as he went down the stairs, he gulped in air to steady himself and began counting backwards from ten.

When Craig opened the door, he stood in shock, his mouth agape.

❧

Back upstairs in the bedroom, Renee got up from the floor and stood on shaky legs. She stared at her reflection in the mirror and saw the flame of desire that burned within her. But she looked heavenward and said a prayer. "Oh, Lord . . . what am I doing? But thank you for that interruption." She glanced at the TV set and wondered why Craig didn't just turn it on to see who had come to the house at that hour. She picked up the remote and turned the set on. It automatically went to the security channel from that morning.

Renee sat on the edge of the bed staring into the face of a beautiful woman smiling up into Craig's face. Then she kissed him, her arms going around his neck and gliding down his back. Renee increased the volume on the complicated-looking remote to hear what was being said as woman breezed into the house. Before the door closed, Renee saw that Craig looked stricken as he dragged his hand across his forehead. Renee looked heavenward again then said, "That really wasn't the interruption I was looking for."

Downstairs Craig spent some fifteen minutes talking to his ex-girlfriend Cynthia, but his mind was on Renee. He told her he was married, which Cynthia confirmed when she looked around the living-room and saw the presents and the wedding-day photos still on the coffee table where Renee had left them earlier. But Cynthia had fired back about his phone message. He'd told Cynthia that she misunderstood his reason for calling. "Look, Cynthia, I did call, but it was about a business opportunity," he lied. No way could he let Renee know that he'd already lined up another woman to be his wife if she hadn't shown up at the courthouse on Tuesday.

Cynthia fanned herself with the two pictures she was still holding. She merely stared at Craig, noticing his nervousness. She knew when he was lying to her. "Okay, Craig, now you are lying to me. Why? And I hope not for this." Her voice rising as she flung the photos at him.

"Look Cynthia, you knew what we were about from day one, so spare me this dramatic scene. But I can see that you're upset, and I'm very sorry," he said, but she had already snatched up her purse and walked to the door and left, slamming it in his face.

Craig paced the floor his hands thrust into his pockets and paced the floor. Then he exploded. "Damn, this is the last thing I need right now." He turned and saw Renee coming down the steps. He remembered what they had just shared upstairs. "Oh, Renee, baby, I'm so sorry. I assume you heard all of that, huh?" He searched her face and reached for her hands.

"Yeah, most of it, but I could tell she was upset. I think you should go talk to her or something." Frowning she continued, "I mean, three months will be gone before you know it, and the two of you can resume your relationship, right?"

"Wrong. I told you we were over months ago." His eyes searched her face for signs of the desire that was bursting from her upstairs. Not even a trace remained. Now she looked at him with compassion, and he felt like crap. "Maybe I'll call her tomorrow. I just hate that her surprise appearance interrupted something special that was happening upstairs."

"Well, I don't think that either of us was ready for that, anyway. But I have a substitute." She grinned and walked backward to the kitchen, with him following and gathering her to him.

Squirming out of his grasp, Renee opened the freezer. "Can I tempt you with an ice cream sundae?" she asked, pulling out ice cream.

"You know, Renee, I think you've tempted me since I got that picture of you from my mother." He perched on a stool, his chin resting in his hand and watched her make two large ice cream sundaes, complete with whatever else she found in the pantry and refrigerator.

He savored the first spoonful of his sundae. "This is very good, Squirt."

Renee explained about the picture he referred to. She told him she had worked at a convenience store to earn extra money. But she was disheartened to see the type of woman he dated; although, just as she had guessed, Cynthia was tall and pretty. "So, Craig, what was the proposition you called Cynthia about last week?"

"You heard that, too? Well, it wasn't like she implied." He sat back and watched her.Craig felt his conscience weighing on him. In his quest to get what he wanted, he really hadn't considered Renee as a person who might get hurt in the process. He'd seen her hurt look when she came downstairs. Already he was tired of his deception . . . he'd even signed the family Bible. He hated the fact that he had to lie to her. But then, Craig wondered, why had she shown up at the courthouse? Truthfully, he was surprised that she did. "Renee, have you ever done something and then later regretted doing it because you knew you would end up hurting people that you care about, people who trust you, but you felt you had to do it anyway?"

Renee's breath caught in her throat to the point that she could no longer taste the sweetness of the sundae. The color drained from her face. He couldn't possibly know about the situation concerning Charles Hunter. When she had decided to temporarily move to Craig's house, Renee thought it an escape from the prison her apartment had become. If she couldn't tell her family about what Charles had done to her, there was no way she could even think about telling Craig. Again, she wondered how she could have fallen prey to such a man. A man she thought she loved and who she believed loved her—a man whose only interest in her was to run a con on her, bed her and then rob her while she slept. She immediately wanted to run back to her apartment and do what she'd done for two weeks after Charles took all her money and left. She wanted to scream into her pillow and curl into a ball and cry. She noticed Craig waiting for her to answer.

"I think we have all experienced that at one time or another," she said in a quiet voice, thinking about her parents.

Misunderstanding what she meant, Craig turned her around to face him and folded her into his arms. "I'm not going to hurt you, Renee. Come on, let's get some sleep. We've had a long day." He took her hand, and for the second time that day, they climbed the stairs to his room.

Renee walked down the hall to her bedroom. "I'll just let my stuff stay in your room until tomorrow, if that's all right," she said.

"No problem. Good night, Squirt." In his bedroom, Craig picked up the red nightie from the floor and went into the hallway. He called out before she entered her bedroom. Grinning, he waved the nightie and said, "I'm sleeping with this under my pillow."

Renee only shook her head and called him, "Freak boy."

When they finally fell into an exhausted sleep, neither would have guessed what the other was struggling with.

And each said a silent prayer that no more surprises lay in store for them.

ه‎

In the week following Cynthia's inopportune drop-in, Craig and Renee lived in relative peace and quiet, with only the usual domestic pet peeves surfacing from time to time. Renee fussed when he left the toilet seat up in the first-floor guest powder room. Craig fussed when she recorded a soap opera over a baseball game he hadn't had a chance to watch.

On the following Thursday they met back at Renee's apartment, where she had gone to pick up more clothing and to check her mail, which included two reports, one from Simon and a one from Det. Skinner. Craig stunned both Renee and her landlady, Mrs. Harvey, when he gave the woman a check covering Renee's rent and utilities for the next three months.

Later, at Craig's house, he tapped on her bedroom door and asked her to come down to his office because he had a gift for her.

"We've had this discussion already, Craig," Renee said, but followed him. She rarely went into his home office, but she liked the room. Bookcases lined one wall, and it had an impressive entertainment center, a working fireplace and a seating area with a futon. But she liked the huge aquarium and the large window that looked out at the waterfall in the yard.

"I got you a gift anyway," he said, grinning as she sat in his chair at the desk. He sat on the edge of it, lifting a large gift-wrapped box from the side and placing it on the desk in front of her. Renee smiled at the yellow and green wrapping paper, telling him he shouldn't have spent any money on her. "Please open it," he insisted, watching excitement brighten her face. Then he sat back and watched her open the box and lift out a brand-new laptop computer. She stood up and squealed and rounded the desk to throw her arms around his neck and kiss him soundly on the mouth several times. "Thank you . . . and, I'm keeping it, Craig," she said firmly.

Craig's arms easily went around her waist, pulling her between his legs. But Renee pulled back and gave him her sternest look, which he knew meant hands off. He'd seen it every time he reached for her in that sexy way. Renee smiled and reached for his hands. "Do you have time to show me all the bells and whistles of my new laptop?"

"For you, baby, I have all the time in the world." And he meant it.

Thursday evening, Lawrence Jennings was sitting in an empty conference room, waiting for the quarterly board meeting of the bank trustees to begin. "Think, man, think," he whispered to himself, holding a fist to his dry lips. On Saturday, no sooner had he started to check the computer further than two patrol officers making their rounds passed the bank, shining a high-powered flashlight into the window and onto his glistening forehead. Lawrence almost passed out before recovering enough to unlock the door to the familiar officers. The printed electronic notes that were attached to the withdrawal request were tucked away inside his jacket pocket. He knew it by heart, having read it several times, but he had planned to look into the stipulation that was attached to that inheritance.

⌒⤸

On Saturday, Renee awoke feeling hot and frustrated; she'd had another dream. Actually it was a dream about something that really did happen the previous week. She had awakened in Craig's arms after they fell asleep together on the couch watching TV. He was pressing against her and kissing her neck—as he slept. Secretly enjoying his caresses far too much, she didn't immediately stop his roving hands. That is, until he moved over her and she had to punch him on the arm, waking him immediately. Craig was shocked that she had hit him, but glad.

So on that sunny Saturday morning, Renee jumped out of bed, with the now familiar ache of longing clinging to her. She donned her bathing suit, padded barefoot through the kitchen to the patio and dived into the pool.

When Craig awakened he went downstairs and walked through the living room to the kitchen to make a pot of coffee. Glancing back into the living room, he saw that Renee had placed his favorite of their wedding pictures on the mantle above the fireplace. His chest tightened. To the world they were really a couple, and something in that made him feel centered and good.

A sound distracted him. Pulling his attention from the picture in the living room to the sliding glass doors that lead to the patio, Craig took a couple of steps to go to the doors, but stopped. He watched Renee bobbing in the pool. She was laughing and flinging water at . . . "Oh no, Steve and Fran's new puppy." Craig smiled watching Renee flinging water at the puppy, but he almost swallowed his tongue when she climbed out of the pool and picked the puppy up and hugged it to her wet body. When she set him down the puppy began shaking water from his short coat of hair and was about to run back under the hedge to go home, but Renee ran after him. She carried him back to the patio and doused him with a handful of water. Then she picked up the now soaking-wet puppy and set him down at hedge and shouted, "Go!"

Craig continued to watch as she adjusted her thigh-high swimsuit and dived back into the pool. As his desire surged, causing his hand to tremble, Craig became aware someone was standing beside him. He pulled his eyes away from Renee to look down into the smiling face of his housekeeper, Maria.

"Oh, Mr. Craig, now this one is very pretty and she looks friendly. You know, I can't believe that was all we had to do to keep that little dog from doing his business on the patio. I would have had buckets of water just waiting for that little pee-pee machine." Maria laughed when Craig stared at her dumbfounded. She grinned and winked at him. This was not the first time she had come to do the weekly cleaning and found him in the company of a woman—not often, but it did happen occasionally.

"Yes, she's very friendly and she's my wife, Maria. So, how was your vacation?" Craig said quickly then jumped back when she swatted at him with a dishtowel.

"It was good. Now why you lie to me? I know how you are with the ladies." She tried to gauge if he was telling the truth. "You marry this one? For sure, Mr. Craig?"

Craig wasn't listening, as he had turned back to watch as Renee stepped from the pool and began drying off. Desire was taking his breath away, tightening his chest muscles and continuing downward. His memory of the feel and taste of her lips, her neck, her breasts was so vivid. "Oh, baby," he mumbled absently, his arm was draped across her wide shoulders.

Realization hit Maria when she looked from the pretty woman drying off and back to him. She had seen his eyes go dark. "Hey, Mr. Craig, this is true?" she asked, pulling his arm from her shoulder and pulling his hand up to her face. The solid gold band on his finger gleamed at her. "You love this one, for sure, and you married her?" She clapped her hands and giggled.

Craig smiled, affectionately hugging Maria. "Yes." Yes, he'd married her. Did he love her, as in the traditional sense? He didn't know, but he liked saying, he was married to her.

Maria beamed up at him then threw her arms around his waist. "Oh, then I am so happy for you." Maria gave him a sly look. "Is there a baby on the way?" she asked, shaking him.

Craig's eyes became wide as saucers. "What? No!" He didn't get a chance to say anything more because Renee slid the door open and stepped into the kitchen, tying a sarong around her waist. She was laughing to see Maria shaking him.

Craig made a quick introduction. He was having difficulty focusing on anything but Renee in the azure blue one-piece bathing suit. "Renee this is Maria, my housekeeper, and I'll keep her as long as she acts right, but if she doesn't . . . well, then like that puppy, she's out of here." He laughed and ducked out of the line of Maria's dishtowel, which she twirled over her head, ready to pop him with it.

"Well, Renee, congratulations. You just tell me what you need me to do differently around the house and I will do it for you, okay?"

"Absolutely not. I think whatever you've been doing has been perfect. This house is very clean. And since I like to cook, I will do the cooking, if that's okay with you."

Maria's eyes widened and ripples of laughter bubbled up from her plus-size frame. "Oh no, Renee . . . did I buy all that food stuff for you?" She lifted her apron to cover her embarrassed face and looked from Renee to Craig as more giggles erupted.

BERNICE LAYTON

Renee's eyes connected with Craig's over the woman's shoulder. But Craig moved out of the line of fire and began filling their mugs with steaming coffee.

For the next hour or so, Renee and Maria talked about the wedding and looked at the pictures. She also told Maria that she was using the guestroom for work and asked the housekeeper not to bother cleaning the room, preferring to do it herself.

Throughout her workday, Maria had no reason not to believe that Craig and Renee weren't what they appeared—a young couple in love and happy. She caught glimpses of it as they lounged around the pool, their hands touching, almost tentatively, and she saw it when she announced that she was leaving for the day. Craig was putting in a new computer workstation he'd brought for her to work at. Renee is exactly what he needed, Maria thought.

As the afternoon cooled down, Renee worked on her new computer at the workstation still in the den while Craig worked at his desk. He looked over at Renee as she was reading her notes. She was twirling several strands of hair. He couldn't even count the number of times he'd seen her do that. Craig decided to take his bride to the movies. She looked up and gave him a smile, telling him her answer was yes. Again, he felt a constriction in his chest that was becoming familiar and comforting.

CHAPTER 7

By Wednesday morning, one week after the quarterly board meeting, Lawrence Jennings had covered his withdrawals—temporarily. His quest for answers was right under his nose; he had made a connection. He didn't know what it all meant, but it was a connection nonetheless.

Since the board meeting, Lawrence had discovered that aside from being very wealthy, this same Thompson fellow had purchased the Davis Advertising for a cool million dollars on June tenth. Lawrence knew he got it for a steal.

Looking out through his opened door, his eyes squinted to bring into focus the wall calendar, hanging above Miss Lilly's former desk. He smiled a not so pleasant smile.

Later that Wednesday afternoon, Lawrence went to pay a visit to someone who could probably fill in some of the blanks. He told himself it was only proper to pay a visit. He smiled down at the gift basket he was carrying in his hands, seconds before reaching up and ringing the doorbell of the neat cottage house.

◦⌒

Lillian was expecting her afternoon visitor because he'd called her an hour earlier. She peeped through the side window at Mr. Jennings's profile and mumbled through pinched lips, "I can't imagine what he wants with me . . . and bringing me that puny-looking little basket, too." She put on her fakest of smiles and opened the front door with a flourish. "Well, hello, Mr. Jennings. Why, I just can't believe you came all this way just to see me."

"Miss Lilly, I must say that retirement was just the thing for you. You're positively glowing." He laughed briefly and handed the little basket to her. "This is just a little something from me to you."

Lillian always thought Mr. Jennings's chuckle sounded as if he was choking on his own spit. *Uh-huh, he wants something. He always did when he had that weird grin,* she thought, smiling at his sweating face. "Well, this is just nice, thank you, and please come on in."

"Yes, Miss Lilly, I can't believe it is so hot." He thought her house was really nice, with fine furniture. When she excused herself to go get glasses of iced tea, he called out, "Say, Miss Lilly, your home is indeed lovely." He looked around, remembering that she hadn't made all that much money at the bank and recalled that extra fifteen thousand deposited into her account . . . on the same Tuesday she retired. It was another connection.

Accepting the tall glass of iced tea, Lawrence gulped the cool brew. "Now, since I missed your retirement party, why don't you tell me all about it? I just bet I missed a grand time." He laughed briefly.

There it was again, Lillian thought. That idiot laugh she'd had to endure for the last twenty years. She also knew that the laugh, with a clearing of his throat at the end, was a cover for when he was cornered. His face was shiny with sweat despite the cool air swirling around them. She sipped her tea and then patted her lips daintily with her napkin. "Would you like me to turn the air conditioning unit up a bit more for you, Mr. Jennings?" She really wasn't about to waste a penny more on her electric bill for the man.

"Oh, no," he said anxiously, "I'm fine. So, you were about to tell me about that Tuesday . . . ah, yes, that was the tenth, I believe." Lawrence thought he could just shake the daylights out of her. Damn old woman, he fumed inwardly, knowing she wasn't all that much older them himself.

"Oh, I will, but first tell me about your cruise to the Bahamas. Did Mrs. Jennings enjoy herself?" Lillian watched him lick his lips and thought, damn old fool. Got his big old brown nose so full of that trifling little witch he married he can't even think straight. His sorry butt up and married her just four months after his sick wife, Naomi, had passed away.

"Oh, yes, yes. She sure did, and did way too much shopping," he said, getting a little uncomfortable just thinking about Vivian's luscious and trim body.

Lillian groaned inwardly as Lawrence gave highlights of the cruise. *I'll just bet why she was shopping, alright. Probably shopping to take her mind off of missing little Ray Newman, up at that shipping warehouse.* She smiled when she remembered what happened a few months ago. She'd decided to drop off a loan approval to Ray's father at the warehouse. She went around to the back of the building where he sometimes worked, or more likely, took an afternoon nap. She recalled she was just about to knock on the door but hearing something, she looked through the open window and to her surprise and shock, she saw two people having sex. Lillian had pulled her glasses up from the chain around her neck and saw that the stuck-up, high-faluting Mrs. Jennings was bent over the desk and there was little Ray Newman, his jeans and drawers down to his ankles, and he was grabbing those melon-size breasts of hers. Lillian recalled it was like looking at a bad car accident . . . you just couldn't pull your eyes away from a scene like that.

"Miss Lilly?" Lawrence asked with fake concern.

Pulling herself back to the present, Lillian was embarrassed beyond words, and one look at the foolish man caused her to giggle. "Oh, I apologize, Mr. Jennings. I was just thinking about some funny moments at the party. It was just beautiful." Lillian giggled again remembering that's just what she'd heard little Ray Newman say to Mrs. Jennings as he grabbed her fake breasts—"jus' beautiful." When Mr. Jennings told her he had time to visit, Lillian was immediately on guard, because in all the years she had known him, this was the first time the man had ever crossed her doorstep. He was after something, and that got her curiosity jumping. She was determined to find out why he wanted to waste her time today by sitting his big butt on her newly upholstered sofa.

❧

Renee and Craig, holding hands, walked out of the movie pavilion and into the warm night air. Although the sun had gone down hours earlier, the evening was muggy and warm. They walked to a nearby restaurant for a light supper.

As they crossed a bridge walkover, Craig stopped and pulled Renee closer to him, sliding his hand up to the swell of her hips. Oblivious to their surroundings, he kissed her and then said, "Let's go eat before I start chewing on you." He watched her eyes flutter open.

Renee grinned, as the idea of him kissing and chewing on her neck thrilled her to no end.

Later, Craig let Renee drive his car . . . much to her delight. When they headed to their separate bedrooms, Craig said, "Thanks for the date, wife. Goodnight."

Renee smiled at him. "You're welcome, husband." Once inside her room with the door closed, Renee realized she liked calling him that.

CHAPTER 8

Well into the next week, Craig was busy going from one meeting to another, scouting and securing new business for the agency, all part of his plan to put the agency in the fast track.

Craig's staff was excited and energized, and why wouldn't they be? Initially, he had put money into the business to upgrade the computer system, which was completed last week, and at the same time he purchased new materials for producing ad campaigns. Craig made it a priority to meet with each employee for feedback, opinions and recommendations. He implemented almost every suggested action, as each promised to do their best under his leadership.

He'd received a call from a Lawrence Jennings, the vice president of the Wayland Bank down in his old neighborhood. More business, he thought, as he met with his staff.

On Thursday, armed with six poster boards and a proposal that would make even him go check out the bank's new loan programs, Craig walked into the cool interior of the Wayland Bank. He was transported back to his first visit there so many years ago.

He remembered his visit there to see Miss Lilly just a few weeks ago when he had come to see her about his inheritance. She had been surprised to see him. Then he was the one to be surprised, in fact, floored when she presented him with an up-to-date statement of his current inheritance balance. Craig had guessed the amount would be a few thousand dollars. After all, his grandfather wasn't wealthy by any means. But never in his wildest dreams did he ever expect to be the recipient of such a gift. *Granddad.*

He was greeted by Lawrence Jennings. "You must be Mr. Thompson. Please come on back to my office. I'm Lawrence Jennings." Lawrence wasn't surprised that Craig Thompson was African American, but he was surprised how young he was. Indeed, he had expected a much older man. Lawrence's lips tightened and stretched briefly over his white, perfectly capped teeth. He studied the much taller man entering his office, taking in the expertly fitted suit, slim gold bracelet and matching neck chain. He looked professional and powerful and walked with an air of confidence.

Looking at the interior of the bank; Craig saw that it was just as it was eons ago when he'd come there with his grandfather. It was also way too dreary and needed a new paint job and new furniture in the lobby, all of which he hadn't noticed a few weeks ago. But, then he hadn't cared what the bank looked like because he was in shock from talking with Miss Lilly. Now he needed to tell this pompous dude that maybe he didn't need to sell customers on a new loan program; instead, he just needed to refurbish the bank. But what the hell, the man wanted his advertising expertise, not his redecorating suggestions.

Before Craig presented his campaign ideas, he passed his three page resumé to Lawrence. He added, "I will tell you that I am highly skilled in all phases of advertising, from creating campaigns to sales and marketing, and monitoring, tracking and managing position reports. I'm hands-on in all phases of my client's portfolio. You will see that I have an extensive listing of clients for whom I have opened and retained accounts that produce measurable revenue." Craig didn't see the need to point out that, in the past few years, business had been declining. "Mr. Jennings, since we talked, my staff and I have come up with a couple of campaign ideas that I know you'll be pleased with."

Looking up from the resumé, Lawrence's smile was tight. He already knew what it said. "I'm thoroughly sold on your impressive and extensive resumé," he said, returning Craig's resumé to him. "Now, let's take a look-see at what you've got, son."

Craig bristled inwardly. He didn't like it when men referred to him as son. In the business world, it made him feel as if he was being seen as young and out of his league. He always nipped it in the bud. "Please, call me Mr. Thompson or Craig, Mr. Jennings; in fact, I insist." Craig met Lawrence's eyes levelly, making his point crystal clear, and then he went about setting up the campaign poster boards along the window ledge of the older man's office. He was aware that Lawrence's shrewd eyes were on him, and not on the boards.

Lawrence sized Craig up perfectly: Yes, he was sharp as well as arrogant. "Absolutely. You know, Mr.

Thompson, your name sounds familiar to me. Are you a customer at this bank? I mean, I don't recall seeing you before." Lawrence was reaching; he needed answers he hoped would lead him somewhere, anywhere, closer to that two million dollars.

"No, Mr. Jennings. I'm not a customer here. Now, if you will focus your attention on the boards, you'll see that, first, we want to go animated. Second, we want bold colors, lots of them. Third, we want the announcement posters of the new low-interest loans program in bold, whimsical letters on glossy paper." Craig finished lining up the boards on the window ledge and stood back to allow Lawrence to see them. "Now, take a look at them going from left to right and tell me what you like and what you don't like." Craig sat down and watched as Lawrence put on his glasses to view the posters. "Everything is negotiable and can be changed and reworked to your specifications. So, tell me what do you like?" For some reason Craig couldn't explain, he didn't like the pompous man, nor did he trust him. It was his eyes. His grandfather used to say you measured a man's character by looking into his eyes, which would show how he conducted business. Whatever it was, Jennings didn't possess it, although it was obvious that he thought he did.

"I just love it," Vivian Jennings purred, and she wasn't looking at the posters.

The attention of the two men turned to her immediately. She saw the stranger's eyes drift down past her face, so she pulled her shoulders back a little knowing that action inched her breasts up. She knew Lawrence looked; he always did. But so did the tall, sexy stranger, just seconds before he pulled his gaze away and stood up.

"Vivian, I'm in the midst of a meeting," Lawrence said as his wife sauntered over to the younger man.

"I am so sorry to interrupt your meeting, but I was running some errands and, well, I sort of needed your input on something." She waved her hand, and said, "Forget all that and introduce me to your visitor, honey."

Lawrence made a quick introduction. "Mr. Thompson is presently putting together some campaigns. Dear, you remember I told you about the new loan programs?"

"Not really," Vivian said, dismissing Lawrence. "It's a pleasure to meet you."

Craig extended his hand to shake hers and smiled down at her. "Craig Thompson. Pleased to meet you, Mrs. Jennings," he said, extracting his hand. He thought, so Jennings has a much younger wife, he thought, and she was stunning.

Vivian picked up on his arrogant dismissal of her, and assumed he must be gay. "So, campaigns you said," she said, keeping her eyes on the visitor. But when she sat down in the empty chair next to Craig and crossed her legs in his direction, which caused her short skirt to rise higher, she caught him looking down ever so briefly at her thighs and smiled. *So he's not gay, just cool.* Vivian's satisfied smile widened, as she sat back and looked at the colorful posters. "I like them. Which one do you like?" she asked Craig, pursing her lips.

Looking at Lawrence, Craig answered, "I like them all, but this is a personal view. I feel that I should point out to you, Mr. Jennings, that you'll want to, well, you'll want to do some inside undertaking when you want to drum up new business."

"What do you mean?" Lawrence asked, forcing his attention off of his wife.

"May I speak freely and frankly?" Craig asked.

"By all means do. I'm interested in what inside undertakings you meant, young fellow."

Craig turned when another visitor interrupted the meeting. It was someone he hadn't seen in many years, James Tinsly.

Mr. Tinsly and Craig's grandfather, Reginald, were respected friends. Craig remembered that as he stood to shake the man's hand. He had aged well and still had that twinkle in his eyes that Craig had seen when he first met the man. But Craig was equally aware that James Tinsly's name had been on both of his inheritance checks. He hoped that information wouldn't be disclosed in this or any other meeting.

James Tinsly smiled up at the tall man who he remembered meeting as a teenager. He thought Craig was a mirror image of his grandfather, including his height and the easy smile now gracing his face. He had gladly signed those checks over to him. "It is very nice to meet you, Craig, very nice." When he came further into the room, he went up to Craig and whispered, "Again." He clapped his hands loudly and walked over to the poster boards, acknowledging Vivian's presence along the way. "Mrs. Jennings, I hope you're well today." He nodded and pulled his eyeglasses from his jacket pocket. He looked at the posters, nodding and humming as he studied each one appreciatively.

Lawrence quickly rounded his desk to walk Vivian out.

The men smiled at each other. Mr. Tinsly said, "I hear congratulations are in order for you, Craig. Miss Lilly says your bride is pretty and as sweet as apple pie." He smiled and patted Craig's arm.

Craig laughed, picturing the pies Renee threw at him. He was sure one was an apple pie. "Thank you, sir, and yes, she is on both accounts."

"Wonderful, and Craig if you ever need me for anything, you just call me." He pulled out a business card from his pocket and wrote a number on it and handed it to Craig.

Craig looked at the business card and glanced at Tinsley for a split second before slipping the card into his breast pocket. He thought it odd the president of the bank would give him his personal phone numbers; after all, he didn't really know him.

Lawrence returned, red-faced and breathing heavily. "I'm sorry, gentlemen. So, Mr. Thompson, Craig, you were talking about inside undertakings here at the bank. Would you like to explain?" he asked, resuming his seat. "You know, James, you don't need to be bothered by this if you don't feel like it. I know you've been under the weather a bit." Lawrence was hoping the old man would go back to his office, or better yet, go home.

"No, no, I feel fine now; just a cold, that was all. After all, I am the bank president. Now go on, Craig, we're listening." James sat and motioned for Craig to continue.

Craig held back a laugh, as he thought, *Touché, Mr. Tinsley.* Then he told them the bank needed a makeover: fresh paint job; new furniture in the lobby; new flooring. "The bank needs cool, clean tiles to compliment a new paint job. Gentlemen, you can run all the campaign ads you want, you can put posters on buses and in community centers, but your potential customers will only see that you're just trying to push your same old products, even if they're new. If you don't do something new with the inside, then who is to say your new loan programs are really new?" Their silence didn't bother him. Craig knew they were thinking . . . and they knew he was right. He then fielded their questions.

Craig had them and had spent the next ten minutes giving suggestions and recommendations. "Trust me, gentlemen, with your new look, fresh paint and your new tile floors shining, the customers will line up after seeing your new ads, and they'll be comfortable sitting in the new plush chairs in your lobby as they wait to fill out all those new loan applications," he said, grinning . . . yeah, he had them sold.

As Craig spoke, Lawrence was acutely studying Craig and thinking . . . step one, the meeting, done; step two, formulizing a plan to get one million dollars. Hearing Craig ask a question, he pulled his attention back to the conversation.

Craig smiled. "Okay, so back to square one, gentlemen. Which ads do you like?"

And with that, the deal was sealed for all the ads. Craig went back to his office and brought his staff up to speed. The graphics and creative departments went to work immediately and, with the use of computers, Craig expected a rough run of the ads within a day or so. He'd already come up with a palette of cool colors and some ideas for cutting-edge décor for the contractor.

Craig had been back in his office for only two hours when he got more good news. The law center downtown called and needed a TV ad. He smiled up at his secretary, Lindsey, as he fielded the call. "Of course we can do that. Just tell me what you'd like to see."

❧

It was seven when Craig finally arrived home. On the drive home, he thought that more business brought with it a greater chance he would be revealed as the owner of the agency. He decided to just tell Renee that he'd secured a bank loan. After all, he figured, that's what people did every day. He smiled, thinking he might even tell her he'd secured the loan from the Wayland Bank. Liking that plan even better, he was smiling when he entered his house and walked back to the kitchen.

He looked out on the patio and his heart soared the moment he saw Renee sitting by the pool with . . . that darned puppy from next door, again. She was talking to the little mutt.

Craig opened the patio door and sang out. "Honey, I'm home."

Renee looked up, and so did the trembling puppy. "Hey, Craig, have you ever been properly introduced to Leo, here?" she asked, playfully fluffing the puppy's ears.

Craig took off his socks and shoes and sat beside her. He enjoyed the simple act of sitting beside her and dangling his feet in the water as she was. He leaned forward and glared at the puppy. "Not really, but I am aware of his favorite spots to leave his surprises on this patio." He looked at Renee questioningly.

Renee just giggled. "Oh, you're just being mean. Anyway, this is Leo, and he doesn't leave any more surprises." She lifted the puppy's paw to wave at him.

"And he hasn't done it?" he asked, looking doubtful.

"Nope," she said, grinning.

Craig leaned toward the puppy and shook his paw. "Well, in that case, hello Leo, but I'll still be watching you," he promised, pointing to his eyes just as they heard whistling from next door. Steve was calling for Leo. Craig and Renee laughed as the dog ran under the table, around two chairs, then around the yard to crawl back under the hedge to go home.

Craig laughed. "Now why did he do all that, instead of just running across the damn grass and going under the hedge?" he asked turning his attention to her. "Hi, baby." He leaned forward and kissed her lips lightly.

"Hi yourself," Renee said, returning the simple kiss. She told Craig the grass was way too much temptation for Leo . . . and also because she and Maria had been repositioning the sprinklers. "I grilled turkey burgers and veggies, are you hungry?" she asked.

"Oh, you know how to get me going, woman." They went back to the patio and fixed their plates. After a few minutes of eating Craig told her about the two new accounts. Her excitement was not lost on him; neither was how sexy she looked, and his abdomen tightened. His let his eyes travel to her thin summer shirt and his mouth watered to taste her again. Coughing, as a distraction Craig sat up, forcing his attention back to what she had just said. "I'm sorry, what did you say?"

"I said, Mr. Davis should be dancing at the thought of all the money coming in."

"You know, I would be, if I were him," Craig said, averting his gaze and looking out at the pool. "Did you swim today?" he asked, changing the subject and feeling guilty.

"No, Annette came out to see me. We sat around talking. I really have missed our talks. You know, we used to talk on the phone for hours," she giggled.

"I remember, but what could two twelve-year-olds have to talk about for hours?"

She smiled at him and bit into her burger. "Mostly we talked about boys and clothes and the cutest actors on our favorite TV shows. But mostly about boys."

"What did you talk about boys?" Craig asked. He liked talking to her. He liked her. He felt very comfortable around her. He was himself and she made him laugh.

"Oh, you know the usual stuff, like have you ever French-kissed a boy, or did you ever let a boy touch your breasts. That kind of stuff, that's all." Renee giggled, only vaguely aware that Craig was intrigued by the conversation.

"Did you French kiss a boy or let him touch your breasts?" Craig bit his bottom lip, trying hard to suppress a laugh, because he knew that at twelve years old Renee had no breasts.

"No, not then. I got French kissed when I was fifteen," she murmured.

"Oh, really? By who?" Craig smiled at her sudden shyness.

"Rodney Donaldson," she said, smiling. "I was so nervous, and so was he."

Craig made a face. "Bucktooth Rodney Donaldson? Yuk, Renee."

She sat back. "Well, what was I supposed to do, Craig? Wait for you to kiss me? Besides, you had moved away by then." Renee immediately wished she hadn't said that; now he knew that she had wanted him to kiss her all those years ago.

Craig got up and went to sit beside her. "Renee, did you want me to kiss you back then?"

She didn't want to talk about that time back then; it always brought on sadness. First, dealing with Bryant's illness and his death, then Craig moving away. She picked up her napkin and wiped her hands before answering him. "Yes, Craig, I did. But you were so clueless that when you walked in the front door, you ended up kissing Meg. And guess what? She felt you when you did." She realized she was still mad at her sister Meg about that, too.

Craig stared at her. "Huh? What? Hey, I never kissed your sister Meg. When?"

"Under the mistletoe in the entryway to the living room . . . that last Christmas. Cecelia and I were decorating the tree and we saw you, and you did kiss her back, too. Both of you were grinning and looking stupid." Knowing she sounded like an adolescent, Renee felt foolish.

Craig wrinkled his brow and thought for a minute, and then laughed loudly. He remembered it just as she said. "Oh, yeah, you're right. I did kiss her. But wait, I never felt her up, Renee. I mean, she was cute and all, but she wasn't much older than you."

"I didn't say you felt her up like that. She said she felt your . . . well, your . . . reaction to kissing her. She told me and Cecelia that after you ran upstairs, grinning all goofy and dumb-like." Renee rolled her eyes at him.

Then it dawned on him what she was talking about. "Oh, you mean I got a woody when she kissed me?" Craig laughed for several minutes before he could talk. "Honey, at that age I got hard if the wind blew against my jeans zipper. It wasn't about her. Look at me, Squirt." He took her chin and turned her face back to him. "Why did you want me to kiss you under the mistletoe?"

Renee didn't like the close scrutiny he was subjecting her to. "Why is it so important now, Craig? We're no longer kids, although I might as well be for fulfilling a promise I made with you." Still sulking, she looked up at him and saw that he was still waiting for her to answer. "Oh, all right, yes, I did. I thought you were the cutest boy ever, Craig, and whenever I looked at you, I smiled and . . . I-I didn't know what the feelings were that I had when I thought about you kissing me. And that day on the swing, it was the first time you called me Renee, and not Squirt or skinny bones or knobby knees, and you put your arm around my shoulders and held me close." When he didn't say anything, Renee went on. "And all I wanted to do was to hold you, too, because I knew how much you were hurting. I knew you were grieving over Bryant just as much as we all were. I felt it in my heart." She became uncomfortable under his quiet, intense gaze. The tension of the night settled in the middle of her chest, and Renee pulled her hands from his. "So there, are you happy now that I've told you all that?" Renee held back her tears, but their glistening pools remained in her eyes.

Craig pulled her onto his lap. "Thank you for telling me that." He held her close, wrapping his arms around her for several minutes. "Renee, I was sixteen and my thoughts were on sports cars and girl's breasts. You were a nice, sweet girl, but you were only twelve, my baby sister's age. If I had kissed you, your parents would have had me arrested, and my parents would have encouraged them to do it." He reached up and caressed her face. "I'm sorry that you were hurting back then, baby," he said quietly and kissed her neck, grinning. "But can I ask you something?"

Renee nodded, unable to speak due to the heat of his lips warming her neck.

"How in God's name could you kiss bucktooth Rodney? You know he ate boogers from his nose, don't you?" Craig was struggling not to laugh, then gave up the effort.

She felt his stomach rumbling. "No, he didn't." Renee sat up and swatted at his shoulder.

"Oh, yes he did, and I know because I caught him doing it up on the bleachers."

"And what were you doing there? Watching the cheerleaders' bouncing breasts?"

"No, as I recall, I was under the bleachers with one hand under Lisa Pullman's sweater, and the other hand . . . well. Anyway, we looked up when someone sat down and we watched him and laughed. But we were trapped, so we ended up having to covering our mouths to keep from laughing out loud. Oh, man, that was so funny. He was just digging away." Craig looked up at her and rubbed his hand against her thigh. "But all joking aside, I'm sorry." He missed kissing her. "Can I now?" When she didn't answer, he moved his hands up to her neck and brought her lips close to his, and he proceeded to give her the French kiss she'd only imagined as a preteen.

Renee kissed him back. She loved the feel of the strong muscles of his back as she glided her hands over his shoulders. She wanted to shout out, 'Yes, this is how I wanted you to kiss me then.' Hadn't she dreamed of him doing this long ago and every night since that Friday night in her apartment? When his tongue easily moved over her lips and connected with hers, Renee could have sworn that a line of fire had been ignited and had moved straight down to the very core of her. Her head felt full and heavy as she tilted it back, inhaling deeply. That gave him access to plant kisses all along her smooth neck, returning back to her mouth. She felt him come to life against her. It was then that Renee knew she wanted him, and she kissed him back with all the passion he had kissed her. She couldn't get enough of him, it seemed.

Craig would have never imagined that he would be sitting on his patio kissing Renee. Since the night on the couch, they had not really kissed, only light touches and light kisses, mostly on the cheek. He missed tasting her lips. Craig inhaled deeply when Renee eased her hands down his chest. He knew the hardest thing would be to go to his room alone. His hands moved up her torso to touch the sides of her breasts; he tried to stop himself, but his hands caressed her breasts until her nipples distended and his mouth watered to taste the swollen buds.

Craig was dizzy from kissing her, and blood pounded in his ears. Easing his lips from hers, he leaned his damp forehead against the swell of her breast. Craig reached up with trembling hands and slowly unbuttoned her cotton summer shirt and gazed openly at her full breasts. As he guessed, she wasn't wearing a bra, so her bareness called out to him. "Beautiful, Renee . . . you're so beautiful . . ." He breathed heavily and looked up at her. Renee's eyes were closed and he knew that she wanted him to touch her, and so he did. His fingers traced the outline of her breasts, first one then the other, then he followed with his mouth. Feverishly, his mouth found hers again when she leaned forward, pressing her breasts into his chest. Craig wanted her so badly, but he was also aware they had set their rules and he didn't want to take advantage of her, regardless of how badly he wanted her. "Oh, baby . . . look, um . . . we need to stop." His eyes strayed to her flushed face.

Renee heard him and looked down at his mouth. Her eyes had darkened with desire. She slowly unbuttoned his shirt. Then, leaning forward, she planted kisses on his chest and found his nipples, as sensitive as her own. Craig's response was immediate, physical and audible, and it thrilled her to no end. He strained painfully against her, and Renee knew that he was like that for her, because of her. She loved feeling his hands in her hair and guiding her mouth across his chest and neck and back up to his mouth, where she eagerly sought his lips.

Craig whispered with effort against her warm mouth. "Renee, please, baby . . . we need to stop right now or I won't be able to if we keep this up." He struggled to speak. He felt as if he was suffocating from their body heat and her tongue mating with his and it seemed the pool was the only place he could escape to. Only he couldn't, because she was sitting on his lap, holding onto him and she wasn't stopping. He had to get his mind elsewhere. *Think of something, work, yeah, work.* No good. *The play-offs.* No good. He wished he could just stop her roving hands, but he couldn't.

Renee drew her lips across his cheek and kissed his ear, then lightly bit his neck. The effect sent waves of pleasure and desire up and down his body. He heard her whispering his name as her breath fanned his neck, then his chest. Craig's heart hammered against his ribs as he gasped for air. He knew she felt him straining. "Renee." He whispered her name in a strangled, hoarse voice that didn't sound like his own.

Renee placed a finger on his lips and traced the outline of them. "Craig, I don't want to stop. I want you." *Beautiful brown eyes,* she thought. "I'm a grown woman now, Craig. And it's been a while, but I do know what I want, and I can feel what you want, too." She shocked him yet again by smoothing her hands down to work the belt and zipper of his trousers. Craig bit down on his bottom lip to keep from simpering like he was a teenager. His arms tightened around her waist.

Craig pulled her hand away and looked at her intently. His mouth opened to speak, but words did not come. His eyes feasted on her and, in that moment, he wanted nothing else but her. He lifted her from his lap and stood up, only inches separating them now.

Silently Renee took his hand and led him inside.

"Are you sure, baby?" Craig asked, stopping momentarily.

She answered by turning and kissing him. "I'll meet you upstairs in your room."

"Huh? Oh, I'll put the food away," Craig managed to say, watching her walk into the house and up the stairs. He hurriedly put the food away, locked the doors, and headed upstairs with two glasses of chilled wine. He stood outside his bedroom door for a minute to calm his raging desire. He hoped that she hadn't changed her mind. He entered his room and found the lights dimmed and soft jazz playing. His breath caught in his throat when he saw Renee standing against the wall near the window. She slowly walked barefoot toward him, her hair fanning her face and shoulders. He'd never seen a prettier sight.

"I thought you changed your mind and were going to leave me up here all alone," Renee said quietly, standing on her toes and running her hands up his chest.

Craig handed her a glass of wine as he leaned down and kissed her cheek, relishing the soft warmth of her face. His mind was still struggling with what she had said out on the patio. She didn't want him to stop. He took a large gulp of wine as she dragged her hand down his chest and began slowly pulling his shirt from his trousers. He took her glass, and reaching behind her, set their glasses down on the dresser. Clasping her hands, he held them to his chest. "Renee, look at me." When she did he saw how heavy and dark her eyes had become. He'd never seen a more beautiful woman in his life and struggled to find his voice. "Baby, I don't want to take advantage of you, or of our situation. But I need to know that you're sure this is what you want and . . ."

Renee cut him off, extracting her hands from his and reaching up to his face. Wordless, she pulled his head down to her lips. She kissed him thoroughly and passionately, answering him in a way she knew he understood. She felt his heart beating wildly under her hand and knew her own heartbeat matched his. Everything in Renee was alive and she was never more sure of anything in her life, despite her history of making bad decisions. No second-guessing, no self-doubts, just feeling and living in the moment . . . a moment that was becoming unbearable as she strained against him.

Releasing a growl from deep within, Craig devoured her mouth as he ran his hands up and down her back, stopping at her rounded bottom. When he lifted her against him, his breath caught in his throat when he felt her trembling in his arms. He knew she was as ready as he was, but still he paced himself. Putting her down on her feet, Craig unbuttoned her cotton blouse again and slid the garment from her shoulders, watching as the flimsy garment floated to the floor. Everything moved as if in slow motion. Everything, that is, except his furiously racing heart. It was as if he was watching a movie with the tape was on slow play. Craig surprised himself by not rushing. He knew that time was of the essence, lest he lose it right then and there.

Renee watched his fingers touching her breasts, then she reached up and unbuttoned his shirt, pulling it from his trousers and down his arms. His bronze chest was in splendid proportion to his large body. His bare chest revealed the softest black hair she'd ever seen on a man. Her fingers skipped lightly over his chest. Her lips followed suit, planting kisses on his chest. She was vaguely aware of her gauze skirt falling in soft heap around her ankles. She was then naked to his eyes except for her black lace panties. As he caressed her breasts, Renee reached up and kissed his mouth again. His body was hot to her touch. She trailed kisses up to his neck and then down to his tight nipples. She couldn't help but run her tongue across them. She smiled at his reaction when she ran her nails lightly down his stomach. She stopped at the waistband of his trousers for a second and met his eyes.

Craig never wanted to please a woman so badly before. But this wasn't just any woman or just any night of lovemaking. This was Renee. His Squirt. His wife. And it felt so right for them to be here, in this space, suspended in time. He picked her up and carried her to the end of the bed, where he put her down and leaned forward to kiss her, his tongue circling hers once again.

Renee unbuckled his belt, her fingers grazing him as she eased his trousers down his muscular thighs and legs. She felt no shame in her exploration of his body. In fact, she was fueled by it, and it her heightened her desire for him. He was all male. Firm and soft, and she loved touching him. She couldn't get enough of touching him. Her warm hands snaked up both of his powerful legs to his thighs. "You're beautiful, Craig, and so perfect," she whispered, as her running her hands down the length of him.

Craig stepped out of his shoes, then his trousers. He literally could not speak as he watched her warm hands glide down his legs, then back up to his stomach, causing his knees to almost buckle from her touch. He knelt before her, bringing her face close to his and kissing her. "No, baby, you're the beautiful one, and you're perfect in every way. Renee, I want you so badly and I don't want to hurt you . . ." His voice was thick with emotion.

Renee touched his face, loving the feel of stubble against her fingers. Her hands traced the lines of his face, the same face that had appeared in her dreams for as long as she could remember. She couldn't contain a smile as she remembered the teenage Craig, and she realized that it was his face she'd longed to see on the faces of her past lovers. "Craig, I'm not the same fragile teenager you remember. I'm a full-grown woman now, and I'm dying for us to make love. Haven't you wanted to since we've been living here together, or maybe even that day in my apartment?" She reached for him again, but he caught her hand, stopping her.

How could she know what was in his heart, he wondered, as his eyes went from her eyes to her swollen red lips. "Yes, I have wanted this for a long time. I've wanted you since the day you ran into me at the courthouse. But Renee, our pact, our deal . . ." He searched her face again.

"Craig, this isn't about promises, or deals . . . it's just about how much we care about each other, right?" Renee had begun to feel more in her heart for him, even if he didn't feel the same for her.

He wanted to say more, but looking into her eyes sent a beam to his heart then down to the juncture of his thighs. "We do care about each other, don't we, and . . ." She reached out, encouraging him to get in the bed. She was about to pull him towards her, but he stopped her, kneeling before her and kissing her deeply once again.

Renee experienced the sensation of floating into space, then she realized that Craig's hand was sliding down her chest and stomach, pressing her backward until she lay back on the bed. She could feel the heat of his arms on her legs.

Craig trailed kisses down her stomach, as his fingers massaged their way down, touching her intimately. He found her ready for him. Her body reacted uncontrollably as his hands glided over her. Each moan, each sigh coming from her was like a wonderful spasm of pleasure running throughout his body. He removed the last piece of clothing she had on and, with the lightest of touches, he explored her.

Renee's heart pounded as blood rushed to her ears, creating sounds of roaring ocean waves. Her thighs were trembling, and she couldn't stop her body from moving about. Renee reached out blindly for a lifeline as her passion mounted. From out of nowhere, his hand captured hers, grasping her trembling fingers, intertwining them with his own. His pace became frantic to take her over the top. His hand came up to caress her breasts and stomach, liking the warmth and texture of her skin. Within seconds, he felt her fall apart as passion claimed her body. Moans escaping her throat were almost overpowering her, and he felt the rhythmic contractions of her release against him. Craig slowly kissed his way up her body as she gulped in air.

Her hand was still clutching his as wave after wave of pleasure ricocheted through her body. Renee had never felt so alive and sexy in her life, and tears seeped through her eyelashes. It would be several minutes before she could steady her breathing, but still she didn't move. She knew he was watching her, waiting patiently, dropping

PROMISES MADE

more kisses on her. Every inch of her body was affected by waves of aftershocks. She blinked him into view; he was running his hands along her thighs. She reached out to touch him. "Craig . . ."

"Baby . . . I'm not rushing you," He said against her lips on a brief kiss. She saw a condom in his hand. "Still, no pressure and if you've changed your mind, just tell me. Remember no deals and no promises here." He leaned over and caressed her cheek.

Renee was touched by his tenderness and gentle caresses. She moved up on the bed, releasing his hand. "Craig, shut up and come up here on the bed with me. I'm not having second thoughts. I was just thinking that you've really grown up nicely, that's all." Renee frowned at what she'd said and then laughed at his reaction.

Craig chuckled and only took a few seconds to prepare himself before joining her on his bed. His body covered her immediately and they began kissing and caressing each other to the point they were weak with want. When he moved her, he noticed her eyes were closed. "Renee, open your eyes. I want to watch you and I want you to see me," he said in a voice stranger than his own.

Her eyes fluttered open and she reached up to touch his face. Her chest tightened with emotion. "Craig . . . you've grown from the cutest boy to the most handsome man . . . and I want to watch you making love to me . . . like now, Craig." She moved beneath him.

He needed no more encouragement than that. He'd held out as long as he could. When he entered the warmth of her body, each stilled their movements for several seconds. Craig was holding on by a thread, but he was determined not to move until she was ready and wanted him to. He kissed her eyes, her neck, down to her breasts, and up to her mouth again. He couldn't get enough of her, and his body trembled when he felt her move under him. Only then did he began to move. Craig felt complete. Their frenzied movements continued, spiraling, taking them further and further away from the current space and time. She touched him and excited him everywhere and his body moved in sync with hers. Craig reached her, lifting her closer, the action taking them closer to the point each was seeking. Their breathing quickened, their moans and gasps incoherent as their passions mounted. Her sounds of pleasure fired electrons in his brain, pushing his desire for her over the limit, and his deep groans filled her head and the high ceiling of his bedroom.

When Craig heard her cries of pleasure becoming deeper and more frantic as her hands clutched at him, he pulled his mouth away from hers and lifted his head to look at her. In a deep voice fueled by his thrusting hips and surging blood, he commanded her to look at him. "Open your eyes, Renee . . . open your eyes . . . I've got you . . ." When she did, each watched as passion took over and claimed their inner souls. Her cry of ecstasy pushed them over the edge of pleasure and he soon followed her with a release that left him trembling.

It would be several minutes before either Craig or Renee could move. The only sound in the room was their ragged breathing and pounding heartbeats. The music that flowed throughout the bedroom was forgotten. Another selection started and finished, and yet they still lay entangled and spent in each other's arms.

Before long, Craig had to get up to remove the only barrier that was between them. Returning from his bathroom a few minutes later, he lay down beside Renee, gathered her in his arms and kissed her deeply. Finally he said, "I hope I didn't disappoint you, Renee," lifting curls from her damp forehead.

Renee hugged him to her and searched his face. She couldn't believe that he was serious, but she could see that indeed he was. "How could you disappoint me? Craig, you're wonderful. Did I please you?"

"Oh, God . . . yes, on so many levels . . . you little screamer." He laughed at her expression and tugged at his ear and pulled her closer. "Can I just hold you in my arms?"

Renee laughed. "Well, what else would you normally want to do?" Actually, she didn't want to imagine him making love to any other woman.

He was exhausted and really didn't want to talk. "You want to know, honestly?"

"Yes, I do." She watched him, admiring him.

He thought for a few minutes before answering. "Renee, some men . . . well, some look at sex on the impersonal level. It keeps us emotionally detached sometimes, and what we want is the physical relief and then we want to be left alone, you know." She nodded her head, her smile wavering. He thought she looked even sexier after making love and caressed her cheek. "That, I think, is how I have been and, in fact, I've been told that more than once. Okay, now let's chill for a bit." He tried to settle her against him as exhaustion claimed his limbs.

"What you mean is that you want the physical aspect of sex and not the emotions, and that women have told you that?" Renee asked.

"Well . . . yes, I think so." He felt her body stiffen and her hand moving away from his chest . . . and he didn't like what he felt . . . her detaching from him.

"So you're not one of those guys who fall in and out of love based on the physical aspects of the relationship?" Renee knew she shouldn't continue the conversation, but she did anyway.

"Baby, look, two people don't have to be in love to enjoy a great physical relationship. You don't really think that, do you, Renee?" He leaned back, angling his head to look at her.

"I-I don't know." She honestly didn't know how to answer that.

"Hum, okay, so are you saying that you've been in love with every man you've ever slept with, in the physical sense?" Craig didn't like the conversation either, and he wondered where she was going with her questions.

First, she looked at him with her mouth agape, then she pushed him away from her as she sat up on the bed staring at him. Her words exploded in a rush, loudly. "Every other man I've slept with? What the hell are you saying, Craig? Do you think I've slept with a lot of men? Is that what you think about me?" Enraged, she could only blink rapidly at him.

Craig sat up, not sure what she was so upset about. "I don't know; how should I know? I haven't seen you in almost eighteen years. Why are you so upset?" He didn't understand, but he knew all he wanted was to kiss her again and hold her in his arms and drift off to sleep, but for some reason she was angry at him.

Renee began yanking the covers from under him, but he wouldn't budge. In fact, he reached for her hand to come back on the bed. She got up from the bed and threw a pillow at him before scrambling around on the floor for her clothes in the semi-darkened room.

Craig got up then and rounded the foot of the bed, where she was still feeling around the floor for her clothes. "Renee, what are you doing?" He spotted his boxers and stepped into them, not taking his eyes off her frantic, angry movements.

From the floor she looked up at him, anger clearly etched on her face. "You're standing on my shirt, stupid," she hissed up with narrowed eyes.

Craig spotted her shirt and picked it up, but Renee snatched it from his fingers. "Renee, come on. What's wrong? Did I say or do something that upset you again?" He watched her yank on her clothes. "Come on, Squirt. You know, I don't think this is the afterglow I've heard so much about."

"Why don't you just shut up, Craig?" After stepping into her skirt and fumbling with her shirt, Renee stomped to the door, yanked it opened, and stormed down the hall to her room.

In the span of some sixty seconds, Craig thrust his hands to his hips and looked from the bed of now-crumpled bed linen to the stereo. He picked his shirt up from the floor and wondered what else had happened, beside the obvious. Surely, he didn't just dream that they'd made love. But he knew that they had because he still felt the aftershocks. He heard the guest bathroom door slam and finally left his bedroom to go after her. He stopped when she came out of the bathroom, ignoring him and going inside her bedroom. Then she turned and slammed the door in his face, sending him back to his bedroom.

Sitting on the edge of his bed, Craig rubbed his head and replayed their conversation, searching for a clue as to why she got so upset. He drew a blank and threw up his hand. "Oh, to hell with this." He got up and went out the door and walked down the hall again. He didn't bother knocking on her door; he just threw it open and found her standing before the dresser mirror, brushing her hair. Her face was red and angry, in contrast to the yellow sleep set she'd put on.

"Get out of here," she said, holding the brush in mid-air, not even looking at him.

Craig walked in and took the brush from her hand, turning her towards him. "Renee, what the hell is going on? I mean, if this is some kind of ah, hormonal, post-orgasmic, traumatic, um . . . whatever, then tell me, like right now, and I'll be prepared in the future." After he'd stumbled through what he thought happened, his eyes bore into hers and he never saw her hand come up and slap him soundly on the cheek. "What the . . ." He stared at her, dumbfounded.

Renee's temper flared and her instinct was to slap the silly look off his face. "We're honest here, right, Craig?" she asked, waving her hand in the space between them.

Staring at her, he answered tightly, "Yes." His mind was still reeling from the fact that she had slapped him.

"First of all, in the future we will not be doing that again. Second, how many women have you slept with, Craig?" She crossed her arms under her heaving chest, waiting.

"What? I don't know. How the hell should I know?" He saw her doubtful look. "I didn't exactly keep a score sheet, Renee." He was still lost in what he believed was a one sided-conversation.

"Okay, then when was the first time you had sex, Craig? And don't you dare say you don't know, or I swear I'll punch your lights out." Renee's hand had balled into a fist as she watched him look into the mirror to examine his face.

He turned and stared back at her, looking puzzled for a few seconds. "I was fifteen, no sixteen . . . I think . . . yeah, sixteen."

"Uh-huh. With who?"

"Oh, I think it was . . ." He thought for a few minutes, his eyes glancing left then right, searching. "Oh, yeah, Emily Wheaterby." He smiled as if he expected a prize for remembering.

Renee snorted and smirked. "Oh, you were really hard up then, if your first time was with that cross-eyed, stank skank, Emily Wheaterby. She was in Cecelia's class and everybody knew that she slept around with boys," she said, forcing away his partial nakedness.

"I didn't think she was cross-eyed or a skank, but where are you going with this?"

Ignoring his question, she said, "Okay, so if that cross-eyed skank was the first girl you ever had sex with, and we just had sex, about how many women do you think you've had sex with in between then and now?" She glared up at him, waiting for his answer.

Frustration forced him to blink at her and shake his head. Throwing up his hands, Craig yelled out. "Damn, I don't know . . . thirty, forty . . . like I said, I didn't keep a score sheet, and I am a grown man. Besides, Renee, men aren't supposed to kiss and tell. Isn't that in all those women's magazines and on your women's channels on TV?"

Renee put her hand up to his chest and backed him out into the hallway and stood on the threshold of her door. "Thirty or forty . . . like a dog, right? Yes, they just hump anything in heat, too, don't they? It's probably more than that, I'll bet."

"And your point is what?" He still wasn't following her, but looking at her full breasts swaying under her nightshirt he wanted to make love to her again.

Renee continued glaring at him. "Craig, I've had sex with four men in my lifetime. You make number four. Number one was Bobby. We were both virgins at nine-teen and he was sweet and kind and we stayed a couple for almost six years. And, yes, I loved him and hoped to even marry him but he fell in love with someone else and dumped me. Number two, was David and, yes, I loved him right up until he decided he didn't want to work anymore and went looking for a sugar mama to take care of him. Number three was Charles. I thought I loved him, and stupid me, I thought he loved me. Only . . . he was a liar and a thief. And number four is you." She held up her hand, preventing him from speaking. "How dare you imply that I've have had sex with so many men that you can say what you said to me!" She then mocked him: "Duh, geez, Renee, have you been in love with every other man you ever slept with." Her voice rose with her indignation. "Yes, you clown! I loved them and they turned around and hurt me! But you wouldn't know anything about loving someone, because the emotionally detached master stud that you are, you can't even remember how many women you've slept with in your lifetime, let alone their names!" When she finally finished, Renee pushed him out into the hallway and slammed the door in his face and locked it.

Craig stood staring at the grain pattern of the wood on the door for several seconds, her words at last sinking in. He touched the door and heard Renee crying. His own chest constricted. He whispered at her door, "I'm sorry, Squirt." He walked back to his room and quietly closed his door. He felt like the dog she implied he was.

Picking the bed covers up from the floor with angry yanks, Craig got into his bed, hoping sleep would claim him quickly . . . but it didn't. His mind replayed their conversation in bed, and when she just cut him up into little pieces a few minutes ago. But, in truth, Craig knew that she'd hit home with him when she said he didn't know the pain of loving then losing because he had never let women get that close in the first place. Not so with his male friends who did and ended up with broken hearts. In a sense, Craig thought he was lucky to have bypassed all that.

Down the hallway, Renee hugged her pillow close to her body and cried until she had no more tears left. Her mind was torn as she struggled between the fresh memories of their beautiful and passionate lovemaking and his belief that she'd had many lovers, as he had. She didn't blame them for hurting her, but she did blame Charles. Because her other boyfriends may have fallen out of love with her or didn't love her as much as she thought loved them, but they never dated her with the purpose of stealing from her. Renee knew she had to get that issue resolved before she could move any further. One thing for sure, she never intended to sleep with Craig Thompson again. Since they were just starting the second month, she'd try to hold on until the end of the three months . . . and prayed that by then Charles would be arrested and behind bars.

The following day was a workday for Craig and Renee, and neither had gotten any sleep the night before. Craig showered and dressed and followed their morning routine: He went downstairs and prepared a pot of coffee and set their travel coffee mugs on the counter.

Leaning against the kitchen counter, his arms folded across his chest, Craig reflected on last night's conversation for the tenth time. He thought she had every reason to be mad at him; hell, he was madder at himself. He was also saddened that she'd been so hurt by the few men she had loved. He had no idea of the number of woman he either had sex with or had inadvertently hurt because he hadn't fallen in love with them. Hadn't he been told at one time or another to open his heart? He even gave up trying to count his past lovers. Renee was right; he couldn't even remember their names.

Craig looked up when Renee walked into the kitchen. He thought she was stunning in a peach-colored dress that fit her curves nicely. "Good morning." He poured her coffee into her mug. Her subtle perfume filled his senses, evoking memories of the previous evening. He recalled the taste of her lips and the feel of her skin. Her faint perfume lingering on his pillows and sheets was another reason he hadn't slept.

Renee didn't answer him as she took her lunch from the fridge, unplugged her cellphone from the counter and left the house.

He watched her leave without saying a word. The cold front had returned to his kitchen.

At lunchtime, Craig was at his desk putting the final touches on the campaign for the Wayland Bank, having earlier received the mock-up of the ads from the graphics department. He dialed Renee's office number and waited.

"Renee Richards. May I help you?"

"So, you're back to Richards again?" he asked, listening to her inhaling deeply.

"I'm busy," she said with an impatient voice. She wasn't really busy at that exact moment, but hearing his voice was like a caress; her pulse raced and her stomach tightened. *Lord, help me,* she silently prayed.

"Renee . . . I'm sorry. I . . ."

"I'm busy," she repeated, determined not to give in.

"Then you shouldn't have answered your telephone," Craig said tightly, holding the handset tighter in his hand. He didn't want her angry. The past few weeks had been wonderful. They laughed and talked, and he knew he would miss that terribly if she was angry, or worse, left him. "Renee, I'm sorry about what I said last night, but I'm not sorry about what happened between us. Listen, baby, can we . . ." Craig winced when he suddenly heard a dial tone; she had hung up on him. He stared at the phone and laughed. It was so like her to hang up on him, but he still didn't expect it.

Renee swiveled in her chair and turned to face the window. For the tenth time she asked herself, "How could I have been so weak and just plain thoughtless?"

After a week of avoiding each other at home, Craig and Renee seemingly had accepted their awkward situation. Neither tried to talk to the other or had meals together. Each often worked late, sometimes arriving home as late as nine.

At first Craig had tried to talk to Renee, but when she refused to even look at him, he just gave up after a couple of days. But he missed her deeply.

The Saturday of the second week, Renee didn't even bother to get up when Maria arrived for her scheduled six-hour workday. But Maria again noticed that something was amiss with the newlyweds. She had first seen it the previous week and now noticed the situation had not changed. Before leaving, she did knock on Renee's door and told her she had made them pasta salad and was leaving it out on the counter.

It was almost ten that night when Renee remembered what Maria had told her. The first floor was dark, except for light spilling in from the patio. She heard a sound outside and looked out toward the patio and saw Craig doing laps in the pool. Standing back in the semi-dark kitchen, Renee's breath caught in her throat when she watched Craig step from the pool, sending water droplets swirling around his body. Her hand flew to her chest when little flickers of remembered pleasure shot through her body. The tension in her body increased as she watched him dive back into the water. She wanted to close her eyes to the sight of his beautiful body moving in the water. His movements were sure and strong, like his love-making.

Renee turned her back on the sight of him as her heart began beating faster. She did not see the casserole dish, so she checked the fridge, seeing it had been put it there. She closed the door and pressed her cheek against the cool stainless steel of the refrigerator door. She hated that she had put herself in a position to be hurt.

Craig slipped out of the pool and began drying off. He saw a flash of light from the kitchen and left the pool area, coming round to look into the kitchen window. He had to squint around Renee's abundance of plants and flowers and was surprised to see her just standing against the refrigerator. Alarmed, he walked to the patio door, opened it and walked in barefoot and stood behind her. She was sniffing. He moved closer until his damp body leaned into the warmth of her back, and when he felt her tense up, he pressed his hands to the refrigerator door to keep her from acting on her instinct to run.

Renee didn't hear him come into the kitchen and was unaware he had been standing there behind her until his body touched hers. She fought to control the treacherous reaction of her body and felt her nightshirt begin to stick to her perspiring body.

"Renee, honey, I'm sorry," Craig whispered. "I didn't mean to hurt you and I never meant to make you cry." He reached around for her chin, his heart breaking that Renee was so sad, and it was his fault, again. He moved closer and brought his arms around his waist, resting his head on the top of her heads.

"I'm sorry," he said quietly, "I wasn't around during those times when someone hurt you. I would have wanted to be there for you, if only to beat those losers up." He slowly turned her to face him and wiped her tears away with damp fingers. "Baby, I never meant to insult you like that." He hugged her tighter, then stooped down to her eye level. "I was, again, incredibly stupid and insensitive. We still have a box of frozen pizza you can throw at me, if it'll make you feel better," he whispered, smiling when she rolled her eyes at him. Then he finally kissed her.

Try as she might, Renee did not possess the energy to respond to him or desire to stop him from kissing her. She blamed herself for her weakness. When she got hurt again, it would be her own fault for being foolish and wanton. When his lips touched hers and commanded her to open her mouth to accept his kiss, she did so without hesitation. They stood kissing until she was weak and had to cling to him for support.

Craig lifted her up in his arms and carried her upstairs to his bedroom. Quickly stripping out of his wet trucks, he then removed her nightshirt and kissed her from head to toe. He took a condom from the nightstand, but without saying a word, Renee took it from him. Craig loved the feel of her touch upon his body, and his breath rushed from his lungs.

Renee and Craig were puppets fueled by their desires. When at last their passions subsided, they lay side by side, facing each other. Instinctively, Craig braced himself. He didn't want to say anything that would send her fleeing from him again. So he kept it simple. "I've missed you, Renee," he said, running his hands down her back. "You built a structure around you that was like a twelve-foot high concrete wall, built for the purpose of keeping me away from you. I hated that and I longed for you and for your company." Craig caressed her cheek and leaned forward to kiss her.

"Craig, I'm not going to say that I'm sorry for that. I won't, because you assumed a negative and low opinion of me as a woman. We don't all sleep around with a lot of guys like that." She watched him to make sure he understood her.

He wanted to clear the air and answer the question she had asked him that night when they first made love. Staring deeply into her eyes, he explained, although somewhat embarrassed, he sought the physical relief, then he wanted to be by himself, left alone.

"What about the cuddling and the affection?" Renee said. "What we're doing now."

"I'm not used to doing this. I didn't need any cuddling and affection, I just wanted my space and I didn't want to talk about a future because there was none, or about the relationship, or the sex itself, except in terms of when it was going to happen again. I guess I got what I wanted from them and I bounced."

Renee knew it took a lot for him to say what he did. "But, Craig, we're talking and you're caressing my face and kissing me. This is affection after the sex. Didn't you ever want love, or something solid to consume you, someone special to promise yourself and your heart to?"

He sat up and thought about what she'd asked him. "Renee, I didn't want mind games, and I was pursuing my career, so I certainly didn't have time for it," he said, letting his eyes linger on her lips. "So when I wanted marriage, I went looking for the one woman who had promised to marry me with no strings or demands attached, just a bag of bubblegum balls." He smiled and began tracing the outline of her lips. "And I like being with her."

Renee sensed that Craig had just made a self-discovery. When he kissed her with such tenderness, her heart wanted the moment to last forever. The thought shook her.

Several hours later, Renee awakened and untangled her legs and arms from Craig's heavy limbs. She stared down at his sleeping face and ran her hand from his face to his heart. She felt it beating soundly beneath her hand. Renee guessed that some woman must have hurt him so badly he just decided to close his heart off to the emotion. She lifted the covers, about to get out of the bed, when she suddenly felt Craig's warm hand on her arm.

Craig felt an instant odd sense of loss; she was trying to leave him. "Hey, where you going?" he asked sleepily, making her smile.

"I'm going to my room to give you space. Go back to sleep," Renee whispered.

He knew why she was leaving. He said simply, "Do you want to stay with me?" Holding his breath, he watched her frown and was glad for the dimness of the room; otherwise, she would have seen the dejected look on his face when he thought she would say no.

"Yes, I want to, but . . ." She didn't get a chance to finish because Craig reached for her, bringing her body close to his. Their lips came together almost desperately.

At the ungodly hour of one-thirty in the morning, Lawrence Jennings was in his den reading the confidential financial report on Craig Thompson. He sat back and a wide grin spread across his face. He was giddy and wished he could pat his own back for deciding to go visit Miss Lilly that day.

When she had excused herself to answer the telephone in the kitchen, he took the liberty of crossing the room to look at the photographs on a shelf in her living room. His eyes zoomed in on a wedding photo of a young couple, specifically the date etched into the bottom of the frame. He even thought they were a striking couple.

Lawrence smiled again, patting Craig's financial papers in his hand. He had found a key piece of information from that visit with Miss Lilly. Craig Thompson had gotten married on the same day he got his inheritance, and coincidently, it was on that same day he officially purchased the ad agency. And Miss Lilly had gotten fifteen thousand dollars . . . a payoff of some kind, he wondered. He smiled; he was getting closer to that two million dollars.

Lawrence had a plan. He was positive that Craig Thompson got married in a hurry to meet the stipulation of the inheritance. A marriage of convenience; yes, that's what it was. "Yes, that has to be it. Clever of you, son," he said, patting the papers again.

Tomorrow was Sunday, and it was also the rededication of the bank. It was going to be a grand showplace. Lawrence planned to have a little chat with Craig tomorrow night. Although the man was an advertising genius and an astute businessman, he had committed bank fraud in order to get his inheritance. Then he purchased that agency, something he was keeping awfully quiet about. Why, he wondered? Lawrence could see that agency pulling in more accounts with that young man at the helm. And he wasn't a greedy man. All he wanted was one million back or else Craig would suffer the consequences.

Lawrence looked at the picture of his wife, his Vivian. She was in a good mood tonight. He didn't care what the busy-bodies in town thought about her; he loved her. Lawrence knew he would do everything and anything in his power to keep Vivian happy, but he needed money to keep her in the lifestyle they had grown accustomed to. He needed Craig Thompson's money to continue to finance that.

CHAPTER 9

Craig hung up the telephone and turned to see Renee coming into the kitchen wearing one of his dress shirts. "Good morning." He handed her half of a muffin he had taken from a box. "You're even more beautiful in the morning, you know that?" He bent down to give her a quick kiss, but when Renee's hands reached up to caress his face, he brought her body up against his.

When he invited her to the Wayland Bank rededication, Renee was excited to see his work. "Great, I'll come home after church, change clothes and meet you there, okay?"

"I can do better than that. I'll send a car for you." Craig smiled, his eyes darkening as he kissed her neck and began unbuttoning the shirt.

"Craig, what are you doing?" Renee smiled.

He took the muffin from her hand and set it down on the island top. "I'm reclaiming my shirt; besides, it's way too big for you." With that, his mouth found something more pleasing than the muffin to nibble on.

Eight hours later, at five-fifteen, the Wayland Bank was officially rededicated by the bank trustees, the board of directors, the bank president, Mr. Tinsly, and Lawrence Jennings, the vice president.

Everyone praised the contractor for an outstanding job, and he too beamed, as did the new marble flooring. The employees couldn't believe the transformation. The bank was bright and airy. The pale lavender paint on the walls complemented the dark purple and gold fabric of the cloth chairs. Everything old was gone. In their place were low bankers' lamps with shiny brass bases resting on cherry wood desks. Craig's vision was the new high tech age of the millennium, complete with chrome, soothing colors, glass and light.

Craig stood back and took it all in. Impressive and professional, he thought. Now add the new commercial ads and little Wayland Bank was going to be a force to contend with. The bigger banks out on the interstate didn't have what the Wayland Bank had—personality and friendly, personable bank staff and tellers.

"Well, Mr. Thompson, you did an outstanding job. You must be very proud of all of this," Vivian said, sidling up to him and resting her hand on his forearm.

"I am and you're looking lovely, Mrs. Jennings," he said, taking in her short gold dress. He hoped her gold stiletto heels didn't leave black scuff marks on the new tile floor. Craig could only smile when her husband walked up and stood beside his wife. He thought her hand slid from his arm like a retracting tentacle.

Lawrence looked up suddenly at the young woman who'd just entered the bank. She looked every bit as beautiful as her wedding day picture. A secretive smile crossed his face.

Renee was dressed in a form-fitting lavender sheath dress that stopped at a discreet length above her knees. The color almost matched the lavender fabric covering the new chairs. However, the sheer colored material of Renee's dress had a full black lace overlay, and it created a stunning effect. Her hair was pulled up and draped down her back in brown waves. The outfit was set off with black and lavender chandelier earrings and black stiletto sandals with the same dark lavender and black straps. She looked elegant and sexy.

Craig looked up and took Renee in from across the bank lobby. Memories of that morning rushed to his head. She literally took his breath away . . . much as she had on their wedding day.

Renee stood in awe. She couldn't believe the transformation of the old bank since she'd last been there several years ago with her mother. Scanning the bright and fresh interior, her eyes suddenly connected with Craig's. She felt the heat of his eyes touch her skin from across the room. She didn't even try to hide the smile that spread across her face. She wondered if he, too, was thinking about their morning together. Lord, she thought, they didn't even make it to the bedroom. What he started in the kitchen was finished in the den. Renee blushed and raised a hand to her heated face.

"My, my, look at you. Marriage sure is good to you, Renee." Miss Lilly's melodious voice filled Renee's head and put an end to erotic memories. The two women chatted for a few minutes, and then Renee asked about the woman standing very close to Craig.

Lillian didn't need to look to see whom Renee was referring to, but the expression on her face told Renee plenty. "That, my dear, is Mrs. Jennings. Trust me, you have nothing to worry about. Your poor lovesick husband has been waiting for you to walk through that door for the last half an hour." She stood back and looked Renee up and down. "Renee, you're lovely."

Renee smiled and put her arm around Lilly. "Thank you. Now I should go rescue Craig."

Lawrence had been watching the two women with great interest. They knew each other well enough for Miss Lilly to be at their marriage. The marriage. That was the crux of everything. It was all there in black and white. Craig Thompson needed a wife in order to get his inheritance. *Craig is one smart businessman*, he thought again. He watched as the younger man seemed transfixed by his wife. *Perfect*, Lawrence thought with a grin.

Miss Lilly made a grand gesture of presenting Renee. "Well, look who I found wondering around, all by herself and looking for her groom." She smiled up at everyone.

With all sets of eyes suddenly settling upon her, Renee was forced keep her knees from knocking together. She decided to reclaim her man. *Well, not really my man*, she thought, reaching out for Craig's hand. He turned to her and was shocked that she kissed him.

"Craig, can we all assume that this lovely young lady is your bride?" James asked, stepping closer to shake Renee's hand. "Ah, yes, Craig, she looks as sweet as apple pie." James smiled, trying to recall where he had seen Renee before.

Craig could not take his eyes off her. "Yes, I'm sorry. This is my bride, Renee." He introduced her to everyone.

"Newlyweds, how nice. Lovely dress, Renee. It's a Dior from last season or maybe the season before that, isn't it?" Vivian asked as she looked at Renee's dress. "I mean, it looks nice for out of season." Then she looked past Renee, dismissing her.

But Renee wasn't about to take a put-down like that standing up. "Actually, it is from last season. That's why I got it for a fraction of the cost. It's one of my favorites. But you must remember how it is when you first get married, don't you, and . . . well . . ." Renee smiled when Craig slid his arm possessively around her small waist and she inched closer to him. "I haven't had a chance to shop for clothes. Isn't that right, baby?" Her eyes narrowed as she looked Vivian in the eyes, then let her eyes drop to Vivian's own sparkly, out-of-season dress.

Aw, shit. Craig cringed, knowing where this was going. He wasn't about to let a catfight happen at the rededication of bank, at least not on his watch. "That's right, honey, and you do look beautiful . . . how about some champagne?" He looked into her mischievous eyes as he spoke, trying to maneuver her away from the group.

Renee smiled and decided to let him off the hook. "Oh, that would be wonderful." Craig led her to where a bar was set up and picked up two glasses, handing one to her. She watched him over the rim of her glass, grinning and waiting for him to say something.

"You're so bad, Squirt," he said, grinning. "You do look beautiful; well, you always do. But tonight, I feel good with you." Craig frowned trying to find just the words to express what he felt, but somehow the words were stuck somewhere in his chest. "You know, I'm glad that you are here with me. Renee, I want to tell you something . . ." Craig looked up just as James signaled him to begin the presentation of the two commercials. He turned back to Renee.

"Craig, I understand. Now go, this is your moment. One of many, I hope."

As Craig walked to the front of the bank, the TV monitors all went blue. Then his image appeared on each one.

Renee smiled, turning to look at each of the monitors. Her eyes connected with Lawrence Jennings for a second, and he smiled and winked at her. Not knowing what else to do, Renee waved at him and smiled back, thinking how excited he must be to see the commercials, too. She returned her attention to Craig just as he finished describing the process of creating the ads, and the first commercial appeared on the TV monitors.

It was fast-paced, with animated and colorful characters and basically said the bank staff were just waiting and waiting to serve customers. But the characters acting as the employees were running around, processing applications and fixing coffee while the tellers were staring into space, yawning or dozing off. When the tape ended, there was a round of applause and laughter from the assembled group. Then Craig announced the second commercial, totally different from the first. It opened with a quiet piano tune, slow and forlorn as several short scenes played out, one blending into the other. An approaching thunderstorm off in the distance came up on the screen, followed by scenes of a house under construction getting caught up in the storm. Then a young girl is seen rehearsing walking to accept her high-school diploma. Next a couple in the delivery room welcoming their new baby. Finally, a woman is shown standing at a graveside. The commercial ended with a simple caption: *When You Need Help, The Wayland Bank Will Lead The Way.* The ending music became uplifting, and the commercial reverses to the beginning and repeats the simple caption again, showing the bank's new logo. Craig pressed the stop button on the VCR tape, but no one moved or said anything. Perfect, he thought, this was the same reaction the staff had when they first viewed the final tape. "Well, folks . . ." he began amidst a thunderous round of applause. Then he introduced his creative staff, one by one.

Watching him, Renee was so proud of what he'd done. At that moment, she couldn't imagine her life without him. And that suddenly scared her. *Oh, my God, please don't let me be falling for Craig.* Stunned by the thought, she looked up at him with wide eyes, then gulped the rest of her champagne.

Craig felt good and spent the next hour talking with well-wishers, but he kept an eye on Renee as she shadowed Miss Lilly and several of his staff members at the buffet tables. Craig briefly worried that someone would say something about his ownership of the agency, but so far so good. He'd already decided he would tell her when they returned home. It would be the perfect time, and she would see why he'd done everything to get to this point. Yes, telling her tonight would be perfect, he thought.

Lawrence stood back and watched as the evening moved along. He felt good, too, and saw his chance when he saw Craig sitting with his wife, who, Lawrence guessed, Craig would do everything in his power to protect from any public scorn, humiliation and embarrassment.

"Craig, wonderful evening, isn't it? But if your lovely wife wouldn't mind, could I speak to you privately, in my office?" His smile was wide and happy when he looked at Renee. *Oh, yes, she'll be his Achilles heel.*

Craig didn't care for the man, but he could endure him for a few more minutes. Between the man and his flirtatious wife, he didn't know which irritated him more. He kissed Renee on the cheek, promising he wouldn't be long, and followed Lawrence to his office.

Once inside his office, Lawrence offered Craig a glass of very old scotch to celebrate. "How about we toast to joint ventures?" Lawrence smiled at Craig and offered him a seat.

Craig sampled the scotch and sat down, crossing his long legs and folding his hands. "Joint ventures, Mr. Jennings? I'm not aware of another project you need my assistance on, or are you talking about future advertising for the bank? That can be arranged, you know."

Lawrence smiled. "Well, son, I wasn't thinking about the bank at all. You see, I was thinking more along the lines of how I can help you and you, in turn, can help me." Smiling, he sat back in his chair, twirling the scotch in a heavy tumbler. He watched Craig.

Craig saw caution signs, like the ones on the road warning of danger ahead. He was suddenly edgy and wanted their little meeting over with. However, he paced himself and set his glass on the desk. "Mr. Jennings, as far as I'm concerned, our business concludes tonight. But when the commercials begin airing tonight on the local channels and you see a problem, then you will deal with our postproduction crew. They will be in contact with the local stations, and they can handle any problems that may come up. Now, if you'll excuse me, there are still a few people I would like to acknowledge before my wife and I leave." Craig was about to stand up when Lawrence's next words stopped him.

"Does Mrs. Thompson know that you're the sole owner of Davis Advertising?" Lawrence remained relaxed and confident in his executive swivel chair and eyed Craig levelly. "Hum, that look tells me she doesn't, right?"

"That is none of your business." Craig looked at a spot beyond the older man's receding hairline and saw more caution signs. *Slow down, caution, bumps and danger ahead.*

Lawrence pulled a piece of paper from his jacket pocket and flipped it open, then put his reading glasses on. "Okay, then, does Mrs. Thompson know you married her on the tenth of June to get your inheritance because you knew there was a stipulation? Does she know that you married her to get that inheritance so that you could purchase that advertising agency on the tenth of June? Does she know any of that, Craig?" Lawrence leaned forward and slid Craig's drink back towards him. He waited for Craig to ask him what it was that he wanted.

Craig hadn't blinked or moved. *I don't believe this son of a bitch.* But he did swallow and slowed his breathing as he saw those virtual road signs floating and flashing before his eyes.

Lawrence continued talking calmly and slowly as if he were talking to someone slow to comprehend what he was saying. "Now, I can see that you're probably surprised that I have this information," he said, patting the papers on his desk. "And I don't want to disclose any of this because, you know son, fraud is, well . . . you know, as surely as I do, that defrauding a bank is a crime. A federal crime," he stressed, with a reptilian smile on his face. "And I tell you I would hate to see anything terrible happen, and I see you have so much to lose should this information come to light. Are you following what I'm saying?"

"So far." Craig decided to remain calm and wait the man out. But on the inside he wasn't calm. He desperately wanted to strangle Lawrence's thick neck until his shrewd eyes bulged out from their sockets.

"So far? I see. Well, where do we go from here? Well, you tell me." Lawrence had expected a different reaction but, like a shrewd attorney, he watched each and every reaction. He could tell Craig was seething inside, but he also knew that Craig didn't want to hurt his wife.

"It's really public knowledge. Do you think I have no intention of telling my wife any of that?" Craig asked in a quiet voice, nodding at the paper under Lawrence's hand.

"Hum, I don't think you do, Craig. You see, she's, well, she sure is beautiful and just a lovely person, isn't she?" He grinned at Craig. "But she also looks like she would be hurt to the core if she found out the only reason for your, well, hasty marriage to her . . . well, I'm sure you two are living as any normal husband and a wife would . . . and women get emotional and all hurt and devastated, you know. They get all embarrassed when things are exposed. Like when things come out in the public light, that is. And it always does comes out, son, always," Lawrence said, his voice deliberate and sure.

Craig cringed inwardly, and in a tight voice, said, "Don't call me son, again." Craig's mind was filled with images of Renee if that information did get out. His Squirt would hate him. After all, he did pressure her to keep her promise to marry him because he needed his inheritance to buy the agency. Then he would be just another man who hurt her—like the others. Finally, he spoke. "Mr. Jennings, you seem to think you're holding a winning hand of some kind. What exactly do you think you're holding?" He felt the beginnings of a headache, but still his eyes did not leave the other man's.

Lawrence smiled. "I'm holding your future. I'm holding your wife's happiness . . . or public ridicule and embarrassment for both of you. But, I'm also holding a way for you to keep everything as it is, all nice and tidy.

May I explain?" He leaned forward, eyes gleaming. He'd made his point that he indeed was holding something.

Craig answered curtly, "It's your party." *Renee*.

Lawrence laughed at the reference to the celebratory party in the lobby. "Okay, you only paid a million for the advertising agency. Anyway, that leaves you just under two million, counting all that interest and such. Craig, that's an awful lot of money for one man to have, especially considering the fact that within the next few months, you are probably going to be raking in millions as you get that agency back up on the fast-track. With you at the helm, I just know it." Lawrence sipped his scotch and licked his lips.

"And your point is?" Craig said with effort.

"Ah, yes, my point, simply, is this. We all have to pay for our . . . shall we say, the pleasures and necessities of one's life. I have pleasures that far exceed my current salary structure, and you have necessities that can . . . well, help me. You follow my point now, son . . . I-I mean Craig?" Craig was cool, his attitude aloof, but Lawrence knew he had the young man thinking, and probably a little scared. Hell, he would be if it were he.

Craig picked up his glass and drained it, not taking his eyes off the man across from him. He set the glass back down, patted his upper lip with the back of his hand and calmly addressed Lawrence. "Yes, I think I understand your point, you spineless cocksucker. You want my money to maintain your pseudo-social life, and with it, you keep quiet about what those papers contain," Craig spat out, pointing to the papers still pressed under

Lawrence's sweaty, beefy hand. "Is that your point? Did I follow you correctly?" He continued to pin the older man with a deadly look in his eyes.

Lawrence had rehearsed this meeting far too many times to back down now, regardless of what Craig said in an attempt to rile him. He had figured that Craig would react this way. "You left out a major point: How much will my silence cost?"

Craig shrugged and waited, but he could only think about Renee. One thing was for sure, he was not going to hurt her.

Lawrence felt heat rise to his neck. He was getting excited at being so close to getting that money back. Well, almost getting back what he'd used so freely over the past twenty years. "One million dollars keeps your necessities yours. It keeps your wife standing proudly by your side, as she was out there, and it keeps your employees happy and employed, as they were out there. It keeps your new business yours, and it still keeps you with enough money to enjoy some pleasures of your own."

Craig hadn't expected that, but still he showed no reaction. "You know what, I have a better idea. How about I just go collect my wife and then call my attorneys and schedule a meeting with the Wayland Bank's board of directors. I think they would be most interested in knowing you were blackmailing a former customer. A customer, I might add, who is the benefactor of a whole lot of money that his grandfather entrusted to this very branch many years ago?" Craig stood and walked to the door, but Lawrence's next words stopped him.

"Defrauding a bank, Mr. Thompson, is a punishable crime, one that far exceeds me losing my position here. I'll be fired, sure, but not a big problem for me." Lawrence clasped his hands under his chin as he spoke. "However, you will be tried in a court of law, and these papers will be the proof that will convict you, and you will not go down alone." Lawrence almost grinned at the look that flitted across Craig's face, but he didn't. He stood up, but wisely he didn't move any closer to Craig.

Craig stepped toward him and waited. "What?"

"Well, you see, these papers also suggest that you had an accomplice, and it would be a shame, just a shame, to take that person down with you." Lawrence dropped his eyes and shook his head sadly. "Maybe she just did it for the fifteen-thousand-dollar payoff. After all, the bank records do specifically document your request for two checks to be personally delivered to you, by her." Lawrence almost hated having to go that far, but it was part of his plan had Craig balked, and he had.

Craig stared at the man incredulously when it dawned on him who Lawrence was referring to. "Miss Lilly? Are you fucking kidding me? No one in this town, or even this state, would ever believe that woman would do anything wrong, and you know that. What she got from me was a gift, you asshole." This is not what he was expecting, and he was beginning to feel nauseated as his tight stomach began combating with the old scotch.

Lawrence assumed his sympathetic voice again. "Oh, I know, really I do, but look at how the authorities will see things. You waited until Miss Lilly's very last two days at this bank to request your inheritance. If there were any improprieties in those transactions, well, then she would no longer be an employee . . . say, if there were any charges, you know, being filed." Lawrence rushed on after patting his mouth with his handkerchief. "Craig, she was even one of the signers of your request for the beneficiary review and on the withdrawal document. That should not have happened; well, at least not in the real banking world. No, no, all of that should have been handled by the president or by me as the VP. Then you asked her to stand in as a witness to your marriage to that nice young lady out there, upon which you received your inheritance—in two checks, just as you had requested she process them. And that, as I said, appears somewhat odd."

He continued in that pseudo-sorrowful voice. "They'll say that you paid her off with fifteen thousand dollars, which she in turn deposited into her savings account, right here in this bank. They may even say that she instructed you to get a wife. After all, she knew what the stipulations of the inheritance were from day one." Lawrence took another sip of his scotch. "Oh, yes, and then there's the public record of the filing of the official transfer of the Davis Franklin Advertising Agency from Mr. Franklin himself to you for one of your inheritance checks on the tenth of June. That, I'm afraid, Mr. Thompson, is how the authorities will see things," he finished, his fingers drumming the papers on his desk.

Craig couldn't speak. He walked toward the door. Lawrence quickly came from behind his desk, stopping him and standing just three feet in front of him.

"Craig, once you think this over, you'll see that I'm offering you an opportunity here to keep all that is important to you, son. Don't do anything rash. Think about it," Lawrence said in a rushed breath. He never saw Craig move.

Craig's right hand lifted quickly and went around Lawrence's thick neck, and he pushed the man's sweating head against the light switch on the wall near the door. Bending down into Lawrence's face, he said, "I told you, don't call me son." Craig straightened up and released the man's neck with a push and then proceeded to wipe his now sweat-stained hand on Lawrence's starched white dress shirt. Then he let himself out of the office.

Once he cleared the frosted window outside Lawrence's office, Craig's body sagged against the wall. Then he steadied himself and walked through the short hallway to go back into the lobby. He was sick and angry, but mostly he was angry.

Neither Craig nor Lawrence was aware that someone had happened to walk down that same hallway and had overheard some of their conversation.

Renee looked up to see Craig standing directly behind her. She sensed that something was wrong, despite the slight smile plastered on his face.

Craig slid his arms around her waist, announcing it was time to leave. As they made their way around the room saying good night, Craig saw that Lawrence had returned to the party and stood beside his own wife, his hand caressing her ass on the sly. Watching him, Craig knew in that moment what a murderous thought felt like.

By the time Craig and Renee got home, he announced he needed to edit a portion of the tape in his den and suggested she turn in.

But ten minutes later, Renee walked into his den and found Craig sat on the sofa, watching the activities of the fish in the two-hundred-gallon aquarium that took up an entire wall of his office. He was so deep in thought that he jumped when she stood in front of him.

Renee sat on his lap. "What's wrong?" she asked holding his face within her hands.

Craig turned his face and kissed her hands. "Just a little tired. I guess." She was innocent of his plan, and now she could get hurt because of his quest to get what he wanted.

"Then come to bed," she said. "This has been a long day for you." She slowly loosened his tie and kissed his lips. He was holding back, she could tell. "What's wrong? Talk to me, Craig," she whispered against his lips.

His mind was still reeling from Lawrence Jennings's extortion and blackmail scheme, but his body was succumbing to her. "Renee." He whispered her name. *I have to tell her.*

When he said her name, Renee whispered, "I have something to show you." Then she stood up and opened her robe, showing him the red nightie. She smiled when he inhaled quickly and raked her with his eyes. "I took it

225

from under your pillow. And guess what? I'll even keep my heels on. That's in one of those videotapes," she confided, grinning impishly as his eyes widened.

Craig was mesmerized. When her hands went around his neck, pulling him into a deep kiss, he let himself fall under the spell she had cast over him and his body. Craig let the pain surrounding his heart retreat to the back of his mind. He would live in the moment and give her what she wanted because the pain in his head and his heart would return regardless.

Lawrence fell back on the bed with Vivian collapsing on top of him. She had taken every last ounce of strength he possessed. He always tried to please her because he didn't want her to go looking to another man for what he couldn't give her. He was aware of her little flirtations, but he knew she was true to him and would never do anything to jeopardize what she had because of him: respectability, acceptance and social standing.

Vivian had a husband who was a member of the society circles she could never have cracked before. Lawrence didn't care what people whispered about his wife behind their dinner napkins. They, too, needed him and the services that he could provide at his bank, even if they were not fully eligible. He had the power to help them, and he knew many of their dirty little secrets, secrets he ignored when he approved their loan requests.

"You're wonderful, honey," Vivian said, sitting up and trying to ignore Lawrence's huffing and puffing. He was such a lousy lover, she thought, but he thought he sent her to the moon. But where he really sent her was straight into the arms of her lover, Ray Newman. Her hand trembled thinking about him. Only Ray did that for her.

Vivian had slipped from that party earlier and caught Ray getting off work.

"Darling, why are you trembling, surely I can't be that good, can I?" Lawrence grinned, watching his wife and thinking she was one beautiful creation, and she was his. His eyes trailed up to her perfectly aligned breasts. They were the pleasures he'd mentioned earlier to Craig Thompson, he thought.

Vivian gritted her teeth and smiled. "Baby, you're that good," she lied, patting his hand.

"Did you have a good time at the party tonight, dear?" He did wonder where she'd disappeared to earlier in the evening, before he was side-tracked with his meeting with Craig. "For a time there, I couldn't find you." He swallowed when she ran her hand down his stomach.

Here I go again, Vivian thought. She needed to explain yet another encounter with Ray. "Oh, you mean around seven-thirty, yes . . . well, I had to come back here to the house and get another pair of stockings." When she saw Lawrence frowning, she said, "Lawrence, you saw those high and mighty women there tonight. They would have started another round of telephone gossip about me." Vivian let her fake sniffles tickle her sinuses and bring water to her eyes, afterwards she turned on him. "I could even imagine a picture of us in the society pages, with me standing there with a huge run in my stocking. I couldn't embarrass you like that, Lawrence. I-I just couldn't," she said, tears glistening in her eyes.

"Vivian, I understand. Tomorrow why don't you drive on up to that shopping mall you like and buy yourself as many pairs of stockings as you want?"

"Oh, baby, are you sure? Because I can just run up to that mart store, you know." She blinked, producing exactly the effect that she wanted. *His wife, the wife of a banker, had no problem at all rummaging through sales bins for stockings at a discount store.*

"I am more than sure, and Viv, we'll soon have the title to that property in the Bahamas all paid for, and I plan on buying us a yacht I've been eyeing down there," he said, his lecherous eyes feasting on her breasts.

Lawrence was on top of the world, and soon he would have a million more reasons to say he was one lucky man. And the best part was that he wouldn't have to worry about replacing what he took from the other account. That had become way too stressful for him, anyway.

Vivian smiled, thinking she was the lucky one. Tomorrow, she would call Ray, and they would have a longer time together. That thought, and the image of Ray's face, fueled her as Lawrence pulled her on top of him.

⌐

Craig couldn't sleep. He was angry that he could not see a way out of Lawrence Jennings' blackmail. If he said no and told the man to go screw himself, he stood to lose everything; especially, Renee. And that he couldn't bear. He slipped from the bed without disturbing her and went to his den. Sitting on the sofa where they'd made love twice that day, Craig closed his eyes and let his memories flow. He would not hurt Renee, but he also knew that if he explained everything to her now she would hate him and end up being hurt by him. Never in his wildest dreams had he thought something like this could happen. Never did he think he would be black-mailed for the very inheritance he had set out to get—underhandedly, at that. Poetic justice was what he believed was happening; his initial deception had become a trap.

He frowned, remembering Jennings' words. *And what about Miss Lilly?* Craig walked over to a window in his den. He couldn't hurt Miss Lilly either. That woman had been a friend to him and Renee, and she had been a lifeline to his grandfather after his grandmother died.

Three hours later, he returned to bed and pulled Renee to his side. It was almost daylight, and his intense mental juggling had him exhausted. He still didn't see a way out. Damn.

Monday morning, Craig's secretary, Lindsey, buzzed in to tell him he had a caller holding. He tensed before picking up the phone, prepared to slice into Lawrence Jennings. Only it wasn't Jennings.

"Hi, Craig, it's Phillip. How you doing in that heat down there, big guy?"

Craig signed with relief. "Phil, man, I'm great. What are you up to, buddy? Oh, did you get my thank-you e-mail?" Phil Peterson was an agent for several high-profile NFL players, so Craig knew he was about to get some free tickets with good seats.

But Craig was getting more than that. Phil was offering him a deal of a lifetime: a commercial spot for the upcoming NFL season. But he had to go to L.A. the following day to pitch the ads. The whole time Phil rattled about a possible ad Craig had been taking copious notes.

"Listen, Craig, I've gotta run, but my secretary will be calling you within the hour. As I said, the flight attendant will have copies of the itinerary for you. See you tomorrow, my friend." With that, Phil was gone. One of Craig's best friends, he was always like a bullet.

Craig sat back, both his mind and heart racing, an NFL campaign . . . that could mean millions. He called an immediate meeting, and once everyone was gathered together the room became a loud excitement-filled happy-fest. The creative department and the research department went to work immediately. Within the hour, the office was abuzz with activity—staff members were running from the video department to the writing department. The production staff was at the ready to put together a preliminary presentation. They all knew this was a big deal and couldn't contain their excitement.

Craig was excited, too, and had to tell someone: Renee. He ran everything by her, and her excitement mingled with his. It was a good thing.

Renee was indeed happy for him. She was happy to hear excitement in his voice. For the past couple of days, he seemed distant from her mentally. "So you'll be going to L.A. tomorrow to wheel and deal. This is a good shot for you, isn't it? I'll bet Mr. Franklin gives you a big fat raise, and kudos and a promotion."

A tightening sensation suddenly gripped his stomach. Damn, for a brief few minutes, he had forgotten about the pain and the deception that had come back to haunt him in the hellish form of Lawrence Jennings. For that brief moment, he'd forgotten about the blackmail. He heard her asking him what was wrong. "Nothing, it's just so much to do before I can leave tonight."

She knew he was putting her off. "Okay, Craig. But you can talk to me about anything. I'll see you at home. Bye." *Home.*

The minute she hung up, Craig turned to a picture of them at their wedding reception. He felt the unfamiliar sting behind his eye. He desperately needed to quash that odd feeling of wanting to cry, followed by a feeling of rage.

After completing dinner preparations, Renee received a call from Simon. He told her that Charles had been tracked to Florida, and he needed to know if he had ever made any calls to Florida from her apartment.

"I'm sure he did; in fact, yes, because I remember asking him about a few calls to Florida when my bill came. So I had to send a letter to the phone company complaining about it before they would even consider removing those charges from my bill. I have a copy and can fax it to you," Renee said, excitement and apprehension building in her, she closed her cellphone, and ran up the stairs, taking two at a time. She had very little time to look through her stacks of paper for her telephone bills. Craig would be home in half an hour.

She sat on the bedroom floor and searched stacks of documents detailing her search for Charles. Having lost track of time, Renee's breath caught in her throat when she heard Craig pull into the driveway. As if lighting was on her heels, she gathered up the papers spread out on the floor, dumped them back into the hard suitcase and rushed down the steps. "Hi," she said, slightly out of breath.

"Hi yourself," Craig said, noticing an impish look on her face that he'd seen years ago when he would look up suddenly and catch her watching him. Tonight it made him smile.

During dinner, another thought filled her head. *How could I have let myself fall for Craig?* Renee watched him, knowing with certainty that she was falling in love with Craig.

Later in his office, Craig reviewed the test video the staff had spent the afternoon putting together. It was just unfortunate that they hadn't the time to come up with something even better. Thank goodness for technology and smart employees, otherwise he would still be at work viewing videotapes and drinking coffee. And he thought he should have told her.

"You nervous about L.A.?" Renee asked from the doorway, her voice filtering through his cluttered mind. There it was again, Renee thought, when she saw a shadow pass over Craig's face. Something was wrong and possibly connected to work.

Craig drained his wineglass. "No, the test video is good. I was just thinking that I'm going to miss you. But I'll take you there whenever you want to go."

She didn't want to think about the future, their future. Their deal was always on her mind. Although neither had brought it up, but only a little over three weeks remained until the end of the three-month deal. Renee heard Leo the puppy yelping at the patio door, looking for her. "Leo's at the door."

Craig pulled her to him and buried his face in the hollow of her neck. *Safe, content, happy.* Those unfamiliar words popped into his head for no reason at all. *I can't hurt her.* He signed deeply when Renee hugged him tightly before going to send Leo back under the hedge.

Several hours later, Renee sat on the loveseat in the bedroom working on her laptop while Craig still worked in his den. And if a shadow seemed to cross his face whenever she brought up work, well, she just didn't mention it.

By ten-thirty the following morning Craig was preparing to leave for the airport. When his private line rang, he guessed it was Renee calling. "Hello?"

"Well, good morning, Mr. Thompson. You sound as if you're having a grand morning. And why not, it's just a beautiful day, isn't it?" Lawrence's smug voice grated on Craig's nerves. Lawrence wasn't about to be put off again. He had way too much on the line and needed that money. Lawrence's voice grew quiet, his sunny voice disappearing. "I'm calling to see if you've given any thought to our previous discussion."

"No," Craig lied. In fact, it had been all he had thought about—that and Renee.

"I don't believe that for a minute. But I can understand you wanting me to think otherwise, almost as much as I can understand you wanting to protect those that you deeply care about," Lawrence said.

"I'm on my way out of town. I'll call you, so don't you ever call my personal number again. We clear on that, you moron?" With that, Craig slammed down the phone just seconds before Joyce walked into his office. He put on his best smile. "Hi, Joyce."

Joyce was a take-it-like-it-is kind of sister, and he liked her. Her computer literacy was off the charts. He would be lost without her skills and her friendship. She hopped up onto the high stool at his drafting table. "You look happy, Craig. Marriage is working for you, and I bet you didn't think you could ever fall in love like this, did you?" She mimicked his silly grin.

"Duh, I did get married, so I'm supposed to feel like this, aren't I?"

Joyce looked out the window and then hopped off the stool. "Hey, the airport van service is here. Let's go do this." Walking to the door, she turned and watched Craig shut his computer down and put it in his briefcase. "Craig, we're all so happy for you about everything, you know, including saving our jobs."

Before he could respond, she was off and running down the hall, singing. He mentally replayed what she had said. He *had* saved their jobs, his included. But this truth didn't bring him any closer to making the decision he had to make . . . keeping them all employed or losing his inheritance if he didn't comply with Jennings' blackmail . . . or losing Renee.

The meeting in L.A. had been delayed. Craig and his staff stayed in L.A. overnight, much to the excitement of his staff, but not so for Craig. He wanted to get home to Renee. He hated leaving her alone, but she said she was okay and felt perfectly safe at his house.

In fact, Renee did feel safe in Craig's house. There was no way that Charles could get to her, and she never answered numbers on her cellphone she didn't recognize.

The following afternoon Renee was filling the vases with fresh flowers when the front-door buzzer sounded. She wasn't expecting Craig home for a couple more hours. Renee glanced out the window, then opened the door and was surprised to see Lawrence Jennings. "Hi. It's Mr. Jennings from the bank, right?"

"Yes, I see you remember me, Mrs. Thompson. I hope I'm not intruding," he said, seeing Renee wiping her hands on a paper towel.

"Oh, not at all. Please come in Mr. Jennings. Call me Renee."

Smiling as he came in, Lawrence openly looked around the first floor. "My, this is a beautiful home, Renee. I just love the high vaulted ceilings and glass block. But I'm old-fashioned. I still like the old houses with lots of original wood doors and floorings with inlaid designs. That is pretty much how my house looks." He turned and smiled at her.

"Sounds like the house I grew up in. I'm sorry to keep you standing here while I babble like an idiot. Can I get you something cold to drink?"

"Well, if it's no trouble to you," he replied, dabbing at his forehead with a handkerchief. Lawrence thought she seemed like such a nice person, someone he could really like. Too bad her husband had lied to her.

"Oh, please, none at all. Have a seat and I'll be right back."

Renee walked off to the kitchen. A few minutes later, he stood when she returned and handed him a glass of cold lemonade.

Lawrence sipped the beverage and smiled up at her. "Miss Renee, this sure hits the spot. Thank you." He looked up at her with a wide grin.

"Oh, by the way, Mr. Jennings, I have called a couple friends and suggested they go down and check out those new loan programs." She sipped her lemonade and motioned for him to sit down. Renee was actually glad to talk to Mr. Jennings about the effect the commercials and renovations were having on bank business.

"Well, you just keep doing that because that is what we're there for—to help people and make their lives better, you know." Renee nodded in agreement.

"How is your wife? Vivian, right?" Of course Renee remembered the woman's name. Renee could just imagine the grief his flirtatious wife gave him.

"That's right, Vivian. Well, she's just fine." Lawrence wished Vivian was really just fine, but he knew something was up with her lately. Still, he just smiled at Renee.

"Well, Miss Renee, I don't mean to take up your time, but I was wondering if Craig might be home. I just wanted to personally show him the projections from all the new business the bank has gotten since those commercials aired. I tell you, people have come in and have just stopped in their tracks when they see how the place has been transformed." He could tell she was thrilled by the news.

"Really!" Renee said excitedly as she looked down at the papers he handed her.

"Yes, really, they sure do. The first thing they do is turn around, you know, thinking they had stepped into the wrong place or something, and then they look around and take it all in." Imitating his customers, Lawrence glanced around wide-eyed, making Renee laugh at his antics. "I'm really happy about all those suggestions Craig came up with, and I'm just so glad that I was able to approve each and every one of them," Lawrence said, smiling even as he lied.

"You know what, Mr. Jennings? I did the same thing." She laughed. "Honestly, I sure did. I stopped right there in my tracks. I was impressed, too." Then she joined in when he laughed at her mimicking his wide-eyed, open mouth expression.

That was the scene that greeted Craig when he stepped into his living room. He was instantly enraged by the sight of Lawrence Jennings in his home, with Renee. But he held back the urge to throttle the man on the spot when Renee looked up, then quickly walked over to him, and slid her arms around his waist. Craig hugged her to him, but nailed Jennings with his eyes above Renee's head.

"Hey, you're home already. You were supposed to call me and here I'm sitting . . . Oh, Craig, look who stopped by." She gestured toward the older man. "It's Mr. Jennings from the bank, and he has good news. Well, I'll let him tell you all about it." Renee grinned up at him and reached for the briefcase dangling from his hand. "Why don't you go on and sit down, and I'll get you a glass of lemonade. And I'll just refill Mr. Jennings' glass." Renee picked up the glass and went into the kitchen. She just knew Craig was going to be excited about the news.

Lawrence stood up. Looking back toward the kitchen, he stepped closer to Craig and spoke in a hushed tone. "Mr. Thompson, ah, we didn't get a chance to finish our conversation the other morning, so I—"

Craig hadn't moved and the front door remained ajar. Without warning he reached out and grabbed Lawrence by the collar of his shirt and pushed the stumbling man out the door, down the short walkway and thrust him against the driver's side door of his Cadillac. Craig stood so that his back was to the house, blocking Renee's view should she come to the door. Finally, he spoke, his voice quiet, slow and deadly. "Do you have a death wish, Mr. Jennings?"

"What? Well, no, of course not. But, listen I-I'm offering you a chance here. I'm not out to draw blood. I just want—"

"My fucking money," Craig finished, drawing out his words while snarling at the man. "I'll call you in a couple of days, but in the meantime, if you ever cross any of my doors, I will give you the opportunity to make that wish . . ." Then Craig bent down to Lawrence's five-foot, nine inch stocky frame and grabbed his necktie, tightening it around his neck. "You understand what I'm saying? Then I'll go to that wife of yours and tell her about your extortion scheme, because she'll be the one who will be ridiculed and trashed in the tabloids. I'll make sure of that. You follow me?" Craig knew that he was holding the necktie too tightly when he saw Lawrence turning different shades of red. "Just nod that you do understand. Good." Craig had opened the car door and proceeded to push Lawrence in behind the wheel. Frowning, he wiped Lawrence's perspiration from his hand and onto the man's dress shirt yet again.

Renee stood in the living room, holding two glasses and looking quizzically at Craig as he came back through the front door, slamming it. "Craig, what happened? Why did Mr. Jennings leave so abruptly like that?"

Livid, he walked past her to stand in the living room. "Renee, are you crazy, letting a stranger in here?" He glared at her. Wearing shorts and a tee shirt, her hair in a ponytail and holding the two glasses in her hands, she looked like a teenager . . . a vulnerable teenager.

Baffled, she wondered what had happened. "What? No, I'm not crazy, and he's hardly a stranger, Craig. You've worked with him, and his wife has flirted with you, so I don't think he's that much of a stranger, do you?" She had to jump back when he snatched the glasses from her hands, sloshing the contents on the carpeted floor. He walked into the kitchen with angry strides and dumped the liquids down the drain. Already in a state of shock, she was further stunned when he threw the glasses into the kitchen trashcan. He turned and saw her standing in the doorway.

"He is a fucking stranger, Renee, and you're a woman in the house alone!" He didn't mean to yell at her, but she needed to know how reckless her action had been. "Can't you understand that? Or do I have to spell out what happens to women when they put themselves in a situation where something could happen to them?" He walked across the kitchen and faced her, arms across his chest. "I don't know him, and neither do you. I can't believe that you could be that thoughtless," Craig said, immediately regretting his harsh words.

Renee stared at him for several seconds and felt sicker with each passing moment. She couldn't believe what he had just said to her. When Craig moved closer to her, he wasn't all that surprised when she pushed him away from her.

"I-I can't believe what you just said to me, Craig . . . to me, about me. Again, you're making assumptions about me." She wagged her finger at him and her tone matched his. "You stay away from me. I'm out of here in a few more weeks and I'm out of your life. Then I can go back to my own life as a thoughtless, mindless woman who wouldn't know how to protect herself from a stranger whom she had met only a week ago . . . or from one she has known for seventeen years!" When she ran up the stairs, his sad eyes followed her. He wasn't surprised when he heard the guest bedroom door slam behind her.

Craig spent an hour out on the patio, staring into the pool. He was the one who had been thoughtless and irresponsible in his quest to get what he wanted. As a result, two innocent and loving women could not only get hurt, they could be destroyed. He couldn't risk that. He'd made his decision. He called Lawrence on his cellphone and set up a meeting for the following day. His choice was not an easy one, but he'd decided to pay off Lawrence Jennings because he couldn't kill the man. But he'd also come to another realization: he had to talk to Renee.

After climbing the stairs with heavy steps, Craig found himself at her door, his heart beating wildly. He knocked, and when she didn't answer, he turned the knob and found her sitting on the window seat and staring out the window. He moved further into the room and pulled the vanity stool from the dresser. He sat down and rolled closer to her. His heart ached when he saw the remnants of tears, and knew she had used the hem of her tee shirt to dry them.

"I'm an idiot, Renee, and only God knows how sorry I am for what I said to you downstairs. All I could think of when I came in was what could have happened to you. How do you think I would have felt, for not being here . . . for leaving you alone in the first place, overnight? I promised you that I would take care of you, didn't I?" He reached for her hand, but she drew away. He rolled the vanity stool closer so that his knees touched hers.

Renee had spent the last hour being angry at him and mad at herself because she did feel stupid. That was exactly how Charles had made off with her money, because she'd let her guard down. She knew that was exactly what people would say if they found out. They would all wonder how someone supposedly so smart could be so thoughtless. Sniffing back tears, she turned her head to face him. "I'm not as stupid and thoughtless as you think, Craig. If anything, I'm too smart. Do you think I would hesitate to protect myself if I sensed or faced harm or danger in any way? We have alarm panels in this house and, as you well know, I know how to punch someone out." She turned away from him. "Mr. Jennings said he had projections of all the new business since the commercials and the renovations, and I was happy to hear all that. I was happy for you." She turned to face him again, stronger now. "It's because you haven't said anything about it . . . nothing, Craig. I've asked you how you think the bank's business has picked up, and you don't want to talk about it. You don't even want to acknowledge that you're responsible for that bank's future success."

He listened to her and ached to touch her, but he didn't. "You're right about everything. I've just been so focused on getting more business for the agency that I failed to be open with you. My only excuse is that I'm an idiot, Renee, and I'm not used to sharing my work with anybody. Although I like when you ask me about work, baby, I just honestly don't know how to share it, or even what to tell you about it. I've never done that before."

She stared at him incredulous, then she told him he had allowed his emotional detachment to spill from his bedroom over into his everyday life. "That's sad, Craig," she said.

He could not disagree with her. And that was how he felt—sad and sorry for himself as he stared down at the wedding band he proudly wore on his finger. In a quiet, emotion-filled voice, he told her, "I like sharing everything with you, Renee." His fingers touched the hem of her shorts, and he couldn't meet her eyes. "I'm so sorry for what I said downstairs. I feel like I'm on some kind of emotional roller coaster." Craig decided to tell her what was uppermost on his mind, even more so than the blackmail. His eyes finally met hers. "Renee, I don't know if I can say good-bye to you in a few weeks; even the thought scares me. Baby, I don't want to. I want us to stay married." She had slowly pulled back from him, but he rushed on anyway. "Look, I know what our deal was and what I promised, but I just don't think I can let you walk out of my life in a few weeks."

Renee faced him, his voice pulling her to him. "Craig . . ." she whispered.

"Renee, I think I'm love with you. Actually, I'm pretty sure of it." He lifted his tear-filled eyes up to hers again. "I didn't plan this, and honestly I didn't want to love you like this. It just happened and in a way, I'm glad I love you, but at the same time, I feel like I'm . . . opened and exposed and . . . I just hadn't expected to feel this way. I hadn't expected that you'd become the center of my world, the center of me," he said, putting his hand to his chest. "This hurts, Renee, and this painful ache I feel is because I don't want to lose you. But I don't want to trap you into a relationship with me based on what I wanted, based on our three-month deal or the promise."

He loves me. This is what she heard and kept hearing in her head. It was musical and it was ringing in her ears. "Craig, you really love me?"

He blew out a steady breath. "Yes. Guess I've found that heart we didn't think I had, huh?" He moved closer to her.

Renee was almost speechless, but did manage to say, "Craig, you do have a heart, you always did, and, and I love you, too. I think I always have, but you didn't know it."

She said she loved him, too, but she didn't say that she was in love with him, and Craig knew there was a difference. But he didn't press her, mainly because he had the blackmail to deal with. Still, Craig was just happy that she didn't hate him or started packing her things. That was something he didn't think he could bear. He lifted her hand to his lips. "Renee, about what you said downstairs, baby, I don't want you out of my life, out of here .

. . our home." His lips feverishly found hers at the same moment she sought his.

He held her tightly against him. This kiss was different, with each feeling the significance of admitting to loving each other. An unspoken, permanent bond was sealed between them at that moment. They kept kissing until she slid from the window seat and onto his lap, and from there to the carpeted floor. His body covered hers in one move, and he continued kissing her as if he had been gone away from her for weeks instead of one night.

Renee was overjoyed. He had said he loved her and that alone made her heart beat faster. She was wonderfully content with this knowledge. The moment when Craig's lips captured hers again, Renee knew without a doubt that she was where she was meant to be. The happiness was bursting through her because she didn't want their marriage pact to end, either, and it had nothing to do with needing his protection and security.

Craig savored the sweetness of just lying on the floor holding her. He was complete. He was saved. He was thrilled in the knowledge that she held his heart in her small hands.

Several hours later, Craig walked back into his bedroom carrying a tray of sandwiches, juice and two roses and sat on the edge of the bed. Renee lay asleep among the tangled bed sheets. "Hey, sleepyhead, wake up. I brought us something to eat." His lips claimed hers when she sat up behind him and began dropping warm kisses down his arm. "Damn, vixen woman, you're killing me, and on an empty stomach at that."

"I never got to fix us dinner," Renee murmured.

"Don't worry about it. Besides, we were treated to a late lunch before leaving L.A."

Renee's eyes widened and she scrambled around on the bed to sit beside him. "Craig, oh, my God, I forgot about L.A. Tell me everything, what happened?"

He laughed and restrained the impulse to call her Squirt. "Okay, in a nutshell, we've got the green light for mock ups and will be putting our ideas in final form." For the next few minutes, as they ate sandwiches, Craig explained what was going to be a busy time at the agency.

"How do you all plan to celebrate?" She asked, her face full of love for him, and watched him shrug his shoulders.

Renee jumped up from him. "I'll plan a celebration cookout and pool party . . . here at the house this Saturday. It'll be fun, please, come on . . ."

He liked the ideas she began rattling off. "I need to start making lists. I have to decide on decorations and the menu. We'll have lots of food and, and . . ."

"Cuddling and affection stuff," Craig said, amused and roused by her enthusiasm.

Renee looked up pushing hair from her face. "Huh? What?" He'd gotten back under the covers, and was motioning for her. Grinning, she pounced onto the bed and into his arms.

Miss Lilly was leaving the restaurant where she'd just had dinner with her daughter Laurel and her two granddaughters, Amber and Alison, when she looked across the pier and saw her former boss, Lawrence Jennings, talking with Craig Thompson. She found this odd; so odd, in fact, the hairs on the back of her neck stood up.

Alison looked up at her grandmother. "Nana, what's wrong? You look weird."

"Hmm? Oh nothing, baby, I'm fine. But I think I'll use the ladies' room before we drive back to town." She smiled quickly, adding, "I don't want your prudish mama here to have to pull over into the woods again for me and then lecture me about being uncouth." Lillian laughed at the tight-lipped look her daughter shot her as Alison and Amber burst into giggles.

Lillian rushed back inside the restaurant and went to a side window, which gave her a better look at the two men in the empty lot across the road. Something was wrong. Lawrence Jennings was grinning from ear to ear. Craig, on the other hand, looked deadly serious.

Miss Lilly saw Craig get in his car, slam the door and speed off, leaving a cloud of dust and dirt all over Mr. Jennings. Her eyes zeroed in on her former boss . . . and there it was, that wide, toothy grin that meant he had just gotten over on someone. "Oh, my goodness, what has he done now? More importantly, what has Craig done?"

Saturday afternoon was perfect for a cookout—sunny and very warm, and thankfully, the humidity was low.

Guests were expected to start arriving by four o'clock, and Renee wanted everything to be ready. It was, with Maria's help. The meats for grilling were seasoned and stacked in the refrigerator. Craig's patio was in the shape of a wide S just outside the kitchen, with the pool area to the left, so several bistro-style table and chair sets were arranged around the patio. A decorative centerpiece was on each table. On the other side of the patio, wicker lounge chairs had been set up with tables and colorful umbrellas for protecting guests from the hot Houston sun.

Craig and Renee were sharing a slow dance in the living room before the party guests arrived. Craig whispered in her ear, "thank you for the party, Renee."

Renee smiled and rested her head on his chest as they swayed to the music. They hadn't talked any more about their argument two nights ago, and they only spoke of loving each other in general terms. Renee knew that she couldn't fully be his wife without telling him about her legal problems, which were sure to come to light once Charles was arrested. Now she had a new worry—how any negative publicity about her could ultimately affect Craig. She had never thought about how sharing Craig's name could be a problem.

Renee felt so protected in his arms, and she was sure he would understand about her falling victim to Charles. But Renee knew she would also have to tell her parents, who had given her that money in the first place. She could count all the times they had told her she was making a reckless decision about one thing or another.

She remembered when she had pulled all of her savings, then two thousand, to buy an 'adorable' used car, even when her father told her it was not a good idea without getting it checked out first. Only Renee fired back by telling him she was an adult and it was her money. One week later, she had to call her father to pick her up from work because the engine was smoking. The next day, the 'adorable' car was sent to the scrap yard with a busted engine. Then there was the time she moved into what she said was a cute little apartment because she wanted her own place . . . against her parents' and sisters' advice. They told her it was a bad area, and it was. One month later her apartment was broken into while she was working. She had to move back home with no money and no possessions. But, then there had been other times where she just didn't use better judgment. Renee just didn't think she could take hearing them say, once again, that she was irresponsible and reckless. They would blame her for allowing herself to be used and duped. That was going to be just as hard to deal with as having to tell Craig, she thought.

It took her several minutes to realize the music had stopped and they were no longer dancing. "See what dancing in your arms does to me? It takes me away from everything." Feeling the sting of tears, she looked away just as Craig's cellphone rang, interrupting anything else she might have been tempted to say to him.

He recognized the name when it flashed up on his cellphone caller ID, and for some odd reason his stomach tightened. "Hi, stranger, can you hold on for a second?"

Looking at Renee, he excused himself to take the call in the den.

While she waited for Craig to come back on the line, Lillian was hoping she was making the right decision. She had thought long and hard before deciding to call Craig. But ever since she watched Mr. Jennings do his stupid happy dance amidst all that dirt and dust, without so much as a care that his designer shoes were getting dirty, she knew something was wrong. And when she walked into her living room after her daughter dropped her off, her eyes immediately went to the wedding picture of Craig and Renee.

It had all made sense then. Craig had married that girl for the sole purpose of getting his inheritance. The idea of Craig doing such a thing to that nice girl weighed her down because she knew that Renee was in love with Craig and he was going break her heart.

Lillian's mind returned to the present when she heard Craig calling out her name. She had totally forgotten he'd asked her to hold on.

"Miss Lilly, I'm sorry I took so long, but I had another call come in. But what a nice surprise." Craig tried to sound upbeat, but his stomach was tight with nervousness.

"Well, I hope I'm not interrupting you, but Craig, I kinda wanted to talk to you."

"Are you busy today?" Craig smiled when she rattled on about having already finished her grocery shopping. Craig had been walking back into the living room as he invited her to come to the party, promising they could talk then. He now handed the telephone to Renee.

"Hi, Miss Lilly. Oh, please come. It's just a cookout, and you can sit back and relax. Bring your sexiest bathing suit to take a swim and that handsome Mr. Stewart." Renee laughed at Miss Lilly's shriek. "I'll take that as a yes, and I'll see you soon."

By 8 P.M. the party was still in full swing and food was still sizzling on the grill. Craig didn't lie, Renee realized, when he'd said his co-workers could put away some food.

Lillian watched Renee, and what she saw was a young woman deeply in love. Since she'd spent time with both of them, she just knew that Craig loved Renee as well. They were just as they presented themselves to be—deeply in love. Maybe she was just imagining things, but then she did see Craig pass that envelope to Mr. Jennings. *It was probably nothing at all.*

Craig sat in the kitchen drinking coffee and reading the Sunday paper when Renee came in from church. "Good morning. How was church?"

"Wonderful. Maybe you'll go with me one Sunday. It's a really nice church family." She kissed his cheek, feeling happier then she'd been in a very long time.

"Maybe I will, just as long as there is no game on TV I want to see." Craig laughed at the disapproving expression she sent him. He decided to bring up the issue of money, something they rarely talked about except for household bills. "Hey, Renee, how are you set for money?" He saw her hand shake slightly when she raised the coffee mug to her lips.

"Wh-what do you mean?" Her mind raced wildly at the mere mention of money.

"It's just that we never really talked about it." Tension surfaced in Renee's face. "Baby, I only brought it up because I want to give you some money. To spend any way you want. I was thinking about seventy-five thousand?" he said. "It's up to you." Here it was again, he thought, another opportunity to tell her about the inheritance, right here and now. "If you need more money, well, you just let me know."

Still in shock, Renee said, "Craig, you can't give me that kind of money." She was silent for several seconds. Then realization hit. "Do you really have that kind of money to give away?"

"I wouldn't be just giving it away. I'd be giving it to my wife to do whatever she wants to do with it. And, yes, Renee, I have that kind of money." He hesitated briefly, then said, "I've invested well and saved well. The seventy-five grand won't make a dent in my account."

"Oh, wow," was all she could say. She had assumed that he was well off, but now sensed he was better than that.

CHAPTER 10

Two days later, dressed for work, Renee stood in the front doorway and waved Craig off to work. After church on Sunday, she had gone to her apartment to look for old telephone bills that might list a Florida number for a call Charles may have placed. She came up with nothing. She recalled having to send in a letter to the phone company; she thought she had a copy in her suitcase but, for the sake of time, she'd just open a copy she had saved on her computer.

As soon as Craig's car was out of sight, Renee ran up to her bedroom to get her laptop. After ten minutes of scrolling through saved documents and biting on her bottom lip, she found the letter but had forgotten she didn't have access to a printer. To save time, she decided to use Craig's laser printer down in his den.

Renee entered Craig's den, feeling as if she was doing something wrong. Then she caught herself and laughed. "Hey, I live here, too, don't I?" She didn't know his computer system all that well, but she did know she would just need to turn it on and insert her disk. Piece of cake. With her heart racing, her fingers drumming on the desk and her eyes flying to her watch, Renee waited for Craig's computer to come to life. Then opened her document and finally saw her two- page letter. She quickly scanned the letter, and there in the second paragraph were the long- distance numbers she was looking for. She hit the print icon and waited and waited. When the pages didn't print out, she hit the print key again. She panicked and almost went through the roof when the printer started beeping and making a grinding noise. Renee quickly rounded Craig's large desk and saw several red and yellow lights flashing on the printer panel, indicating the paper tray was empty. "Oh, no," she said, and began frantically searching for paper. She found none. She threw her hands up then searched his desk and the bookshelves for scrap paper. Not even a single sheet was found. "I don't believe this . . . I'll bet Darrin Stevens on *Bewitched* never ran out of copy paper." Same thing when she searched the desk drawers. No paper. "How can an ad man not have any copier paper? This is crazy."

With perspiration dotting her forehead, Renee ran upstairs to the guest bedroom and found several sheets of yellow paper in her suitcase. She ran back down the stairs, coming to a screeching halt when she heard Craig mumbling as he put his key into the keyhole. "Oh, no."

Renee stood just ten feet from the den, where the printer was still flashing and beeping intermittently, waiting for the paper now shaking in her damp and trembling hand. With her eyes flying from one deadbolt lock to the other, she flew into the den. She dropped to the floor and yanked the power cord from the wall, shutting the printer off. She ran back to the foyer just as Craig came through the door.

"Hi, I see you're still home. Good. I forgot something." Craig kissed her forehead and stood back and touched her forehead. "Renee, are you hot?" His concern put a smile on her face.

"What?" Her hand flew to her own forehead. "Oh, yeah, I ran out to the yard to water those plants I got from Leslie. You may have noticed I have a green thumb," she heavily.

"Oh, yes, I've noticed. How could I not, with all the flowers and plants growing up the kitchen wall, and just yesterday I discovered a potted plant in the bathroom. What's the paper for?" he called over his shoulder as he walked past her into the kitchen.

"Huh, what paper?" Renee pulled her other hand from behind her back and stared dumbfounded down at the sheets of yellow paper she was clutching. "Oh, these, I was hot, that's all." She smiled and briskly fanned her face, following Craig into the kitchen. "What did you forget?" she asked, watching him.

Renee made a point of loosening her grip on the yellow sheets of paper.

"Oh, right, I forgot your account number. I wrote it down on a pad last night. Have you seen it?" he asked, scanning the kitchen counters. "Maybe I left it in the den," he said, heading in that direction.

"No!" Renee said in a strangled voice, causing Craig to look at her curiously. "I mean, it is on the side counter, right there next to the coffee pot." She said, pointing a trembling finger at the counter. She absolutely did not want him to go into the den.

Craig just looked at her with curious eyes. "Great, I'll make that deposit today. Don't be late for work," he said, tearing a single sheet off the pad and then folding it and putting it into his vest pocket. There it was again, he thought. Renee was nervous. "I've got to run; I'll call you later. Have a great day baby." He kissed her wet lips and hurried to the door.

Renee followed and closed the door behind him, then sagged against the doorframe for several seconds. She smoothed out the wrinkled sheets of paper and quickly walked into the den and proceeded to copy the document. When she was finished, Renee felt like a cat burglar, wiping off the desk with her hands and neatly restacking two books on Craig's desk.

Twenty minutes later, Renee was on the interstate headed to work. She planned to fax the letter to Simon at the number he left on her cellphone and then shred the other three copies that came out of the printer at work.

At lunchtime Craig headed over to Renee's bank to make the deposit. On the ride there he thought back on his last conversation with Lawrence Jennings, which had been a couple of days after he'd showed up at his home. Craig had arranged to meet Lawrence at a restaurant several blocks away from the bank.

He'd purposely arrived half an hour early for their one o'clock meeting. He could only imagine Lawrence's reaction and closed his eyes to shut out the man's larcenous face. He absolutely hated being forced into a corner this way. But Craig knew he had too much to lose, and he didn't want to lose those things that were so important to him now. Like Renee and his agency. Craig was so tempted to just get up and walk out, he turned and looked out the window. He really didn't notice when a shadow fell over his table, but steeled himself when a hand rested on his shoulder. His instinct was to back-flip Jennings onto his ass. Instead, he turned slowly in his chair and looked up at the man looking down at him.

"Hello, Craig," James Tinsly said, patting Craig's shoulder to keep him from standing, as he was about to do.

"Mr. Tinsly, how are you, sir?" Craig watched his grandfather's old friend pull out a chair and sit down across from him. He did his best not to appear flustered, but that is exactly how he felt.

"Good, good," James said, resting his hands on the table as if deep in thought. "Craig, as you young folks say, I'm just going to lay it out there, so bear with me. You're in a bit of trouble—of your own doing, of course—but that's neither here nor there. You've backed yourself in a corner, and I feel justified in doing something. Let's say as a favor to my old friend, Reggie." James watched Craig and let his words sink in.

James smiled patiently at Craig, noticing him checking his wristwatch. "Don't worry, Craig, I sent Lawrence to a community meeting in the next county. I'm sure he'll be contacting you on your cellphone to tell you he's been detained."

Craig finally spoke. "Mr. Tinsly, I'm afraid you must be confused, I, don't . . ."

James raised his hand to stop Craig and smiled. "You're so much like Reginald. He, too, believed he was doing what he thought was right, like adding that stipulation to your inheritance." He sat back, the smile easing from his face. "You know, Craig, that day the two of you came into the bank, you smelled the place up of fish something awful, making me wish I'd gone fishing, too." He smiled, sending crinkles around his eyes. "Anyway, I said to him, 'Now why the hell would you do that, Reggie? Look at that boy, already tall and handsome, no way is he going to stay single. He'll meet up with some pretty young lady and she's going to knock his socks off.' But your grandfather said you were stubborn and he wanted to make sure. Craig, he wanted to make sure that you found the love of your life and that you married her before you touched your inheritance. He wanted you to have a home and not have to worry that you'd be stuck under your father's get-rich-quick schemes and the mismanagement of his own money. You understand, Craig? Your grandfather wanted you, your wife, and, one day, your children, to be sound and secure financially."

Craig said nothing as he listened to the older man for whom he had a great respect.

"Craig, I finally remembered who Renee was. She used to work in an ice cream shop. She used to give me extra scoops of ice cream in my sundae. Then she'd just go crazy and put all kinds of stuff on it, and all I ever wanted was one scoop of vanilla and one chocolate. But I ate it all, because it gave her the biggest smile, and she was so nice. So I was thrilled to learn that you're the one she married. I saw how much you two love each other, Craig. That was obvious at the rededication. I think she's that pretty young lady Reggie was talking about." He looked at Craig pointedly. "Is she, Craig?"

Craig swallowed hard, his voice quiet. "Yes, sir, she is, and I love her very much."

James smiled. "I'm so glad about that. It makes me helping you much easier."

"Help me? How do you mean?" Craig asked, unable to break James's steady stare.

"Your marriage, Craig, for whatever reason, has happened. You and Renee have found love, and as far as I'm concerned, that follows the stipulation of the inheritance, and therefore there was no fraud on your part." He slowly shook his head and took another sip of water.

"Fraud, sir?" Craig's throat was so dry it caused his voice to crack.

"Uh-huh," James answered.

Craig was suddenly very tired. He couldn't lie to the man, and the weight of what he'd done was just too much for him to bear. "Mr. Tinsly, I didn't mean to cause any problems to the bank, or your staff. I-I just wanted the opportunity to purchase the ad agency. For myself, yes, but also—"

"To keep a lot of people working," James finished for him. "I understand that, Craig. There is nothing worse than seeing a business close its doors because it cannot compete with the bigger companies. I've seen it happen, and I admire Davis for holding out for you. Did you know that he got his first business loan from my bank? You probably didn't. But way back then, when Davis came to my bank for a loan, he was one of the first white businessmen to do that, and I gladly approved it. Back then, his staff was made up of local folks and he kept them employed, pretty much like I did." He looked out the window, lines creasing his forehead, and then back at Craig. "One staff person in particular I should have let go years ago, and I didn't. You follow?"

"I think so, sir." Craig saw a light and held onto it.

"Lawrence Jennings needed to be gone a long, long time ago. But his business sense is good enough that the board of directors and the bank trustees see his business skills as the next best thing to sliced bread. He secures outside contract loans from established businesses. You know, Lawrence's first wife, Naomi, was on the board for many years before she passed, so he remained at the bank, really as a courtesy to her. Anyway, his latest issue is a more personal one for me. You see, your grandfather entrusted Miss Lilly and myself to look over your inheritance, and we did. At first, that is. But with so many years of inactivity on the account, we just stopped checking so often, and then the account fell under Lawrence's management. Then one year turned into another and yet another and still you never showed up to collect the inheritance and, well . . ."

James drew in a deep breath. "I've been watching Lawrence for the past couple of months. Just recently,

I've had some of his office calls monitored." He grinned when Craig raised his eyebrows. "I know a lot of people son, and one is an expert in telephone transmissions, nice fellow. Anyway, when I overheard part of a conversation between you and Lawrence at the rededication party, I arranged to get a tape of a call he made to you last week. Well, I could no longer ignore what I now know to be fact. Lawrence is blackmailing you." His eyes met Craig's with a stern look that almost dared him to say he was wrong.

Craig sat back in his chair and met the eyes staring back at him. James was daring him to say differently. It was a look his grandfather often gave him as he waited him out. Craig nodded his head, yes. "I'm meeting him here today to give him this." Craig slid the envelope to James. It contained a cashier's check for the one million dollars Lawrence demanded from him.

James put on his reading glasses and looked at the check, and then he passed the envelope back to Craig. He took a sip of water. "Listen to me. Your grandfather worked hard for his money, and with my help, he invested well. He profited so well, in fact, that he left that inheritance for you, and I'll be damned if I'll let Lawrence Jennings get his filthy fingers on any of it. You'd better believe that," he said, his lips tight.

Craig's cellphone rang, and he saw that it was Lawrence calling. His eyes met James's briefly, listening to Lawrence explain not being able to keep their meeting. "I'll meet you here tomorrow, same time, and if you fail to show up, then our business will be concluded." Then he snapped the cellphone shut. Craig sat back. "Okay, what now, Mr. Tinsly?"

James didn't answer Craig's question. Instead he rubbed his hands together and said, "You know, I could use a bowl of vegetable soup." His eyes twinkled with mischief as he added, "And maybe a grilled cheese sandwich, too. You see, we've got a plan to work on for your next meeting with Lawrence, and that is best done with food in our stomachs."

Craig closed his eyes to say a silent prayer. Immediately, his grandfather's face floated before him. When he opened his eyes again, James was smiling knowingly over his menu.

Craig and Renee had enjoyed an early evening swimming in the pool later that day. It was yet another hot, humid Houston evening. They'd stepped from the pool and stood side by side, drying off. That's when Craig picked up the deposit receipt showing her new hefty savings account balance and passed it to Renee. He needed no thanks from her, but when she threw her arms around his neck and kissed every inch of his damp face and neck, it was well worth it.

The early evening proved way too hot for anyone to keep cool. That was Vivian Jennings's thought as she pulled her car behind the aging gas station off Highway 14 and drove another fifty feet to Cooper's, the small, out-of-the-way motel.

Vivian couldn't believe Ray had rented a place there, but he said it was what he could afford. But then, she didn't have to worry about being spotted by anyone who knew her or Lawrence. She also knew she couldn't keep taking chances and risk getting caught.

But Vivian didn't care what the stuffy people in town thought of her. She knew they just thought she was someone who made good by marrying a respected businessman. In social settings, they were all proper and respectful, but she knew they talked behind her back. *Those old dried-up witches,* she thought, looking in the rearview mirror and reapplying her lipstick. Not far from her car, she spotted Ray's beat-up truck behind room number 10.

Before getting out of her car, Vivian covered her head with a wide scarf so that no one would recognize her. Better to be safe than sorry, she thought. It was just such a trashy area of low-rent housing, liquor stores and honky-tonk hangouts. Vivian puckered her lips and smiled; she felt quite safe there. Smoothing down her tight yellow sundress, she knew that Ray was going to practically rip it from her body, especially when she let him see that she had on a black thong beneath it. But Vivian was smart. She had brought extras of each, which were rolled up in her large canvas bag.

She climbed the stairs to Ray's second-level unit. The minute she tapped on the door, Ray opened it, and Vivian's world suddenly lit up like Christmas morning.

"Hey, baby . . . 'bout time you got here. Come on in."
Ray's smile touched her everywhere, causing her to giggle
in response.

Vivian loved Ray. She loved everything about him.
Ray could take her to heights of passion that Lawrence
could only imagine.

CHAPTER 11

Lawrence couldn't believe how bad his day had turned out. To make matters worse, it was almost seven-thirty and he was running low on gas. He cursed himself for not filling up before he left that community meeting. Lawrence thanked his lucky stars when he spotted a dusty gas station on the outskirts of town just off Highway 14. He hadn't talked to Vivian since earlier in the day, but he remembered her mentioning going to the hairdresser. Lawrence chuckled, knowing how she was going to fuss at him for messing up her hair when he got home and made sweet love to her tonight. That alone would make him feel better and take away the stress of his lousy day. Most disappointing was missing that meeting with Craig Thompson.

Stepping from his car when the attendant rushed over to him, Lawrence stretched and said, "Just fill it up with unleaded, son, and please use the premium gas. My car will choke on that cheap stuff." He smiled briefly at the young attendant, who was happy for a premium gas sale. "Say, do you have a soda machine in the office there where I can buy a bottle of soda, preferably a cold one?"

"Oh, yes sir, we sure do, and they're nice and cold too 'cause I filled 'em up myself early this morning, but they in the cans, though, so go on in." The attendant just knew the man in the business suit would give him a nice tip.

Lawrence walked across the lot to the station's office. He absently looked to the right where a cheap motel stood. His eyes squinted to bring into view a gold and black mustang that looked similar to Vivian's car. *Couldn't be. No way would she be anywhere near this dump.* He shook the thought off, pulled some change from his pocket and stepped inside the office.

With a cold cola in hand, Lawrence walked back outside and to the side of the gas station. The sun's last purple-orange rays had dropped behind the horizon and the gas station's lights had flickered on. Lawrence looked back in the direction of the mustang again. He frowned, thinking the front tire looked fairly new. Recently he'd had a new driver's-side tire put on Vivian's car after she ran over another nail. His face filled with tension and his eyes hooded, he walked toward the motel. He called back to the attendant, "Say, young man, I'm just going to stretch my legs and walk around a bit. While you're at it, check the pressure of my tires as well . . . I don't want to get a flat so close to home." He nodded at the happy attendant.

On shaky legs, Lawrence walked along a sidewalk that was overgrown with brush until he reached the front of the mustang. As he stared at the car, a sick feeling crawled into the pit of his stomach. It was Vivian's car. Looking around, he spotted only two other cars, neither of which looked drivable. And there was a rusty pickup truck. He looked up at the bottom units, which were dark and probably unoccupied, but two top units had lights on. One room was just at the top of the stairs; the other one was at the opposite end.

He set his soda down on the bottom step among several empty beer cans, bottles and cigarette butts and quietly walked up the stairs. He listened at the door of the first unit and heard a television game show and loud snoring, but his attention was drawn to the unit on the end. His stomach knotted painfully as he moved along the concrete walkway. It was dark now, and he knew he wouldn't be seen because the light had been busted out on that end of the motel. He listened at the door and heard the unmistakable sounds of people having sex— only guttural, and laced with profanity. Then Lawrence heard Vivian's voice crying out, begging and pleading. *Oh, good God.* Lawrence almost threw up the tuna salad and crackers he'd eaten at that community meeting. Then he heard a man's voice responding to his wife's in that same vulgar tone. He instinctively raised his hand to touch the door, but let it drop. Instead, he balled it into a fist and inched closer to the low window where dim light spilled out. Lawrence knelt down and looked into the window beside the air-conditioning unit. He couldn't tear his eyes away from what he saw. With tears filling his eyes, he saw his Vivian on the bed, her face in the throes of passion, something like he himself had never seen before. She was never vulgar, never trashy, but in that cheap motel room, she sounded and looked like some ten-dollar street prostitute. Although he didn't want to, Lawrence let his eyes slowly move up from Vivian's

thrashing body to the man's face. And then he got
another shock. He recognized the man who was violating
his wife . . . Ray Newman from down at the warehouse.
Ray and his father were customers at his bank. Lawrence
felt the air being sucked from his lungs, and when he
inhaled, all he was able to bring in was humid, muggy air,
making him feel lightheaded. He saw as Ray grab Vivian's
breasts, and felt on the verge of throwing up for sure
when he realized she was enjoying it.

Lawrence forced himself to look away. Because his
bad knee was now painfully sore from his weight bearing
down on it, it was difficult for him to rise, but he was
finally able to struggle up from his stooped position.
Wiping sweat and tears from his face, he quietly walked
unsteadily down the stairs, gripping his stomach with
one hand and the banister with the other, trying to side-
step the beer cans, bottles and cigarette butts. When he
reached the landing, he practically ran to his car, kicking
up dust on his leather shoes. Lawrence didn't even
remember flinging money to the stunned attendant, who
stood grinning at the crisp one-hundred-dollar bill.
When he looked up in his rearview mirror, the station's
call sign was flickering and waving its red letters. Only
the sign wasn't flickering or waving. But that is how it
appeared through Lawrence's hot rush of fresh tears as he
pushed his car along the dusty gravel trail out of the gas
station and back onto Highway 14.

By the time Lawrence opened the back door to his
house, his mind was grappling with two facts. First, he
still loved Vivian, in spite of the fact that he had just seen

her having sex with that young man. Second, he planned to keep that meeting with Craig Thompson because he needed that money, now more than ever. He couldn't risk having Vivian leave him for that lowlife warehouse worker.

Lawrence thought he would find solace in the bedroom, but one look at the bed brought on flashbacks of what he had seen in that motel room. He pressed his knuckles to his eye sockets as a forlorn moan escaped his lips. "Not my Vivian, my sweet, sweet Vivian. How could you? How could you do this to us, to yourself? Dear Lord, how could you act like that? Th-that gutter slut wasn't you. No, that was not you." He picked up the silk robe hanging on back of the chaise and brought it up to his face, inhaling her scent with a sob. "Dear God, no." He imagined her mouth on Ray's body and squeezed his eyes shut. "No, no." His mournful wails mingled with his tears until he heard Vivian coming into the house, slamming the front door. He heard her heels clicking on the marbled foyer and quickly poured himself a double shot of scotch from the bar Vivian had set up in a corner of their bedroom. Then he heard her heels clicking on the hardwood steps as she came upstairs.

In the darkness of the room, Lawrence sat quietly and watched as his wife came into the bedroom. She threw her purse onto the dresser and kicked off her shoes, one of which landed where the hallway light spilled into the room. Dust clung to the shoe, just as it clung to his.

Vivian walked over to the mirror and shook out her shoulder-length hair. "Lord, I am so addicted to that," she said in a low but audible voice. She looked into the mirror again and gasped, "Oh, my God . . ."

Vivian whirled around so fast the hem of her replacement dress flounced around her legs. "Good Lord Lawrence, is that you sitting there?" She flicked on a small dresser lamp and stared at her husband, and then immediately went over and knelt beside him. "Honey, wh-what's wrong? Are you sick?" Vivian was scared and worried. She wondered how long he'd been sitting there. *What did I say about Ray?* "Baby, what's wrong?" Vivian asked, easing down onto the floor and patting his hand.

Lawrence just watched her. He had heard her talking to herself. He felt somewhat relieved. *That was it! Ray had given Vivian drugs she was now addicted to.* He heard it from her own mouth. *My Lord, drugs.* "Yes, dear, I think I'm feeling a little under the weather, and I haven't eaten well today. I've got something of an upset stomach from the food at that town meeting, that's all." His eyes misted when he saw genuine concern in her. And then his eyes lowered to her swollen, reddened lips and dropped further to her neck. He saw faint red circular marks and his stomach turned over. He saw her face at the motel flashing over the face she was now showing—a face filled with love and concern for him. *Yes, she still loves me.*

"Well, look, honey, you've got to take care of yourself, and you don't need this," Vivian said, taking the heavy tumbler from his hands and placing it on the floor beside her. She removed his shoes and socks. "Honey, where have you been to get your shoes so dirty?" Vivian frowned at the familiar dust, but then dismissed it. "Well, no bother, I'll just have Grace to clean and polish them. Oh, and speaking of our dear housekeeper, I had to have a word with her again today," she said, glancing up at Lawrence with wide, innocent eyes.

Lawrence tuned out hearing the details of yet another issue Vivian had concerning Grace. His mind was on the countless times Vivian had gone missing for hours of the day or early evening. Now, his mind raced; he knew without a doubt that she was probably with Ray, and not shopping or getting her nails done, either . . . her usual excuses.

Vivian was still talking about Grace. "So anyway, that was it, honey. I missed you today." She began unbuttoning his shirt.

She never gave him a chance to say a word. Lawrence felt the sting of tears behind his closed eyes as she pressed kisses to the back of his hand, soothing his painful thoughts. But the memory flashes still returned, and he kept seeing her on that bed with Ray. He heard her disgusting language, begging and pleading with that piece of trash boy. She never, ever acted that way with him—like she was nothing more than a street whore. But he saw her acting that way with Ray. That is what he made himself believe her addiction was doing to her. Lawrence understood that, because he was certainly addicted to her. With Vivian now sitting on his lap cradling his face, ready to pamper him, he damned Ray Newman as he put his arms around her waist. But, try as he might, Lawrence couldn't force away the smell of another man clinging to his wife's body. *She has a terrible addiction . . . yes that's all it is.* His mind clung to this thought, screaming over and over.

CHAPTER 12

Renee took the call on the patio she had been waiting to get for almost a year. Simon had found Charles in Florida. Before hanging up, she told Simon she was wiring him more money. Since accepting her case, Simon had accepted payments from Renee. She knew he charged her a fraction of his usual rates.

Renee was determined to see Charles punished to the fullest extent of the law, even if it did cost her all the new money in her account. She just had to. But at the same time, she was afraid to see Charles again. She knew she should have told Simon about the additional threatening messages Charles had been leaving her cellphone, but she didn't. "Please call me again the moment you get anything new, okay? Bye."

Renee walked back into the kitchen just as Craig came downstairs. They kissed good-bye and then each drove off to another workday.

Craig smiled for the first time in a long time. Funny, he thought, how being blackmailed could weigh down a person's soul and entire being. When it is lifted, so is the spirit.

Miss Lilly decided to stop in the bank to say hello to her ex-coworkers. The woman who now held her former position was a woman who looked smart and efficient. This was unexpected. She expected to see a leggy, busty, big-haired vixen in her seat, so it was hard to mask her shock when she saw her replacement.

Efficient-looking and professional, Racine Hilton came over to introduce herself to Miss Lilly. "Well, I'm so happy to finally meet you. I've heard so much about you, and I just have to say a big thank you to you, Miss Lilly."

Lillian smiled and shook hands with the welcoming woman. "Well, it's so nice to meet you, Racine." A frown creased the woman's face before disappearing behind a polite smile—but not before Lillian saw it.

"Miss Lilly, if you have a few minutes, could you come sit with me for a quick chat?"

Lillian sensed something was wrong when Racine touched her arm. "Sure, why not," Lillian said, following Racine to her desk. Her eyes took in the new sectioned off area of the finance department. Individual cubicles were also sectioned off for privacy, but open enough for those working in that department to be a part of the bank.

Racine spent some twenty minutes detailing to Miss Lilly discrepancies she had found in dormant accounts and was clearly relieved when her predecessor showed no surprise at her revelations. "Oh, Miss Lilly, we're talking hundreds of thousands of dollars that has gone missing over the years, and possibly more. Once I incorporated all the customer accounts and ran the reports, I was floored. I mean, for so many years someone has been just taking money out of these accounts. One was recently closed out, though; that was the Thompson account."

Lillian had a strong suspicion about what Racine had found. What she had always sensed, but could never prove, this young woman found after installing a new database. She asked where the information was stored at.

"It is stored internally in the computer program, but only my system and Mr. Tinsly's have access to the database programs. These programs I told you about tracked all that missing money. A few days ago, I gave the printout to Mr. Tinsly. I don't think he understood it."

"Why is that?" Lillian asked, absently repeating "Thompson account" in her mind.

Racine smiled. "Oh, he just looked down at the printout as if it were in a foreign language. Then he said he would take it home to study it."

"Well, don't let that gray hair of his fool you. James Tinsly is one smart man. Tell you what, Racine, I'll just call him and have a chat with him; besides, it's time I went to see him and his wife, Ruth anyway." Then she lowered her voice. "But don't you tell nobody else about what you have found." The two women were caught off guard when Lawrence Jennings came out of his office and limped down the short hallway toward them.

"Well, isn't this a surprise, Miss Lilly. Surely you're not missing your old job already, are you?" he asked, plastering a tight smile on his face.

"And a good day to you, too, Mr. Jennings," Lillian said, and looking down at his leg. "Goodness, are you limping there Mr. Jennings? I sure hope you haven't rein-jured that bad knee." She could only imagine what he'd been doing to cause the bad knee of his to act up again. She gave him a smile of pure innocence. "That was some kind of pain you had to endure before."

The mere mention of his painfully sore, now swollen knee, ignited flashbacks of his discovery of Vivian with Ray Newman. Lawrence fumed inside. *How dare this old woman make him remember that painful and vivid memory.* "No, I'm not limping like an old man," he protested, then turned to Racine. "Racine, you must remember that Miss Lilly is now just a bank customer, and if she's not back here for business . . ." he let his words trail off, pinning Racine with a look as he slowly handed her paycheck to her. His meaning was crystal clear.

Racine's lips tightened as she nodded and looked at Miss Lilly briefly.

As for her, Lillian's expression remained pleasantly blank, but she, too, understood what he had meant. The smile with which she had greeted her former boss was unchanged. Patting Racine's hand she said sweetly, "He's right, dear. I'm just a bank customer now, and I shouldn't have come back here interrupting you. Good day." She got up from the chair and walked away.

"Racine, I'll be gone for an hour or so. I have an important lunch meeting."

Racine smiled shakily. "Oh, all right, Mr. Jennings." She turned to her computer monitor. She didn't like or trust that man, and if her suspicions were correct, they all pointed to him. A few minutes later, she watched him passing her window out on the sidewalk. When Racine looked back at her computer screen, she saw there was an e-mail from one of the bank tellers, and Miss Lilly's home telephone number was flashing before her eyes.

She smiled at Miss Lilly's retreating back as she quickly walked to her car.

At one o'clock, Lawrence was sitting across from Craig, who looked comfortable and relaxed, sipping a cola, in contrast to his own nervousness. He'd been shaky and agitated ever since seeing his Vivian with Ray, and still cringed whenever he thought about the two of them. And that is why he hoped this meeting with Craig Thompson would be an answer to all his problems. And he could finally wean himself off his dependence on the baby accounts before something happened . . . like getting caught.

Dismissing whatever ailed his blackmailer, Craig said, "I'll give you two hundred and fifty thousand dollars now and I'll match that in two weeks. That will be all you get from me. You see, I've done some thinking, and if I must, then I'll just take my chances and risk losing everything. I am not giving you an entire million dollars of what was entrusted to your bank, my money." He extracted a cashier's check from his jacket pocket and slid it across the table. "And believe me . . . I don't want to give you this."

Lawrence picked the check up and stared at it. He was not getting the one million he had sought . . . what he needed. Even with the matching balance in two weeks, it wasn't enough. He plastered a tight smile on his face. "Clearly, you misunderstood what you really stand to lose if I go public," Lawrence said quietly, all the while plotting how he was going to push Craig further to get the full million for his silence.

Meanwhile, Craig pushed his chair back and stood up, dropping a couple bills on the table for his soda. "Our meeting is adjourned, Mr. Jennings. I'll call you in a week or so about the balance." With that, he walked out of the restaurant and got into his Mercedes-Benz, which was parked at the curb in front of the restaurant.

Lawrence said nothing as Craig dropped the bill on the table and left. He glanced at the check again. He replayed in his head what Craig had said. "No, son," he said sneering. "I don't think this will work for me." He tucked the envelope in his pocket, looking out the window. "I have responsibilities just as you do, and like you, I'll do what I have to to protect what's dear to me, regardless of the fact that you think you have the upper hand today."

CHAPTER 13

A few days later, Craig came home and told Renee to put on her dancing shoes. She gladly complied. She decided to wear a cute little black dress she had treated herself to the previous week. Craig thought the hour he had been waiting in the kitchen for her had been well worth his wait. His chest swelling with pride, Craig closed the distance between them and took her hand. "You are absolutely beautiful."

"Well, you cleaned up pretty good yourself." Shaking her head up and down, Renee circled him, approving of his beautifully fitted navy suit. "Nice eye candy for me." She laughed and pushed Craig away when she saw his eyes warming. "Oh, no, you don't; we're going out for dinner and dancing." Laughing, Craig let her push him out of the kitchen and straight through the living room. He liked this feeling of oneness with Renee, his wife. He even liked when several of their neighbors, who happened to be outside on the warm evening, spotted them and whistled appreciatively as they walked to his car at the end of the driveway.

After they were seated and had ordered, Craig slid a black velvet box over to her.

"Hey, what's this for?" Her eyes lit up, recognizing the jewelry box from a well-known jeweler.

He leaned over and kissed her cheek, then her lips. "It's a belated birthday present." She was still staring at the box, so he picked it up and placed it in her hands.

"Belated? Craig, my birthday is in February." She slowly opened the box and her eyes shimmered with tears. Craig had given her a gold chain with a bicycle pendant made of diamonds. Giggling, she looked into his dancing eyes and knew that he remembered giving her rides on his bicycle. When her giggles subsided she struggled to tell him what the gift meant to her. "You know you told me, that first ride, to let go of the handle bars, and you said I would be okay. You always said that to me, and I always believed you."

"And I always said that I wouldn't let anything happen to you on my bike," he finished for her, lifting the chain from the box and hooking it around her neck.

She buried her face into his collar and inhaled his cologne. It was in that moment that Renee knew that she had always loved him. "Craig, thank you. I absolutely love it." she murmured against his cheek, and found his lips at the same time he found hers.

Cynthia Gaines was slow dancing with her date, David. Her eyes zeroed in on Craig the moment he and his wife were being escorted to their table, and she watched him tenderly putting a necklace around her neck. When Craig kissed his wife again, a muted sob escaped her lips. She had long ago released him from her heart when he had broken their relationship off. She knew all along exactly what their relationship really was about. It was purely physical. She watched Craig's wife head to the ladies' room.

When the dance ended, Cynthia excused herself to the ladies' room.

Above the rim of his glass, Craig watched Cynthia walk toward him, waved hello, then turned in the direction of the ladies' room.

"Aw, damn," Craig said, with a sigh. Since he couldn't go into the ladies' room, all he could do was wait and pray.

In the sitting area of the ladies' room, Renee sat at a vanity table touching up her lipstick. She looked up and recognized the woman now standing beside her. She smiled tentatively. "Hello . . . Cynthia, right?" Of course, she recognized Craig's ex-girlfriend.

Cynthia sat next to her. "That's right. How are you? It's Renee, isn't it?"

Renee didn't hate this woman, so she had no reason to be rude to her. "Right, I'm okay."

"Craig told me you heard most of what I said to him the night I came to the house. I'm sorry. I know I must have sounded cruel," Cynthia said, noticing Renee's nervousness. Except for the fact that Renee was married to a man she wanted for herself, she didn't have a reason to dislike her. "Craig told me from the beginning that there would be absolutely no committed relationship, so I was truly in shock to hear him say that he was married."

"I told him that night to go after you, or to at least call you and explain things, because I could hear how upset and how hurt you were." Renee turned to face her then, understanding on her face. It's how she now knew she would feel if she lost Craig, especially now that she'd admitted to loving him.

"Thanks, and he did. We had lunch the next day. So I've done what any smart sister who got dumped would do." Cynthia inhaled deeply and said, "I've let go and moved on." She smiled and turned to look at Renee. "But he seems happy, though, and I guess he's gotten what he always wanted." She sighed, admiring Renee's necklace, then frowned. "Is that a bicycle?"

Renee laughed. "Yes, Craig used to give me rides on his bike when I was twelve." Renee reached up and touched the two-inch, diamond-encrusted charm.

Cynthia sat back, stunned. "You've known Craig since you were twelve years old?"

"Yes, but what did you mean when you said Craig has gotten what he's always wanted?" Renee didn't understand what Craig had gotten that he had always wanted.

Cynthia said, casually, "Oh, I just meant buying that ad agency. It's nice, you know. He's now the president and CEO of an agency that I'll bet he'll turn into a Fortune 500 company. Just wait and see." Cynthia pumped lotion into her hands and inhaled the fragrance. "You, Mrs. Thompson, will be very wealthy," Cynthia said, putting on lipstick.

"What do you mean buying the agency? Craig's not the president or CEO. He's the senior advertising executive there," Renee insisted, staring at Cynthia's profile.

Cynthia in turn stared at Renee's puzzled expression. "Renee, Craig bought the Davis agency, let's see . . ." Cynthia's expressive eyes searched the ceiling. "Actually, I think it was around the time the two of you got married. I read that he paid like a million dollars cash for it, then put in a hundred grand of his own money in upgrades. I swear, girl, I didn't even know he was rolling in money like that," Cynthia continued, expertly applying lipstick to her lips.

In shock, Renee stared at her. *Craig bought the agency.* "I'm sorry, Cynthia, but I-I don't believe that. He would have told me. That's major news; he would have told me."

Cynthia pulled a palm pilot computer from her purse and tapped the screen a few times. "It's true, and it did make news, Renee. There it is; read it for yourself." She passed the pocket-sized computer to Renee.

Renee quickly read part of a magazine article reporting the acquisition of the Davis Franklin Agency by senior advertising executive Craig L. Thompson on the tenth of June. Scrolling through the article, she read bits and pieces and then looked up at Cynthia. "You're right," she said, in a quiet, emotionless voice.

Renee closed her eyes. June tenth was their wedding day. Questions tumbled about in her head, way too many for her to grasp all at once.

"Renee, he didn't tell you? Why not? How could he have kept it a secret? Haven't you been to the agency? Davis is long gone. He's sunning himself somewhere in Costa Rica or Brazil." Cynthia stopped talking when she realized that Renee was in shock.

Answering in a weak voice, she said, "No, I didn't know." Renee suddenly remembered seeing his impressive office and jokingly telling Craig it looked like it could be the boss's office. He had only laughed and quickly shuffled her out. Right down to the parking lot. He did everything except start the ignition for her, she thought. Yes, he was strange that day.

"Oh, I'll just bet he's waiting to surprise you with the news." She pointed to her PDA, still in Renee's hands. "This is only one magazine that picked the story up. Several other magazines also did stories, as did the business networks on television for days after the deal was set. It was big news; actually, it still is. Many business magazines picked the story up. I mean, come on, and why wouldn't they? This up-and-coming black man, not even thirty-five, has done what men twice his age only wish they could do. That's large, Renee. Still, I'm happy for him, and you, of course," Cynthia said, brushing her hair.

Renee stood up quickly and sucked in air as a distant memory flashed into her head—the night their parents called after finding out about the marriage. Renee could clearly see herself walking from the kitchen and seeing Craig's picture on TV in front of the news media, only he had turned the set off when they became focused on the message from their families. Forcing tears away, Renee shook her head. *How could I have forgotten that? Why didn't I remember that, until now?* Her mouth went dry as her heart thumped madly and her pulse raced.

Cynthia stood up and walked over to where Renee stood with her back against the wall, her fingers touching her wedding rings. "Renee, you're pale. Oh, my God, what's wrong? Look, you check things out, but I'll just bet Craig is probably just waiting to surprise you with the news, that's all." Cynthia patted her hand, then filled a paper cup with water from the cooler in the corner. "Here, drink this," she said, pressing the cup in Renee's cold hand. "Renee . . ."

Renee took the paper cup with shaking hands and gulped the water down. "Thank you, Cynthia. I'm glad you told me about this."

"Well, now I wish I hadn't ruined the surprise." Both women stopped talking when other women spilled into the ladies room.

She steadied her breathing and thanked Cynthia. They both left the powder room. Renee saw that Craig was waiting for her and stood up when she approached the table.

"Hey, what happened? I saw Cynthia go in there. Did she say something that upset you, baby?" he whispered, taking for her hand and guiding her to her seat.

She'd decided to let it drop until she did just what Cynthia had suggested: check things out for herself, starting with June tenth. "No, we talked about make-up and stuff." She smiled briefly up at him, although now her mind was still processing the news that he was the owner of the agency and he hadn't even told her. *Why keep something like that, something so significant, a secret? But if others knew . . . why did he keep it a secret from her?*

"You sure you're okay, Renee?" She nodded yes. Craig could only imagine what happened in the ladies' room, but let the matter drop.

Although her heart was heavy and she kept seeing Craig's face on that magazine cover, Renee stayed in the moment. She even remembered the time she had asked him where all his business magazines were. There were none in the house, only magazines on computers and cars. He told her they were all at the office.

Even as they prepared for bed and Craig reached for her, Renee's mind was retrieving bits of information. Things she thought odd—things she had never questioned before, but had just shrugged off. Like why he really wanted to get married, and his witnesses, Davis Franklin and Miss Lilly. There were no best friends there, not Steve or Dan. She didn't believe that he'd been in touch with Miss Lilly like that. Then there's the money. How could he just give her seventy-five thousand dollars? And he'd told her it wouldn't put a dent in his money. So where did the money come from? *He told me he had never committed a crime.* And hadn't Cynthia said he paid a million dollars cash for the agency and then turned around and put thousands of his own money in for upgrades? A million dollars, that wasn't just a business loan—he didn't have that kind of capital. That first time at her apartment, he said he had hoped to buy that agency, one day. One day, she reflected, as in years into the future . . . not in two days.

Renee realized that Craig was kissing her neck. She didn't want those stressful and worrisome thoughts to deprive her of the sheer pleasure of love-making with him. It was like nothing she'd ever experienced. When his mouth captured hers, his kisses took her breath away and comforted her troubled soul. Renee banished her troublesome thoughts as Craig took her to heights so intense she forced her eyes open, thus allowing her tears to flow. It was then that Renee was positive she was deeply and passionately in love with her husband, who was still, after all, a stranger to her.

Craig had sensed something was wrong the moment Renee returned from her trip to the powder room, but he hadn't pressed her. He figured Renee had stood right up to Cynthia. When he reached for her their shared passion-filled night cast his worries away. And when he thought he would die, he cried out her name and knew in that very instant that he would never be able to live without her.

CHAPTER 14

As soon as Vivian Jennings saw the little warehouse clerk leave for lunch, she walked around to the back office of the warehouse where Ray worked. She knew it was his lunch break, and she was hoping to catch him before he left.

Ray was not happy about her visit. "Vivian, you've got to stop taking these chances coming over here. You can get me fired, and if your husband ever finds out, I'm a dead man."

"Oh, Ray, hush up. I don't want to talk about Lawrence. Besides, he's been moody as hell lately; must be a lot of stuff going on at that damn bank. I love you, Ray, and I miss you."

Ray threw his head back in frustration. He didn't want to be hearing this again. "Look, Vivian, stop talking like that. You don't love me; we're just having a good time kickin' it, you know that. We've had this talk before." He saw the shimmer of tears in her eyes and softened his tone. "Look, we're gonna stop this creepin' around real soon, okay?" Seeing the dejected look on her face, he pulled her into his arms, then walked her to the back room where they often shared what he considered just a quick and easy afternoon lay.

But to Vivian, it was heaven. The times she spent with Ray were her reason for breathing.

The lovers were unaware of a pair of eyes watching them with mounting anger. Lawrence had followed his wife the moment she had left the bank. The minute she pulled her car from the bank's parking lot, he knew she was going to meet that low life Ray Newman. Lawrence drove around the back of the warehouse and parked his car on the side street and waited. Within minutes he looked into the dirty side window and was sick and disgusted as he watched the younger man throw his laughing wife onto the dirty couch. But, he forced himself to remember, that was what her being addicted was about. It caused madness and a lack of morality in her. What drug, he wondered, was Ray giving his wife to make her act like that, forcing her to forget who she was and her place in society? Heartsick, Lawrence could no longer watch. He walked stiffly to his car, thinking and praying that nobody would come to the back of the warehouse and see what he'd just witnessed. He had to get Vivian away from that trashy boy.

Thirty minutes later, Ray stood at the metal door watching Vivian pull out of the back parking lot of the warehouse. He'd decided a few weeks ago to break things off with her, but she wouldn't take no for an answer. She kept coming back. He was tired of the creeping around. He wanted a steady girlfriend he could take out on dates. He wanted the little clerk, Carrie. She was so pretty and kind and sweet. Ray had just gotten up the nerve to ask Carrie out when Vivian called him on his cellphone, telling him she was at the back door. Ray closed and locked the metal door and walked back to the front office. His heart lurched when he saw Carrie hurry into the office and punch her time card. He became lost in her mocha complexion, her dark eyes and her cute, petite body. He even thought she might still be a virgin.

"Hi, Ray, I got some fresh cookies. Want some?" Carrie held up a plastic bag.

Ray decided to take a chance and just ask her out right then, and to his surprise, Carrie said she'd love to go out with him.

Almost shyly, he thanked her for the treats and practically ran back to his post at the back end of the warehouse. He was happy. He had a date with Carrie, and he was determined not to be with Vivian again.

CHAPTER 15

Renee had remained awake long after Craig fell asleep last night, her mind almost obsessively processing what she now knew to be facts. Somehow, it all started with her marriage to Craig. Tomorrow she was determined to find out what he was hiding from her, and why.

The day had turned into yet another hot day in a string of hot days, and that didn't help her already frazzled nerves. That morning she had told Craig she needed to get into work early to prepare for a morning appointment. So by seven Renee was at her desk sweating, despite the air conditioning. She was not perspiring because she hot, but because she was mad and getting madder by the minute.

Renee had begun an extensive Internet search of the Davis Franklin Advertising Agency, right up to the date of transfer to and acquisition by Craig L. Thompson on June tenth. Working in an accounting and investment firm had certain advantages, affording the opportunity to search deeply into an individual's financial history. After typing in key identity information about Craig, Renee sat in shocked disbelief as her computer monitor began flashing his financial data before her eyes.

"Oh, my God," she said, "he lied." Craig wasn't just well off. He was a millionaire, and would get richer with all the new business the agency was pulling in, mainly, for now, the NFL campaign. On June tenth he had deposited almost two million dollars into his personal account. Tracing the deposit, Renee saw that a lump sum of almost three million dollars had been initially withdrawn from the Wayland Bank and deposited into his personal account on June tenth. They were married on June tenth.

Renee looked at her calendar and counted backward to that date. She looked over at the small wedding picture on her desk, the one she and Craig had taken with their witnesses, Mr. Davis and Miss Lilly. Her memory of that day became clearer and clearer as she stared at the picture. She focused on the smiling, friendly man, Mr. Davis, and had a clear visual memory of Craig passing the man a white envelope. She remembered Mr. Davis giving Craig a thick set of papers with a blue binder backing. *Thick legal papers.*

She refocused on the picture, this time looking at Miss Lilly, thinking back to a conversation she had with Craig. They were sitting on the patio reminiscing about the old neighborhood and Miss Lilly's name came up. Something clicked . . . if Craig hadn't seen Miss Lilly in such a long time, then how did he come to ask her to be a witness to their marriage? Why hadn't he asked one of his friends?

Renee scanned more articles, write-ups and several website links, all praising Craig's acquisition of the agency. There were too many to count, and yet she knew nothing about it. How had he kept that a secret from her all this time? And why had he? Renee needed answers, and she knew just where to get them. But even as Renee stared at her computer screen, she knew she should have done some checking on Craig long ago. However, she had not, and now she was learning that he was a stranger to her. Once again, her parents and sisters were proven right: she jumped into action before she looked.

⌒

When her doorbell rang, Lillian frowned. She wasn't expecting anyone. She opened the door and beamed. "Renee! Oh my, what a nice treat this is. Come on in here, girl," she said ushering Renee into the living room.

"Miss Lilly, I hope I'm not interrupting your day. But, you know, I was in this area on my way to my parents and just thought I'd drop in to say hello."

"Oh, I don't mind you dropping in anytime you want. Have a seat and I'll get us some refreshments." She'd grown quite fond of this young woman.

"Oh, okay, if it's no bother to you."

"Not at all, honey. You sit down and relax and I'll be right back." Lillian scampered off to the kitchen saying again how nice it was of Renee to come visit her. But it hadn't escaped her eagle eyes that the young bride looked nervous.

Renee looked around the comfortable living room, her eyes going to a shelf and landing on a larger version of the wedding picture on her desk. A sharp sting of threatening tears came.

Why is she nervous? Lillian wondered, filling their glasses with iced tea. Then her hand shook slightly. *Oh, Lord, she knows!* She arranged chocolate-chip cookies on a plate, and bracing herself, carried everything into the living room. Lillian set the tray down on the coffee table and sat beside Renee on the couch. "Okay, we done shared the pleasantries, now out with it. What's wrong?" Renee's sadness was breaking her heart.

"Oh nothing, really, it's just . . ." Renee looked at the picture again and then back at her hostess. "Miss Lilly, why did Craig marry me?" she asked, her tearing eyes both pained and melancholic. She came there for answers, but did she want to hear them? Accept them? Just the thought of an unwanted answer frightened her. She heard Miss Lilly say, "Because he loves you," but Renee persisted. "Yes. But let me ask you this, was there a reason that you know of that Craig had to get married? Maybe something connected to the bank?" Renee watched closely as the now-troubled woman lowered her head. She knew she had come to the right place for answers, and now she had to toughen up to hear them.

Lillian raised her head and reached for her glass. She was not a liar; in fact, she'd never outright lied to another living soul, and she wasn't about to now. Craig had put his own butt into a hot seat. Putting her glass down, she began telling Renee what she knew.

"Honey, Craig called me out of the blue about an inheritance that his grandfather, Reginald, left in a trust for him. Craig had really forgotten about it, had never even inquired about it. That money was in an interest-bearing account that just grew up, for years and years. When he came in to see me, I explained how the inheritance was set up, and that included a stipulation, added a couple of years after it was initially set up." She took a small sip of tea and continued. "I asked Craig if he'd gotten married. Then kind of joking like, that boy asked me if I was proposing to him, can you believe that fool?" Lillian chuckled, remembering Craig's antics that day. "Well, anyway, I told him that his inheritance could only be released to him if he was married and he brought in proof."

The fine hairs on Renee's arms suddenly stood up, so she braced herself. "What was the stipulation, Miss Lilly?"

Lillian didn't see a reason to hold anything back now besides she knew they were in love. "I told Craig that he had to be married and remain married for no less than three months to gain full control over his inheritance. Honey, on that day it totaled almost three million dollars."

Renee felt a migraine coming on. Her mouth went dry, despite having almost drained her glass. "Three million dollars." Renee had already read that in his financial statement. "When . . . did he first come to see you?"

"Oh, that was around the first week of June. He asked what he needed to prove marriage, and I said a marriage certificate, of course. He laughed and looked up at the ceiling saying, 'Good old Granddad.' It was funny, you know, because he just kept saying that," Lillian said absently. "Well, anyway, he called me a couple days later, and he told me that he was well aware of the stipulation and that he had just wanted to know if his grandfather had indeed kept it in there. And then he told me to get his inheritance ready for withdrawal, all of it. He said he would call me back on Monday, and when he did, he told me he was indeed getting married on Tuesday morning at ten. That is when he asked me to be a witness. He just came out and asked me. Of course, I was delighted to be there, you know." She took Renee's small hand when she saw the girl's stricken look.

The tension in Renee's arms began to ease. That was it. Their three-month deal was just long enough to satisfy the stipulation of his inheritance. And why? Because he'd already spent one million buying the agency from Davis, and then he paid her off. For her time and services as a live-in wife, Craig paid her seventy-five thousand dollars. He had said he'd never wanted a committed relationship before, had walked away from those getting too close, and even Cynthia had told her that last night. Renee heard Miss Lilly calling her name as if she were far away.

"Renee, honey, regardless of what you're thinking right now, that man loves you and you know it. So forget all about whatever led up to your marriage. Enjoy being young and in love."

"He's lied to me from the beginning, Miss Lilly. How can I enjoy anything ever again? His marriage to me was just a means to get what he wanted, his inheritance to buy that agency." Renee choked back tears.

"You don't know that for sure. Renee, I was at your wedding and at the reception and again at the cookout at your house. Honey, you two love each other." Lillian waited anxiously for Renee to answer.

"Yes, but love built on a lie is a lie. He didn't want me, Miss Lilly. Well not as he said he did. He needed a means to get that money for the agency." She finally unleashed her tears and they flowed down her cheeks silently.

"Oh, Renee, you can't possibly believe that." Lillian grabbed a napkin and dabbed at Renee's tears, but hadn't she wondered the same thing? "Don't do this, Renee. You have a wonderful husband who loves you. Yes, he may have not given you the whole story up front. But you obviously loved him enough to marry him in the first place. And now the two of you are just starting your young married lives together. Trust me, down the road you and he will make more mistakes, but you'll learn from them and get closer than ever before." Miss Lilly held Renee's hands tightly and spoke in a sympathetic but firmer voice. "Now trust me on that. My Bob and I made a ton of mistakes, and we both were hurt by some of them, but we stayed together as a couple, and with God's help and family support, we toughed it out. We didn't quit because of a misunderstanding or a half-truth, you understand me?" She asked, pinning Renee with a look of stark honesty.

Renee stood up. "I have to leave now, and please don't call Craig and tell him I was here." She saw no point in telling Miss Lilly how Craig had cornered her into marrying him using a promise they'd made, probably right around the time his grandfather added the stipulation.

"Okay, baby, I won't. But you think about what I said, and you call me if want to talk again." Lillian hugged Renee and opened the door for her. Watching Renee get into her car, her thoughts were on Craig. "My, my, my, Craig, you did just what I'd hoped you had not done. You have broken that girl's heart. And you lied to me to get that inheritance." When she closed the door and re-entered her living room, Lillian found herself drawn to the wedding photo—the same photo that Lawrence Jennings had shown particular interest in on another very hot day.

Driving somewhat aimlessly, Renee somehow ended up on Craig's old street. Not knowing what else to do, she parked her car across from his old house and let her head fall back against the headrest. She was transported back to the day he moved away. Her heart had been broken that day, too. The tears came again, but this time they were hot and angry. When she opened her eyes, in despair, she stared vacantly out the windshield.

Renee didn't return to work; instead she drove home and went into the living room, going directly to the pictures on the mantel above the fireplace. She picked up the picture of her sitting on the swing in the backyard when she was nineteen, remembering vividly how she had felt that day. She had decided to take the accounting course at the university, much to her parents' dismay. They'd always dreamed of Renee becoming a nurse because that's all she'd ever talked about doing. But she'd stood her ground and had told her parents and her sisters that it was her decision to make and that she was taking the accounting degree program. In fact, she'd already registered. She told them she wasn't asking for permission; rather, she was informing them of her decision. To Renee, that marked the beginning of adulthood. But it also marked the beginning of the impulsiveness that, unfortunately, led to a succession of bad decisions that she had not fully thought through.

She reached up to the chain around her neck and touched the diamond bicycle pendant. She sighed mournfully, curling her fingers around it. She thought about how she had been the one to set the course of her life then—not her parents or sisters . . . and definitely not Craig Thompson now. How dare he put her in this situation because he wanted his money? He was no better than Charles Hunter. His betrayal had the same effect as Craig's. Both hurt her in the process of getting what they wanted from her. But Craig had bought her for the cut-rate price of seventy-five thousand dollars. Feeling hurt and angry, Renee looked at the picture again, this time without seeing it, and then tossed it carelessly back onto the marbled mantle, where it fell against the others. She had made her decision. She was leaving.

Renee walked up the stairs to the guest bedroom and pulled out her luggage, which now consisted of three large suitcases. She changed into a pair of jeans and a tee shirt and spent the next two hours packing her belongings. Then she lugged the suitcases, including the hard case containing her personal papers, out to the garage and put them in the trunk of her car.

Craig was going to tell her everything. He was in love with her and wanted their marriage to be real in every sense of the word; that meant being totally honest with her. He expected her to be upset with him at first, but he'd planned ahead. After leaving Lawrence that afternoon, Craig returned to his office and had his secretary book a complete honeymoon vacation for him and Renee. He felt good, and the dark cloud had lifted. Once he told Renee everything, he was sure she would understand.

Pulling into the driveway at six that evening, Craig saw that Renee's car was backed into the garage. He figured she probably had brought in groceries. Even better, he thought, they could throw a couple steaks on the grill and maybe take a swim. Whatever. It didn't matter, because his Squirt was there, home and waiting for him. It felt good when he came home now. She made him feel good.

With happiness enveloping him, Craig walked into the house and called for her. "Renee . . . Renee. Hey, Squirt, you upstairs?" He went into the living room and then into the kitchen, thinking she might be out on the patio with Leo. But Craig stopped in his tracks when he saw her sitting at the island, working on her laptop. "Hi, baby. You didn't hear me calling out for you?" She was staring intently at the laptop screen and asked if she brought work home. "Tell me you didn't bring work home again?" He cupped her chin and turned her head from the computer to his lips and kissed her.

Renee broke off the kiss. "No, I didn't bring work home," she said, watching him go to the refrigerator, grab a bottle of beer and take a hefty swig. His kiss warmed her lips and his familiar cologne filled her senses with unwanted longing. Fighting back a renewed urge to scream, Renee hit a key on her laptop to engage the screen saver.

Craig smiled and sat on the stool beside her. "I thought about you all day today." He traced the bicycle dangling low on her chest. His fingers grazed her skin and their eyes met briefly, then she looked away. "How was your day, baby?" Something felt off to him, but he shrugged off the feeling.

Renee glanced up at him. "Informative." Keeping her eyes locked on her keyboard, Renee replied cryptically, "It wasn't a good day for me." She couldn't meet the eyes she knew were trained on her.

Sensing something ominous afoot, Craig's stomach tightened. Concern evident on his face, he set the bottle down and leaned closer to her. He reached for her hand, but she quickly moved it away. "What's wrong, baby?" He searched her face for signs that she was ill. Then he saw a large teardrop fall from the corner of her eye. She wiped it away impatiently. Craig's heart lurched, now certain he was about to get some very bad news. He prayed that no one had died. "Renee, tell me what's wrong?" He soothingly rubbed her back.

She couldn't talk because her pain had become a physical pain. Instead, she reached for a stack of papers that were face-down beside her laptop. The papers were a printout of what her Internet search on him had yielded, even his confidential holdings statements. She turned the papers face up and covered them with her hand as she spoke. "Craig, I told you not to pull me into any drama that was going on in your life, didn't I?'

"Honey, what's going on? What's that?" he asked, pointing to the stack of papers. She removed her hand and he saw his name on a copy of a legal document. He didn't need to read further; he knew that she'd found out that he bought the ad agency. Damn. "Renee, I was going to tell you about that tonight, really I was," he said in a rush, watching another tear fall.

Renee fumbled with the papers and one by one laid each page out, ten in all. The first paper was a copy of their marriage certificate. She'd taken a neon green highlighter and circled the date. Craig could only stare at it.

"Renee, let me explain how I came to purchase the agency." When she turned to face him and Craig saw the anger burning in her eyes, he retreated and tried to regroup. Besides, he reasoned, hadn't he planned to tell her anyway, and hadn't he expected she would probably be a little upset? Still, he was in a panic.

Renee held up her hand to stop him from saying anything else. She turned the laptop to face him and hit a key to disengage the screen saver.

Craig stared at the monitor and saw himself as he had appeared on several business magazines. Then each magazine cover or article headline flashed on the screen. He closed his eyes for a full five seconds before opening them. When he did, Renee had picked up her carry-all bag and dumped several magazines onto the island countertop, causing some of the papers to fly about. Some landed on the floor.

"Craig, I've told you over and over again that you could talk to me and tell me anything. But you purchased that agency and it's a secret. Why, Craig?" Renee pointed to the magazines. "All of these magazines, as well as the stories on the Internet, are full of praise for what you have accomplished. They all applaud that maneuver, but you don't even mention it to me. Why hide that from me?"

Her quiet voice gave him a false sense of security. *Okay, maybe she wasn't all that upset.* "I-I don't know why I didn't tell you, but you're right. I should have told you, baby. I came home tonight to tell you all of this . . ." He waved at the papers and reached for her then, his lips feverishly claiming hers. Renee turned away.

"I'll bet you didn't tell me because then you would have had to tell me where you had gotten so much money from." He stared back at her, looking frightened and she ached to smooth the worry lines from his forehead. *Stay strong, girl . . . he hurt you . . . no matter how you feel about him.* "Stupid me, here I thought maybe you'd committed some sort of crime, and I even told you that I didn't want to get caught up in any business that was unethical that you may have gotten yourself into. But the joke was on me, wasn't it?"

Craig said nothing. His eyes searched her face for a glimmer of something, anything, he could latch onto. His chest tightened with each passing minute.

Renee turned over the last two papers in the stack. "Well, that was a wonderful thing for your grandfather to do. You know, he used tease Annette and me whenever I came to your house. You know how we'd make up our faces and paint our nails and act like dancers in front of the mirror? Well, one day he walked by Annette's room and just stood there shaking his head at us. Then he laughed and said, 'You gals had better pick another career to bank on or eat a whole lot of potatoes.' She laughed. "You know, Craig, I think his sense of humor is what probably prompted him to add a stipulation to your inheritance. I'll bet he did it to put you in your place after you were mouthing off about something. What do you think?"

Craig couldn't think; just breathing was becoming an effort. He closed his eyes, knowing she was probably correct that his grandfather added that clause to teach him a lesson.

Renee saw the pain and shadows crossing his face and again her heart ached to comfort him. *Stand firm, you're nobody's doormat . . . not anymore, and never again.* "Look at me, Craig, and tell me I'm wrong. Tell me that you didn't just marry me for the sole purpose of getting your inheritance." Seeing the truth in his sad eyes, her tears renewed themselves. "It wasn't about you wanting to get married because you were ready. You had to get married and that is all I was, just a means to your money. It wasn't about the promise. It was just about you getting your money, wasn't it?" she shouted, her voice and face tightening with anger.

Finally finding his voice, he croaked, "No, you were not a means. I love you, Renee," he said, looking into her eyes. "We love each other." She stepped down from the stool and walked around him to pick up her purse from the side counter.

He jumped up and walked over to her. "Baby, listen. I know it may sound like that's what happened, but it wasn't like that. I honestly was going to tell you about this tonight." He pointed at the papers, his voice pleading. Frantic, he wondered what she was going to do. "Renee . . ."

Renee got a tissue from her purse. "It doesn't matter now, Craig."

"Yes, it does matter." He reached into his jacket pocket and pulled out the airline tickets and hotel confirmation. "Look, I've been planning a honeymoon for us. Baby, let's just sit down, order some dinner and talk this all out. Please, Renee. Let's talk this out and I'll make everything right again. I promise." He tried to pull her into his arms.

Renee backed away and looked up at him and laughed bitterly. "You promise? Craig, you should never say that word ever again. You can't promise me anything because you don't know the meaning of the word promise." When he reached for her again, Renee slapped his hand away and jabbed her finger into his chest. And this time when she spoke, little doubt was left as to how angry she was. "You've held my teenage promise over my head, and after seventeen years, you call out of the blue to hold me to that promise . . . but never again, Craig. I was such a damn fool for believing you would or could sue me if I didn't marry you. In fact, you must think I was a fool to buy into that load of bull, because I did. But I'm not totally blaming you, Craig. I allowed myself to get in this situation, which shows my faults. I was reckless and I didn't think about the ramifications of my hasty decision. I take ownership of that," Renee said, shaking her head and snatching up the marriage license, papers and magazines from the island and throwing it all at him. Despite her intense effort to suppress it, an anguished sob managed to escape. "I bet that's exactly what you must have thought when I showed up at the courthouse on June tenth! It was such a busy day for you!" Having said her piece, and having dismissed his feeble efforts to explain, Renee stepped around him and walked into the living room, stopping briefly by the marble coffee table to pick up her car keys.

Craig watched her helplessly, a sinking feeling in the pit of his stomach, "I never thought that, any of that." He followed her as she walked to the door. "Where are you going?"

Renee reached the front door then, her hand was on the knob. She blew out a breath and turned to face him. "I'm out of here. What's the point of me staying and talking it out? There's nothing to talk out. Craig, in case you're not getting the big picture, this . . ." she said, spreading her arms wide, "this marriage isn't real. This marriage defiles the reasons people get married. This defiles what we said before God because it wasn't really in our hearts then. People get married for love, Craig. Like my parents did and your parents did, and even Miss Lilly and Mr. Bob did. That is what real marriages are based on—real love and honesty, not money." She bit her lip. "This hasn't been real from the beginning; it has all been make believe, and it has been of your own creation, orchestrated to the point that you even set the terms of our deal." Just as he reached for her, she turned back to the door. "And you paid me for my services, didn't you?"

"What?" Craig thundered, knowing she was talking about the money he had given her. "That's a damn lie. I gave you money, and it was not payment for anything. You know that." He knew everything else she'd said was right, at least initially. But things changed; he changed. He fell in love with her. Craig searched his brain and tried another approach. "Renee, listen to me, I gave you money from my heart. We're not a lie, and neither is our marriage. Honey, listen, I'm sorry that you found out about this before I had a chance to tell you. But I was going to tell you tonight . . . and I get that you're upset right now, but please, let's just sit down and talk this out. But, baby, don't go out like this. I can understand if you want to get some air, but not like this. Squirt, everything's going to be okay, I promise you that." Craig winced inwardly at having used that word again. "Baby, I'll make everything right again. I will. We're going to be okay." He moved closer to her until he was near enough to caress her cheek. Then he leaned forward to kiss her,

moving closer still, desperate to hold her in his arms. He was desperate to keep her from leaving.

Renee was suffocating. He just didn't get it. Turning her face away from his kiss, she moved out of the circle of his embrace. With her hand behind her back, she turned the knob and said, "Goodbye, Craig." Then she turned and walked out the door.

Craig stood in the doorway and watched her walk to her car and drive off, and only then did he turn and go back inside and rest his back against the closed door.

"Shit!" Craig exploded, storming into the kitchen, stepping over the papers and magazines to grab another beer. He gulped it down and grabbed another. Then he saw that Renee's laptop was still on. He went over to look at it and began scrolling through the documents saved on the desktop under his name. Craig felt as if his world had just crashed and was slowly burning. But more important, he didn't know where Renee had gone, or when she was coming back.

He got a bag of chips from the cupboard and another beer and carried them both into the living room, where he flipped on the TV and flopped down on the couch. "Okay, I'll give the Squirt two hours to go to the mall or the bookstore and calm down. Then she'll come home."

But almost three hours later, Craig was awakened by an overly loud commercial on TV. He fumbled for the remote and turned the set off. Realizing he'd fallen asleep and it was dark outside, Craig thought of Renee and became alarmed.

He went into the kitchen and turned the light on. He reached for his cellphone and dialed Renee's cellphone number, praying she was maybe still at the mall and on her way back home.

Renee had finished unpacking. She took a call from her sister about gift for their parents' upcoming anniversary, took a call from Simon, put the groceries away she'd picked up at the mini-market and now she stood back, looking around her kitchen. Renee now felt disconnected from the place that she enjoyed cooking in so much. Her windowsills were bare because she'd taken her few plants over to Craig's. The floral curtains hanging at the window looked foreign. Walking back into the living room, Renee stared up at the stained-glass window and hugged herself in an effort to hold her tears inside. They fell anyway, so she just let them. "Oh, God." Renee blamed herself for her own weakness. That was something she couldn't blame on Craig. It was she who allowed herself to be duped and made a fool of because she had thought he could protect her from Charles. As she sat on the couch and stared into space, Renee suddenly realized the thought of Charles no longer seemed so frightening to her.

When her cellphone rang again, she grabbed a couple of tissues and angrily wiped at her eyes before answering it. She saw it was Craig calling, and she prepared herself. In her state of anger, she'd resolved not to let his voice and silky words pull her back. "Hello."

"Renee, baby . . . it's late. Where are you? When are you coming home?"

She shook her head against the longing just hearing his voice stirred. "I am home, Craig . . . my home, where I should have always been."

Craig stood in the living room staring at the TV screen. "What? Renee, this is your home, here with me. Please, baby, come home." Craig thought he sounded like a lovesick wimp, but at that moment he didn't care. He needed her. "I'm sorry, Squirt. Please come home."

"I told you, I am home. Leave me alone, Craig," she said, snapping the cellphone shut.

Craig just stared at his cellphone for several minutes. "Okay, so she went back to her apartment to chill out . . . okay, she needs a little space. I can deal with that," he muttered as he headed up to his bedroom. He stripped off his clothes and stepped into the shower, hoping that would ease the pain he felt. After ten minutes, he realized he didn't feel any better. Reaching for a towel, he noticed for the first time that Renee's toiletries were gone the vanity counters.

The sinking feeling he initially had after speaking with her on the phone returned. Why had he brushed it off? Wrapping a towel around his waist, he went into the bedroom and saw that the few items she had on the dresser were also gone. Craig rushed down to the guest bedroom. Everything had been cleaned out. He went back to his bedroom and sat down on the loveseat, his mind tumbling. His stomach lurched painfully when he saw Renee's wedding rings on the table. But everything else in the room that was hers was gone. He knew then that she was really gone. She had walked out. She had left him.

❧

Ray opened the door to his motel room and was taken aback to see find Vivian standing there. "Vivian, I told you we needed to stop. We have to," he said, backing away from her.

Vivian saw the freshly starched shirt and pressed slacks hanging on the closet door. "It looks like you're going out, Ray," she said, her tone accusatory as she slammed the door closed.

Ray was tired of this scene and told her he had a date with Carrie.

"Oh, please, you mean that little country girl down at the warehouse?" She stared at him unbelievingly. "Spare me, Ray, she's barely out of high school," she sneered at him.

Her hard words, delivered in a condescending tone, upset Ray and he responded in kind. "She's not a little country girl, and she's twenty. But then you must have forgotten that I am younger than you by a lot of years, so that makes me closer to Carrie's age than yours, now don't it?" He knew then that he'd hit a nerve, at the same time bringing her down a peg or two.

With rising heat, Vivian glared at Ray. She was furious at him now. That was a weak spot for Vivian, and although she was attractive, she was much older than him. "So what then, Ray, you going to bring her back here to this dump?" she asked, her anger now blazing.

"That isn't any of your business." Ray walked to the door and opened it. "Please leave and let's just let things end on a positive note. We've had a lot of fun, but it's over."

"She can't give you what you really want, now can she, Ray?" She stepped out of her dress and walked over and kissed him.

Ray was still torn, but he succumbed the moment her hands went around his neck. She did make him feel good. When she laughed at his weakness, Ray promised himself that would be the very last time that he would allow this to happen. He glanced at the broken wall clock. He had less then forty minutes to pick Carrie up, and he would be damned if he'd let Vivian prevent that from happening.

In the empty motel room below Ray's room, Lawrence could hear Ray and Vivian above him. He could hear Ray's grunts as he forced himself on his wife. He heard each creak of the bed. He also heard Vivian practically offering herself to Ray. She couldn't help herself; after all, Vivian was addicted to the drugs Ray gave her. Still, hearing her guttural sounds and gutter mouth was more than Lawrence could bear to hear. But he did hear, and he beat back the urge to cry like a baby. *Damn you to hell, Ray Newman.* Thirty minutes after he saw

Vivian go up the concrete steps to Ray's room, Lawrence watched her traipse back down. He watched her get into her car and drive off, and he didn't miss the angry look on her face, either.

❧

Renee awakened after tossing and turning all night long, and her body was loudly telling the tale. Then she forgot that her apartment was closer to her job than to Craig's house, and she ended up arriving an hour early for work. She was surprised to find her friend Leslie was there. "Leslie, what are you doing here so early?"

After Leslie briefly explained the baby being fussy that morning, she turned to Renee. Although she had gotten past her friend's quick marriage, Leslie was anxious to hear how Renee was handling married life and her husband's new job title and took that opportunity to ask her. "Is your hubby working longer hours already?"

"What do you mean, Les?"

Leslie grinned shyly then said, "Well, we know it's all still kind of hush-hush, but with Craig now running that agency, I can just imagine he would be spending a lot of time there and, well, maybe you're feeling a little neglected. That's all I meant, but I understand. Actually, Renee, we all do. Girl, that's why we haven't pressed you for details and all. We all remembered what happened when Shelia's husband won that big lottery. Well, it was all over the news and people were following them, and she was a wreck. Remember, she told us in this very room that her only solace was here at work because she didn't have to hear everybody talking about it, looking at her and asking her a bunch of questions." Leslie didn't mention that the receptionist, Maryann, even went so far as to remove many of the magazines with the story of Craig's ownership of the agency from the lobby. "Too bad they packed up and left town. I really liked Sheila."

Renee stared at Leslie's mouth as she talked. *She knew . . . they all knew.* All she could mutter was, "Yeah, you hit the nail on the head, Les."

"But you and Craig are okay, right?" Leslie asked, passing Renee a bagel.

Get a grip. Renee looked blankly and said, "Uh huh."

Leslie let the subject drop as she turned the TV set on to check out the morning news. The two women were so busy talking, they never heard the news report of a hit and run accident out on Highway 14. The anchorwoman said that a young black man had been seriously injured by a driver who had failed to stop. The young man had suffered several broken bones in both his legs and one arm, according to police. His other injuries included a ruptured spleen, head trauma, and a massive loss of blood. The young man's family and friends were said to be standing vigil at the hospital and waiting for hopeful news on the condition of Ray Newman. His mother, a prominent member of Hayview Baptist Church and a well-known community member, had made a plea for the driver who had plowed into her son as he crossed the highway to turn himself in to the police.

❦

Lawrence had just watched the morning news. "Oh, good Lord," he said, as his housekeeper, Grace, poured him his first cup of coffee.

"Isn't it awful?" Grace declared. "I mean, who would do such a thing? Just left that poor young man out there, all hurt and broken up like that. Tsk, tsk, tsk." She looked up when Vivian breezed into the dining room. "Morning, Miss Vivian. I trust you slept well?" Vivian held her cup up for Grace to pour her coffee.

"I slept just fine," she said, eyeing Lawrence as he peered at her over his own cup. "So what's all broken up now, Grace?" she asked, casually lifting her hair back off her shoulders.

His eyes still on Vivian, Lawrence made a mental note to talk to her again about the dismissive tone she used with Grace.

Grace handed Vivian a watered-down cup of coffee cup. "Nothing's broken, Miss Vivian, we were just commenting on that terrible hit and run accident last night," she said, walking back to the kitchen.

Vivian ignored Grace and sipped her coffee, feeling content and thinking about Ray.

"Dear, aren't you the least little bit concerned about one of the residents of this town being injured in such an accident?" Lawrence asked, looking at Vivian above his glasses.

"I guess. Lawrence, when do you plan to talk to Grace?" She met his stare by tilting her head in the direction of the kitchen. "She hates me and she always does or says things to really annoy me, like this coffee for one . . ." Vivian was about to set her cup on the saucer when her hand started trembling. Her eyes had strayed to the TV set in the corner of the dining room. The local lead story was about Ray. A smiling picture of Ray Newman was in the background of the screen. In the foreground, a hospital representative was describing major trauma. *Major trauma* . . . Vivian's entire body began to shaking from head to toe. *No. God, no.* She heard Lawrence say something and forced her attention off the TV screen and looked at him.

Seemingly engrossed in the morning paper, Lawrence glanced up, anxious to see his wife's reaction to her lover's accident. "What's wrong, dear?"

"What? Oh, nothing. I-I just have a headache, that's all." Lawrence was staring at her. "Oh, this is terrible news, isn't it?" Vivian wanted to run out the front door and to go to Ray. He was hurt. Tears pricked painfully at her dry, unblinking eyes. She silently prayed for Ray as she looked into her husband's curious, watchful eyes.

"Yes, terrible. I believe that reporter said it was a hit and run. Too bad." Lawrence reached for another piece of toast. "You're looking quite thin lately, or are my eyes tricking me?" He smiled, glad that Grace fixed the raisin bread the way he liked it, only slightly toasted.

Vivian was irritated by his rambling. "What are you talking about?" she asked, immediately feeling remorse for her tone. "I'm so sorry. I haven't been feeling well, and I've been coughing a lot." Vivian was all the while silently praying, *Ray, please, please be okay . . . I'll get to the hospital as soon as I can.*

"Then, Vivian, I expect you to make an appointment with that doctor you used to work for, Dr. Strass." He sipped his coffee, his eyes steadily watching her as she picked up the remote from the table and began flipping through TV channels to catch more snippets of the news story on other local stations. "You know what, Vivian? I think I know that young man," he said lightly as he reached for his orange juice. He knew he had her full attention then.

Vivian's hand trembled, forcing her to put the remote down. "What?"

"Yes, yes, I sure do think I know that young fellow. He comes into the bank every week to cash his paychecks. I think he's kind of taken with one of the new tellers." He let out a little laugh and said, "I tell you that boy will stand at that girl's window for the longest time, turning the poor girl all shades of red."

"Really? That's interesting," Vivian replied weakly.

"I'm going to put some scrambled eggs and toast on a plate for you," Lawrence said, getting up and walking over to the breakfast buffet, aware that her eyes were trailing after him. "Here you go, dear," he said solicitously, placing the filled plate in front of her. He leaned down and kissed her forehead, saying nothing about her suddenly clammy skin. "So what's on your schedule today Viv? Going to get your hair done?"

To Vivian, Lawrence's voice sounded like a horn being blown directly into her ear. "I'm meeting a couple of girlfriends for lunch." *Trauma and internal bleeding . . . yes that's what I heard that newsperson said,* Vivian thought.

Lawrence knew his wife's few friends and she rarely met any of them for lunch . . . for a game of poker, maybe. He knew she would be at the hospital, taking care to keep a discreet distance from her lover. "Well, my dear, I'm off to work, but you finish eating and then have Grace draw you a relaxing bath. You'll like that, especially if you're coming down with something." He kissed her dry lips and left the dining room.

The second his car backed out of the driveway, Vivian pushed her plate across the table, knocking over her forgotten coffee cup. But she took no notice of the spreading brown stain on the lace tablecloth. In utter despair, she let out a mournful wail and hugged her body as she cried silently.

Grace was only mildly concerned as she went about cleaning the kitchen. She was used to Vivian's wails, moans, complaints and nasty comments about everything from her cooking to her cleaning. She decided at that moment to put a load of towels into the washer.

Craig's morning fared no better. He overslept, making him late for an appointment. When he returned to his office and sat down at his desk, he immediately looked at the picture of him and Renee at their reception party. His throat tightening with emotion, he picked up the picture as if it was a fragile thing and then he reached for the telephone.

Renee's office phone rang six times before she answered. "Hello, this is Renee." She heard an intake of breath and knew that Craig was on the other end.

"Hi, please don't hang up," he pleaded quickly.

"What do you want?" Renee had already decided she wasn't going to act as if things were fine when they weren't. She listened as he explained about waking up late and missing the start of an important meeting. "I never oversleep, baby."

Please don't call me baby. "You overslept last weekend and missed your tennis game with Dan." *Now, why did I go there? I'm the reason he overslept last Saturday.* Renee closed her eyes and wished she hadn't brought that up.

"That was because I woke up with you in my arms. Renee, I . . . I miss you. Please come back home. Let's talk. Let me explain things."

Enough of this, Renee's mind screamed, but she told Craig she was not coming back to his house, as it was all part of the Big Lie, the fake marriage, and there was nothing to straighten out and nothing for him to explain. Renee's eyes drifted to the wedding picture on her desk, but she forced herself to be strong.

"Our marriage is not a lie. I love you, Renee, regardless of everything else, and I know you love me, so why can't we move past this?"

Renee recognized that he was pushing for what he wanted . . . her. "Craig, you didn't trust what you now call love to be honest with me in the beginning, so now you want to move past this? What you mean is for me to forget what you've done. Well, that is not going to happen. And in case you haven't noticed, I'm not that same little preteen who used to believe that the sun and moon came and went upon your shoulders. So again, I'm not even going to entertain your need to work things out . . . to explain things and move past this situation, because *this situation* is of your own making, not mine." Renee was breathing fire, her angry words filling her office. At that point, she didn't care who might have heard her.

Craig just listened to what was basically a rant. And if he'd had any doubt about the depth of her anger, it had disappeared in the face of her unflinching fury. She was right about everything. It was his fault. But he refused to give up. "Can we get together for dinner tonight?"

"No, Craig." *Don't let the tears fall,* she prayed. Then she heard him begging her to call him, if she needed anything, like money . . . *Oh, no, he didn't.* Through clenched teeth, Renee snapped, "I was paid, remember?"

Hearing her stinging words, Craig felt like shouting in frustration and pain, but he didn't. "I gave you a gift, and you know damn well it wasn't any kind of payment. Look, if you need something, please just call me, Renee?"

"No," Renee assured him, her voice tired, slow. "I won't need you for anything."

He didn't want to ask the question pressing him most; he didn't want to hear the answer she would probably give. But he had to ask, "So what happens now? To us, I mean?"

Renee's tears slid down her cheeks upon hearing the emotion in his voice and in contrast, seeing his smiling face in the picture. She remembered his touch and what she thought was a happy marriage and a beautiful relationship in the making. "There is no us, Craig. There never was. I guess that, um . . . we just divorce then." She angrily plucked several tissues from the box on her desk and wiped her eyes.

Craig couldn't even wrap his mind around the word divorce. He'd just gotten accustomed to being married— and liking it. Divorce meant not having her in his life, in his heart and in his bed. "No, Renee, I won't divorce you. I don't even want to talk about that."

"I'll file for divorce, but I'll let you have the honor of going to my parents' house and recording it in the family Bible. You'll have to do it, because you created this situation."

"No, Renee, I . . ." Taking a deep breath, Craig steadied himself. Speaking in a firmer voice, he said tightly, "We love each other, damn it. Why should we end our marriage without so much as talking about what happened? Why won't you let me explain the situation that, yes, I created? But I'll tell you one thing, I won't be recording anything in your family's precious Bible, either." He didn't wait for her to respond. He hung up the telephone and got up from his chair. He stood by the window and was about to call her back to apologize for hanging up on her when a knock on his door pulled his attention away from his misery, momentarily.

$\backsim$

The rest of the afternoon seemed interminable, Renee so she decided to leave work thirty minutes early and by the time she reached her apartment, loneliness hung over her like a dark and menacing cloud. The absolute quiet, bothered her, and she wondered why, it hadn't before. She made her way to her bedroom and crawled into bed, pulling the covers over her head and went to sleep. She never checked her answering machine, never knew about the missed calls.

Craig's afternoon ended on a sour note when he took a call from Lawrence Jennings. He had put the man off long enough, and it was time to make the final payment. But he detected a new desperation in Jennings's voice.

His friend Dan had called earlier and, hearing something in Craig's voice, he had decided to stop by the house. He was waiting by the pool with the neighbors' puppy, Leo, when Craig arrived home. "Hey, man, you look like hell," Dan greeted Craig when he stepped onto the patio. Getting a cold beer from the bar refrigerator and passing it to Craig. One look at his friend's face and he knew what had happened. "She found out and she walked, huh?"

Craig nodded and gulped down the beer before dropping his tired body down into a chair across from Dan.

Craig watched Leo anxiously looking into the kitchen through the closed patio door. The puppy let out a little bark and stood on his hind legs, his wet nose pressed against the sliding glass door, looking for Renee. Leo walked to the other glass door, looked in and then padded over and sat on the edge of the pool staring into the water. Craig almost laughed when Leo turned and looked back at him. "Yeah, Leo I know. I miss her, too."

Taking in the scene, Dan could only shake his head again. "Oh, great, two lovesick puppies I gotta deal with. Okay, I'm here, man, so talk to me and tell me how you plan on getting your wife back." Just as Craig was about to speak, Dan held up his hand and called out to Leo. "Hey, Leo, come on over here, boy. I think you might want to hear this, too."

Craig and Dan laughed heartily when Leo ran over and jumped up into Craig's lap, something he'd been too afraid to do before.

CHAPTER 16

A full two weeks had passed since Renee had moved out of Craig's house. She had decided to take Friday off to spend a three-day weekend at her parents' to help celebrate their anniversary. She was glad to be leaving the apartment because the loneliness and lack of sleep were getting to her, and she'd been receiving a lot of hang-up calls at all hours of the day and night. She screened her calls because she believed most of them to be either Craig or Charles.

Early Friday morning Renee drove out to her childhood home. Everyone was expected to arrive at the house Friday morning to prepare for the event . . . her parent's thirty-fifth wedding anniversary and a renewing of their wedding vows. The ceremony and party were planned for Saturday afternoon in the Richards' backyard. She knew she would be way too busy to even think about Craig or to focus on how much she missed him.

Coming into the back door, Renee was glad to see the kitchen full of family. But she was shocked and stunned to see Craig standing in the kitchen helping her mother cook breakfast.

When Craig saw Renee, his heart thumped madly. "Hi, baby, you made it," he said, making a show of checking his watch. He walked over to Renee and stood with his back to everyone. His eyes touched her everywhere he'd dreamed about.

Renee was in shock. She hadn't expected him to be there. "I didn't expect to see . . ." The voices of so many people fixing breakfast plates prevented her from saying more.

Craig and Renee seemed to be in a state of suspended animation until he took Renee's chin and kissed her, lightly. Then he pulled back and reached into his jeans pocket and extracted her wedding rings, easing them onto her finger.

Renee looked at her rings, feeling detached. She didn't want to kiss him, didn't want to feel her body heating up at the very nearness of him, but it did. But the voice in her head screamed, *You dummy, he used you.* Despite the fact that she missed him, missed the way his smile touched her soul, she was going to stand firm. "Craig, can I talk to you out on the back porch?" Renee walked out the back screen door.

Craig turned and whispered to the family, "Bet she thinks I forgot the gift, but I didn't."

With everyone laughing, he stepped out on the porch and sat down, watching Renee pacing. "What's that look, Squirt?"

She sat down beside him. With her voice just above a whisper, she asked, "Craig, what are you doing here?" She merely rolled her eyes when he simply said he was invited and, like her, he was staying all weekend. She stared at him. "You can't stay."

Several moments passed before he answered. "I'm staying. Honey, regardless of what's going on between us right now, your family is now my family and I'm here for them, too. I think it's wonderful they're doing this, renewing their vows, recommitting to each other," he said, his eyes voice heavy with meaning.

"What about our divorce, Craig?" she asked with a sinking feeling.

Craig stood up then leaned over and whispered in her ear. "And . . . there will be no divorce. I love you and I'm going to fight to get you back into our marriage, even if that means giving up everything else . . . and I mean everything else, Squirt." He kissed her cheek and then walked back into the kitchen, leaving her on the porch, wretched and befuddled.

Going to the edge of the porch and flopping down on the back step, Renee replayed in her mind what he'd said. She looked up at the sky. She vowed to avoid him as much as possible and try not to let her family know that something was amiss with them.

⌒

By five, the house had been cleaned, cleared and decorated. The backyard had been transformed into a sight to behold, worthy of yet another wedding reception. Renee walked to where Craig was sitting on the swing in the yard.

"This is really nice, Renee. Kind of reminds you of our reception here, doesn't it?"

"Yes, it's nice." Renee watched him unfold his tall body from the swing, grinning.

"Only difference I think is that . . . well, I'm pretty sure that by this time tomorrow night, old boy Harold and Lena will be getting busy doing the wild thing," Craig laughed, moving his hips suggestively. He began walking backwards when he saw her livid reaction over what he'd said, then he took off running.

She shrieked, then she sputtered, then she advanced on him, her eyes deadly. Renee's hands were balled into fists. "I can't believe you said that. Craig, I'm so going to strangle you!" she yelled and took off chasing him around to the front of the house. There she was pulled up short and stood speechless. Craig was sitting on the front porch swing, which had been taken down years ago due to worn beams.

Craig smiled at her as she slowly climbed the steps. "Surprise."

"Who put the swing back up?" Renee asked, running her hand along the heavy chain and remembering the hours she'd spent on that very swing—far too many hours to count, most of them daydreaming about the boy she had a crush on . . . now her husband.

Craig smiled. "I did. I started working on it before you arrived, but I managed to finish it." He took her hand, encouraging her to sit beside him. "Didn't you wonder why everyone found some way of keeping you off the front porch today?" Her reaction told him that she'd just figured that out. His heart beat faster when she finally sat down beside him. Studying her face he said, "Renee, honey. Please talk to me."

Renee swallowed hard. Turning to look at him, she said, "This weekend is way too important for Mom and Dad; there isn't room for our drama." She kicked her foot and put the swing into motion, enjoying the gentle swaying and reveling in the cool breeze that came with it.

They remained like that until someone inside called out that it was time to go to the club for the combined bridal shower/bachelor party. Craig silently vowed to talk to Renee again before the weekend was over.

Four hours later, everyone was back. The minute Lena told Craig that he and Renee were set up in Bryant's old room, Craig wasted no time in lifting a stunned Renee up over his shoulder and sprinting up the steps.

Renee looked from him to the double-size bed. "We're not sleeping together," she said.

"Renee, we're married, and your family expects us to share this room and that bed," he said, pointing to the bed.

She knew he was right and shook her head in defeat. "Whatever. I'm too tired to think about it." Her mind was in turmoil as she went to take a shower, but truthfully, she didn't trust herself to be in such close confines with Craig. She returned to the bedroom thirty minutes later and found it empty. From the voices drifting up from the first floor, everyone was still up and playing cards. She was almost asleep when she felt him sliding into the bed. She turned to face him with a tight, angry expression. "I thought you decided to sleep downstairs."

"Nope, I played a game of cards and then took a shower in the downstairs bathroom," Craig said, ignoring her scowl and adjusting the covers. "Let me tell you, Renee, your parents need a bigger hot-water tank in this house." Ignoring her protests, he eased her to turn back around to spoon with her, murmuring against her neck. "But I think the cool water helped things a bit." Craig was glad she couldn't see the wide grin spreading across his face, though he did laugh out loud when she punched her pillow and threw her head against it, and then bunched the covers up behind her to create a barrier between their bodies. Craig's plan was a simple one . . . he was going to make Renee fall back in love with him, starting with that weekend.

Both Craig and Renee slept soundly for the first time in two very long weeks.

∼

Craig presented his in-laws with a wedding gift from him and Renee. A honeymoon cruise to the Virgin Islands. Renee pulled Craig to the front porch and said, "Craig, that was a very generous gift. It's going to make them wonder about your financial situation."

"No, they won't. I told them that I'd gotten an inheritance. I didn't specify how much, and they didn't ask. I reassured them that I plan on taking care of you." He recalled looking at her purposefully when her parents signed the family Bible again, daring her to say something.

As the reception wound down, Renee found Craig sitting on the swing and sat down beside him. She saw that he was hurting as much as she was. "You look tired," she said. She missed them sitting on the patio and talking for hours, until they were both yawning.

"I am. I've been busy, but glad to be, you know." His eyes met hers.

She only nodded and turned her head. She recalled her conversation with Simon that morning. He'd told her that the local authorities had found Charles Hunter in Florida and that, once taken into custody, he would soon be extradited to Houston. Simon also told Renee that she was only one of four other women in the Houston area Charles had swindled out of their money. "Craig."

"Hmm?"

"I know we have played the married couple this weekend for my family's sake, but it does not change things between us. I'm hurt by what you did. But I'm also angry at myself for falling into your deception. For all my smarts, I feel so dumb for not checking things out, things that were right under my own nose." She shook her head, recalling the conversation with Leslie, then met his eyes. "I've made a lot of mistakes since the last time we sat on this swing together all those years ago, Craig, but I won't again . . . I cannot do that to myself."

"I'm sorry I hurt you, Renee. I honestly never thought you would be hurt. Please don't be angry at yourself for anything. I hate myself for what I've done to you. I only wanted . . ."

Cutting off his pleading voice, she said, "I know what you wanted, and you got it, Craig."

"But I don't have you, Renee, so nothing else matters."

Renee stood, looked up at the sky. "Craig, you never really had me, nor I you. For now, we're just married strangers, with secrets between us."

Renee turned and went back inside the house, leaving Craig outside. She returned to the bedroom and thought about the irony of her situation. Craig's secret was out and yet she could not tell him the secret that brought her to the courthouse that day.

CHAPTER 17

Vivian Jennings had been a physical and emotional wreck from the moment she'd heard the TV reports describing Ray's broken body, and she could get no information on his condition. It was now nine in the evening and she had disguised herself by dressing down, by wearing sneakers and tucking her hair under a baseball cap. She spotted a nurse she'd seen previously and pulled her aside, all but begging the woman to let her in to see Ray.

The nurse finally relented, and Vivian's weak legs carried her to Ray's bedside. "Oh, dear God . . . Ray. I'm so sorry this has happened to you. What monster did this to you?" she whispered, touching his fingers, which dangled from the cast on his right arm. She crumbled against the bed and buried her face against his upper arm, the only part of his body that wasn't cut or stitched or badly bruised. Sobs wracked her body and tears flooded her anguished face.

Fighting through a fog of pain medication, Ray's eyelids jerked and his eyes finally opened a crack. Looking down at the baseball cap, he would have laughed, but he instinctively knew that it would be too painful. He heard Vivian, her voice calling out to him.

Vivian felt a slight movement and raised her head. It was Ray's hand. His fingers curled weakly around hers, and her eyes flew to his face. "Oh, Ray . . . you're okay, baby. Ray, you were in a car accident. You just keep healing inside and your body on the outside will heal, too. Do you understand me, Ray?" When he blinked yes, she sagged with relief. "Don't be scared, because I know that you are, baby. I have been praying for you every day, all day." She saw that he was struggling to speak and she lifted a corner of the tape holding a tube in place, in the corner of his mouth. "What is it, honey?" Her eyes darted to the various monitoring screens.

Although it was difficult to move his tongue, Ray did manage to say, "Pretty Viv . . . ugly hat." He managed a faint smile through swollen lips, and Vivian had not seen a more beautiful sight in all her life.

Vivian gazed upward thankfully, her prayers had been answered. "I've got to get the nurse, but Ray, you're going to be okay inside," she urged. Vivian ran to the door at the same time the nurse burst in after the monitor at the nurse's station indicated Ray's status. She rushed out. "He's awake."

The nurse rushed to Ray's bedside, then said to Vivian, "I guess you're just what he needed then. Okay, you go now," she said, just seconds before pressing the emergency call button. Suddenly, lights flashed and an insistent beeping could be heard coming from Ray's room. Vivian backed down a corridor as several nurses and doctors rushed into Ray's room.

Vivian ran to her car on the back parking lot and rested her head on the doorframe, then she stepped back and threw up. Only one thing mattered: Ray was awake.

Lawrence had just left a meeting with Craig Thompson and was sensing that the young ad man was stalling, buying time. Passing around the front of his car, he briefly glanced at the new fender and hood. He drove home thinking about what Craig had said about the money being tied up for a couple more weeks because some people at the bank had some inquiries about the inheritance. But Lawrence hadn't bought it, even as he reminded Craig of all he stood to lose.

Craig had charged back at him, suggesting Lawrence check with his bank people. Lawrence was desperate. He needed that money, and he needed it now.

Lawrence drove home, anxious to check on Vivian. She'd been sick all week, but he knew what was really wrong with her. "Ray," he uttered the young man's name with a disgusted feeling and blinding fury as he drove. He figured that whatever it was Ray had given Vivian to get her addicted in the first place, it was most likely the cause of her being so ill. Probably some kind of withdrawal, he assumed. He vowed to keep an eye on Vivian for her own good.

Renee was at a busy downtown pasta and pizza eatery with Simon Donovan. It was lunchtime and office workers had to scramble for every available seat. She was thus sitting rather close to Simon. She felt very small but also very protected next to the large man.

At forty-two years old and married, Simon was good-looking man, with his Italian heritage showing i his black hair, dark eyes, olive skin and his love of any thing Italian. In the months since she'd known Simon Renee had come to trust and like him. She watched him smile as the waitress set their steaming plates of baked zit in front of them.

Renee remembered the calls from Charles had beer on-going for a couple of weeks, and then Charles threat ened to kill her. That was the weekend before she'd mar ried Craig. She reflected Charles's voice, which used to sound laid back, seductive and funny, had turned angry vicious and serious. Renee recalled her heart beating wildly when Charles threatened to kill her. And so she sought what she thought was a safe haven . . . in Craig.

"Renee . . ." She looked up, embarrassed for having let her mind drift back to that conversation with Charles that day. "Sorry. What'd you say?" she asked, tackling her ziti.

"I said so how was it living with your folks again?" Another lie. She debated whether to tell him Simon about Craig, and then decided against it.

"Well, I only stayed there a few weekends, just to re center myself and tune out Charles's calls. That's why I told you to only call me on my cellphone. I'm back home now."

"Yeah, it's hard to go back home sometimes. When Rhonda put me out last year, I stayed with my folks." Remembering, he shook his head sadly. "After six days I called Rhonda and begged her to let me come back home

BERNICE LAYTON

because the last thing I want to do is to have to move back home with my folks," he said angrily, piercing his baked ziti with his fork.

Renee laughed. "Oh, Simon, they were probably just glad to have you home."

"Bullshit! Renee . . . it was weird," he said, his lips tight. "Okay, here's the deal, and don't you dare laugh, but I found out, well . . . they . . ." Looking painfully embarrassed, he leaned closer to Renee's ear and continued, "Those two still have sex, and I heard 'em." He pulled back and grimaced. "I was sick. I couldn't even look at my mother the next morning. And there she was humming while she was making the pancakes. I took my cellphone to the cellar and begged, pleaded and cried to Rhonda to let me come back home. I promised to buy her a top of the line SUV and I ran my ass home that morning." He shook his head and resumed eating his ziti.

Renee couldn't help laughing, and couldn't stop. In seconds, she had dissolved into a giggling mess. His eyes fixed on his ziti, Simon saw no humor in the situation he'd described.

Craig would recognize that laugh anywhere. He turned and saw Renee sitting with a large man. He watched her trying hard to stop giggling. Then he saw the man lean closer and whisper something, causing her face to turn even redder. Craig's nostrils flared as he experienced a range of emotions—jealousy, anger, pain. He felt them all as he glared at the man whispering in his wife's ear.

Dan tore himself away from his lunch long enough to check out what his friend was staring at so intently. "Hey, isn't that Renee, Craig?" He turned back, but Craig was already standing. Looking doubtful, he said, "Hey, be careful, he looks bigger than you and me."

"Oh, eat your stuffed shells," Craig grumbled. He had no awareness of walking across the crowded restaurant, but he was suddenly standing in front of the still laughing Renee and the mystery man. "Good afternoon, Renee," he said quietly.

On hearing Craig's voice, Renee sobered instantly. Her heartbeat quickened when she looked into his eyes. His intense eyes pierced hers. She looked from him to Simon, and swallowed nervously when she saw the tight look on Simon's face. On guard, he had eased his hand from the table to inside his jacket, where his holstered gun rested. "Oh, I-I'm sorry, Simon, this is my old friend, I told you about him, remember?" Renee quickly stammered, resting her hand on Simon's arm.

"Vaguely," Simon said, standing to shake the stranger's hand. But he was very much aware of Renee's discomfort in the presence of the tall brother.

Craig took Simon's extended hand. "Craig Thompson, pleased to meet you."

"Likewise," Simon said with a steel edge to his voice.

Both men remained standing until Renee tugged on Simon's sleeve to let him know everything was okay. Then her eyes returned back to Craig. "How are you, Craig?"

"Fine, and you?" The man remained standing, eying him with suspicion.

"Fine," Renee was definitely not going to invite him to join them, as good manners would dictate. What she really wanted to do was run out the door and leave both Simon and Craig there staring each other down. "Well, thanks for stopping over."

Craig knew a dismissal when he heard one, and that is what she was doing. "Okay, then, you take care." He offered a curt nod to the stranger before turning to go back to his table.

After Craig walked away, Simon sat down and pinned a look on Renee. "Okay, who was that? And don't lie. Just act like I'm your big Italian brother and start talking, lady."

She desperately wanted to tell him everything. She wanted to tell somebody what she'd foolishly gotten herself into. "That's Craig. I told you he'd called me out of the blue, after many years, so we have been sort of, dating."

"Oh, so that's the guy you had a crush on when you were a kid, huh?" Simon smiled. "Well, why the hell didn't you say so? I wouldn't have given him my killer stare." Simon's arm was now resting on the back of Renee's chair.

"Oh, is that what that was?" she asked, trying not to look in Craig's direction.

"Renee, you're my client and my friend, regardless of the fact that you pay me. I usually don't become friends with my clients. Now my goal is to protect you. Even when you don't sense danger, I do, and that guy seemed very possessive of you. So, why is that? And don't bother feeding me any bull 'cause I can smell that over my now cold ziti here."

Craig watched Renee with the man and didn't like the fact that he seemed very possessive of her. He shook his head to chase away even the thought of Renee having an affair with the guy. No, he wouldn't let his mind go there. He fumed within when the man draped his arm across the back of Renee's chair, as if he was quite comfortable doing it. *That sonofabitch!* his mind screamed. He tore his eyes away as a series of expressions crossed the man's face as he listened intently to whatever Renee was saying.

Dan wiped his mouth with his napkin. "Man, that was good," he said. "So who is he?" he asked, looking at a scowling Craig.

"I don't know. Some guy she barely introduced as Simon. Let's go." Craig didn't want to stay a minute longer. He extracted a few bills to pay for their lunch and strode out the exit door—in the opposite direction of from Renee. He didn't think he could just walk by her without pulling her into his arms—after punching that Simon guy in the face, of course.

That thought clung to Craig back at the office. Justin and Joyce were working on the mock-ups for the NFL campaign. Try as he might, Craig was just not up to sharing their enthusiasm. He walked out of the conference room, feeling their puzzled eyes on his back.

When Craig passed the reception area, heading to his office, the receptionist announced he had two visitors. Craig was surprised to see James Tinsly and Miss Lilly waiting to see him. He immediately braced himself, knowing this would not be a pleasant little visit.

"This is a surprise, you two here," Craig said, once they were in his office. He hugged Miss Lilly and shook James's hand. The two men shared a look that didn't escape Miss Lilly.

After a conversation he'd had with Lillian a few days ago, James had decided to stop in to see Craig personally. "Craig, please forgive us for just dropping in on you like this, but things have taken a new spin regarding Lawrence Jennings." He was all but whispering. "Can you spare a few minutes? We won't take up much of your time."

"Sure, James," Craig said, looking from him to Miss Lilly. Not knowing how much the banker had told her about their plan for Lawrence, he decided to speak cautiously. "Please sit, and I'll get you both a cold soda."

As Craig prepared them sodas, Lillian noticed the same sad look on his face, was what she'd seen on Renee's when she visited her. Glancing around his office, she also thought his grandfather would have been so proud to see his grandson come so far.

The three sat around a conference table in Craig's office. "Okay, James, since Miss Lilly is here, I can only assume you've told her everything and things are worse."

James nodded, "Yes, unfortunately, it is worse. And yes, Craig, I've told Miss Lilly everything. But she in turn told me some things that I think you need to be aware of." James paused, his troubled eyes meeting Craig's. Lawrence's betrayal went deep with him. "I trusted that man. I have trusted him with other people's money, and those people had put their trust in me and my bank. But,

Craig, your inheritance account had been compromised for years and . . . and I never knew it because Lawrence had managed to cover his tracks using money from other accounts. One in particular, maybe two."

Craig listened as they told him of the discrepancies, all the while assuring him that he had received his full inheritance.

Miss Lilly said, "A few years back, Mr. Jennings told me—ordered me, really—to stay out of those dormant accounts when I asked him about them once. He said he could assure me that all was right with them. He said the account holders were getting their proper quarterly statements and annual reports. He even told me he'd received calls from those customers to personally thank him for handling their accounts so well."

Craig listened carefully as James reported tracking, thus far, eight hundred and fifty thousand dollars that had disappeared from the accounts, including his. Finally, he said, "Well, that doesn't sound good."

James said, "When you and I met, we put things in place to catch Lawrence dipping into that other account. I'd planned to call him on his deceptions and fire him, right?"

"Right. So what's changed, other than the fact that Lawrence is getting antsy and has been pressuring me for the balance of the money he's extorting from me?"

"Craig, that other dormant account holder is a Mrs. Esther Henderson. She and her husband entrusted a scholarship fund to my bank back in the early eighties. Even after they moved to Boca Raton, Florida, when he retired, the account remained in my bank. The grants were college scholarships for underprivileged African Americans kids. Those grants are still being made, but now in much smaller amounts. The grants were to be dispensed in allotments of five and ten thousand dollars for each year the student stayed.

Craig sat up straight. "Are you telling me that Lawrence stole money intended for underprivileged kids?"

"Yes, I believe so." James continued on. "The account should have been transferred to a bank in Florida. Her grandson was to be the trustee, only it never happened."

"Well, I hope you've talked to Mrs. Henderson about finalizing those changes in light of these suspicions concerning Lawrence," Craig said. James' lips thinned.

"No, I didn't. I can't talk to her at all now. Mrs. Henderson passed away some eighteen months ago. I just found out three days ago," James said.

Craig could see that the man was in turmoil, so he looked to Miss Lilly. "If this Mrs. Henderson has been deceased for eighteen months, and the grandson was never named trustee . . . wait . . . are you telling me that the account was never transferred from your bank to the bank down in Florida?"

Lillian looked from James to Craig. "Yes, that is correct, and the account is active, with withdrawals filtered through an account at the Wayland Bank. About three weeks ago, money was put back in to cover a previous withdrawal from the Henderson account."

Craig could only stare at her, dumbstruck. That is until James said, "Lawrence deposited two hundred and fifty thousand dollars into that account. Craig, we've traced the original check that I gave you to pay off Lawrence, and he did just what I thought he would. He deposited the money in an account he had at another bank, then he turned around and withdrew it, only to deposit a check into the Henderson account. Oh, it has different account and routing numbers, but it's the same account. I'm quite positive money from those accounts has paid for Lawrence's lavish lifestyle, like his cruises and vacation trips. His spending far exceeds what he's paid by me. His money never came from his deceased wife's estate. I have discovered that Naomi Jennings left him a mere fifty thousand. Oh, she sent him a message," James said with a shake of his head.

"Elaborate of Jennings. So you got him by the balls? Sorry, Miss Lilly," Craig said.

James twisted his hands and rushed on. "Yes, in a sense we've got him. However, a visit by Lawrence to Boca Raton, Florida, eighteen months ago has given rise to new questions."

"What?" Craig bolted from his. "Are you telling me you think Lawrence had something to do with the woman's death? Would he have had a reason to go Boca Raton?"

"No, not really, Craig, but the coincidence of him being there for a mini-vacation and the woman dying around that same time, well, you can see where I'm going, can't you?"

Craig was aghast. "Theft is one thing, but murder? I don't know, James, that's a hell of a stretch, even for a greedy bastard like Lawrence." But then he thought about his own situation and what he had done for money. "But then men have done far worse for money."

"Or for a woman," Lillian said quietly.

Neither man chose to comment on her observation.

"Well, the figures don't lie, but I'm having a reputable investigative firm check it all out. They'll do the rest of the legwork, but when the time comes, Lawrence will not just be kicked out of my bank. I intend see him behind bars."

"I'll do whatever you need me to do to help James."

"Thank you, Craig, but what I think we'll need is your promise to prosecute Lawrence when the time comes. Would you have a problem with that?"

"Hell no, not at all," Craig said with conviction, and he meant it.

But Miss Lilly made him think about what prosecuting Lawrence really meant. "Craig, if you agree to see that Mr. Jennings goes to jail for what he's done, well, for you that means disclosing all the financial information relating to your inheritance . . . *everything* concerning your inheritance," Miss Lilly stressed. She took his hand. "Honey, that means anything that Mr. Jennings could throw back at you in court. That could cause some embarrassing revelations for you and Renee both." She knew she'd hit home when he sat back in his chair.

He closed his eyes briefly, then opened them. "Well, as James said, the figures don't lie, and neither will I. But, in any case, I'm on board with seeing Lawrence pay. I wonder if his wife is a part of this," Craig said absently.

James shook his head. "I seriously doubt she could even plan something so devious. Besides, he's been married to her for only four years, and his thefts go back almost twenty. Vivian Jennings is only hanging onto Lawrence either because he has money or because she is waiting for something better to come along. Unfortunately, Lawrence hadn't wanted to hear any of that when folks tried to warn him about getting tangled up with a young woman like Vivian. In any case, the warning had come too late because by that time she'd already begun to weave her spell around his . . . heart."

Lillian pursed her lips with a knowing look. "Yeah, and he was too stupid to realize it. But, trust me, Vivian Jennings has her own thing going on, and it doesn't include Mr. Jennings." She sat back and crossed her arms disdainfully.

The two men laughed, but stopped short when Lillian shot them a disapproving look.

"Well, I don't think that boy getting hurt like that was funny. I like him and I like his mama. She's a real good friend of mine, and she is devastated," she said, sniffling.

"Miss Lilly, who are you talking about?" Craig asked with raised eyebrows.

"I'm talking about Ray Newman. Didn't y'all hear about that hit and run out on Highway 14 a little while back?" Craig shook his head no. "Anyway, that poor boy was run over and left for dead. Thank goodness that motel where he lives had an early-morning delivery of supplies, cause it was the deliveryman who found him and called an ambulance. It's just so sad." Lillian cried into tissues she had pulled from her purse. Craig and James were immediately at her side. "The deliveryman, bless him, said that he had thought it was some large animal. He told the news reporters he went to take a closer look, and poor Ray was so mangled and bloody that it looked to him like Ray was hit and then backed over," Lillian related, crying harder.

"Wait, are you saying that Vivian Jennings is having an affair with this Ray fellow and he was involved in a hit and run?" Craig asked her.

"Uh-huh, and I wouldn't say it was so if I hadn't seen the two of them doing it with my own eyes down at that warehouse," she revealed. "But regardless, he's a nice boy," she said sadly. "I mean any healthy man would take what was so freely given to him, you know. Still, it's just so awful."

"I can't imagine anyone hitting someone and then just driving off, not even stopping to help. That is just shameful, a terrible thing to do," James said.

"But if someone hit that guy on purpose and left him to die out on that road, well, that would be criminal." Craig didn't like where his thoughts were going.

"Right. What if, let's say, a jealous husband found out about his wife's affair, maybe by following her—that's not hard to do—wouldn't the husband know exactly where to find the guy?" Lillian offered, seemingly unaware that she had even said aloud a thought that had crossed her mind more than once since she heard about Ray's accident.

The two men seemed lost in their own thoughts, but they heard her loud and clear.

❧

A few days after her lunchtime encounter with Craig, Renee arrived home and found more recorded messages from Charles. His voice was rushed, almost panicky. The messages had an urgent edge to them. She wasted no time calling Simon. Within an hour he was at her apartment armed with another recording device for her telephone. He was accompanied by his wife Rhonda, who stressed to Renee that she should not be alone.

Renee liked Rhonda the moment they had met, months ago, and even than Rhonda told her the same thing she was telling her again, now. "Renee, you need to talk to someone about what happened to you before your pent-up angry fuse blows," she said.

Renee just shook her head no. "You know if I had been conned out of my money by a stranger, I would have screamed it from the roof-tops of buildings and plastered up billboards of Charles's picture. But the fact that I was involved with him, intimately, well, I'm just not prepared to tell anyone about it. Most of all my family, they're all aware of my history of making bad decisions and even worse judgment calls. Rhonda, I'm just not ready yet," Renee said.

"Listen, Renee, regardless of this guy being an ex-boyfriend, he is the one who made a bad decision, not you, and he needs to be caught. But you have my number whenever you are ready to talk," she said.

Simon ignored the exchange as he prepared to listen to the messages, but his attention was immediately drawn to a stack of papers laid before him on the coffee table. He saw what looked like a certificate with Renee's name on it.

Simon had never taken his wife on a case with him, but was glad he did a few months ago. In fact, Rhonda had insisted tagging along after he told her about the calls Renee had been receiving. Then Rhonda reminded him that Renee could be in serious danger if the ex-boyfriend made good on his threats, and came after her. Simon knew the dangers all too well also.

∽

The following morning, Simon sat in his office reading. A friend down at the Bureau of Records had faxed him—a marriage license issued to Renee Richards and Craig Thompson on June tenth. He re-read the document and said aloud, "Renee, what were you thinking?" Sputtering a stream of profanities, he reached for the phone and dialed her home phone.

Renee had just sat down to work on her laptop when Simon called. "Hi, Simon, what's up?"

"Why don't you tell me, Mrs. Thompson?" Simon said, hearing a sharp intake of breath and her feeble, 'huh.' "I didn't stammer; you heard me." Simon wasn't going to give her any leeway. "What did I tell you? I expect my clients to be what with me? Come on, tell me, my one requirement is . . ." He was waiting for her to say it.

Renee felt her throat constricting. "To always be honest with you," she choked out.

"That's right!" Simon exploded. "So what happened, Mrs. Thompson? Oh, and let me guess. I met hubby at lunch the other day, didn't I?" Simon's voice was edgy but controlled.

"Yes . . . oh, Simon, I wasn't thinking." By now, Renee was well into an-all out cry.

He hated when women started crying. Damn. He softened, visualizing her sad face. "Hang tight, I'll be right over. Aside from this new issue you've gotten yourself in, the tail I've had on Charles Hunter hit pay dirt earlier today. The local cops will be serving the arrest warrant sometime tonight. There was a wrinkle in the plan, but I'll tell you all about it when I get there."

Renee hung up and steeled herself mentally for the tongue-lashing and lecture she knew she was going to get from Simon. He really was like an older brother to her. He was protective and didn't want to see her get hurt again. But his anger would be no different from how she felt about herself. At that moment, Charles Hunter wasn't her primary concern, Craig was.

Sick with a migraine and an upper respiratory infection, Vivian believed she was bearing the pain and discomfort of guilt while Ray was steadily improving. She had left the hospital thirty minutes earlier. He was still horribly broken and swollen, but he was conscious and enjoyed having her visit him when she was able to sneak in. She sat down wearily on the edge of her bed, cursing the motorist who had hurt him.

Lawrence was in his office waiting for the monthly employee meeting to start. He was chairing the meeting. Included on the agenda was his presentation of very impressive figures that showed new business was up by 62 percent.

Glancing down at his watch, he wondered if Vivian was making yet another of her trips to the hospital to see her lover. Over the past three weeks, he'd tried talking to her, but she'd completely shut herself off from him . . . and he hadn't counted on that happening.

Lawrence closed his eyes. Vivian had never refused him before. That had infuriated him to the core. But that night, and every other night since Ray's hospitalization, she had completely shut down. But Lawrence wasn't a stupid man. He knew she wasn't ill just because of the drugs, either. He was watching her downward spiral, and he was powerless to help her without letting her know that he knew of her relationship with Ray Newman.

Racine Hilton called out from his doorway that the meeting was about to start, putting an end to his thoughts. He dismissed Racine with a curt nod. He didn't like Racine, not at all. He felt her watching him, and had the distinct feeling that she talked about him behind his back. Lawrence didn't trust Racine Hilton, not one bit.

Lawrence was surprised to see James at the meeting. He almost never attended these monthly meetings. Lawrence wondered why the bank president was really there. Too bad. Lawrence had planned on slipping away to process a check through his baby account. But with James there, he couldn't. He told himself, once again, that he was doing nothing wrong.

To Lawrence, it was the ultimate in respectability to be accepted by upper-class society folks, and money was the tangible proof of that respect. He had been there once before—when he was married to his first wife, Naomi. She'd been kind and generous to everyone except him. Upon her death, she left the bulk of her estate to her daughter from a previous marriage. All she had left him was the house he now lived in and a mere fifty thousand dollars of her vast estate.

Lawrence recalled being handed the sealed letter she'd left for him with her attorney. In it, Naomi detailed Lawrence's womanizing and affairs during the course of their marriage, especially early in the marriage. She described the humiliation she felt when she knew her friends talked about her behind her back because of his lecherous ways and the whores he preferred over her. She said she could never forgive him that and wished him to suffer the same kind of humiliation and embarrassment that she had endured daily as his pitiful wife, who stayed with him throughout a twenty-five-year marriage that had produced nothing but heartache.

As the discussion dragged on around the conference room's large table, Lawrence's mind wandered and Vivian's face floated before him. *Well, Naomi, you've gotten your wish,* he thought, feeling heat rising to his face. He was sure that Vivian would be better away from

Ray Newman, and away from this town, but only he would know it would be a permanent residence change.

⌐⌐

Renee waited for Simon in the lobby of the downtown courthouse. He had called her to reschedule the previous night's meeting because he'd forgotten he and Rhonda had plans. Renee was glad he rescheduled. Last night she hadn't looked forward to their talk in the first place.

Meanwhile, Craig continued his barrage of calls and e-mail messages. Her response was always the same, their marriage was over. His lies had blinded her to the possibility of any kind of relationship with him. After this business with Charles was over, she'd vowed she would never be that thoughtless ever again. She couldn't understand how she could have let Craig box her in like that. But then she did know why . . . she needed his protection. That was her deal.

Renee heard laughter coming from a couple walking toward her hand in hand. She could tell they'd come to the courthouse to get married. The happy couple practically skipped their way past her . . . so in love and so full of expectations for their future. The emotional tugging on her heart was so intense a sob escaped her and echoed in the hallway. Renee quickly covered her mouth and looked around, but nobody was paying her any attention.

Although she at first hadn't seen a future with Craig beyond the three months, she knew she wanted to be his wife forever. Her heart beat just a little bit faster when she recalled the sheer happiness she'd had with Craig—a happiness she'd been longing for her entire adult life. She recalled the times when she'd wake up in the middle of the night and stare at his face in slumber, seeing the grown-up face that she could only imagine when he was just a teenager.

Taking a deep breath, Renee still loved Craig. With all her being, she loved him. But as much as she loved him, Renee couldn't get past his betrayal and his lies to get his money. She looked up when Simon touched her shoulder. But when another sob escaped, Simon reached down and pulled Renee up into his arms.

"Are these tears for the tall, serious brother?" Simon asked sarcastically. Renee just bobbed her head. "Uh-huh. Why?" he asked, handing her a handkerchief. When she didn't answer, he asked, "Renee, are you in love with this asshole?" He knew what her answer would be, but when she didn't answer him, he released her and rolled his eyes upward.

"Yes, I am," Renee admitted, sitting back down on the bench.

Simon ran a hand through his short hair and sat down beside her. "Okay, first thing first. Here's the deal: Your first asshole, Charles, was arrested by U.S. Marshals in Tampa, and his sorry butt is being transported back to Houston today. He tried to run, but they caught him. He'll be officially charged at the arraignment today, and let's hope he doesn't make bail."

Renee's tears stopped immediately. "He'll be back here today?"

"Yep, and I'll be there when he's brought before the booking facility commissioner." He asked if she wanted to be there and explained the process. "That's when he'll be officially charged and bail will be set. There's a strong possibility that he won't get bail considering the level of threats and the fact that the bank folks want their piece of him, too. They won't want him free, he is a flight risk. You really don't get to say anything, but as one of his victims, it's a good show for you to be there, but not required. But, I should tell you that if he gets bail, then he'll be out on his own until his trial date. He'll be free to walk the streets." Simon avoided looking at her directly.

"Well, let's just pray he can't make bail because he'll make good on his threats and come after me, won't he?" Fear gripped Renee. "I know he will."

Simon knew that was a risk. "Look, let's just hope he doesn't and we'll go from there. But Renee, why not take a vacation about now? Or, better yet, go on out to your folks home."

"No, I'm not running away again."

"Okay, how about we put you up in a hotel, something nice with lots of pay-per-view and a mini-bar and mini-fridge?" He nudged her. "Come on, splurge on a five dollar candy bar."

"No," she said with conviction this time. She refused to let Charles force her from her apartment. Not again. She'd already done that and it was costing her dearly.

"Okay, but you call me if anything, and I mean any-thing, happens that you think may be somehow con-nected to Charles. Don't think about it, just call me." She nodded yes. He took her hand and stood up and led her down the hall. "I'll speak to a couple of the patrol guys in your area and ask them to keep a look out for anything odd, and I'll make sure they get a picture of Charles," he said, trying hard to reassure her. "Let's go get something to eat and then you can tell me all about loser number two. Sorry, make that husband. I expect you to be honest with me, Renee as to why you felt you had to marry that loser, okay?"

Renee smiled up at him. "Okay. But, Simon, Craig isn't the bad guy you think he is. Really, he's actually a wonderful man, who . . ."

Simon stopped and turned her to face him. "Who broke your heart. Now, in my book that makes him a loser." He could tell by the way she curled her lips that a smart retort was coming.

"You're just jealous because he's good looking," she said with a sarcastic grin.

"Bullshit. I'm good looking. He broke your heart." He was daring her to say he was wrong as he stared at her. "You feel like pasta?"

Renee laughed at him, "Pasta again? How in the world do you and Rhonda stay so trim with both of you eating so many carbohydrates. It's not good, you know?"

He laughed with her, pulling her to his side and kissing her forehead. "Oh, we work it off, sweetheart, trust me, we work it off." When Renee's jaw dropped open, Simon's laughter could be heard up and down the hallways of the old courthouse.

⌁

Minutes earlier, Craig had rounded the courthouse hallway from the opposite end and spotted Renee standing with Simon's arms around her. He thought the two of them had looked rather close sitting together on the bench. He then altered his first assessment that there was nothing going on. He couldn't believe that Renee would have gotten involved intimately with her number five so quickly. But watching them leave, he saw Simon kiss Renee and put his arm across her shoulder as if he had a right to.

Craig sat down on an empty bench and pinched the bridge of his nose. His life seemed to be spinning out of control and he was falling, head first, to the cement ground. He had barely slept since Renee had left him, except for the two nights at her parents' home. At his home everything was a reminder of her, making him miss her even more. When he fell into bed, sleep was elusive, but thoughts of Renee weren't. She filled his dreams, and he would wake up angry and lonely. He missed the cuddling and affection thing with her more than ever . . . he missed having her in his life.

He was also worried about her, but was powerless to help her. She evidently didn't want any involvement with him. And he desperately wanted to know the extent of her involvement with this Simon guy.

Craig couldn't imagine not having Renee in his life. She had branded him with her touch, her smile and her love. She loved him. She'd said it to him freely and without hesitation. And he loved her, but it seemed to him that she'd moved on already, and that was something he just couldn't accept. Not having her in his life was one thing, but Renee in the arms of another man. No. The possibility was real and heartbreaking and unacceptable. He loved Renee with all his heart, and she hated him. Once again, he found himself on the verge of tears.

Thankfully, he didn't break down, because he looked up and saw Alex and Dale walking toward him. The three headed for a meeting with city solicitors regarding a district rezoning area south of downtown Houston. If it all worked out as he was expecting, Craig saw another profitable venture for the agency. But try as he might, he couldn't get excited even about that.

❦

Simon leaped up from his chair. Glaring down at Renee, he bellowed, "Damn it, Renee, you can't possibly be that dense! That idiot couldn't have charged you with breaking a freaking promise that you made with him on some freaking swing when you were, what again? Twelve years old! Come on, give me a freaking break!" His outburst had attracted the attention of several patrons and wait staff. Simon wiped his forehead and sat back down, pulling his chair closer to the table.

Renee patted his arm, trying to get him to calm down. "Simon, I was scared to death. That weekend all I thought about was how vulnerable I was sitting there, and how I could escape Charles's calls. I didn't sleep at all. You had to leave town on that emergency, and then you had an arrest on that other case. I couldn't reach you, Simon. What else could I do?" she said angrily, thinking she sounded as dumb as Simon's expression showed.

"Duh! You could have told him to go screw himself . . . or better yet, you could have called my office to send me an S.O.S., and then I would have told him to go screw himself. Is any of this ringing home for you? Renee, have you slept with this nut case?" He already knew the answer. Shaking his head, he leaned back, looking as though he had reached the upper limits of his patience. He watched her nod her head.

"And now you love him, right?" When she nodded again, Simon dropped his head forward and moaned. "No, no, no! We all say what's necessary to get laid, honey." Fighting the urge to curse at her, Simon tried another approach. "Okay, well, does he love you?" he asked, biting his lip.

"He said he does. And yes, I believe him."

Simon remembered the look of possessiveness on Craig's face in the restaurant. He picked up his glass and signaled for the waitress to bring him a drink. Somewhat calmer now, he turned back to her. "Well, for what it's worth, I'd say he seems hung up on you, too. Look, Renee, I care for you like my own sister. I'm not like this with other clients. I don't give two shits about their personal lives beyond my job. If they screw up, oh well," he said, throwing his hands for emphasis. "But, sweetheart, you know I only have your best interest here. Did that idiot force himself on you . . . I mean . . ." At a loss for words, Simon grabbed up a breadstick and angrily bit into it.

"I know what you mean. No, he didn't. But he did hurt me with his deceit. Simon, I only thought about how he could protect me if Charles came after me," she said.

"Uh huh, and that somehow ended up with you marrying him and jumping into the sack with him, right?" Simon drummed his fingers on the table, still trying to control his mounting anger. Fighting the urge to shake the living daylights out of her, he blew out a long breath instead. "Renee, you know those women in those sappy, black and white movies? You've seen them, damsels in distress, right?" He didn't wait for her to answer. "Well, anyway, they're always in some sort of peril or some shit like that, and they have to get away from the villain, you know, the bad guy, the rogue," he said, punctuating his words with his hand gestures. His lips tightening, he continued. "Anyway, these dumb ladies, damsels in distress, always take off running away from the bad guy and they always end up falling down in their dumb-ass high-heel shoes. Well, sweetheart, right now you remind me of those women in those movies. And you should get up right now and go running away from me because, right now, I'm the villain here, the rogue," he said, jabbing his chest. "Well, honey, I would just push you to the floor and that way, I wouldn't have to sit back and watch you make some stupid attempt to run, only to fall flat on your face." When he saw the pools of tears fall to her cheeks, Simon stopped talking to his words sink in for a few minutes. He snatched his drink from the startled waitress and gulped it. Only then did he reach for her hand.

Renee went hot with anger and snatched her hand away. "You're right, Simon, I am stupid, but you're wrong calling him an idiot or a loser or an asshole, because he's not. He's, he's . . ." Renee lowered her head and dabbed at her tears.

"Yeah, yeah, yeah, sweet as apple pie, smooth as honey and great in bed, right?"

Renee's fuse blew then, and she immediately regretted telling Simon anything at all. Her hands slapped the table. "That's right! He is all of that, and don't you dare call him names again. If anybody is an asshole and a villain, you're right, it's you. That's why Rhonda kicked you out before. Now get out of my way." Renee had had enough of Simon at that point. After having had her say she stood up, scraped her chair back and barged past him. But as she made her way to the door to leave, she heard Simon call after her, as did everyone else.

Simon didn't care that everyone was watching them like spectators at a tennis match. "Be careful of those villains, and don't fall in those damn high-heels," he called out to her.

To her chagrin, everyone looked from him to her, then down at her high-heeled shoes.

Simon evaded the narrowed eyes and then the pinched look the waitress gave him as she dropped his plate of spaghetti in front of him with a thump. He turned to the window and he saw Renee waiting to cross the street. He watched as she pulled a tissue from her pocket. *Damn crying woman,* he thought.

By the time Renee had collected her mail and climbed the stairs to her apartment she was an emotional wreck. She was just glad that Charles was behind bars for now and she didn't have to constantly keep looking over her shoulder and driving around the block before parking her car. She entered her apartment and let her weary body lean against the closed door. When goose bumps suddenly pricked her forearms, Renee was immediately on guard and silently flipped her keys in her hand into a defensive stance. The room was dark, with just a sliver of light coming from the street lamp outside her living room window. Her body remained stationary as Simon's parting words leaped into her head and she eased one foot, then the other, out of her high-heeled pumps in case she had to run.

Her hand on the doorknob, she called out in a strong voice, "Who is in here?" She blinked when the light came on and was startled to see Craig lounging on the couch. His face was angry and weary.

"It's me, your husband." Craig stretched and sat up but remained on the couch.

"This is getting old," Renee said, dropping her mail on a table and walking further into the living room. "And you're only my husband until the divorce is final."

Craig kept his eyes on her. She was just as she was in his dreams, beautiful and walking toward him, her hair framing her face. And she was barefoot. "I told you, I'm not divorcing you, Renee," he said, rubbing his tired eyes. Again he could see Simon kissing her forehead, his arms around her shoulders. He looked at her hand, bare of her wedding rings. They were back in his jewelry box because she'd returned them to him at the end of the weekend festivities celebrating her parents' renewal of their wedding vows.

She walked back to the door and opened it. "Craig, I want you to leave."

He walked up behind her and pushed the door shut. "I'm not leaving. I want to talk to you. I've been trying to talk to you since you moved out, but you have denied me even a simple conversation. Why is that, Renee?" he asked quietly.

She turned and looked up at him. Standing so close, she could smell alcohol on his breath. "Because I have nothing to say to you, Craig. What did you plan to say to me, huh?" She mimicked his deep voice. "Oh, geez, Squirt, I really am sorry for lying to you and I didn't really mean to screw up your life?" When he reached out to touch her shoulder, she shrank away from him and walked over to the fireplace.

Her imitation of him brought a tiny smile to Craig's face. "Yeah, something like that."

"Well, don't bother. I don't want to hear anything you have to say. That is why I haven't returned any of your calls, or answered your e-mails. And stop sending me those e-mail cards. They're clogging up my inbox." Okay, she thought, some of them were funny and cute, but others were just sad, especially the ones with kittens and puppies. "Craig, our three-month deal is over and you got what you wanted. Now I want it over with so that I can get on with my life." She hadn't meant for her voice to take on such a hard edge, but it had anyway.

"With your new friend?" Craig threw the word at her as an accusation.

"What are you talking about?" she asked, mystified.

"I'm talking about your chummy friend, Simon. The one you barely introduced me to, the same one you were arm in arm with at the courthouse earlier today." He towered over her, but his heart was breaking. "How could you do that, Renee? I'm dying here, and every day it is just an effort to get up. How could you do that?"

"Do what? Besides, Simon is none of your business, you hear me?"

He turned away and then whirled back around and faced her again. His voice rising, he said, "I'm officially making him my business. You got that?"

"You've been drinking, and you need to leave . . . better yet, I'll call a cab." Renee said, finally grasping what he was talking about. *He thinks I've got something going on with Simon!*

"Is he honest with you, Renee? Is he perfect and doesn't screw things up like I do? Is he what you want?"

Craig's words were slurred and he was having trouble swallowing past the stabs of pain he felt.

She saw it then and she heard it in his voice. He was hurt. But more than that, he was jealous. He thought Simon was someone special to her. "Simon is my friend and, yes, he's . . . well, he's painfully honest with me. I never expected you to be perfect, Craig . . . just honest. You're the one who put that expectation on yourself and on everybody else. So don't you dare stand there accusing me of doing whatever when that's what you've done. You alone thought you could play God to get what you wanted—and I guess you did."

He knew she was right, from her moving out, right down to Lawrence Jennings' extortion. "You're right." He touched her face briefly and then sat back down on the couch.

It was then that saw the bottle of scotch on the coffee table. "I don't think that will help anything, do you?" she asked, pointing to the bottle as he refilled his glass.

"Helps me . . . helps me not to miss you so much." He lifted his eyes to hers. "I thought you were fair, Renee. You told me that I could talk to you about anything. Do you remember saying that to me?" Craig was so tired it was an effort to talk. He gulped his drink and welcomed the burning sensation he felt from his throat down to his empty stomach. It meant he could feel more than just pain and anger.

"Yes, I remember." Renee sat down in a chair across from the couch.

"But when I wanted to talk to you—to tell you everything, and there's a lot going on—well, you just turned your back and closed me out. How is that fair, Squirt?"

"That's just the thing, Craig. At the point *you* decided you were ready to talk. You controlled even that. You decided to talk to me when you thought it was safe to do so, but then I found out first." She blew out a breath. "Okay, Craig . . . I'm here, you're here, so let's talk and get this out on the table and then I'll call you a cab, deal?"

"No deal. I want you back. Baby, I love you. Please don't make me leave." His sad eyes searched hers. "I know that everything is my fault, and I take responsibility for that."

His emotion-filled voice covered her like a blanket. Renee desperately wanted to throw her arms around him, just as she wanted his arms around her. She wanted him to tell her things were going to be all better. "So talk to me," she said, holding back threatening tears.

He started to speak several times, but stopped, only to start again when he looked into her eyes. His voice quiet, he finally spoke. "It started when I wanted to help twelve people, including myself, keep our jobs. That's all I wanted initially, Renee. To be honest, I had always seen that agency as my security blanket. From the moment I landed that job, I knew I was there to stay. Period. Then Davis offered the agency to me, but I found out that my inheritance had that stipulation that Granddad stuck in there to teach me a lesson. And the second I heard about the stipulation, I could see his face when we talked one day while we were out fishing. You were right, though, about why he did it. He was teaching me a lesson for running my big mouth. You see, that day I had gone on and on, telling him that I wasn't going to get married." He smiled briefly before continuing. "After I left Miss Lilly at the bank, I went home and I fell asleep on the couch. The second I opened my eyes, I looked up at the mantel in the living room and there was the picture of you on that swing in the backyard. It was like a beacon. I remembered our promise and that's why I called you. If you had said absolutely no, then I had planned to, and did, call Cynthia. I left her a message that I had an interesting proposition for her. And I'm pretty sure I called another ex-girlfriend . . . maybe two, I don't remember."

"I figured that out," Renee said. "But you somehow knew I'd show up. How?"

"I don't know. I saw you in my dream and I just knew. So when you did show up, willing to marry me, I wasn't all that shocked, but I was happy." Craig stared at his hands before meeting her eyes again. "Renee, I love you so much. You may have thought our marriage was a fake, but after the first few weeks, you know, past our fighting stage, I just couldn't see my life without you in it. So I set out to make you fall in love with me. I mean, really fall in love with me and want to stay with me as my wife so that when I did tell you everything you would still love me. I envisioned us happy, building a life and having children. That shocked the hell out of me because I never imagined myself as a father. But when I thought of you and me staying married, I thought about us as parents, too." He looked up to see her watching him. "I'm in hell right now Renee and you're right. It is all my fault."

She thought about what he'd said. "You could have told me, Craig. I would have understood you wanting to buy the agency. I wouldn't have married you, but I would have understood." His face said there was more. "Besides us, why are you in such hell right now? What else is eating away at you?" Renee braced herself.

Craig kept his hands still and his eyes down. "Somebody found out that I'd basically lied to get my inheritance and he began to blackmail me for hush money." Looking up and seeing her shocked expression, Craig rushed on. "The threat was that he would tell you and then go to the bank officials. You would be humiliated and paraded in the local papers and tabloid magazines as someone I'd married just to get my inheritance and I'd be charged with bank fraud. It's a federal crime, you know." He grimaced, remembering Lawrence Jennings's words.

Renee got up and sat beside him the instant he stopped talking. "What? Who is it? How much money did he want?" Of all the things she thought he might say, blackmail was not even remotely one. Yes, she was shocked.

"One million dollars," Craig said, taking her hand.

"Oh, my God, who is it?" she rushed to ask. Her heart thumping, she grasped his forearm.

"I was approached the night of the bank rededication." He desperately wanted to kiss her.

Renee remembered the night well. After his meeting with Mr. Jennings, he'd been distant when they returned home. She recalled later finding him in his den, sullen. She also remembered seducing him that night. But Renee also knew that it was from that night on she'd noticed there were times he seemed so withdrawn. Although he would seem to shake it off, she still sensed that something had been bothering him, but didn't push him to talk to her.

At times she had even wondered what seemed to trouble him so much. Then there was that time when Mr. Jennings stopped by the house and he had blown up at her. She saw the look then, too. Renee's hand flew to her throat. "Oh, my God, it's that Mr. Jennings, isn't it?"

Craig only nodded. He was reveling in her nearness to him. Her perfume was a soothing balm for his alcohol infused brain. He heard her ask if he'd paid Jennings. "I paid him most of it, that whiny son of a bitch."

"Why did you pay him anything, Craig? You could've gone to the police."

"No, Squirt, I couldn't have." When she asked him why, Craig knew he had to be totally truthful. "Because of you, and because of my staff. They have been thanking me from day one for saving their jobs. But, Renee, I was saving my own ass. It just happened that in the process of looking out for my own ass and trying to save my own career, I helped them as well. It was purely a business decision to pull them along with me. They could have left, gone to another agency, but I didn't want anyone jumping ship. You see, I needed their skills and expertise as I moved the agency forward. Can you understand my motivations?" He pleaded for understanding.

"Yes, I can. But, Craig, that man has committed a crime and he has to be punished."

"I'm working on that, but there's more." He told her about the visit from James and his offer to help, but he stopped short of mentioning anything about the suspicion hovering over Lawrence's connection to the dead woman down in Florida or the hit and run of Ray Newman.

"What can I do, Craig?" Renee's anger was gone; she wanted to help him.

He brought her hand to his lips. "Don't give up on me . . . on us yet. I'll make things right again, I will. I wanted to tell you everything right away, but something always came up. I just didn't want to lose you." He caressed her face, searching, hoping. "Have I lost you, Squirt?"

Renee had never thought he was being blackmailed, and by a man that she initially liked and had invited into Craig's home. She now thought had every right to get upset with her; after all, she'd invited his blackmailer into his home for lemonade. "We've both lost a lot already." That was all she could say before he pulled her to him.

"I can't lose you now. Give us some time to heal, Squirt," he said, leaning forward, his lips gently touching hers. He whispered, "Have you stopped loving me already, baby?"

The question immediately flew from her head when Craig kissed her. She truly felt bad for what he had been struggling with, and so she meant the kiss as a sympathetic gesture. But it turned into anything but when she melted against him.

It was not lost on Craig that she didn't answer him, but he forgot all about the question the moment her lips parted. Everything flooded back to him . . . the feel of her in his arms, how he felt enclosed in hers. He tightened his hold on her, he lifted her to sit onto his lap.

Renee pulled back and looked into his eyes. Yes, she loved him and missed him, but that didn't change the fact that he'd lied to her and that lie was still the basis of their relationship. But when she felt his hands curve around from her back, holding her within the comfort and strength of his arms, his deception disappeared for the moment. And all she could think about was feeling alive in his arms once again.

When her reasoning returned, she was about to pull away from him but realized that his seeking hands had already worked the front clasp of her blouse and her bra. Renee watched as he leaned forward and lavished her breasts. Even if she wanted to stop him, she didn't. When his hands moved up her thigh, pulling her closer to him, Renee released a deep sigh of longing.

That was all Craig needed to hear, the sound of her yielding to his touch, to what he had to offer her . . . his life, his heart. He loved watching her and caressed every part of her. When his lips sought hers again, Craig didn't care that she no longer trusted him and that she believed the worst of him. He didn't even care about her friend Simon, because at that moment all he wanted was her, his wife. It only took him a few minutes to remove her clothes; not wanting to break the connection with her seeking lips, he stood up and carried her into the bedroom.

They spent the night entwined in each other's arms and rediscovering what they'd missed in the long weeks since their separation.

Several hours later, Craig awakened. He was alone. Sitting up in bed, he heard her muffled voice coming from the living room. Easing his exhausted body from the bed he went to the partly opened door. He listened for a few minutes; Renee was talking to Simon on her cellphone. When he returned to the bed, Craig's heart was as heavy as his aching head. Despite everything he'd told her and what they shared, he had already lost Renee to another man.

Minutes earlier, Renee had gotten up when her cellphone signaled a message waiting. It was from Simon. She hadn't heard back from him since their argument, and dialed his cellphone. "I'm sorry," she said, quietly.

"I'm sorry, too. I shouldn't have fussed at you like that today. Do I still work for you?"

Dropping her head back against the couch, she said, "Yes, and I didn't mean to be nasty like that, about what I said about Rhonda kicking you out. Really I didn't."

"Oh, yeah, I forgot about that. Ouch. But listen, Renee, it's because I do care about you that I wouldn't let some loser, um, I mean some guy do another number on you. That's all."

"You were right. I should have gotten in contact with you first place. I'm sorry I didn't." She sat on the couch and rested her head on the back. She heard him ask if she was okay. "You know what they say about the truth hurting. That's why I think I got so angry at you today when you were only being honest with me. It is the same type of tongue-lashing I expect to hear when my family finds out. You forgive me?" She recognized that begging for his forgiveness was no different than Craig begging her for hers earlier.

Simon hesitated. "Forget about it. We have another pressing matter to deal with. Our boy made bail—five hundred and fifty grand."

Renee bolted upright and turned towards her bedroom door; it was ajar. "That wasn't supposed to happen, was it?" she whispered in a weary voice. "That's a hefty bail. He had it?"

"His girlfriend, Pamela, fronted the money. She was a teller at your old bank. So he's back, and you know the drill: Call me immediately if there's any trouble. I've talked to the patrol cops I know in your area, and they will ride through. If Charles contacts you in any way, you call me. You got that, baby sister?" Simon tried to sound stern, but knew she was upset and scared.

Renee choked back a sob and laughed lightly. "Yeah, I got that, big brother. Goodnight." When Simon told her to sleep well, Renee didn't think she would ever sleep well again. Charles was out on bail, and she knew that he would be looking for her. She double-checked the locks on the front door and headed back to her bed . . . and to the safety of Craig's arms, if only for a little while longer.

It was nearly eleven o'clock when Vivian got home, having spent most of the evening waiting for a chance to see Ray. At some point between her visits Ray had suffered a serious setback. His airway had become so constricted that he had to have an emergency tracheotomy. He was now unable to speak. The helpful nurse had told her that Ray could have died if the floor nurse wasn't at the nurse's station when Ray managed to press the emergency button before he went into cardiac arrest.

Vivian couldn't understand it. Before the setback, the nurse said that Ray was doing so well he could be released in a matter of days. She would no longer be able to see him.

Vivian pressed trembling hands to her parched lips in a futile attempt to stifle the sobs wracking her body. She finally gave up and ran out the back door to the garden, where she sat with her face buried in her hands. She couldn't imagine her life without Ray. But she was nothing if not practical; she also couldn't bear to lose the life she had with Lawrence, either.

Hearing a noise, she squinted in the darkness and saw the garage door was open. She thought that was odd, because they rarely parked in the garage. Because the latch on the garage door was tricky, they would just pull their cars into the circular driveway. Curious, Vivian went inside the garage and looked around inside. At first she saw nothing out of the ordinary, but when she turned on the light she saw something strange. A car fender was propped up behind an old wooden picnic table. It was dented, mangled and was almost covered in what looked like brownish paint. What was it doing up behind that old table? she wondered.

Vivian walked over to the mangled piece of metal and began pulling it from behind the table. "Now why would this piece of junk be out here?" she mumbled, struggling to pull the table away from the wall. And then she noticed a car hood, also badly dented and mangled. Her search—and her curiosity—came to an abrupt end when she saw a spider dangling inches from her forehead and she went running from the garage. She made a mental note to have Grace call someone to clear out all that old stuff and get the door latch fixed as well.

When Vivian finally made it to the bedroom, Lawrence greeted her with a smile. "Vivian, dear, I was just about to call you on your cellphone. How is your friend, Beverly?" Of course, he knew she had been visiting Ray again.

Vivian had been using her friend who recently had back surgery as an alibi to cover the time she spent at Ray's bedside. "Oh, she's coming along nicely. Her husband is back home, so I won't be needed anymore," she said, sounding dejected. She picked up her robe from the chaise and used it to cover her trembling hands lest Lawrence wonder what was really bothering her.

Lawrence pulled her into his arms. He noticed her cheek color was returning. "Well, I'm glad you're feeling better and I'm glad Beverly's husband is back home, too, because I've missed you," he said, kissing her neck.

"Honey, you know, I'm still having side effects from the medication for this respiratory infection. It has made me really sick, so would you mind if I grabbed a shower and just curled up in bed with you?" She kissed him lightly on the lips, knowing he was disappointed that she wasn't going to let him have sex with her again.

"All right, dear. Say, let's have lunch tomorrow. I think I might have some good news for you," Lawrence said, but the smile he flashed stopped short of his eyes.

"Oh." Vivian stood in doorway, listening with feigned interest. She noticed for the first time that he watched her with shrewd, calculating eyes, as though he was suspicious of her.

"Well, it's about our vacation home, but I don't want to spoil anything." He thought he saw a spark in her eyes. In that moment, Lawrence knew that all he'd done had been worth it. "You run along and take your shower, and then we'll stretch out and watch TV for a while."

Vivian stepped into the steamy shower and just stood there and let the hot water run over her aching shoulders. But when she reached for the soap and the water hit her hands, she saw blood on them. Alarmed, she stepped back from the water and examined her hands and arms for cuts. Finding none, she suddenly realized that what was she was seeing was that brown paint from those dented and mangled car parts she examined in the garage. Her mind was tumbling. *Dried car paint wouldn't wash off with plain water like this.* She rubbed her fingers together, and the metallic smell of blood filled the shower stall. Her mind raced to grasp what her eyes saw. "Oh, my God . . . this is blood . . . did Grace or Lawrence have an accident and hit some animal . . . or hurt somebody?" she wondered aloud, the words leaving her mouth in a panicked rush. The water streamed down into her cupped hands, causing a pinkish puddle to form. Vivian became faint.

Her back hit the tiled shower wall. The news reporter's voice bounced around in her head. *Tragic accident . . . hit and run . . . critical . . . internal bleeding . . . Highway 14 . . . Ray Newman.*

Vivian used bloodstained hands to cover her sobs, which were muffled by the still-running shower. The enclosed shower stall provided soundproofing of sorts. "No, no, dear God no. Lawrence, you didn't . . . you couldn't have done that. Please God, don't let that be true." She thought about the suspicious eyes he slid over her in the bedroom, and then she looked down and saw that she was standing in bloody water; her washcloth, which had slipped from her hand, and had closed the off the drain. And she now knew with certainty that she was standing in Ray's blood, and she knew that all the pain he had suffered was because of her.

Waiting for Vivian to come out of the bathroom, Lawrence drifted off to sleep with his mind on Ray Newman. Too bad that young man had a seafood allergy and had been inadvertently given a food tray with shrimp broth instead of a vegetable broth, he thought. That was just an awful shame he thought, hugging his pillow. He blamed the hospital for carelessly keeping patients' food trays in the hallway like that. Any stranger could tamper with a patient's food.

Lawrence was smiling when he finally fell asleep. He was thinking about getting another seafood platter from that diner down on Mason Street . . . the shrimp were delicious.

Vivian didn't sleep at all; she was sick from grief. Today she planned to go see her doctor for her follow-up visit. She got up very early and went out to the garage, taking a small plastic jar and a plastic knife, something she remembered seeing on a popular crime show. She scraped samples of the dried blood off the fender and planned to take it to Dr. Strass. She knew he could pull some strings and have it sent somewhere for a DNA test. Vivian had not thought beyond this initial step and had no idea what she would do if tests proved the blood was Ray's. Still, she prayed it wasn't his, or even human.

CHAPTER 18

Craig awakened late Saturday morning. Renee was still sleeping, sprawled across his chest. He missed waking up next to her and realizing he missed that as much as he missed making love to her. As memories of last night flooded over him, his eyes lit on her ringless hand resting on his chest. When had such a small thing like Renee wearing her wedding rings become so significant, Craig wondered? But he knew the answer. As long as she wore her rings, as he continued to do, their marriage was real. Craig felt Renee stirring against him and tried to shake off the sudden constriction in his throat. He let her awaken gradually, being in no hurry to get up at all. He would sooner forget the Saturday mornings he'd awakened alone after having dreamt that she'd slept beside him.

Renee was dreaming that she and Craig were dancing in her parents' backyard under the stars. Her body was alive and the heat from his body seared her cheek where it rested against his bare chest. That's when the dream ended and she became fully awake. Memory came crashing back, and she slowly raised her eyes and met his dancing brown ones.

Craig's first instinct was to laugh, knowing exactly what she was thinking. "Good morning," he said, running a hand down her back. "I want you back home with me, baby."

Renee finally found her voice. "Good morning," she replied. She wasn't prepared for the 'morning after' with Craig. She didn't want to hear loving sentiments in the light of day, but here he was expressing exactly that. She reminded herself that she had to be strong to regain control over the course of her life. That applied to both Craig and his lies and to Charles Hunter and his theft. A night of loving in Craig's arms had changed nothing.

"Craig, this is my home." She saw a shadow pass over his handsome face, and she saw the hurt when he lifted his body from hers and angrily started dressing. "Craig, listen to me." She got up and rounded the bed to where he stood buttoning his shirt, not looking her way.

"Listen to what, Renee? Listen to you telling me that I'm a liar again, regardless of what I told you last night, regardless of what happened between us, repeatedly, last night? Listen to you close the door on us? No, I don't want to hear any of that." He went into her bathroom and shut the door. Ten minutes later, he emerged and found her pacing the bedroom floor.

Renee watched him walk over to the window and look out. "Craig, last night was special. It always has been, but we need to talk, because I don't want us to be angry with each other."

He didn't want to talk anymore. He'd awakened with her in his arms. He felt alive again and he wanted them to stay married, not because he'd told her the truth about things, but because she loved him as much as he loved her. Craig turned to face her. "Do you love me, Renee?"

"Yes, I do," she answered honestly, moving closer toward him.

"And I love you, and we've made a home together and we were happy there, so why won't you come back to me?" In his mind, Simon didn't matter; he wouldn't let him matter.

Renee shook her head sadly. He just didn't get it. "Craig, it's your home. It was your home long before I went there. I became a pawn in events you set in motion to get your inheritance. It was a marriage of convenience and a three-month deal." She was now directly in front of him. "Neither was based on love, not real love, don't you realize that? Have you forgotten what would have happened at the end of our three-month deal? None of it was about love." Renee tried to be as gentle as she could, but she saw growing tension in his face.

"That's bullshit, Renee. You said you love me and I know you were happy living with me as my wife and my friend. What difference does it make how we became married now that the truth is out? Renee, we fell in love in those three months."

"Just hold on a minute, Craig. Are you saying that regardless of everything that's happened . . . your initial lie, our marriage, legal or otherwise, the blackmail, and—" She stopped when something dawned on her. "Wait a minute . . . what happens if Mr. Jennings does report you to the bank officials?" She watched as his face became guarded and he stood up straighter.

"What are you talking about? The stipulations were fulfilled as my grandfather set them, and we stayed married for the three months." Craig spread his hands, waiting for her to challenge what he'd said.

"No, I mean, what if the bank finds out about Mr. Jennings' blackmail and extortion. They would fire him instantly. But he would be a fool not to tell everything he knows. He would tell them you only got married to get your inheritance and the ad agency was transferred to you on June tenth. What would happen if the bank found out about all of that?"

He knew what she was asking him. He'd already knew the answer—the only answer—was that he would lose it all, everything . . . including her. "Well, I guess you want to hear me say it again. I would lose everything that I'd set out to have in the first place." He paused briefly. "And that's a price I'm willing to pay. I would gladly pay it to have you back."

"Ah, I thought so. But, if I'm still married to you and living in your house as your wife, you would be making a liar out of Mr. Jennings and annul his claims that you had committed bank fraud. And you could just turn around and say Mr. Jennings was greedy and tried to extort money from you, right?" She made no effort to soften the accusation in her voice.

He processed what she'd said. It was certainly something he'd thought about himself. And he wasn't at all surprised that she came up with the same scenario that he did. "I seriously doubt that Jennings would go running to the bank officials and just say to them, 'Hey, y'all, guess what, I've been blackmailing Craig Thompson and here's why.' " He walked past her and out into the living room. He didn't like what he knew she was thinking.

But Renee followed him, not letting up. "Just be honest with me. You want me back with you so that you don't lose that agency." She watched him pick up his jacket from the couch.

Craig needed some air. His chest was tight and he had a full-throttle headache. "Renee, I don't want to lose you, period. The business I could deal with losing, and that also goes for the inheritance. You mean more to me than all of that," he said, walking to the front door.

"Where are you going?" she asked. "Let's have coffee and talk some more."

Craig stopped and turned, facing her. "If you want to keep rehashing how I brought this all on myself, then no. I don't want to stay and talk about that shit again. Trust me, Renee, I've beaten myself up enough. I'm going into the office and work. At least there I don't feel like such a failure. Remember, I've got to keep work flowing. I've got eleven thankful people, and their families, counting on me to do that." He dropped a kiss on her forehead and then unlocked the door, letting himself out, leaving Renee standing in the doorway of her apartment watching him.

Craig's car was parked up the block from Renee's apartment building. When he got behind the wheel, he glanced up in his rearview mirror and saw the dark haired man, Simon, standing at the curb, several car lengths behind his car, watching him with hostility.

Simon was leaning against the lamppost. His eyes connected with Craig's in the rearview mirror. He'd gotten a call from one of the patrol officers about an unfamiliar car parked near Renee's apartment building all night.

Craig was immediately on guard as he exited his car at the same time Simon walked toward him. Craig spoke first. "You waiting out here until I leave to go up and see Renee?" Craig asked, pinching the bridge of his nose and then looking at Simon.

Simon was surprised that he and Craig were about the same height and build, but all similarities ended there. "That's funny, man." Simon could guess what Craig meant.

"So what then, are you out here waiting for me?" Craig was ready.

"Look, friend, I just want to make sure you don't hurt her, that's all." Simon couldn't say but so much, as Renee was still his client, so his words were guarded.

"First of all, I'm not your friend. Second, how is whether I hurt her or not any of your business?" Craig's headache was running double time in his head. Not to mention his body was tensing, gearing up for the first move in a fight.

"She's my friend, and I don't want to see her hurt again. Least of all by some joker who suckered her into marrying him," Simon said, pointing at Craig.

"Well, it is obvious she's told you that we're married. So, again, how is my business any of your business?" Craig stepped closer to Simon, drawing looks from several passersby.

Simon pointed in the direction of Renee's living room window. "She's my business. I really don't give a damn about your business," he said, closing the distance between them as he spoke. "You just remember that." With that, Simon walked around Craig, down the street and climbed the steps to Renee's apartment building.

Craig turned and watched the man go up the steps, a sight that brought on a return of that tightness in his chest. His instinct was to follow him and throw Simon out the door on his ass.

He looked away and then angrily got into his car and took off, his tires squealing.

Lawrence had just about all he could take of Racine Hilton's stares and her quick comments. He'd asked her to do a simple task—print him a report on the loan repayments of several business account holders. Her response was that she was right in the middle of setting up a new checking account. "Excuse me, Racine, but my request is somewhat more important than your data entry, don't you think?" he asked, standing by her desk, smiling.

"I'm sorry, you're right. But if I don't complete this now, the customer won't be able to access his new checking account." Racine was getting frustrated under his suspicious gaze.

"I suppose that could seem important to you. Who's the customer?" When Racine told him the name,

Lawrence sent her a surprised look and relished in telling her that the customer had closed two other checking accounts at the bank for insufficient funds. "Didn't you pick up on that from his application?" he asked, thinking this was just what he needed to fire her.

"Oh, no, Mr. Jennings I-I didn't see that," Racine said, leafing through a stack of applications. "There have been so many new checking accounts opened, I must have missed that."

"Well, dear I suggest you check through that program you insisted we install here. Considering the cost for it, I wouldn't expect you to miss something as important as this."

"I'm sorry. I don't how I could have missed that, Mr. Jennings. The program can track everything, every previous account and customer," Racine said, still searching through her stack of applications. She didn't see the look that crossed Lawrence's face.

Track everything, every previous account . . . Lawrence's mind tumbled over Racine's words again. His mouth had gone dry. "I was under the impression it was just a mailing list of some kind, with addresses and such. How exactly can it track everything?"

She stopped her paper shuffling and looked at him. "The program is more of a financial-tracking database than a mailing list." Lawrence's steely stare made Racine so nervous she totally forgot Miss Lilly's advice not to share the full details about the program with anyone, especially Lawrence Jennings.

"Well, there must be a kink in the program if it didn't pick up that bit of information about this customer's past accounts. Maybe you should run me a report right now of the new and previous account holders. I want to make sure we have not extended credit to folks who have cheated us or skipped out on us before." Lawrence walked away and then turned back. "Oh, and since this database is so phenomenal, I would like to get that before you leave today. Will that be a problem, Racine?" He thought, *Yes, I'll make her stay late and work.*

"Oh, no, sir," Racine answered, glancing at her wall clock.

"You sure? That is a lot of old information to pull up, isn't it?" Lawrence said.

"Yes, but the program is pretty fast. If I just run you specific information, like the account holders and their demographics with some date ranges of transactions, that'll take less than half an hour," she said, as her fingers moving quickly over her keyboard as she began entering specific commands into the computer.

"So how far back did you say you can track?" Lawrence could feel perspiration began collecting under his armpits and dampening his pale blue dress shirt.

"Oh, as far back to an account's very first transaction. I've set the commands to start with the most recent transactions first. This report will take longer, it will go all the way back to the first account opened." Becoming increasingly uncomfortable with his questions and in his presence, Racine quickly finished typing and sent the report to her printer. In seconds the printer began printing out pages.

Lawrence kept one eye on Racine and the other on the printer. "Say, Racine, I just remembered hearing you telling Jackie about an appointment after work today. Tell you what, you can leave now and I'll just collect that report before I leave, or I'll pick it up in the morning."

"Well, okay, if you're sure." Anxiety mixed with doubt lined Racine's forehead. In the end, she decided she simply couldn't miss her appointment.

"Yes, dear, I'm sure." Lawrence smiled encouragingly. "Just go on now, and I'll even turn your computer off." He practically ushered her to the door, the ever-present smile on his face, as he bade her good evening.

Lawrence waited until most of the tellers and other bank staff had left before he went back to Racine's office. The full report was in the printer tray—over one hundred and sixty pages total, in small print. He quickly scanned the documents and was flabbergasted by the amount of information that had been at Racine's fingertips. He had no idea that program could track that much information. Right there in his hands were his doctored balances. Information, he realized, that had been at Racine's fingertips. His first thought was, *Who has she told?* His second was about gaining access to the database and making changes in the program. A closer look the report yielded the names Reginald Thompson, account holder, and Craig Thompson, benefactor. His hands trembled when he saw that some of his earliest withdrawals, then only five hundred dollars or so, were later covered by a deposit. He remembered being giddy about those little withdrawals. But then he checked his other 'babies,' and his withdrawal and deposit transactions were as clear as day. To Lawrence's own banker's eyes, the report showed undeniable signs of questionable activity on accounts that were supposedly dormant. When Lawrence sat down at Racine's computer, perspiration was running down his neatly trimmed sideburns.

CHAPTER 19

Renee!

Renee had no idea what had awakened her, but she was immediately on guard. She thought she heard someone whisper out her name. In the semi-darkness of her bedroom, instinct told her to stay perfectly still. She didn't dare move, but she felt the presence of *something*. Tension gripped every inch of her body. She forced herself to keep breathing steadily, her body rigid. She let her eyes very slowly roam the room. *Did she hear someone swallow, or was it just she herself trying to swallow past the lump blocking her throat?*

I'm all alone and it's the middle of the night. Oh, God . . . why did Simon get that emergency call from his office? Now, as paralyzing fear was closing in on her, she wished she hadn't sent him away. But she had to keep her wits about her. *A weapon, that's what I need. But what?* She remembered the heavy lamp on her nightstand. That would be ideal, she thought, but she would need two hands to lift the thing. But she could knock it down.

Scraping, rustling movement. Those were the sounds she heard near her bedroom door. *Oh, God, it's almost closed.* She never closed her bedroom door. Someone was in her bedroom, trying not to be heard. *Craig . . . Simon . . . someone help me.* But she knew there was no one to help her. *I'll be dead before I get the first lock open. Wait, no I won't. Think.* Renee quickly calculated the position of all three door locks on her front door. *The bathroom light is on, turn it off. Too much light if someone follows me. Okay, close the bedroom door, hit the bathroom light, then the locks.*

Rustling. Panic engulfed her body, causing tremors and her muscles started to cramp. It was becoming an effort to lie perfectly still. That's when she felt the presence of someone moving, coming closer to her. Suddenly, it was as if a voice called out to her, *Go, now!*

Everything happened quickly and all at once. Just as a gloved hand reached out for the light blanket covering her, Renee bounced up and dropped down to the floor. Her hand reached up to the lamp and pushed it down onto the foot she felt near her bed. Then she was up and running through her bedroom door, slamming it shut behind her. *Don't forget the bathroom light.* Her eyes fought against her fear as she ran through her living room and headed for the bathroom. *Forget the bathroom door, get out! Turn the locks and go.*

Then it was over—she was safe, she'd gotten out. Now what, she wondered, her panic only slightly eased. Her chest heaving in the humid night air, she stood on the front steps of her building, barefoot and in her nightshirt. She had no keys, no money. Mrs. Harvey, her landlady, was her only hope. Renee ran next door and began ringing the woman's doorbell, her eyes frantically searching the quiet street as perspiration ran down her face and into her eyes. No one was out, but then it had to be close to two in the morning. She continued ringing the doorbell until she saw Mrs. Harvey peek through her side window near the step railing. "Oh, please open the door. Help me."

"Renee, is that you, girl?" she asked, looking beyond Renee just as a lone figure quickly crossed the street up the block and rounded the corner.

"Yes, yes, please let me in, Mrs. Harvey. I-I think somebody broke into apartment. Please hurry and open the door." Renee's voice was little more than a whisper as she pleaded to the woman, pressing her face against the door; then she heard the door locks and chain being released. Once she was inside and the heavy brown door was locked behind her, Renee felt safe and slid to the floor, immediately passing out at her landlady's feet.

People were everywhere around her. Renee focused on the wristwatch of a paramedic. Two forty-five. She brought the fuzzy number into focus and was overcome by nausea. It was difficult to get her thoughts straight as she tried to remember what could have happened. *I took a shower and got into bed with a new novel and . . .* In an instant she remembered and began to fight at the hands now pressing against her shoulders, keeping her down on the unfamiliar couch.

"Renee, baby, you're okay . . . you're safe. Everything's okay now." Craig's voice was as shaky as he felt. From the moment he'd gotten the call from Mrs. Harvey, his mind and body raced to Renee. She had called him moments after calling the police and ambulance. Craig would never know how he'd made it to Renee's apartment so fast, so fast in fact that he didn't even remember when Simon showed up. His eyes met Simon's for a split second as the PI talked to a couple of police officers, and then his attention returned to the paramedic, who had administered another ammonia capsule under Renee's nose, awakening her instantly this time. Craig bent over and kissed her hand.

Renee came fully awake just as Simon came and stood at the end of the couch. She looked up and whispered his name, "Simon . . ." Then she saw another worry-stricken face looming up and staring down at her. "Craig, what are you doing here? Wh-what's happened?" she croaked, looking from Craig to Simon.

Simon moved closer and ignored Craig's hostile glare as he sat down on the side of the couch, holding Renee's hand. "Hey, sweetheart, looks like you had an unexpected visitor. The police are here and need to talk to you about what happened in your apartment tonight after I left." Simon said, feeling Craig's eyes rake over him. "Can you tell us what happened?"

Now everything came back in a rush. Her eyes met Simon's and then Craig's. "I was so scared." She said with effort, "I was asleep and I woke up when I heard a noise in my bedroom."

Craig's hand tightened around hers. Regardless of what had happened between them, Renee was so glad to see him. "Oh, Craig, I was so scared, I thought he was going to kill me. I just know that is what would've happened if I didn't get out."

Craig was pretty much beside himself thinking of what might have happened. Renee hating him was one thing, but to lose her would kill him. He might as well die himself. His voice was thick with emotion and he had to force the words out. "Oh, God, Renee, if anything had happened to you . . ." he stopped, loath to even put words to the thought. But he plunged ahead anyway. "You must know that I would blame myself." Craig glanced at Simon and briefly wondered why he was holding back from comforting Renee.

Listening to Craig and watching his interaction with Renee, Simon had no doubt the man was in love with his wife. He decided to hang back for a few minutes before trying to squeeze a bit more information out of Renee. "Renee, can you tell me what this man looked like? Were you even able to get a brief look at him before you ran out of your apartment?"

"No, there was just a sliver of light from the guest bathroom. I was too scared to turn around when I knew would be right behind me." She dabbed at her eyes and tried to steady her breathing as she relived the feeling of doom that wrapped itself around her when she knew for sure that someone was in her bedroom.

The police officer taking the report asked if she remembered anything about the intruder. Then Simon piggybacked the question and asked if she saw the intruder's hands.

Renee looked up as something did pop into her head. "Actually, I just remembered that I knocked over a heavy lamp that was on my nightstand, and I'm pretty sure it landed on his foot because I heard him groan when it hit the floor. When he reached out, I saw a gloved hand."

Craig directed a hostile glare at Simon. "Unless you're a cop, why don't you let these officers here ask the questions and maybe they can get out there and find whoever broke into Renee's apartment?" The men's eyes clashed for several tensed seconds.

"But who would break into my apartment and try to—" Then Charles came to mind. She *had* to tell Craig. She looked at Simon, as if silently asking for guidance.

Craig did not miss the direction she looked. He was suddenly seized by an overwhelming sense of hopelessness, of unrecoverable loss, as he watched Simon sitting there holding her hand. The painful stab to his soul was unbearable and the tears burning behind his eyes were telling him he had to let Renee go. He had to if she'd moved on. He brought her hand up to his lips and kissed it, before letting go of her hand. "I guess I should go. Renee, if you need anything, just call me." He stood and faced Simon briefly before practically fleeing Mrs. Harvey's apartment.

Watching Craig leave and seeing the raw pain and look of defeat on his face was more than she could stand. "No, Craig. Simon, make him come back," she wailed, almost incoherently.

Simon was torn. His first instinct was to go after Craig and tell him he had misinterpreted his relationship with Renee. But he couldn't, as Renee was first and foremost his client. His allegiance was to her, not to her husband—a husband clearly inconsolably distraught by what almost happened to his wife. His second instinct was to shake the living daylights out of Renee. She couldn't be so blind as to not see what Craig must have been thinking about the two of them. "Renee, the crime scene techs are over at your apartment. Maybe they can pick up a print from your intruder." He hesitated briefly then said, "It wasn't Charles who broke in."

Renee looked aghast. "What?" She assumed it was Charles. "Are you sure?"

"I still have a tail on him, and I know for sure that he spent the night with his girlfriend, Pamela. In fact, they were still arguing when I got a call to come here. It's possible he could have hired someone to go after you, but I somehow doubt he'd be that stupid, knowing he was tailed from Canada to Florida and back. I just can't see that. So, I'm thinking what happened was that you're a victim of a random break-in."

The police officer who had been taking notes was listening intently to Renee. Then he related what Mrs. Harvey had reported about seeing a dark-figured man running up the street when she looked out her window and saw Renee on the front step.

He hadn't expected that. She had to have been awake and knew that he was there in her apartment. Otherwise, he would have taken care of her, at the very least given her a definite scare; instead he was nursing a painfully sore and swollen foot. He hated the thought of hurting her, because that wasn't his style, but he had to put more of a scare into her in order to accomplish his goals.

Craig hung up the telephone, almost crashing the lightweight handset onto its base, and ground out an expletive. He was tired and edgy and the last thing he needed was to hear another empty threat from Lawrence Jennings. But Craig's main thought was not on Jennings. Instead, he was deeply concerned and worried about Renee. He knew she was scared, but he was powerless to help her.

Craig tried to clear his mind to so that he could at least participate in an upcoming meeting. There was so much business coming into the agency that his meetings were starting to run together. He went over to his drafting table and looked down at an ad in its early stage. The ad was special to him, but at the moment he didn't feel the excitement he'd felt when he'd first started it. He wasn't focused, and he didn't have the energy to even attempt to finish it, despite how important it once was. His thoughts kept going back to Renee.

His cellphone rang, pulling him away from his thoughts. Not recognizing the number, he answered cautiously. "Hello?" Craig was more than a little surprised when the caller asked to meet with him. "Yeah, I'll be there." Snapping his cellphone shut, he frowned and wondered what this was all about. He had the next thirty minutes to wonder.

Vivian sat in her car in the hospital parking lot trying to process Dr. Strass's news that the brown flecks she had taken to him were human blood, type O-positive. The confirmation and its deadly implication had been shattering, because she had also learned that Ray's blood type was O-positive. She knew Lawrence was responsible for the hit and run on Highway 14 . . . he had tried to kill Ray. But she needed more proof.

As if driven by some strange force, Vivian went home and rummaged through the dry-cleaning bin for clothes Lawrence had worn in the past ten days or so . . . and she was thankful the items were still in the bin. Just the day before, Grace mentioned needing to go to the cleaners. Lawrence was a creature of habit. He kept every receipt for every purchase he had made, and she was banking on that habit to find something, anything. She found another shocker—two receipts for lunch. She thought it odd that he had ordered two seafood lunch specials within two days from a diner he had once described as a greasy spoon and said he wouldn't be caught dead in. She didn't know what it meant until she called the diner and was told the receipt was for the steamed shrimp platter. Ray's life-threatening setback immediately came to mind. Vivian now suspected that Lawrence had tried to kill Ray

ot once, but twice. She quickly stuffed the receipts into
er purse. She blamed herself for everything, mainly for
ushing her husband to the point of making two
ttempts on Ray's life. And why would he do something
o extreme, she wondered? But Vivian knew why . . .
ecause Lawrence knew about her affair with Ray.

As the hot afternoon sun beamed down into the
ackyard, Vivian sat in her favorite lounge chair under
he canopy covering the deck. She was staring intently at
he closed garage door. She thought about what she'd
een when she had gone to see Ray that last time. To her
dismay, Ray wasn't alone. The clerk from the warehouse,
Carrie, was sitting at his bedside reading a book to him.
She saw Ray smiling at Carrie with loving eyes. Vivian's
heart broke into pieces as she watched their hands touch
tentatively, shy smiles on their faces. She could see that
they loved each other and knew she'd lost Ray for good.
She had left the hospital still unsure as to how she was
going to deal with Lawrence, but she was sure of one
thing. She wouldn't let him hurt Ray again.

Renee had just finished cleaning her apartment. The
police crime-scene techs had concluded the intruder had
simply come up the back stairs and entered through her
kitchen window. No fingerprints were found, and no
blood was found in her bedroom or the living room. If
the lamp had landed on his foot, it hadn't broken the
skin.

What threw Renee into a state of panic was Simon's belief, shared by the police, that she had been targeted. Someone went for her window on the second floor, not the one on the first floor . . . which conveniently had a window open.

Her sense of security in her own home was now gone. Simon and Rhonda insisted she check into a hotel, go to her parents' or stay with them for a few days. She accepted their invitation. If she had refused, Simon threatened that he was going to sleep on her couch.

∽

The hostess approached Craig as soon as he entered the restaurant. Already knowing whom he was meeting, she directed him to the table. And so there he stood, watching the man eat a breadstick. "Well?" he said, spreading his hands.

Simon nodded at the empty seat across from him. "Why don't you have a seat?"

Craig pulled out the chair and sat down. His face gave no indication of the emotions burning inside him. He couldn't imagine what Simon wanted to talk to him about, but he sure as hell didn't need or want to hear this man telling him to stay away from Renee. He'd already decided that he wouldn't bother her again.

Simon, too, had made a decision, one he felt was in the best interest of his client and friend. He knew she was going to be mad at him. Oh, well, it wouldn't be the first time, he reasoned. It was his job to protect her, and this was the best way to do it. Ignoring Craig's open hostility, he said, "You know Craig, you really wear some nice suits. They look tailored."

Craig stared at Simon in disbelief. "I'm out of here," he said, pushing his chair back.

Simon raised his hand. "Hold up, I wasn't joking, but I do need to talk to you. So please, why don't you have a drink and order some pasta? I'm having the manicotti and garlic bread." The waitress appeared and took his order and then looked at Craig.

Craig cleared his throat. "Nothing for me. I won't be staying long enough for dinner."

"Oh, yes, you will," Simon said, looking up at the confused waitress. "Just bring two of what I ordered, sweetheart, and two tall glasses of iced tea," he said, rubbing his hands.

The server looked at Craig, but he merely returned her questioning look. Hearing no further objections, she left to put their orders in.

"Simon, is it? Listen, friend, I'm not accustomed to being arbitrarily summoned to a meeting that is probably pointless. It's a waste of my time, so why don't you tell me what the hell you want and I'll leave you to your double order of manicotti and garlic bread."

The waitress returned with their beverages. She sensed the men were not friends.

Simon picked up his glass and tipped it towards Craig in a mock toast. "Okay, friend, it's like this. I need you to help me protect your wife from someone who is out to get her."

Craig sat up, dumbstruck. It was then that he noticed Simon wearing a wedding band. He couldn't believe the gall of this man. "Renee doesn't want anything from me, least of all my protection. From what I've seen, friend, isn't that your job now?" Craig took a gulp of his iced tea and sat back, staring at Simon.

The waitress returned with two steaming plates of pasta and baskets of aromatic breads. She set the food down and then retreated back to the safety of another table.

"No, Craig, that's not my job in the sense that you mean. It is, however, my job to protect her, as any hired private investigator would. Renee is my client, Craig, but she's also my friend, and I don't want to see her hurt." Noticing Craig's shocked expression, Simon paused to let what he'd said settle in. "Now I suggest you drop that chip from your shoulder, dig into that manicotti and talk to me, man to man, so we can come up with a better way to protect Renee, apart from her staying with me and my wife. I mean, we really don't mind, but the wife isn't giving me any play while company's in the house, if you know what I mean. Now, can we talk about that, friend?" Simon lifted his plate to his nose and smiled appreciatively.

Thrown for a loop, Craig tried to wrap his mind around what he'd just heard. "Renee hired a PI for protection? Why would she need one, and for how long?"

"Because she dated an asshole almost a year ago who turned out to be a con artist and a thief. They dated only a couple of months. One night he drugged her and stole her bank book and bank cards. While she slept off the drugs, he wiped out the thirty grand in her savings account and skipped town."

"Oh, my God," Craig said, but relief flooded him. *They weren't a couple.*

As Simon explained what Renee had been through and how he came to be in her employ, he also saw fear on Craig's face. "When I met with Renee, I immediately wanted to help her. I mean, she's like the sister I never had. I'm committed to seeing this guy pay for what he did to her." Simon paused to dig into his food and sighed. "Oh, that is good."

"This guy stole thirty thousand dollars from Renee?" Craig remembered the argument he and Renee had the night they'd first made love. She'd described her past loves; this guy must have been her number three, the one she said was a liar and a thief.

"Uh-huh. Her parents had won a lawsuit against an insurance company that refused to pay off an insurance policy." Simon shared how Renee's parents fought the insurance company for benefits on a death policy and then divided the money amongst themselves when the case was settled. Simon watched Craig processing what he'd said.

Craig felt the pinch of tears behind his eye sockets. "Bryant." Craig's throat almost closed up, forcing him to gulp in air. "Bryant was my best friend growing up," Craig said simply, reaching for his drink. He felt like a selfish dog. While he was pulling in money as an ad man, Renee's family was fighting with the insurance company to pay off a minimal policy they'd had on Bryant. *Damn.*

"Listen, Craig, I know what you must have thought about Renee and me, but my loyalty is to her as a friend. I love my wife, who happens to be the one who set up the wiretap on Renee's phone when she started getting threatening calls. I'm worried about her. You see, I've had the ex-boyfriend until surveillance since he was extradited back to Houston. He's out on bail. I don't think he's the one who broke into her apartment, but I haven't quite given up on the idea that he may have hired someone to off her. If she's out of the way then he won't have to worry about her testifying at his trial, and he's facing a whole lot of years behind bars."

"I personally think he's too chickenshit to do that, mostly because he happened to run into a fist—well, okay, two fists—as payback for his nasty phone calls with her . . . the little puny punk." Simon smiled as he flexed his bruised knuckles. "You gotta work them out sometimes." He grinned, recalling punching Charles in the face and stomach after he was released from jail and skipped his happy self up the steps to his girlfriend's second floor apartment. Simon had jumped him.

Craig smiled. "Simon, thank you. I've just hired you. What I can do to help?"

"Well, first eat that food—looks like you can use it—then we'll talk. I'm also glad you just hired me, because when Renee finds out that I told you everything, she'll probably fire me. Another thing, Craig . . . Renee's family knows nothing about what's happened. She feels embarrassed and humiliated and that's been eating away at her. Well, that and the fact that you talked her into marrying you with that promise business." He raised his hand to prevent Craig from saying anything. "But that's water under the bridge now. You guys love each other." Simon's expression challenged Craig to deny it, which he didn't.

For the first time since Renee left him, Craig was filled with a sense of hope. He now remembered times she'd seemed pensive and worried, as though she had the weight of the world on her shoulders.

Craig pulled his chair closer to the table and ate all of his manicotti and garlic bread.

⌒

Lawrence sat in his den, nervously reflecting on several troubling things. Something weird was going on at the bank, and something equally weird was going on with Vivian. His first concern was Vivian. He knew it was more than just Ray Newman's injuries. Two days earlier, when he'd slipped back into the hospital and approached Ray's room from the service-elevator entrance, he had overheard a young woman telling Ray that he was going to be released in the morning and that the ambulance would be transporting him to the rehabilitation center. Lawrence thought how lucky Ray was. Had it not been for that clerk staying at the hospital and reading to him that night, Ray wouldn't be alive in the morning to be transported anywhere.

Lawrence's focus on Ray Newman was so intense that he almost collided with Vivian as she ducked around a corner, headed for Ray's room. It was long past visiting hours and he was determined to make one more effort to free Vivian of Ray Newman. He didn't even have a plan, unlike the time when he had switched the vegetable broth for the shrimp-infused broth he'd doctored. He thought he would just smother him with a pillow. But when Lawrence rounded the hallway, he'd seen Vivian. Her face was pressed against Ray's door . . . listening. Lawrence had seen absolute dejection on her profile.

Again, he cursed Ray for what he'd turned his wife into. Day after day, ever since the accident that was meant to take Ray's life, he'd watched his wife slide deeper into the pits of utter despair. She was still visibly depressed and had lost weight. She no longer dressed up or bothered with makeup. She now preferred jeans and sweat-suits. His attempts to get her to talk to him were met with empty eyes. She would try to mask her emotions, but he'd seen the sadness in her eyes. And try as he might, Lawrence didn't believe the lie that he'd talked himself into . . . Vivian wasn't addicted to any kind of drug that Ray gave her. Pure and simple, she'd been unfaithful. She was not only having an affair with Ray, she was in love with the younger man.

Lawrence felt he had no choice as to how he'd handled the situations that had come up, situations that threatened his way of life . . . his wife. Like Craig Thompson. The man had lied to him and was stalling in paying him off. But he was confident in how he was going to deal with Craig. He knew where to hurt him . . . with his little bride. How dare Craig turn the tables on him and expect him not to take action?

Lawrence thought about the report Racine had printed out for him. There in black and white he could see the hundreds of thousands of dollars he had taken from those accounts over the years. His attempt to crash the program failed, as it had been blocked to everyone except James Tinsley. Lawrence thought his last recourse was to sabotage the program somehow to eliminate the transactions. Problem was, he'd run out of time. In the event Racine had already shared those account activities with anyone else, especially James Tinsley, he'd set the bank's data center up to crash. He'd already wired a lot of money from two other accounts to his private and untraceable account in the Bahamas. Everything was in place. The villa he'd purchased was ready for their arrival. Everything was in place for that to happen . . . everything, that is, except convincing Vivian that the move would be permanent and that they could never return to Houston. His final plan was to deal with Craig Thompson for setting him up. He reached for the phone to make a call.

Vivian snapped her cellphone shut and prayed she'd done the right thing. She was certain Lawrence was aware of her relationship with Ray and that he was determined to keep her away from him. "Dear God . . ." she moaned, remembering the helpful nurse at the hospital telling her that someone must have switched Ray's food tray. The woman told Vivian that Ray's food tray and chart were clearly marked with a warning that he had an allergy to seafood. His allergy was so severe that his food tray was faithfully and routinely checked before it was taken into his room. His nurse clearly remembered doing so just minutes before the hospital server took it to him. According to the nurse, there was no seafood on the hospital's menu.

Vivian inhaled, praying again that she'd done the right thing in making that call.

〜〜

Renee looked up from her computer screen and was surprised to see Rhonda at her office in police uniform. "Oh, Rhonda, what's going on? Did Simon send you to pick me up today?" Since she'd been staying at their house for the past few days, it had been Simon who had picked her up from work downstairs in front of the building.

"Actually, Renee, I'm kind of here on semi-official business. Can you leave work now? Simon will meet us back at the station."

Renee looked up at Rhonda and noticed something odd in her expression. "Yes, I can leave now. Just let me shut my computer down." Rhonda seemed distracted, and Renee didn't know what to make of it. She hoped she was not wearing out her welcome staying at their house. "So, Rhonda, you're still on duty?"

Rhonda shook her head, as if to free herself of distracting thoughts. "Yes, just for a few more hours. I just want to go over a few things with you down at the station first, and then Simon will drive you home. Oh, Simon is fixing sandwiches for dinner, so prepare yourself." She grinned.

"Oh, okay. Thanks again you for opening your home to me." Renee really was thankful because she felt safe with them.

"Hey, girl, I'm having a ball," she smiled. "Besides, I just love how you've cut and styled my hair." Rhonda grinned, shaking her sleek, carefree hairstyle.

"Well, I'm glad you like how I did it. I developed lots of skills growing up with two sisters with heads full of hair, too."

The two women left and headed to the police station.

⌒

At the police station, the news Renee had just received was shocking. But then it occurred to her that although she was in shock, she was also relieved.

Two hours before Rhonda showed up at Renee's office, she'd been on the scene of a shooting in a downtown Houston apartment complex. The victim, Charles Hunter, had been shot and killed by his live-in girlfriend, Pamela McHenry, in what police described as a domestic dispute, one of several involving the couple in the days before the shooting.

One look at Pamela McHenry's bloody, swollen face, her cut lip, and bruised torso, and there was no doubt in Rhonda's mind that the young woman was a victim of abuse at the hands of Hunter.

In her statement to the police, Pamela charged that Charles had beaten her repeatedly since his return to Houston. She said his final abusive act occurred after she had read the charging documents and the victim's statements. She said he had sworn to her that he had never slept with his marks, that he'd only wined and dined them. When she confronted him with the information she had read, Charles had become violently angry and had attacked her. She reported that when she tried to run out of the apartment, he grabbed her and began to attack her again. She said she had shot him in self-defense with the gun he had recently purchased on the street.

Pamela was told that she would still be charged for aiding and abetting Charles in his thefts of tens of thousands of dollars from helpless, unsuspecting women. Pamela clammed up on the advice of her attorney, but not before stating that Charles had forced her to provide him with the names of single female account holders with hefty savings or checking accounts. She said he would then plot to meet the women by posing as a helpful passerby coming to their aid—after he himself had donned a disguise and had run up, knocked them down and grabbed their purses.

Renee felt sick. "Oh, my God, that's exactly how I met Charles. I had left the bank one afternoon and, just as I got to my car, this thug came out of nowhere and pushed me into the door and snatched my purse," she said, looking up at Simon. "The next thing I remember was this well-dressed man carrying a briefcase running to my aid. He said he saw the guy drop my purse on the ground and he'd picked it up. I-I just don't believe this. How could anybody be so heartless? How could I be so stupid?" She shook her head in anger and disgust.

Simon said, "Look, Renee . . . it's definitely over for that loser Charles. And his girlfriend, trust me, she'll serve some time for her part. I'm just sorry the police didn't get the call of shots being fired until it was too late; he was already dead by the time they arrived. But I for one would have wanted to see him behind bars for all he had done, you know?"

For Renee, the shock of Charles's death had begun to wear off, replaced by her anger that, once again, Charles had gotten away with his deceit and lies. "So what happens now?"

Simon sat beside her and took her hand. "Renee, listen, sometimes the law gets the bad guys—you know, those villains and rogues." He smiled when her eyes narrowed, showing she remembered what he had told her before. "And sometimes . . . well, the bad guy gets what's due him or her by a higher calling. Either way, it's still a kind of justice. In this case, he got a hole blown into his chest by his partner in crime. And she'll pay for her part in his scams, because if she hadn't disclosed confidential information in the first place, then you and all those other women wouldn't have lost so much. The bank is separately pursuing charges against her."

Renee seemed to breathe a little easier. "Will I have to testify against her?" she asked Rhonda.

"Not if you don't want to. A lot of Charles's victims won't either, Renee. Several of them here in Houston had already gotten notices of the pending trial and have already said they've let it go or won't press charges. They've decided to put the matter behind them and get on with their lives. They too were embarrassed for having been duped by that man's smooth-talking ways. You can do that as well, you know," Rhonda said.

"Yeah, I guess that's what I should do," she said, but seemed uncertain.

Simon agreed with Rhonda. "Renee, you've given Charles a whole year of your life. Your quest for revenge has taken a year from you. Sweetheart, I think it's time for you to burn everything in that suitcase of yours and start that living I've been talking to you about for months."

Knowing he was talking about Craig, Renee rolled her eyes. "No, I'm not about to close the books on one smooth-talking brother only to reopen the book with another one. No, I can't do that, Simon. But what I can do is go home," she said in a tired, but stronger, voice.

"That's what you want, Renee, to go home to your empty apartment?" Rhonda asked.

Renee stared down at her hands. In a room with two people whom she considered friends she felt totally alone. "Yes, I think I should go to my apartment—that *is* my home." Turning to Rhonda, she said, "I have to go so I can begin to feel centered again. Do you understand?"

Rhonda hugged her. "Yes, and you're going to be fine, Renee. But I still want you to stay at our house for the rest of the week. Besides, you promised to help me redo my bedroom in blue and white." Rhonda had decided to keep Renee busy after her workday because she could see her slipping into a state of depression. So far, they'd already painted the bedroom.

"Well, okay, if you're sure." Renee took a deep breath and smiled for the first time in many days. "Actually, I have been getting really excited about redecorating your bedroom, and I've got tons of swatches for the drapes and paint samples for the crown moldings. Oh, and I found a little antique shop with the nicest lamps that'll go so nice with your new bedroom suite. I've got a brochure here in my bag."

As Renee searched her carryall bag for the brochure, Rhonda smiled over her bent head and sent Simon a triumphant look.

He just rolled his eyes.

⌒

Three days later, Renee was jolted when Simon parked in front of Craig's house. She whirled and fixed him with a deadly and fierce look. "What are we doing here, Simon? What's going on? We're supposed to be going back to your place so I can get my bag."

As usual, Simon had picked Renee up from work. Today, instead of going to his house, he'd made a planned detour.

Simon turned the car off and turned to face her. "Renee, what's going on is simple. You hired me to find Charles, and that led to protecting you. Now, since you took it upon yourself to get secretly married on my watch, I had to involve your husband in this unclear threat that's targeting you. That threat is not entirely over; in fact, we don't really know the source. Let's go." He was out of the car and around to the passenger-side door in seconds.

"No, I'm not going back to Craig's house. I don't believe you, Simon. I don't believe you would turn on me." She tried to snatch her arm away, but Simon tugged her from the car, pushing, pulling and almost carrying her up the walkway to the front door. Between angry sobs, she lashed out at him. "You're fired, Simon. I trusted you as my friend and you turn around and cross me like this. How could you?" Renee had balled her hand into a fist and tried to punch him in the stomach, but Simon anticipated her move and just held her away from him.

He was also saved from answering her because at that moment Craig opened the front door and stood watching Renee's angry face. He stood aside for her and Simon to come inside. Once inside, Simon walked an angry, crying, foot-stomping, fire-breathing Renee over to the couch and gently pushed down on her shoulder until she sat down.

Renee looked up to see both men watching her. "I hate the both of you and I'll never forgive either of you!" she yelled and dropped her face into her palms.

Simon blocked Craig from crossing the living room to comfort her. Instead, he handed her his handkerchief. "Renee, listen to me. Someone other than Charles made an attempt on your life. Up until I got you out of your apartment, that someone had been following you from your job to your apartment. Now listen, you hired me to find Charles, and that included me protecting you. So I'm only doing my job. You got that? Charles is gone, but there's something else going on. I had no choice but to bring your *husband* into this."

Renee pinned him with a withering look, then did the same to Craig, who so far had remained silent. "Oh, okay, I get it now. You two have hooked up and now you both think you know what's best for me? Is that it?"

Craig ventured a response. "Yes, baby, it's something like that."

Renee turned her eyes on him. "Don't call me baby and, Craig, since we're going to be divorced, you don't have a say in my life whatsoever. I don't need either of you. I trusted Simon with confidential information and he betrayed me, just like your lies destroyed us, Craig." She turned to Simon and gestured at Craig. "How could you join forces with him?"

Simon shrugged and said, "Well, if you're like my sister, then that makes him what?"

"Oh, shut up," Renee said, wishing she hadn't asked him anything at all.

"I love you, Renee. Please stay here with me and let me protect you," Craig pleaded.

"Protect me? You clown, I need protection from you!" She stood up and walked to the center of the living room. "Craig, don't you see you're doing it again? You're playing God and making decisions that you think are best for me."

413

"Renee, I'm not going to stand by and watch you get hurt. How do you think I would feel if I didn't do all I could do to protect you? That makes me as bad as you. You didn't tell me things up front either." He moved closer to her. "You also came into our marriage on self-serving terms. Although your reasons were different from mine, they were still dishonest, weren't they?" He didn't expect her next move, but wasn't surprised by it, again.

Renee slapped him with all the anger and heartache she had in her. She was angry at him for telling her the truth, and full of heartache because he made her love him. "Don't you dare try to equate my reason for coming into the marriage to what you did. You hurt me, Craig. And so okay, you say you love me, well, that's very nice. But what if you didn't? What if I had been just as you expected me to be, fat and homey? You would have had divorce papers drawn up well before the end of our three-month pact, and I would still have been hurt. So spare me your crap in trying to compare our situations. They are nothing alike!"

Simon let out a piercing whistle. "Ouch, I just bet that hurts." His snickering was lost on both Craig and Renee as they stared each other down.

Renee moved past Craig and faced the collection of wedding pictures on the mantel above the fireplace. When she turned around to face Craig again, tears flowed freely down her cheeks. "So I guess Simon told you everything." She let her hand flop to her sides. "Well, go on, tell me what a fool I was to get involved with someone who would deceive me so. Go on Craig say it. Say all the things that I feel and then you'll know my humiliation." She didn't wait for him to respond; instead, she turned to Simon. "You told him everything, all the details, didn't you, Simon?" Renee bit her lips when she saw the look in his eyes.

Simon had been walking around admiring the house. He stopped beside her and picked up one of the wedding pictures from the mantel. "Yeah, I did. Besides, I had to. He hired me at triple my normal rate, plus expenses, plus incidentals and a bonus. Nice wedding pictures, you two," Simon said, ignoring Renee's menacing glare.

Craig ached to hold her in his arms. "Renee, why would I say any of those things to you? Nobody would blame you for giving your heart to a man who pretended to be honest and caring. Honey, you were a victim of a crime by a thoughtless, unscrupulous man who had one goal in mind: your money, not your heart. He used your kind and generous heart to do that, can't you understand that?" Craig inched toward her. "Listen to me, Squirt, that doesn't make you a fool. It makes you a loving and trusting woman. But do you think so little of me that you'd think that I would think that about you, huh? Do you think that I wouldn't have fallen in love with you if you were fat or whatever? That would not have mattered to me, because I would have loved you, regardless." His eyes searched her face, lovingly.

Renee swallowed the lump in her throat. "Craig, we've had lies between us from day one. How would I know what you think?"

"You've lived with me as my wife, Renee. I'd say you know me better than anybody else. I've opened my heart to you. Let me tell you, that was astonishing because I never thought I was capable of actually falling in love. You said it yourself when you told me I had never opened my heart enough to fall in love. You were right. I hadn't done that with anybody else, but with you, I did. I opened my heart to you, and I like it. Renee, all that affection and cuddling stuff, I like it with you. I only want it with you, and I promise, I'll never lie to you again," Craig said, staring into her tear-filled eyes.

"Aw, that's so sweet and touching," Simon cooed as he listened to Craig spill his heart out. He thrust his hands into his pants pocket and nudged Renee with his large shoulder, grinning from ear to ear. In the last week, Simon and Craig had talked several times. One such meeting was to discuss getting Renee to Craig's home. He now could say he liked Craig and thought he was as good for Renee as she was for him. "Well, Squirt?" he asked, snickering as he used Craig's nickname for her.

Renee stood staring at Craig, processing what he'd said. Then she was moved again, literally, by Simon's shoulder. "Well what, Simon? And don't call me that," she said in a quiet voice, her tears having stopped.

Simon laughed. "Renee, right now I don't see what the problem is. He loves you and we know it. You love him and we know it. Charles is in a freezer, soon to be sucking dirt, but someone is still out to get you for some reason. In any case, we both want to protect you. Now come on, it's time for you to let all that other stuff go.

You both were dishonest for what you both felt were valid reasons at the time. But now you're husband and wife. You have families and friends who love and support you. Many couples have far less." Simon pursed his lips and nudged Renee again, pointing to Craig. "Besides, sweetheart, he's loaded. He's a millionaire." Simon only grinned when she gave him a 'so what' expression. But Simon also saw her melting in front of him. "Hey, Craig, you got something to snack on in the fridge?" he asked, rubbing his stomach.

"Help yourself," Craig replied, never taking his eyes off of Renee. "He's right, Squirt. It's time to let it all go. I know it's been like a twenty-ton weight you've been carrying on your shoulders, but I'm here to help you carry it. I know that's how I felt when you found out about my inheritance and the agency. I wanted to share that with you, Renee. Nobody else, just you. It was like I had a need to share all of that with you, baby. Remember I told you I'd never shared my life like that?"

"Yes, I remember," Renee said quietly, her shoulders slumped with exhaustion. But she did feel that a twenty-ton weight was being lifted off her shoulders. She could see Craig's love clearly. It was evident in his face. "Oh, Craig, I've messed up so much, and I do love you, I always have, but what do I tell my parents about the money? They fought that insurance company for so long only to have what they gave me stolen."

Yes, she said she still loves me. "Stolen by a man who has met his maker, Renee. You don't have to tell them anything. They gave that money to you to do whatever you wanted to, but if you feel that you absolutely have to tell them, then we'll tell them together. Besides, I don't think your parents are going to be too upset about thirty grand since their checking account is now rocking with an additional two hundred thousand dollars in it," he grinned.

"What?" Renee gasped, as did Simon around a mouthful of cold-cuts.

Craig shrugged, grinning at them. "What? A son-in-law can't share with his in-laws? Besides, Renee, I told you your parents needed a bigger hot-water tank in that house." He was finally standing in front of her. "And Bryant would have expected me to do that."

"But Craig, that's money your grandfather left for you," she said.

"Exactly! Renee, he left it for me to share with my wife and to do whatever we wanted to do with it. I chose to share it with our families. Well, some of it." Craig caressed her cheek. "We're going to be fine financially, not to mention we got that NFL gig for not one, but two commercial spots." He held up two fingers. "And the agency has gotten a bunch of new work."

"Hey, that's nice, Craig. Congratulations. You remember your friend and brother-in-law here if you get game tickets," Simon said, pointing his thumb toward his chest and sending Renee a wide grin.

The dark clouds lifted away. Renee forgot everything else; she was genuinely happy for him. "That is wonderful. You must be on top of the world." A smile tugged at her lips.

"Hum, I'm not there yet."

Renee smiled at the darkening of his eyes, as she felt the sting of fresh tears, happy tears. "Hum, so what would put you up there?"

"Just you, Squirt . . . just you."

Renee quickly closed the distance between them and threw her arms around him and kissed him. Craig lifted her up in his arms and circled the floor with her, and then he unashamedly let his happy tears flow. The only thing that pulled them apart was Leo excitedly jumping and yelping at the patio door.

EPILOGUE

James Tinsley and Miss Lilly, along with Craig and Renee, stood behind a one-way window in the Fourth District Police Station. They listened attentively as Lawrence Jennings was charged with several crimes—two attempts on Ray Newman's life and five counts of embezzlement and fraud involving the Wayland Bank. And although there was never any proof to tie Lawrence to the death of Esther Henderson down in Boca Raton, Florida, James made sure that those underprivileged students who were eligible for half or full scholarships got them. Then he officially transferred the scholarship account to the bank in Miami, as Mrs. Henderson originally wanted. Her grandson was named trustee.

Since James pulled money from Lawrence's retirement fund and refunded Craig the initial money he had paid out to Lawrence, and Craig had received his full inheritance benefits, Craig decided not to press charges. That was to Craig's benefit because, as Miss Lilly had said that day in his office, had he pressed charges against Lawrence for blackmail and extortion, Lawrence would have revealed the details of his marriage to Renee and how he'd lied to the bank to get his inheritance. Both of which would have caused Renee embarrassment, and neither of them wanted that.

Another person was watching Lawrence being charged. With slumped shoulders, Vivian Jennings stood with her lawyer beside James and Miss Lilly. She sobbed softly as she listened to the detective recount all her husband's crimes. But she already knew Lawrence had done much more after talking to Craig, Renee and James. "My God, this is all my fault," she said with bowed head.

James patted her hand. "No, dear, it's not. Lawrence's schemes go back long before he married you. His first wife, Naomi, pulled tight on the purse strings. It was her way of keeping him in line and attached to her, and in some ways it did. But as we now know, he'd obviously developed survival skills."

"But, to try to kill Ray, all because of me . . . I just don't understand. I mean I loved Lawrence, in my way. Ray and I were over at the point he got hurt. This is all so tragic."

When Craig put a comforting arm around Vivian's shaking shoulders, she looked up with sorrowful eyes, expecting his scorn. She didn't get it.

"Vivian, we men do a lot of crazy things in the name of love . . ." His eyes met Renee's briefly. "Most of us are just pigheaded and sometimes stupid, but only the sick ones would ever go to the extremes that Lawrence did. You did the absolute right thing by calling me. I appreciate that and, trust me, I know that was hard for you because you could have boarded that airplane and left Houston." He actually felt sorry for this dejected, jeans-clad woman standing before him looking scared and fearful. It was the look he'd seen on Renee's face after the break-in. "From this point on, Vivian, just do the right thing and you'll be all right. If either me or my wife or James can be of any assistance to you, just let us know, okay?"

Swallowing hard, Vivian nodded and said, "Thank you, I appreciate that."

Vivian was taken by surprise when Renee hugged her also and gave her several tissues from her purse, thanking her for calling Craig when she had.

Walking over to the water cooler in the corner, Vivian tuned out the voices of the detectives talking to Lawrence on the other side of the window. Vivian was going to testify against Lawrence because she had proof of both the hit-and-run and the attempted poisonings at the hospital.

She recalled the night she found Craig's cellphone number in Lawrence's home office. She was searching for something to connect Lawrence to Ray's hit and run. What she found was more than what she was originally looking for. Vivian found an auto-repair receipt for ten thousand dollars for a same-day rush repair job. Later that night, she had overheard Lawrence on the phone with someone—someone, she told Craig, Lawrence had hired for several thousand dollars to follow Renee. In her phone call to Craig, she'd told him that she believed the man may have also been instructed to harm to Renee in her apartment. The man, it turns out, was later apprehended by Simon and two patrol officers when he was caught attempting to again break into Renee's empty apartment at two-fifteen in the morning.

Vivian recalled being in a state of panic when she decided to call Craig's cell number and tell him what she'd overheard. She knew something terrible was going on after she and Lawrence met for lunch the day before. Yes, something was terribly wrong. He'd told her they had to leave Houston right away and could not return. When she pressed him for more details, he simply said that their villa was ready, as if that would stop her barrage of questions or calm her sudden fears. It didn't. But when Vivian told him that she wouldn't leave her family and friends, he then turned into a raving lunatic. Lawrence had looked at her menacingly and asked, "What friend, in particular, are you afraid to leave behind, Vivian? We're leaving Houston tomorrow night and never coming back. Do you understand that, or do I have to give you an illustration of why we're never coming back here?" That alone told Vivian he knew about Ray and that knowledge had pushed her over the edge. That evening, she overheard Lawrence telling Grace to call a junkman to come clean out the garage and take everything, for free.

The next morning, after Lawrence left for work, Vivian sat on the back patio, pretending to read a magazine as Grace drove off to the store. It was her only opportunity, and she took it.

She took pictures of the mangled car fender and hood, and then donned a pair of Grace's garden gloves and pulled them from the garage. She managed to pull them onto the small moving trailer she'd rented and parked on the next street over the day before. Then she drove to the storage unit she'd rented out near the interstate.

As Vivian took the solitary ride, she kept checking the rearview mirror to see if she was being followed, but she saw only the dark brown spots of Ray's blood covering the fender and hood from Lawrence's car. She cried all the way to the storage facility and back. She cried for Ray and all that he'd suffered, and all that he was going to suffer during his rehabilitation and recovery.

Vivian returned to stand beside Miss Lilly and was surprised when the woman eased a comforting arm around her waist. "Miss Lilly, Ray didn't deserve what happened to him. I should be the one to be punished, not Ray. He's kind and wouldn't hurt a fly, you know?"

Miss Lilly encouraged Vivian to sit down before she fell down. "Yes, we know, dear, and I think enough people have been punished already. Now it's his turn," she said, glancing back up through the large window at a depressed, sickly and scared-looking Lawrence Jennings.

Renee and Craig had just returned home after a week-long honeymoon in Hawaii. She wondered what was taking him so long to join her in bed.

Craig bounded up the steps and walked into the bedroom, grinning. "Sorry I took so long, but I had to view a videotape Dale sent over."

"A videotape? But that's work, Craig and you're still off for another three days," Renee said, braiding her hair. She didn't notice his broad grin.

"Well, Squirt, this tape is very special to me. It's a finished commercial that I'd been working on, and it will start airing in two days. I'm very happy and excited about it. Want to see it?" Craig put the tape in and flopped down on the bed with the remote.

Renee watched him. "Hum, happy and excited. You bet I do." She sat up and watched the commercial begin with soap bubbles popping, and then she let out a long squeal when she saw her mother's beautiful face glowing as she talked about the moisturizing benefits of the restored original soap they used to love. Renee turned to Craig with love overflowing her heart. "Craig, you did this . . . for me."

Craig pulled her into his arms. "I sure did. I shared all of your comments with the manufacturer and they, too, were excited about a way to keep that soap on the shelves. Turns out you were right. The manufacturer started using some new essential rose oils that changed the consistency of the soap. Then I introduced them to your mother, and, well they were hooked and hired her. Your mother was great during production of that commercial. She was fun to work with, and as I told her and I'm telling you now, Squirt, don't blame me when you both receive a lifetime supply of that damn soap." Laughing, he shook his head.

Renee replayed the commercial and then turned teary eyes on her husband. "Thank you, Craig. I love you so much."

"I love you right back, Renee." As he kissed her, Craig fought against grinning. He couldn't wait until she went into the backyard tomorrow and saw the two surprises he had for her . . . the wooden swing he had installed while they were away on their honeymoon and a counter-sized bubblegum ball machine sitting on it . . . filled with bubblegum balls.

THE END

ABOUT THE AUTHOR

Born and raised in Baltimore, Maryland, Bernice Layton works full-time and is an avid reader of novels, mostly romantic suspense. She is a member of Romance Writers of America and happily resides with her husband. She is the mother of one daughter. She plans to write several more books and you can visit her at *www.myspace.com/booksbyb*.

Coming in December from Genesis Press:

A VOICE BEHIND THUNDER
by
Carrie Elizabeth Greene

CHAPTER 1

Glory, Hallelujah!

The choir director of the New Life Temple Church observed the newest member of his Men's Chorus tugging at his suit jacket, searching for something to wipe the sweat that pooled on his forehead; while the other members of the group shouted praises and adoration as the Spirit moved them. It was obvious that something had the soloist uncomfortable as he kept reaching from pocket to pocket, his hands coming up empty each time, at the same time everyone in the pew behind him squinted to see if they could make out the designer's name embroidered on the jacket's silver lining. Finally, the choir director pulled out one of his own handkerchiefs and handed it over.

"Brother Donovan, you'll be fine. It will soon be over," he said.

Donovan Kerr nodded taking deep breaths to slow down his heartbeat. The atmosphere was electrified. The morning worship had already begun and the congregation swayed from side to side as they sang "Amazing Grace". Someone belted out a "Hallelujah Lord" to the left and somebody else a "Thank you Jesus", to the right. The organist ran his hand over the keyboard sending out a riff that seemed to bounce off the ceiling's wooden beams, leaping to the back wall, only to spring right up the middle aisle to the choir stand.

At that moment Donovan could only yield to the energy that filled the sanctuary and thrust him to his feet. He was oblivious to anything and anyone. All the rehearsing was over and he knew this was the final moment. Somehow he found himself standing in front of the 16 member male chorus, the choir director motioning him to stand by the microphone and get ready on his signal to begin singing. It was the first time Donovan had ever sung before a crowd and the nervous twinge in his stomach just wouldn't settle. The music began and he belted out the first line of "Take me back" by Andre Crouch. With each pulsating note he felt his voice grow stronger and his confidence increase. Until finally he was able to open his eyes and look out over the congregation.

The first thing he noticed was that nobody was paying attention to him. Instead they were focused on a woman slowly making her way to the front row pew. She was wearing a wide rimmed orange hat and a matching qiana knit dress—a *clinging* qiana knit dress. The hemline barely reaching past her mid- thighs, and her bulging cleavage bounced naughtily as she hurried past the ushers. Shock and revulsion radiated from the faces of the female onlookers, some shaking their heads and other's mumbling out loud "Jezebel!"

Three saintly men seated at the front of the church, kept their eyes straight ahead, or picked up their Bibles to thumb a quick verse or two. The other males gazed at the woman like the Goddess of Love had just entered the room and prayed that she wasn't a supernatural vision but a real person they could connect with after the service. It wasn't until the woman sat down and crossed her legs that Donovan recognized her.

"My God, it's Rachel!"

His wife.

* * *

2008 Reprint Mass Market Titles

January

Cautious Heart
Cheris F. Hodges
ISBN-13: 978-1-58571-301-1
ISBN-10: 1-58571-301-5
$6.99

Suddenly You
Crystal Hubbard
ISBN-13: 978-1-58571-302-8
ISBN-10: 1-58571-302-3
$6.99

February

Passion
T. T. Henderson
ISBN-13: 978-1-58571-303-5
ISBN-10: 1-58571-303-1
$6.99

Whispers in the Sand
LaFlorya Gauthier
ISBN-13: 978-1-58571-304-2
ISBN-10: 1-58571-304-x
$6.99

March

Life Is Never As It Seems
J. J. Michael
ISBN-13: 978-1-58571-305-9
ISBN-10: 1-58571-305-8
$6.99

Beyond the Rapture
Beverly Clark
ISBN-13: 978-1-58571-306-6
ISBN-10: 1-58571-306-6
$6.99

April

A Heart's Awakening
Veronica Parker
ISBN-13: 978-1-58571-307-3
ISBN-10: 1-58571-307-4
$6.99

Breeze
Robin Lynette Hampton
ISBN-13: 978-1-58571-308-0
ISBN-10: 1-58571-308-2
$6.99

May

I'll Be Your Shelter
Giselle Carmichael
ISBN-13: 978-1-58571-309-7
ISBN-10: 1-58571-309-0
$6.99

Careless Whispers
Rochelle Alers
ISBN-13: 978-1-58571-310-3
ISBN-10: 1-58571-310-4
$6.99

June

Sin
Crystal Rhodes
ISBN-13: 978-1-58571-311-0
ISBN-10: 1-58571-311-2
$6.99

Dark Storm Rising
Chinelu Moore
ISBN-13: 978-1-58571-312-7
ISBN-10: 1-58571-312-0
$6.99

2008 Reprint Mass Market Titles (continued)

July

Object of His Desire
A.C. Arthur
ISBN-13: 978-1-58571-313-4
ISBN-10: 1-58571-313-9
$6.99

Angel's Paradise
Janice Angelique
ISBN-13: 978-1-58571-314-1
ISBN-10: 1-58571-314-7
$6.99

August

Unbreak My Heart
Dar Tomlinson
ISBN-13: 978-1-58571-315-8
ISBN-10: 1-58571-315-5
$6.99

All I Ask
Barbara Keaton
ISBN-13: 978-1-58571-316-5
ISBN-10: 1-58571-316-3
$6.99

September

Icie
Pamela Leigh Starr
ISBN-13: 978-1-58571-275-5
ISBN-10: 1-58571-275-2
$6.99

At Last
Lisa Riley
ISBN-13: 978-1-58571-276-2
ISBN-10: 1-58571-276-0
$6.99

October

Everlastin' Love
Gay G. Gunn
ISBN-13: 978-1-58571-277-9
ISBN-10: 1-58571-277-9
$6.99

Three Wishes
Seressia Glass
ISBN-13: 978-1-58571-278-6
ISBN-10: 1-58571-278-7
$6.99

November

Yesterday Is Gone
Beverly Clark
ISBN-13: 978-1-58571-279-3
ISBN-10: 1-58571-279-5
$6.99

Again My Love
Kayla Perrin
ISBN-13: 978-1-58571-280-9
ISBN-10: 1-58571-280-9
$6.99

December

Office Policy
A.C. Arthur
ISBN-13: 978-1-58571-281-6
ISBN-10: 1-58571-281-7
$6.99

Rendezvous With Fate
Jeanne Sumerix
ISBN-13: 978-1-58571-283-3
ISBN-10: 1-58571-283-3
$6.99

2008 New Mass Market Titles

January

Where I Want To Be
Maryam Diaab
ISBN-13: 978-1-58571-268-7
ISBN-10: 1-58571-268-X
$6.99

Never Say Never
Michele Cameron
ISBN-13: 978-1-58571-269-4
ISBN-10: 1-58571-269-8
$6.99

February

Stolen Memories
Michele Sudler
ISBN-13: 978-1-58571-270-0
ISBN-10: 1-58571-270-1
$6.99

Dawn's Harbor
Kymberly Hunt
ISBN-13: 978-1-58571-271-7
ISBN-10: 1-58571-271-X
$6.99

March

Undying Love
Renee Alexis
ISBN-13: 978-1-58571-272-4
ISBN-10: 1-58571-272-8
$6.99

Blame It On Paradise
Crystal Hubbard
ISBN-13: 978-1-58571-273-1
ISBN-10: 1-58571-273-6
$6.99

April

When A Man Loves A Woman
La Connie Taylor-Jones
ISBN-13: 978-1-58571-274-8
ISBN-10: 1-58571-274-4
$6.99

Choices
Tammy Williams
ISBN-13: 978-1-58571-300-4
ISBN-10: 1-58571-300-7
$6.99

May

Dream Runner
Gail McFarland
ISBN-13: 978-1-58571-317-2
ISBN-10: 1-58571-317-1
$6.99

Southern Fried Standards
S.R. Maddox
ISBN-13: 978-1-58571-318-9
ISBN-10: 1-58571-318-X
$6.99

June

Looking for Lily
Africa Fine
ISBN-13: 978-1-58571-319-6
ISBN-10: 1-58571-319-8
$6.99

Bliss, Inc.
Chamein Canton
ISBN-13: 978-1-58571-325-7
ISBN-10: 1-58571-325-2
$6.99

2008 New Mass Market Titles (continued)

July

Love's Secrets
Yolanda McVey
ISBN-13: 978-1-58571-321-9
ISBN-10: 1-58571-321-X
$6.99

Things Forbidden
Maryam Diaab
ISBN-13: 978-1-58571-327-1
ISBN-10: 1-58571-327-9
$6.99

August

Storm
Pamela Leigh Starr
ISBN-13: 978-1-58571-323-3
ISBN-10: 1-58571-323-6
$6.99

Passion's Furies
AlTonya Washington
ISBN-13: 978-1-58571-324-0
ISBN-10: 1-58571-324-4
$6.99

September

Three Doors Down
Michele Sudler
ISBN-13: 978-1-58571-332-5
ISBN-10: 1-58571-332-5
$6.99

Mr Fix-It
Crystal Hubbard
ISBN-13: 978-1-58571-326-4
ISBN-10: 1-58571-326-0
$6.99

October

Moments of Clarity
Michele Cameron
ISBN-13: 978-1-58571-330-1
ISBN-10: 1-58571-330-9
$6.99

Lady Preacher
K.T. Richey
ISBN-13: 978-1-58571-333-2
ISBN-10: 1-58571-333-3
$6.99

November

This Life Isn't Perfect Holla
Sandra Foy
ISBN: 978-1-58571-331-8
ISBN-10: 1-58571-331-7
$6.99

Promises Made
Bernice Layton
ISBN-13: 978-1-58571-334-9
ISBN-10: 1-58571-334-1
$6.99

December

A Voice Behind Thunder
Carrie Elizabeth Greene
ISBN-13: 978-1-58571-329-5
ISBN-10: 1-58571-329-5
$6.99

The More Things Change
Chamein Canton
ISBN-13: 978-1-58571-328-8
ISBN-10: 1-58571-328-7
$6.99

Other Genesis Press, Inc. Titles

A Dangerous Deception	J.M. Jeffries	$8.95
A Dangerous Love	J.M. Jeffries	$8.95
A Dangerous Obsession	J.M. Jeffries	$8.95
A Drummer's Beat to Mend	Kei Swanson	$9.95
A Happy Life	Charlotte Harris	$9.95
A Heart's Awakening	Veronica Parker	$9.95
A Lark on the Wing	Phyliss Hamilton	$9.95
A Love of Her Own	Cheris F. Hodges	$9.95
A Love to Cherish	Beverly Clark	$8.95
A Risk of Rain	Dar Tomlinson	$8.95
A Taste of Temptation	Reneé Alexis	$9.95
A Twist of Fate	Beverly Clark	$8.95
A Will to Love	Angie Daniels	$9.95
Acquisitions	Kimberley White	$8.95
Across	Carol Payne	$12.95
After the Vows	Leslie Esdaile	$10.95
(Summer Anthology)	T.T. Henderson	
	Jacqueline Thomas	
Again My Love	Kayla Perrin	$10.95
Against the Wind	Gwynne Forster	$8.95
All I Ask	Barbara Keaton	$8.95
Always You	Crystal Hubbard	$6.99
Ambrosia	T.T. Henderson	$8.95
An Unfinished Love Affair	Barbara Keaton	$8.95
And Then Came You	Dorothy Elizabeth Love	$8.95
Angel's Paradise	Janice Angelique	$9.95
At Last	Lisa G. Riley	$8.95
Best of Friends	Natalie Dunbar	$8.95
Beyond the Rapture	Beverly Clark	$9.95

Other Genesis Press, Inc. Titles (continued)

Blaze	Barbara Keaton	$9.95
Blood Lust	J. M. Jeffries	$9.95
Blood Seduction	J.M. Jeffries	$9.95
Bodyguard	Andrea Jackson	$9.95
Boss of Me	Diana Nyad	$8.95
Bound by Love	Beverly Clark	$8.95
Breeze	Robin Hampton Allen	$10.95
Broken	Dar Tomlinson	$24.95
By Design	Barbara Keaton	$8.95
Cajun Heat	Charlene Berry	$8.95
Careless Whispers	Rochelle Alers	$8.95
Cats & Other Tales	Marilyn Wagner	$8.95
Caught in a Trap	Andre Michelle	$8.95
Caught Up In the Rapture	Lisa G. Riley	$9.95
Cautious Heart	Cheris F Hodges	$8.95
Chances	Pamela Leigh Starr	$8.95
Cherish the Flame	Beverly Clark	$8.95
Class Reunion	Irma Jenkins/	
	John Brown	$12.95
Code Name: Diva	J.M. Jeffries	$9.95
Conquering Dr. Wexler's Heart	Kimberley White	$9.95
Corporate Seduction	A.C. Arthur	$9.95
Crossing Paths, Tempting Memories	Dorothy Elizabeth Love	$9.95
Crush	Crystal Hubbard	$9.95
Cypress Whisperings	Phyllis Hamilton	$8.95
Dark Embrace	Crystal Wilson Harris	$8.95
Dark Storm Rising	Chinelu Moore	$10.95

Other Genesis Press, Inc. Titles (continued)

Other Genesis Press, Inc. Titles (continued)

Hard to Love	Kimberley White	$9.95
Hart & Soul	Angie Daniels	$8.95
Heart of the Phoenix	A.C. Arthur	$9.95
Heartbeat	Stephanie Bedwell-Grime	$8.95
Hearts Remember	M. Loui Quezada	$8.95
Hidden Memories	Robin Allen	$10.95
Higher Ground	Leah Latimer	$19.95
Hitler, the War, and the Pope	Ronald Rychiak	$26.95
How to Write a Romance	Kathryn Falk	$18.95
I Married a Reclining Chair	Lisa M. Fuhs	$8.95
I'll Be Your Shelter	Giselle Carmichael	$8.95
I'll Paint a Sun	A.J. Garrotto	$9.95
Icie	Pamela Leigh Starr	$8.95
Illusions	Pamela Leigh Starr	$8.95
Indigo After Dark Vol. I	Nia Dixon/Angelique	$10.95
Indigo After Dark Vol. II	Dolores Bundy/ Cole Riley	$10.95
Indigo After Dark Vol. III	Montana Blue/ Coco Morena	$10.95
Indigo After Dark Vol. IV	Cassandra Colt/	$14.95
Indigo After Dark Vol. V	Delilah Dawson	$14.95
Indiscretions	Donna Hill	$8.95
Intentional Mistakes	Michele Sudler	$9.95
Interlude	Donna Hill	$8.95
Intimate Intentions	Angie Daniels	$8.95
It's Not Over Yet	J.J. Michael	$9.95
Jolie's Surrender	Edwina Martin-Arnold	$8.95
Kiss or Keep	Debra Phillips	$8.95
Lace	Giselle Carmichael	$9.95

Other Genesis Press, Inc. Titles (continued)

Last Train to Memphis	Elsa Cook	$12.95
Lasting Valor	Ken Olsen	$24.95
Let Us Prey	Hunter Lundy	$25.95
Lies Too Long	Pamela Ridley	$13.95
Life Is Never As It Seems	J.J. Michael	$12.95
Lighter Shade of Brown	Vicki Andrews	$8.95
Love Always	Mildred E. Riley	$10.95
Love Doesn't Come Easy	Charlyne Dickerson	$8.95
Love Unveiled	Gloria Greene	$10.95
Love's Deception	Charlene Berry	$10.95
Love's Destiny	M. Loui Quezada	$8.95
Mae's Promise	Melody Walcott	$8.95
Magnolia Sunset	Giselle Carmichael	$8.95
Many Shades of Gray	Dyanne Davis	$6.99
Matters of Life and Death	Lesego Malepe, Ph.D.	$15.95
Meant to Be	Jeanne Sumerix	$8.95
Midnight Clear (Anthology)	Leslie Esdaile	$10.95
	Gwynne Forster	
	Carmen Green	
	Monica Jackson	
Midnight Magic	Gwynne Forster	$8.95
Midnight Peril	Vicki Andrews	$10.95
Misconceptions	Pamela Leigh Starr	$9.95
Montgomery's Children	Richard Perry	$14.95
My Buffalo Soldier	Barbara B. K. Reeves	$8.95
Naked Soul	Gwynne Forster	$8.95
Next to Last Chance	Louisa Dixon	$24.95
No Apologies	Seressia Glass	$8.95
No Commitment Required	Seressia Glass	$8.95

Other Genesis Press, Inc. Titles (continued)

No Regrets	Mildred E. Riley	$8.95
Not His Type	Chamein Canton	$6.99
Nowhere to Run	Gay G. Gunn	$10.95
O Bed! O Breakfast!	Rob Kuehnle	$14.95
Object of His Desire	A. C. Arthur	$8.95
Office Policy	A. C. Arthur	$9.95
Once in a Blue Moon	Dorianne Cole	$9.95
One Day at a Time	Bella McFarland	$8.95
One in A Million	Barbara Keaton	$6.99
One of These Days	Michele Sudler	$9.95
Outside Chance	Louisa Dixon	$24.95
Passion	T.T. Henderson	$10.95
Passion's Blood	Cherif Fortin	$22.95
Passion's Journey	Wanda Y. Thomas	$8.95
Past Promises	Jahmel West	$8.95
Path of Fire	T.T. Henderson	$8.95
Path of Thorns	Annetta P. Lee	$9.95
Peace Be Still	Colette Haywood	$12.95
Picture Perfect	Reon Carter	$8.95
Playing for Keeps	Stephanie Salinas	$8.95
Pride & Joi	Gay G. Gunn	$15.95
Pride & Joi	Gay G. Gunn	$8.95
Promises to Keep	Alicia Wiggins	$8.95
Quiet Storm	Donna Hill	$10.95
Reckless Surrender	Rochelle Alers	$6.95
Red Polka Dot in a World of Plaid	Varian Johnson	$12.95
Reluctant Captive	Joyce Jackson	$8.95
Rendezvous with Fate	Jeanne Sumerix	$8.95

Other Genesis Press, Inc. Titles (continued)

Revelations	Cheris F. Hodges	$8.95
Rivers of the Soul	Leslie Esdaile	$8.95
Rocky Mountain Romance	Kathleen Suzanne	$8.95
Rooms of the Heart	Donna Hill	$8.95
Rough on Rats and Tough on Cats	Chris Parker	$12.95
Secret Library Vol. 1	Nina Sheridan	$18.95
Secret Library Vol. 2	Cassandra Colt	$8.95
Secret Thunder	Annetta P. Lee	$9.95
Shades of Brown	Denise Becker	$8.95
Shades of Desire	Monica White	$8.95
Shadows in the Moonlight	Jeanne Sumerix	$8.95
Sin	Crystal Rhodes	$8.95
Small Whispers	Annetta P. Lee	$6.99
So Amazing	Sinclair LeBeau	$8.95
Somebody's Someone	Sinclair LeBeau	$8.95
Someone to Love	Alicia Wiggins	$8.95
Song in the Park	Martin Brant	$15.95
Soul Eyes	Wayne L. Wilson	$12.95
Soul to Soul	Donna Hill	$8.95
Southern Comfort	J.M. Jeffries	$8.95
Still the Storm	Sharon Robinson	$8.95
Still Waters Run Deep	Leslie Esdaile	$8.95
Stolen Kisses	Dominiqua Douglas	$9.95
Stories to Excite You	Anna Forrest/Divine	$14.95
Subtle Secrets	Wanda Y. Thomas	$8.95
Suddenly You	Crystal Hubbard	$9.95
Sweet Repercussions	Kimberley White	$9.95
Sweet Sensations	Gwendolyn Bolton	$9.95

Other Genesis Press, Inc. Titles (continued)

Sweet Tomorrows	Kimberly White	$8.95
Taken by You	Dorothy Elizabeth Love	$9.95
Tattooed Tears	T. T. Henderson	$8.95
The Color Line	Lizzette Grayson Carter	$9.95
The Color of Trouble	Dyanne Davis	$8.95
The Disappearance of Allison Jones	Kayla Perrin	$5.95
The Fires Within	Beverly Clark	$9.95
The Foursome	Celya Bowers	$6.99
The Honey Dipper's Legacy	Pannell-Allen	$14.95
The Joker's Love Tune	Sidney Rickman	$15.95
The Little Pretender	Barbara Cartland	$10.95
The Love We Had	Natalie Dunbar	$8.95
The Man Who Could Fly	Bob & Milana Beamon	$18.95
The Missing Link	Charlyne Dickerson	$8.95
The Mission	Pamela Leigh Starr	$6.99
The Perfect Frame	Beverly Clark	$9.95
The Price of Love	Sinclair LeBeau	$8.95
The Smoking Life	Ilene Barth	$29.95
The Words of the Pitcher	Kei Swanson	$8.95
Three Wishes	Seressia Glass	$8.95
Ties That Bind	Kathleen Suzanne	$8.95
Tiger Woods	Libby Hughes	$5.95
Time is of the Essence	Angie Daniels	$9.95
Timeless Devotion	Bella McFarland	$9.95
Tomorrow's Promise	Leslie Esdaile	$8.95
Truly Inseparable	Wanda Y. Thomas	$8.95
Two Sides to Every Story	Dyanne Davis	$9.95
Unbreak My Heart	Dar Tomlinson	$8.95

Other Genesis Press, Inc. Titles (continued)

Uncommon Prayer	Kenneth Swanson	$9.95
Unconditional Love	Alicia Wiggins	$8.95
Unconditional	A.C. Arthur	$9.95
Until Death Do Us Part	Susan Paul	$8.95
Vows of Passion	Bella McFarland	$9.95
Wedding Gown	Dyanne Davis	$8.95
What's Under Benjamin's Bed	Sandra Schaffer	$8.95
When Dreams Float	Dorothy Elizabeth Love	$8.95
When I'm With You	LaConnie Taylor-Jones	$6.99
Whispers in the Night	Dorothy Elizabeth Love	$8.95
Whispers in the Sand	LaFlorya Gauthier	$10.95
Who's That Lady?	Andrea Jackson	$9.95
Wild Ravens	Altonya Washington	$9.95
Yesterday Is Gone	Beverly Clark	$10.95
Yesterday's Dreams, Tomorrow's Promises	Reon Laudat	$8.95
Your Precious Love	Sinclair LeBeau	$8.95

Order Form

Mail to: Genesis Press, Inc.
P.O. Box 101
Columbus, MS 39703

Name _____
Address _____
City/State _____ Zip _____
Telephone _____

Ship to (if different from above)
Name _____
Address _____
City/State _____ Zip _____
Telephone _____

Credit Card Information
Credit Card # _____ ☐ Visa   ☐ Mastercard
Expiration Date (mm/yy) _____ ☐ AmEx ☐ Discover

Qty.	Author	Title	Price	Total

Use this order	Total for books	_____
form, or call	Shipping and handling:	
	$5 first two books,	
	$1 each additional book	_____
1-888-INDIGO-1	Total S & H	_____
	Total amount enclosed	_____

Mississippi residents add 7% sales tax